The Secret of Sekhmet

Eugenia Oganova

Also by Eugenia Oganova

MISSION ALPHA
The Wise and Passionate You

AWAKENING THE HARMONY WITHIN
How to Create with Spirit

The Secret of Sekhmet

Why Akhenaten Challenged the Gods of Egypt

Eugenia Oganova

for Sekhmet

CONTENTS

AUTHOR'S NOTE

This book is about Maat (Truth), Zep Tepi (The First Time of our history) and Sekhmet (a multidimensional person who taught wisdom to the people of ancient Egypt), and about the time of Akhenaten and Nefertiti (during this time Egypt let go of many gods for the sake of one god - Aten the Light).

One of the biggest tragedies of our present time is that we do not remember who we are – and because of it we are trying to reinvent the wheel with our current technologies, thus feeling superior to our ancestors. At the same time, even more absurdly, there are a few people who still hide the knowledge of the past, which was kept intact for generations, but their own consciousness is not high enough today to understand the information they are protecting. For centuries it was considered that we, as a species, were not ready to know who we really are because we would corrupt it due to our unconsciousness. The snippets of the knowledge released into the masses became diluted until they contained almost no truth at all. The few who still held the knowledge secret, initially with good intentions, became corrupt, political, and greedy. They forgot their role as sentinels of truth, instead basing their value on the ability to manipulate for personal gain.

This world's condition pains me because I see so much of the beauty, creative power, passion, courage and love in our species, yet we tend to squander it all on entertainment and false powers of the ego.

This book is about Sekhmet and her journey of love, hate, despair and awakening through pleasure. I feel that I know her very intimately and understand her journey. The current events and the characters in this book are fictional, but the references to the past, the information, the energy, and Sekhmet herself, are as real as I know them to be.

The Secret of Sekhmet

PROLOGUE

Current time
Boston, United States

Craig readjusted the position of his body. He had been sitting with his back against a large worn leather armchair for more than an hour, hoping that Simon, his animal guide who enjoyed the form of a large orange tabby cat, would show up. But he had not.

Craig had had his share of strange experiences, and he always attributed these experiences to his being part Native American. His mother claimed to be a descendant of the famous Anasazi who had disappeared without a trace a very long time ago in the Four Corners region. She died when he was two, and his grandmother Betty took him to her home in Lynn, north of Boston. Grandma Betty was a calm, educated Bostonian who had moved out of the city because she could not afford the rent. She told him many stories of his mother's assumed genetic past, but all Craig remembered about her was her voice – she used to sing to him. His father was a very tall white man who died from cirrhosis of the liver. All Craig remembered about him was the smell of alcohol, so it was good to not think of him. Craig's grandma worked at a convenience store to add to her modest pension. She allowed Craig to grow up restriction-free. He was not afraid of life, and in general felt good.

His first four years in Lynn went by uneventfully. But in the fifth year, when Craig was preparing to go to school, strange things began to happen. He had very vivid and odd dreams. He also noticed that when he looked at someone, he knew things about that person that he should not really know. He didn't ask for these insights, but when he began to

1

mention them to grandma Betty, she listened very intently and always wanted to know more. Craig didn't realize that other people didn't have this ability; he always assumed that this was how everyone else was. Craig's intense dreams were filled with vivid pictures. Some had large statues that he walked between, and others were about tall strange-looking people. There were also many dreams about underground places, and Craig always had to crawl into a cavern and find something, but he never remembered what it was when he woke up.

Then school started. Craig didn't really like school, but he knew a lot because he could read. All of the hours grandma Betty spent working at the store, he spent reading. The teachers treated Craig as if he were a child and this confused him. He had never felt like a child. He remembered coming home and asking grandma Betty: "Grandma, am I a child?" She had smiled and said that she was not sure, but probably not. Craig was seven then.

As time went by, Craig grew tall. He had very white skin – somehow he had not inherited his mother's dark complexion, but his face did look somewhat like a Native American: he had high cheek bones, almond shaped eyes, and mostly straight jet black hair. Craig found the fascination others had with his appearance strange, but considering that looks seemed to be important in American culture, he looked at himself with curiosity. His dark brown eyes and black hair made his white skin look whiter. He thought that he might even be good looking when he grew up.

Unfortunately, Craig's nightmarish dreams became regular. His grandma tried to find out why he was so unusual, and what his dreams meant. She didn't believe in doctors, medications, or even psychologists, but she did believe in psychics. For an educated woman this was odd, but then again Craig's life was filled with oddities. Grandma Betty took Craig to one psychic after another. Those dark rooms invariably had red and black curtains, lace and crystals scattered around everywhere, a few statues and, always, something from Egypt – Nefertiti's head or a Sphinx. Craig wasn't keen on most of the décor or the smell of dust and incense, but he always asked about the Egyptian objects. None were ever real, they were cheap plastic imitations. But Craig liked them nevertheless. The psychics gave many answers, and none made any sense to Craig. But he patiently followed his grandma.

Then his grandma got sick. She wouldn't tell Craig about it, but he knew. He had a dream, and in it his grandmother had a black spot in her belly, which grew and grew until it took over her entire body, like ink from a squid. Craig knew that this was not good at all. She began to feel worse and worse. She made potions and drank them; she boiled a strange concoction and ate it. Finally Craig confronted her. She had cancer and there was nothing any medical doctor could do. But she was damned if she would die in some hospital! And so she drank the potions and went on with her life, as much as she had left of it.

Soon Craig took over all the household's positions – he cooked, cleaned, took care of grandma, and still occasionally went to school. He didn't mind because he loved his grandma and school was boring anyway. Life was what it was. Spending time with grandma seemed to make sense. Going to school didn't.

One day, as Craig was coming home from school, he saw an excited look on his grandma's face. A momentary hope that she had found a cure and would not die soon disappeared, as Craig could tell that this was not about her. She was dressed and ready to leave. Her girlfriend had told her that a Native American shaman was a guest at a friend's house. Grandma Betty had to show Craig to this shaman before she died! Craig didn't know why this was such a big deal. He had never met a shaman, but whoever this shaman was he could not have been much different from all the other psychics Craig had been introduced to. Apparently this shaman was on a private visit and did not see people, but when he was told about Craig, he asked that the boy be brought to him immediately. And so they went.

The shaman was a short man with brown eyes, darkish skin, prominent cheekbones and a hooked nose. He was dressed plainly in jeans and a button-down shirt, and besides a long braid and a pendant there was nothing unusual about him. He stared at Craig for a long time, and Craig realized that he couldn't feel anything from him; it was as if the man was not standing in front of him at all. Craig felt something from all people all of the time, so this was very intriguing.

The shaman told Craig to sit down on the sofa, and he sat beside him. He asked Craig questions about his dreams and other things. Craig answered truthfully. And then Craig asked why he couldn't feel the shaman. But by the time he had finished his question, all sorts of feelings suddenly flooded him and... he fainted.

Opening his eyes, he could only see the ceiling and hear muted voices. He lay like that for a while, thinking about what had happened. There was no immediate reason to sit up. What he felt and saw was a multitude of pictures and sounds and feelings connected to them, but they had come at him in an avalanche and he hadn't been able to stand it.

The shaman came back into the room.

"So, you have come back to our world then," he stated.

"I saw you, but also many other things, rooms and faces, and different places..." Craig blurted out.

"You are not trained, that is why I blocked this from you."

"Trained like how?"

"People with your abilities are rare. In my tribe I was the only one, and I inherited it from my father. Your grandmother tells me that neither of your relatives had this gift. It is very unusual, but sometimes a spirit will just pick a body and activate the talent. You seem to be one of these; your own spirit decided to have you conscious."

"What do I do now?"

"I do not know," replied the shaman simply. "You need a guide."

"Can you be my guide?" Craig asked cautiously, sitting up on the sofa.

"I have asked my spirit guide and she says I am not the one."

"How do I find a guide?"

"You need to ask your spirit guide."

"How do I ask my spirit guide?" Craig was confused; he thought he had just asked that question.

The shaman stood up and left the room. When he returned he moved the coffee table aside and sat on the rug by the sofa. Craig was curious about a leather-wrapped package that he held in his hands. The shaman opened the package and laid it flat on the floor, inviting Craig to sit opposite him. On the piece of leather were spread some small objects: a tooth, a round rock, a multicolored feather, and a small plastic spoon.

"This is my medicine bundle," explained the shaman. "The feather is a gift from my mother, the rock is to hold me onto the Earth, the spoon is from the time when I had no spoon and the tooth I found in the bones of a mountain lion."

"Whoa..." Craig could not stop staring at the objects.

"Close your eyes, boy," said the shaman. He began: "I am the Kuinana of the Sanaya family. Spirits, I ask you to offer help to myself and this boy next to me..."

And so it went, on and on. Craig was not sure what it all meant, but this was way more fun than any psychic he ever went to. He gingerly followed everything that the shaman told him – to relax, to open his eyes on the inside and look around the space he was in while his body was still sitting on the floor. It was strange, but somehow easy to do. Craig's internal vision had immediately come up with a picture: surrounding him was a rocky desert. Instructed to look for his spirit guide, Craig had fully expected a mountain lion. He looked around carefully, afraid to throw off the vision. But no creature came forward. The shaman's voice continued to recite his instructions and Craig followed them. Inside his vision he walked, climbed, fell off cliffs and climbed again, got lost and even saw a gopher – but the gopher disappeared, a desert mirage, not a spirit guide. Craig was about to give up. After all, his back ached from sitting in that uncomfortable pose on the floor, and his feet felt numb. Then he heard a "meow." It was a very distinct, clean sound, so close that Craig was about to open his eyes – he assumed there was a cat in the house and that it had come into the room. But to his surprise he saw a cat, a large orange tabby cat, inside his vision. Staring at it in confusion, he thought, "How did this cat get into my vision? There are no cats like that in the desert…" and before he could think of anything else, the cat spoke: "Well, you're the one who had to make this into a desert, you know. I would have much preferred a soft couch."

"What???" said Craig out loud, and opened his eyes.

That was how Craig met Simon for the first time, years ago. Since then he had discovered that his cat guide was independent and quite easily annoyed; he had his own ideas and thoughts, and was anything but little and meek. The cat always knew more than Craig, he was a spirit after all!

Craig felt a little embarrassed at this memory – he had been so disappointed that Simon had not been a mountain lion. For a while he had secretly hoped that Simon was just masquerading as a cat. Craig even asked him about his "true appearance." To his surprise Simon understood the question, explaining that he looked different "at home" and that here he was just visiting. Craig was about to say "then why can't you visit as a mountain lion?" when Simon's intense stare told him to shut up. It took a while to remember that Simon could read Craig's thoughts.

Craig's grandmother died just two months after he met the shaman and was introduced to Simon. The meeting was fortunate. If it wasn't for Simon-the-cat, Craig might have been in serious trouble. As no relatives could be located, the authorities filtered him into the foster system. He lived with many families, some compassionate and kind, others unscrupulous. Simon told Craig that life was a path and he must walk it; he couldn't just get off any time he didn't like the scenery. He also told Craig that every person Craig met was a message. "Some people are lousy messengers, but once in a while there will be a very good message." That did not mean that it was pleasant, just more intense and to the point. Craig learned to trust himself, not people. "People lie and people change; it is the rule of things. They do not mean to be mean, they are just lost. It is your job to be found. You are the only one who can find yourself, no one else can. But people sometimes can help you on that path." And so Craig walked the path, no matter how nasty his foster siblings or parents were.

*   *   *

Craig took a deep breath. It had been more than an hour and still Simon refused to show himself. A small candle burned in a cup with a broken handle in the medicine bundle on the floor in front of Craig's feet. There was almost no candle left; a melted mess had filled the cup. "Where are you?!" thought Craig, as he closed his eyes and tried again.

This time he opened his eyes in *that* room, the room he always saw in his dreams, the bad ones. For some reason that dream room scared the hell out of him. He was a six-foot-tall adult now, but he felt the same nervous, cold jitters that he had as a child. The room was a space he saw through a door-like opening in a wall. Inside the room was a large cube, and on top of the cube, a pyramid. The base of the pyramid matched the dimensions of the cube and for a while Craig had thought it was a "very fat obelisk." But when he had told Simon about it, the cat explained that it was a cube *and* a pyramid: "Can't you see they are made of different materials?" said the cat, annoyed. "Besides, no obelisks are this fat, they are made to precise proportions." Craig could never tell why Simon was always so annoyed. But as he was Craig's only friend, he was, annoyed or not, the best cat that Craig had ever known.

With the open doorway in front of him, Craig nervously looked around inside his vision. Simon finally appeared by Craig's feet. He was thinking of petting the cat behind the ears.

"That would be nice…" purred Simon next to his leg. Looking down Craig could see that the cat's arched back was almost to his knee.

"Can we get out of here?" whispered Craig.

"But you asked for *this* one."

"No, I hate this place. You know that! Simon, please, can we leave?"

"You told me you wanted to know *why* Egypt hides the truth. Don't you want to know anymore?" teased the cat.

Craig did want to know, very much so. For the last five years he had studied everything he could find on Egypt – its ancient history fascinated him. He was convinced that there was some very big truth about humanity's origins hidden in the land of Egypt, but for some

6

reason the government of that country did not want to make it public. He read lots of conspiracy theories, carefully filtering reality from insanity. But even after discarding the ego-maniacal junk the mystery remained. He knew Egypt held something, he just didn't know what.

"I want to know! But why must we be here to talk about it?!"

"An orange woman will take you where you need to go," replied Simon. "You need to be there, to help the 'why' become the 'what'."

Then everything disappeared – the pyramid, the room, and the cat. Craig opened his eyes. It was dark, and the candle had burned out. He shook his head. "What *orange* woman?"

CHAPTER ONE

Over one hundred thousand years ago
Agartha of Earth
The fourth dimension of the Solar System

Bright light is everywhere. It is a space between slow matter and fast energy – Agartha. It is beyond the material planetary form, yet inside it. Contained within the vibratory range of Agartha is a Crystalline Sphere, a place for the meetings of the Solar Council. All affairs of the Council concern Earth; they speak for her to the Universe. The Earth herself, a conscious entity, is always present at all meetings.

Tall pylons hold the upper and the lower domes, and beams of bright light interpenetrate the space in all directions. Filled with an astounding sound and yet silence, as if space itself were alive and singing, this crystalline spheroid is maintained by the consciousness of the entities, formless and light, who silently glide through it. The gravity of Earth is almost completely suspended here, creating a feeling of weightlessness. Newcomers are prone to disorientation and vertigo... The formless, shining entities witness and share in the Crystalline Sphere's communal consciousness. When an entity expresses itself, it takes form, becoming a separate self.

Agartha is outside of Earth's linear time, yet it is in relationship to it. Inside the Crystalline Sphere time is eternal, one can remember the future as easily as the past...

The Earth's Solar system is permanently linked in a helical motion with the Sirian star system, rotating together in galactic space.

The Solar Council is anticipating the arrival of the special guests.

8

CHAPTER ONE

*   *   *

The foggy screen makes it almost impossible to see the shiny white ground. Thirty-two beings, their thin white bodies resembling tall frozen statues, are searching intently. They have never seen Earth, and their shiny eyes reflect the new world as they peer through the window of fog…

They are a family, officially locked together by their own choice and attraction. Sixteen of one gender and sixteen of the other, united as one to generate life, as required by Sirian biology. But even though they are matched energetically, this particular family cannot produce a new being. The Sirian High Council has determined a mission for them: they are to develop a quantum tunnel to the sister world and create a new entity there with the help of the planetary being.

They come from the sixth dimension, where all technology is internal to each being. Together they resonate inside a pyramid, whose walls are substantiated by the force fields, and held by the conscious focus of these entities. These thirty-two are individuals but sense reality as one being, together in unison. An opalescent glow surrounds the vibrating pyramid, and the charge flows stronger until everything disappears. Underneath the vessel time-space is compressed, opening a tunnel. The thirty-two are weightless, bound to the same location inside the pyramid, yet each of them now has a separate and unique perception of events. They are no longer together in the same point of time-space: they are inside the pyramid but each is alone, traveling on an individual path, a separate wormhole inside the larger tunnel opened by their communal consciousness.

Then, transparent and whitish, the fog rises again. Time moves very slowly until it is suspended completely. Bright, rapid-moving specks of light swarm so fast that each entity feels its form no longer: the conscious "I" stretches… All that is left is the desire for the destination. In a split moment the commotion stops and the space is calm again. The bright light remains. This is the light of Earth's sun.

The thirty-two beings observe the Earth's sun from underneath the clouds. This position is an illusion, for the crystalline pyramid hovers suspended in space, far above the clouds. The entities' awareness has overshot their bodily forms inside the pyramid. In space, the walls of the pyramid are invisible and only the blackness and the stars can be seen all around. But consciousness persists, and eventually confusion subsides;

matter is reconnected with perception, and the thirty-two see the stars. Unmoving, supported by each other, they rest.

*   *   *

The Solar Council is about to begin its meeting – all of the members, from Agartha and elsewhere, are present. This is a special meeting, for there are guests to be considered: the thirty-two beings from a star called Sirius.

It is 103,388 BC, 292 years into the Age of Pisces.

CHAPTER TWO

Current time
Boston, United States

Bailey hung up the phone. That was the last phone call she had to return this evening. Or was it night already? With the blinds drawn she couldn't tell whether it was night or day. It must be nighttime, damn it! One look at her little fake-gold watch made it clear that her last patient had left two hours ago – she had gotten tied up with her notes again. She took a breath and promised herself for the thousandth time that she would watch the clock more carefully so she could return home before ten. That had not happened since she had been in this office. It was a nice place, much better than her previous hole in the wall in the hospital. Eight years of her life Bailey had given to that hospital, and she had hated every minute of it – the noise and constant commotion, emergencies and fluorescent lights. The last two years she had drifted away, working privately with a colleague and maintaining a few hours per week in the hospital. Although early on she realized that she would be much better off having her own psychology practice, the starting capital had only materialized a year ago. She had wanted to purchase her colleague's practice when he retired as she had already substituted for him on many occasions and knew most of the patients. And now Bailey had finally done it – she was sitting in her own office. It was softly lit and painted a warm hue, and had furniture the color of dark wine. She smiled to herself. No wonder she stayed at work longer. She was in love with her new office!

She slipped her feet into her shoes and stretched as she approached the window. The lights of Boston looked alive, mostly because of the wetness – it had been raining all week.

Her condo was a twenty-minute stroll from her office, but in the rain it took longer. Wet brown leaves whipped around and stuck to her body, and a gust of wind almost ripped her umbrella out of her hands. She held on to it stoically. Somehow this action brought her sister to mind.

"Maybe it's the struggle… Abby's whole life seems to be such a struggle…"

Identical twins often share everything, and certainly Abby was the mirror image of Bailey. But there the resemblance ended. Thirty-one years ago their parents died in an accident, and Abby had been the sole witness. The experience had altered Abby. Why had their father insisted on going on that trip? Even Bailey coming down with chickenpox didn't stop them, the family simply went without her. Her father and mother arrived home in coffins, and Abby returned with her mind so broken that she now spent her days heavily medicated at a mental health facility. Whenever Abby managed to go off her meds she believed that she was receiving "messages." She would talk about the "Solar Council people," whoever they were, and how "they" were here to "support" all of us so that we could "become part of a larger family later." Perhaps, thought Bailey, Abby's shattered mind concocted these voices as a way to cope with the death of her parents. Could the "larger family" mean that she thought one day her parents would return? Bailey didn't know.

As she waited on the crosswalk in the wind and rain, Bailey circled the topic of her twin. Abby's "messages" stuck in Bailey's mind; that's what happened with anything she couldn't understand or control. She had used analyzing as a survival mechanism since the death of her parents. Struggling to regain control of her life, she dug her little mental claws into any problem until it fell under the control of her comprehension. But when it came to Abby – and only Abby – Bailey refused to dig. She didn't want to acknowledge the fear that rose up every time she thought of her twin's threatening condition. When Bailey looked at Abby she saw herself, and it was as if she was also crazy and should be locked up. How illogical! But the puzzle of her parents' death was frightening, and her sister surely was a part of that. She didn't feel up to the challenge of detangling this lifelong mess, preferring to look at it from a circumstantial point of view. In the dummy version: shit happened when they were kids; her sister went insane after a horrific accident in a foreign country; and the death of her parents had not made for a cozy, balanced environment growing up. It was easier to ignore the little nagging feeling of fear, to override it. But it reared its ugly, undeniable head every time Bailey thought of Abby.

She walked down the street, thinking back to one of the recent occasions she had visited her sister. Abby had brought up the Egyptian locket, telling her that the *"universe inside it can open the door to time before the beginning."* Bailey had immediately gotten nervous – her sister didn't talk about such things unless she was off her meds. Usually when that happened Abby was unbearably intense, but that time she had been fairly calm. Bailey had desperately tried to change the subject, but then, to her surprise, Abby had taken Bailey's face in her hands, looked intently into her eyes, and said: *"the Egyptian locket leads deep into the earth; there is a door, Bailey, the locket with the universe inside knows the door!"* That was the last straw – something snapped inside Bailey. Fear and anxiety overcame her, and she felt she had to end the conversation that very minute…

She stood in front of her door without noticing where she was, deep in thought. Thinking about Abby always unbalanced her. Frustrated, she could not find her key.

Bailey's condo was on the second floor of a brownstone. It was a corner apartment with two windows facing the street and another facing a small, quiet alley. She tossed her keys on the side table, hung up her raincoat, kicked off her shoes, and walked to the windows. Across the street from her house was a small store that sold vegetables and prepared food. She often stopped there on her way home on workdays so that she didn't have to cook. Cooking was detestable because it had been one of her parents' favorite things to do, and being reminded of them pained her. For Bailey, they were the subject of an internal dilemma – she simultaneously missed and hated them – and dealing with that was the reason she had become a psychologist. She still felt that, in a way, they "got what they deserved" by getting killed. No good parent would go on vacation and abandon their five-year-old daughter when she was sick!

She closed the curtains. Pulling her auburn hair away from her face into a ponytail, she cleaned off her makeup and changed into flannel pajamas. It took under five minutes to warm up the plate of leftovers from the previous night's dinner, which she had bought at the store across the street. *That* guy in the store had sold it to her. He was strange, but much easier to think about than Abby…

13

Craig must be connected to Abby somehow. How, she wasn't sure, but she felt that the connection was definitely there. She had met Craig only a month ago. That day she had stopped at the little store on the way home to get food, as usual. She had noticed a new person working there, a tall, thin young man. He had a beautiful face with high cheekbones, and a long, thick braid of jet black hair rested on his back. He had noticed Bailey too, she was sure of it. She could feel his curiosity as if it was a palpable thing – her skin had gotten warm and her face flushed, as if she was embarrassed. She could tell that the young man's interest in her wasn't sexual, yet she could feel this strange depth, a sort of intimacy between them. And it kept getting stronger. "What the hell is wrong with me? Intimacy? Have I finally joined Abby? It's just some guy looking at me, that's all." But she knew that it was not all. She was intrigued, because she had never before experienced this deep of a connection with a stranger. Every time she went into the store she sought him out. But as soon as he saw her, he always retreated to the back. It was as if he was hiding. Before long, she was so strongly drawn to him that she recognized she had to do something about it. Her supervisor therapist suggested she just talk to the guy. Oh, if only it was that simple! She was a thirty-six-year-old professional and he was what? Maybe twenty years old and cleaning the floor every time she saw him? What could they possibly talk about? Consumed by curiosity and anxiety, she even began to dream about him. In her dreams he always talked to her about something terrifying and important, but she could never remember what it was when she woke up.

The kettle on the stove began to whistle. Quickly snatching it, Bailey poured water over the hot chocolate mix in her mug. This whole thing with Craig was way too unsettling for her measured world. It was two weeks ago that she finally did something. She had seen the young man leaving the store, and moving as though hypnotized, she approached him and asked him to walk on with her to the park. She couldn't believe she had done that, and had already begun to feel like an idiot when she heard him agreeing to go, saying something bizarre like "you are very orange." Perhaps it was her brick colored trench coat, or was it her hair, or her orange umbrella? That was when Bailey found out his name, and that he lived in a tiny studio over the store, the room with the upper part of the round window. She was surprised at his level of intelligence. His clothes, his words; his whole life's story had not led her to expect it.

14

She noticed that Craig took smaller steps to match hers – otherwise his long legs would probably have taken him much farther with each step. Walking together this strange way felt totally normal, as though she knew him. The feeling of déjà vu was so strong she could hardly stand it! When Bailey stopped, Craig asked her if she felt déjà vu! She knew then that the curiosity in Craig's eyes was not general, it was about her. And the intimacy she felt between them, the familiarity, the déjà vu... Why? She was sure she had never met him before. Was he feeling what she was feeling? Feelings always made Bailey uncomfortable. Feelings were there to be analyzed and catalogued, not experienced – experiencing them could only lead to loss of control. But Craig was ... different: strange, but somehow unafraid; unambitious, but not lost. One moment he seemed so immature, and the next he acted like a balanced, well adjusted, even wise, adult. He looked as though life had just happened to him. He had not done well at school, mostly because he found it boring. When Bailey asked about his friends, his answer was that he had never had one; he was always alone, well, except for his cat of course. But when Bailey inquired about that special cat he fell silent.

Everything about this man was odd. As they walked in the park, Craig asked about her parents. She had reluctantly begun to answer, ready to derail the question to some trivial hypothetical statement. She did not notice that Craig had slowed down. Then he began to fall, and Bailey caught him just before he fainted. Was it a seizure? Was he epileptic? Was this something psychological? Neurological?

When Craig came to he mumbled incomprehensibly, his eyes in obvious terror of something he had seen. "It has to be psychological," decided Bailey. She felt almost embarrassed witnessing his private agony, as she tightened her grip on his motorcycle jacket. She walked him to the corner Starbucks and pushed him inside. They sat down, both glad for the calming music and muted conversations. She offered to buy him some juice or water, but to her surprise he asked for hot chocolate.

As she sat across from Craig, Bailey inquired what caused him to faint. Craig's smile, brought on by the hot chocolate, disappeared, and he became silent again. She knew she had asked not out of concern for him, but out of her own discomfort, trying to regain her footing. His face pale, Craig continued silently sipping his cocoa. Bailey stared at him, and felt lost. This young man looked and acted like a child, yet she felt as uncomfortable as if she was dealing with a father figure.

Assisted Psychiatric Facility
Outside of Boston, United States

The room with the white walls is the common room, and besides the nurse there are eight people in it. One of them is a thin woman with skin so white it is as if it had never been exposed to the sun. Her name is Abby, and she is afraid of the sun, among other things. There are large, dark circles under her eyes from another night of poor sleep, and she twists the strands of her long, dark red hair. She sometimes lets one of the other residents in this place braid them. But Abby likes her hair just as it is – long, wavy, and loose. Her hair is her favorite feature. Right now Abby feels very tense and nervous, but she is doing all she can to not show it. She skipped her medication again last night and the night before. She doesn't like the drugs; they keep her dead inside. When she has been off medication for a long time, she becomes deathly scared from all the memories flooding her. But when she takes the stupid white pills she is dead, she has no feelings at all, even though she is able to think. And what's the fun, if you can't feel anything? She hates the pills, but if she went without them completely she would be too scared to live; her memories and the voices take over, and it is not good. Without the pills she feels somewhat normal for only a few days. Her feelings and thoughts are clear then, and the fear would not yet be overwhelming. And right now, sitting in the large armchair with her legs curled under her, Abby is on her second day without the pills.

She had a nightmare again last night, but luckily enough her roommate had been sleeping too deeply to notice. Abby woke herself from it. It was the same the night before. The nightmares are always the same. They are about the time when she was little: at first her parents are alive, and then they are not. Oh, that was such a horrible time. She remembers only bits and pieces, but she remembers. Egypt was such a magical place. She had been so bummed that her sister had not been able to come with them. Abby remembers a large, busy market with many people and smells – everything was different from what she knew, it was all so interesting! She remembers the bright orange shawl she got as a present on her first day in Cairo; her mother had put it over her head that same night. She loved that shawl.

Then this strange old man had come, smelling like the perfume oil that burned outside. Her daddy liked him, she could tell. And her mommy hated him. Mommy was unhappy with daddy, Abby was not sure why, he was so good to her…

And then all she remembered was the locket, a magical golden thing. Maybe it was not magical, but it was so very pretty and shiny. It was hidden in her father's briefcase, but she knew it was there. She must have taken it at some point, because she clearly remembers it on her neck. It was on a twine, like the one they kept in the kitchen.

"That is when it happened the first time, I think," remembers Abby. "There was this darkness and then a very bright white light, and some tall people looking at me, taller than daddy by a lot…"

Abby stares into space as she tries to put her memories in order, like a beaded necklace. Only bits and pieces come to her conscious mind and she struggles to put them together, patiently skipping her medication here and there to allow the memories. It had taken her years to assemble only a few precious beads. She used to write them down but the nurses always took the papers away, so she had learned to memorize the memories. Sometimes she would draw them to remember. And of course she would call Bailey, her trusted sister. She knew that if she could only remember the whole thing, Bailey would keep her secret, she would understand.

The nightmare was similar to the ones that had started in Egypt. "The tall people looking at me… they were so white, everything was so bright…"

It was OK until they began to talk. They talked inside Abby's head. "They said" – she had repeated the words many times since, so that she would remember them – "*We are the Solar Council, welcome, Abigail.*" This had really scared Abby. "They know my name!" She had felt she was in trouble for sure, if some huge shiny grown-ups knew who she was; that somehow she had caused this event to happen, caused the tall people to show up, or that she had gone there, to their bright home… Abby always got confused at this point. She stops twirling her hair and tightens her fingers into fists, hiding them in her pockets. This was her strategy for staying calm and clear. It works only partially – she is still unclear, but at least she feels braver. She looks around the room. The other patients are scattered around the large space. Many are drawing, a few are playing a domino game and Sophie, her roommate who sometimes braids her hair, is standing by the large window, as always. Everything is calm and as usual. Abby smiles to herself. She has done well, no one suspects anything. She isn't sure what happened the last two times she went off her medication; somehow they had known. "Well, at least I managed to call Bailey," she thought.

"What did they say? They said more, I know it." Abby struggles to remember. More scattered pieces return to her conscious mind. "They

17

said *We are the Solar Council, and these people,* as they pointed to some bluish-white tall people and a different looking woman, *came from a star, Abigail. They are from…"* – she can never remember that part. Last night she had remembered more. Not where the people were from, but what was so different about that woman they pointed to. She wore a mask that looked like a cat face to Abby, and she wanted to talk with Abby; she insisted on it. "This was the nightmare, yes, in Egypt…I remember…" thinks Abby, twisting a strand of hair between her fingers faster and faster. "She said she is Sek-Met… She came towards me, stood right in front of me, and she told me again and again something… She said *I am Sek-Met, I am Sek-Met…*she said more…she said *You are not the one, remember, you are NOT the one, your enemy is here…"* – Abby bolts upright in her chair, startled by her memory. She looks around sharply, making sure no one noticed her abrupt move. All she needs is for them to realize that she skipped her pills and put her back on the medication. She would never remember anything that way! She has to call Bailey. Phone hours are almost over; she had better hurry.

Boston, United States

Bailey finished her cocoa and sighed, then stacked dirty dishes into the dishwasher. The work week was over. She could relax now. As she passed by her phone, she stopped and stared at it. There were fourteen messages on her machine! This must be some sort of emergency. She pressed the button and nervously listened.

All fourteen messages were from her sister Abby. And all of them were about the "locket," someone called "Sek-met," and the "Solar Council." As she listened to Abby's intense whisper on her machine, a cold wave passed through her blood. It was as if Abby's voice itself was delivering the chill, and the waves were only amplified by the repetition of the messages. "*You are not the one, she said, you are not the one, Sek-Met told me, she told me, you are not the one she told me, the enemy is here, beware, she told me beware…"*

Bailey's mind was racing. It had been only twelve days since the last time Abby went off her medication. What was going on? She called the facility. A male voice on the other end of the line assured her that Abby had not had any mishaps and was asleep.

She contemplated the issue of the locket through her shower and into bed, where she lay staring at the ceiling. Now she was angry at her sister for bringing it up, at her parents for damaging Abby by their irresponsible actions, and at herself for not being able to drop it and go to sleep. "What is this thing about the damn locket?!" she said out loud. "It's meaningless! These are just the words of a person experiencing an acute psychotic episode, which my sister was kind enough to share with me, of course! Why does she feel this need to include me in her madness every time she gets off her medication?" Bailey was near tears. If she was not careful, she would end up having her own psychotic episode. She got up and went to her medicine cabinet, returning to bed with anti-anxiety pills in hand. Quickly swallowing them, she hoped to god they would help. Why couldn't she be strong? Why did she need this crap? What was she anxious over? She should be able to handle this. She knew that anger wouldn't help her sleep, but it was now too late to regret the emotion.

After two hours of struggle Bailey finally fell asleep, but she was soon awakened by her own broken breathing. Her clothes were soaked with sweat and she could barely catch her breath. She had had nightmares since she was a child, after her parents died, and all of them were about being left behind or having to fend for herself. But this nightmare was different – a tall strange woman was telling Bailey again and again, "*look* at the locket, *look* at the locket!" When Bailey refused and started crying, she saw that Abby was there too, and next to her stood their father; both were gently telling her the same thing. In her dream she felt trapped and unsure. Now awake and sitting on her bed, she understood the futility of her attempts to shut out her subconscious mind – "When it wants to send you a message, it will try until you give in." Tomorrow she would have to do something about the locket. "Taking action should resolve the issue," Bailey decided, and the decision being the first move toward resolution, she lay down again and prepared to go back to sleep.

*   *   *

The next morning Bailey walked to the bank. There, in a safe-deposit box, was the locket, round and gold. It had been on Abby's neck when she arrived from Egypt so many years ago. No one knew how she came into possession of it; surely the family had no heirlooms of this type and no money to purchase anything of the sort. Maybe it was a cheap item in Egypt, and her parents had gotten it. Bailey had been told that it was from Egypt, and a gift from her father. Of course Abby had never been able to clarify the matter. Bailey had always thought it amazing that this gold thing was overlooked by Egyptian security when

Abby was shipped back home. Maybe gold jewelry on the neck of a white kid did not look strange to Arabs. They may have thought that all Westerners were wealthy.

Bailey was led to the special room in the back of the bank and left with her safe-deposit box. Her fingers gripped the metal box for a moment, then she opened it. The "locket" was not actually what would normally be thought of as a locket – it did not open to reveal a picture inside. This locket was a disk about an inch and a half in diameter, convex on the front and flat on the back. It was heavy, and seemed to be sealed shut. Bailey had always assumed that it was a solid pendant, not a locket, and that the thickness was only for decoration. It would take a lot of gold to fill it. It might also be hollow and filled with some other metal on the inside that made it heavy.

Her grandmother had taken the locket from Abby's neck, where it was hanging on a long dirty twine – not something anyone would use for gold jewelry. All of this was a blur to Bailey. She only remembered that grandma talked to someone, secretly, and that after she saw that man she put the locket in a safe-deposit box along with other things of value.

As a teenager Bailey had wanted to know about her parents. Her grandma, who was very old by then, told her: "You might as well know... there was a locket on Abby's neck when they brought her back. I had it tested by a jeweler I knew. He said he had never seen anything like it; it was made of orange gold, he thought. He could not open it and he didn't want to break it. I had such a headache carrying this locket. You know, I was afraid something might happen to it, so I always had it on me, but my head was just hurting so much... That jeweler told me that it was very valuable and probably very old, but he also got a headache just from handling it for a few days. So I thought that maybe it was the locket that was giving me headaches. Since it was valuable, I put it in the bank. It is under both of our names, dear. I don't think you should ever sell it, though." Bailey wanted to see the locket, and the next day they went to the bank. But when she saw it she immediately felt disappointed – the piece of jewelry, although very pretty and shiny, looked Egyptian. For some reason she had not thought it would be. This piece of gold jewelry her father had gotten in Cairo for Abby could have been anything. He had to have also gotten one for Bailey, but it just hadn't made it into the States in all the commotion. She wanted to think that perhaps her father had at least thought of her in Cairo – Bailey, his little girl left at home sick with chickenpox – and had not bought jewelry for Abby alone. Grandma had no idea how this locket had made it home safely with Abby. Maybe it was because it had been on her body and under her

20

clothes, and Abby had been so very angry – screaming, even biting – that perhaps no one had noticed it.

At the bank with grandma, looking at the locket had shattered Bailey's teen fantasy. She had hoped that her dad had bought one just like it for her, little Bailey, but since, if it existed, hers had not made it into the States, and Abby was sick and didn't need it, Bailey had felt totally justified in taking it and wearing it as though it were hers. She had planned to take it home with her that day. But seeing its odd design and Egyptian look, Bailey felt appalled. She would never wear anything Egyptian on her body – it would betray her pain! She didn't like anything Egyptian. She had mixed feelings about Egypt: an intense fascination and an equally intense blame. Fascination elicited curiosity but only in connection to her parents; it wasn't about the land of Egypt or its culture. Blame raised hatred and coldness: she still saw Egypt as the place that took her parents away from her. Even after her grandmother's death, she never went to see the little gold locket again. But she never sold it, choosing instead to pay a small yearly fee for the box.

Abby almost never brought up the locket. She seemed to have forgotten about it, and Bailey had been successfully avoiding the topic until last night. Fourteen messages and a nightmare were the last straw – she now felt compelled to look at that damn thing again.

And here she was, in the back room of the bank, looking at it.

It was amazing. She almost could not believe she had not come sooner. There were strange symbols on it that looked Egyptian. Of course, Bailey didn't know enough about Egypt to tell.

She stared at the locket. Her hand drifted to her chest and her fingers found a tiny ladybug pendant hanging on a chain. She wanted to feel the locket on her body. Quickly she took the chain off her neck, opened it and slid the locket into the loop, then replaced it on her neck, fingers trembling. There was no mirror. As she searched through her purse for one, a bank worker entered and asked if she was finished. She was startled, as if the woman had caught her doing something illegal. Bailey hadn't realized that she had been there for over an hour, staring at this locket. How could time fly so fast? Why was she missing almost forty-five minutes? She promised the woman she was just about done. The woman wouldn't leave. "I'll be right out!" she snapped, and the woman stepped out. Bailey started to lift the locket off of her neck, then changed her mind. She needed more time with it. She would return it to the bank another time. "Why do I have to return it? Jesus, I feel like a little kid in trouble!" She left the bank, the locket on her neck hidden from view by her shirt.

It was raining again, and Bailey grabbed her umbrella as the wind tried to take it from her. But this time there was no struggle, no fear or nervousness. Her heart was beating hard, as if it were trying to jump out of her chest, and the locket on her neck felt heavy and hot. Everything had changed; everything felt exhilarating – the wind and rain were not annoying and the colors around her were bright, smudged by the running water. She caught herself smiling.

* * *

At home there was a message on her phone. Craig wanted to see her. Since they met she had seen him almost every night. They were definitely having some sort of relationship, but Bailey could not classify it. They were not lovers, for sure. She cared for him as a sister would for a younger brother. Bailey was not certain how to be friends with Craig; she kept confusing this young man with a child, a brother, a father… "And who is the therapist here?" she wondered every time Craig gave her some great advice. "How the hell does he know this? I had to go to school, plus put in years of practice, to get this good!" She was almost jealous – Craig was insightful to a high degree, almost suspiciously so. Considering that she had told him more about herself than she had told even her best girlfriend, Bailey could see that Craig had a special place in her life. Somehow, she trusted him. For as long as she could remember, trusting people had been hard: they had given her more reasons to keep her distance than not. Analyzing from afar was safer; intimacy was too close and way too scary. Yet it was easy with Craig. He acted like he knew her, and he never judged her. He was comfortable with her, as he was with himself. She was never comfortable, with herself or anyone else!

She was preparing a tuna salad lunch when Craig arrived. Before she could speak, Craig blurted out: "There's this ancient secret in Egypt about the origins of the human race, and I think maybe also time travel. People should know, we are ready, but there's a conspiracy, they're hiding it from us…"

"Who are *they*?" asked Bailey, before she could think. Starting a conversation about Egypt suddenly seemed so natural that for a moment she had not even been surprised when Craig brought it up. "Why are you talking about Egypt?" she asked him suspiciously.

"Ah? I was just reading…"

22

Bailey could see that look Craig got on his face whenever he was not going to tell her the truth. She knew he did not want to lie to her, but it was an unmistakable facial expression that signified that this subject was off limits. "I wonder what I haven't earned his trust for yet?" wondered Bailey, watching Craig's face. His eyes had suddenly found the floor very interesting. "There is something about this man…"

But she herself was all wired up about the locket and had to talk to someone, and Craig was the best candidate. This was the first time since they met that Bailey had ever mentioned Egypt. To her amazement, Craig was very knowledgeable on the subject. Apparently Egypt was one of his interests, fascinations, even obsessions. He knew a lot about many pharaohs, temples and their histories, and she was quickly inundated with information. Craig was practically a different man: animated, confident, passionate, and sure of himself. Her own thoughts of Egypt always made her feel somehow defeated and hurt.

As they ate, the conversation strayed to the subject of parents. Bailey never talked about her parents unless she was in therapy. In fact, everything to do with her parents was exclusively associated with therapy: with studying to become a psychologist, supervision therapy sessions, private therapy sessions – the very mention of her parents existed only as an analysis. Yet here she was, eating a triangulated tuna sandwich and telling Craig about the death of her parents in, of all places, Egypt.

"Sometimes I'm not even sure if they were real…" mused Bailey. "I thought of them so much as a set-up of my life that they lost their humanity."

"We have a lot in common, you see," Craig said, folding his legs comfortably under him as he sat. "You didn't have parents either. My mother died when I was two, my father a bit later, and then my grandmother died too. They all are dead, just like yours. And we both are on the path, and are both afraid of people…"

Bailey was about to protest that last statement but no words came out. She knew Craig was right, and was shocked at how apparent this truth was to him.

"On what path?"

"On the life path, you know? Living a life is like walking on the path."

"Oh, I guess…" She had never thought of it that way.

"You and your sister have such different paths in life… an interesting variable she picked to explore."

"What variable? She didn't *pick* anything, she was horribly traumatized as a child by the events in Egypt, resulting in a mental illness. That's why she is so… sick now."

"You were gonna say '*messed up*'."

"She is mentally ill. It is very unfair that she won't have a normal life."

After an uncomfortable pause, Craig mumbled, "We all choose our lives; I don't think any life is 'normal'… Everyone is messed up a little…"

Taking a breath, Bailey realized she had to phrase things differently: "Yes, we all have issues. But when someone's behavior is abnormal…"

"I should go." Craig stood up.

"No, wait. I am not saying it right. I'm sorry… I just can't imagine my sister having any say in what happened to her…"

"Maybe it didn't happen *to* her…"

"What do you mean?"

"Maybe it was meant to be… A path she *chose*. And maybe her path is not as bad as you think. She just has to be given a chance to figure it out."

"She can't have a normal life!"

"She is not a victim," said Craig quietly.

"She is!"

"*No one* is a victim, no matter how hard their path is."

"So she chose to be crazy?" snapped Bailey.

"You think that your sister is *crazy*?"

"I shouldn't, I know, sorry… she is ill. When my emotions attach themselves to my mental statements, I guess I end up judging instead of classifying."

"Have you tried just feeling? Instead of classifying, I mean?"

"I feel…"

Craig interrupted:

"Promise you're not gonna be mad at me?" His eyes explored the floor while his hand fiddled with the zipper on his motorcycle jacket. He was still standing and Bailey felt confused.

"Why would I be mad at you?"

"Promise. Or I won't tell you." Craig looked intently at Bailey.

"Ok, I promise." She was frustrated with this childish game, but she was consumed by curiosity and she knew it.

Craig sat down again.

"I'm a shaman."

24

"Okaay..."

Bailey had not expected that. If this had been a patient talking, she would probably have classified him as someone with delusional tendencies, maybe visual or auditory hallucinations, insecurity – many other things. But this was Craig.

"I'm a shaman," he repeated. "I see... visions... and dreams, and they tell me things."

Craig did not look like a shaman to her. Shamans were smelly and old and weird, they did not know how to use computers, and they did not work in grocery stores!

"What do you mean by that?" ventured Bailey cautiously.

"By what?" Craig smiled, and seemed satisfied with himself.

"You talk to ghosts?" offered Bailey.

"No, not ghosts, just a spirit. But I can't tell you anything about him, that wouldn't be polite."

"To that spirit...?" said Bailey, wanting clarification.

"Yeah, he wouldn't like it if I talked about him, so I won't. Oh, I am so relieved that now you know! I've never told anyone before!"

Bailey was definitely unsure of what to do. "This has happened a lot lately..." she thought.

"So, you hear voices and see visions?"

"No, I only talk to one spirit, and I do see things... But it is either a dream, or I have to go on a vision quest, then it is like a vision." Craig looked ready to say more.

"How do you know it isn't just an intense dream?"

"Oh, I know. It's like... when you wake up you know you were not alone."

"Oh..." Bailey was not sure that she understood, but she had started to feel uneasy. She knew the feeling that Craig was talking about, but she had never connected it to having a vision or, for that matter, having some spirit nearby!

"So every time you have an intense dream that means there is ghost next to you? Sorry, a spirit..."

"No, I have nightmares sometimes, but those aren't visions. It's different. I can tell."

"And a vision quest is some sort of meditation? Like a guided visualization?" She knew about those, and even applied them to her patients sometimes.

"No... In those things you know where you will end up, and I don't."

Bailey knew that guided visualizations could be used to uncover buried trauma and that sometimes the patient ended up where his mind did not want him to go – he would be led there by hidden emotions.

"So, you guide yourself somewhere and then see what happens?"

"No… I go on a quest – I mean I open my eyes and I am somewhere else, and I can see my spirit guide and we talk. And sometimes he takes me to other places and shows me things. He is funny…" smiled Craig lovingly, caught in his own thoughts.

"And you are not aware of where you are?"

"Of course I am – I'm in the vision."

"I mean, you don't know what your body is doing?"

As if to check it out, Craig looked at himself.

"I know what it's doing…" He sounded dumbfounded by her question.

"I mean, when you are in the vision quest, do you know not only what you are doing in the vision, but also what your body is doing?"

"My body is in the vision."

"But you don't disappear from here, do you!?" Frustrated, and thinking that she must not be asking the right questions, Bailey hoped like hell for a "no" answer!

"Oh, no! Of course not! I usually sit, that's the most comfortable position – so I can't fall or walk into things," clarified Craig.

"So, what does a shaman do? Give people potions? Or say some words to make the illness go away?" she said sarcastically. Craig got up.

"I'd better go."

"Wait, I didn't mean that. I don't think you're crazy…not really…"

"You think your sister is nuts, and that I'm too," pouted Craig.

"Of course not! My sister has developed a paranoid disorder because of severe childhood trauma. We still don't know what that was exactly, only that she probably witnessed the death of our parents… You are much more together and you are not sick. You have issues…"

"That's true."

"I would rather you stayed. I never talk about this stuff… My family, I mean."

He sat back down.

Eventually the subject of the locket came up. Bailey unhooked the chain. Craig stared at the locket, fascinated, while his fingers explored its surface. The pictures resembled Egyptian hieroglyphics, and concealed beneath this main design was a spiral. Right away he got onto Bailey's computer to search the Internet for anything similar, but his search came up empty. Unwilling to admit defeat, he kept on looking.

Bailey, curled up on the sofa, stared into space. Could it be that this piece of jewelry was worth more than its weight in gold? Was it truly ancient? Did her father know? She jumped up, looking for her shoes – the paper trail for all his work was in the storage space upstairs. When she bought the condo she had debated dumping those papers – she thought she would never go through them anyway, and Abby certainly wouldn't need them. She couldn't make a decision; in the end she kept them, and they had been accumulating dust in her storage space for many years.

After searching through what seemed like the hundredth plastic container filled with her father's stuff, Bailey spotted a dust-covered bundle of small, yellowed papers, held together by a large paperclip – dad's Cairo receipts! Why would this little pile of useless papers be kept in the first place? And for so many years? The receipts were clipped to a file folder of drawings – some looked like copies of Egyptian statues and temples, and others had odd hieroglyph-like characters, spirals, and numbers. Flipping quickly through the drawings, Bailey froze. She was staring at the drawing of the design on her locket – an exact copy! These papers were from *before* the trip. When her father didn't come back from Egypt, grandma put all his documents and odds and ends into boxes. That meant he knew about the design before he went to Egypt and got the locket for Abby. How could this be?? But the pile of dusty yellowed papers revealed no more information.

*   *   *

Bailey's mind was addicted to the locket. She wore it day and night – at the office, at home, and to bed. She didn't get headaches like her grandma, but she did feel different – a sort of exhilaration, as if she was high. Curiosity about her parents intensified with each passing day. She was finally feeling brave enough to face the truth!

Clutching a pen and notebook, she sat on the sofa with her feet under her. The notebook page was quickly divided in half and she began to write. On the left went everything she knew about her parents, and on the right everything about the locket. But after only a few lines she stopped. To her shame she didn't know much! She had a report from the medical examiner recording the deaths of her parents. There was another official paper clipped to the report – an account of the incident by Cairo police. But it had few details, stating only that "the three American citizens, a family traveling to Cairo, were assaulted in Giza; the two adults were killed while the child survived and was hospitalized." Bailey shrugged her shoulders, wondering what kind of care little Abby had gotten in Cairo. The report continued: "After clarifying the child's identity, the American Embassy was contacted and the transfer of the child to the US was facilitated. The assault case is currently open." That was all. Was the case ever closed? Did they find out who assaulted and killed her parents, and why? Neither she nor her grandma ever inquired further and now, biting the end of her pen, Bailey was shocked that it had never occurred to her to ask these questions before.

Her column for the locket was even blanker. She had researched the locket's design on the Internet and found four Egyptologists interested in taking a look at the picture. After prolonged puzzlement all four concluded that the locket was not ancient Egyptian but was something very similar to it, possibly coming from a culture existing parallel to the Old Kingdom culture. But when they were asked which culture they were referring to, all Bailey got was what it was not – not Mesopotamian, not Nubian, not Hittite, not Mittani, not Assyrian, etc. When she pressed further, suggesting that perhaps it was from a culture that had been unrecorded in history, she was accused of being "one of those New Age people." Three Egyptologists then refused to see the design as ancient, suddenly saying that it was fake, and claiming that she was wasting their time. The fourth scholar asked to have the locket shipped to him to determine its authenticity. Craig exploded when she told him she was thinking of shipping the locket to the fourth scholar.

"Once they know what the locket is they will take it from you, maybe the government will seize it or something."

"What government? Why would they take it from me?" The idea of parting with the locket made Bailey nervous.

"You know it is *the* real thing, right?"

Bailey's mind hated to admit that her intuition agreed with Craig, but it did. And that scared her. She did not send the locket to the scholar, not because she believed Craig's assumption that they would take it from her, but because she was afraid to find proof of what she now suspected to be the truth – that the locket represented something ancient. This posed an even bigger question – how much of human history did she hold in her hand? How much was she willing to go against established beliefs?

Putting the locket's mystery aside for the time being, Bailey searched for more information on her parents. There was a record of the shipping of her parent's bodies home, but nothing more. She called the

Cairo police, and hit yet another wall. After a very long wait, a voice in accented English recited to her the words from the report she held in her hands.

"I already know that, I have that report. I would like to know more about the case." She was told to call a different number – the Police Archives. After a prolonged hold more papers were located, and a tired voice eventually replied:

"Yes, ma'am, the Rixsons were assaulted and killed. The papers say their bodies were found in the morning by the market vendors, lying on the street. And the child was not well, she was delivered with the bodies."

"You put her in the morgue?!"

"The papers say the child was put in hospital. After this the American Embassy took her away."

"What killed them? I was told they were not shot..."

"The papers say the Rixsons had no determining wounds and the assailants ran away."

Frustrated, Bailey asked if the case was ever closed.

"It is deemed an accident, an unfortunate coincidence in which the cause of their death could not be definitively linked to the assault, ma'am. We are sorry for your misfortune. I want the best for you and wish a great day for you now."

"Jesus, there's got to be more information out there!"

Bailey's international phone bill grew – she called the Cairo Governorate Office, Giza Governorate Office, Ministry of Foreign Affairs, the American Embassy in Cairo – but it was all useless, she got nothing. There was one more number to try – the Cairo Bureau of Tourism, Department of Incidents. The happy answering voice was replaced, after a long wait, by a tight one.

"Ma'am, it is useful to remember that thirty years ago Cairo had lots of robberies, but now it is safer. We welcome American citizens." Hearing the disconnected tone Bailey furiously slammed the phone down – another useless call.

There was no reason to keep asking. It was easy to see that no one would take the time to investigate a murder that happened thirty-one years ago. Perhaps there were some details hidden in the dusty papers, but surely no one in Cairo would willingly go searching for them.

"If I could only go through those papers myself... Just walk into all these places one by one and demand information. They would have to give me more of an answer than what they just told me!" Bailey imagined herself interrogating Egyptian authorities. But her heartbeat suddenly got faster than she could handle as she realized she had already made the decision to go to Egypt – Egypt, the "evil place that took her parents from her."

She dialed her colleague, the one whose patients she had taken care of during his vacations before she bought his practice. He was willing to take over her practice for two weeks. By the time Bailey hung up, she had her travel dates marked on her calendar.

As the trip materialized in front of her, she felt the reality of it and her excitement faded, replaced by intense fear, sadness, and hurt. Caught in this overwhelm, she naturally thought of Craig. "He is perfect for this – he knows the story, he knows stuff about Egypt, he is calm and he…has no money. Oh well, I will just buy him a ticket. I have to pay for the hotel anyway, we'll share the room. Considering the current situation in Egypt, I'll feel safer having him around." Afraid that she might become sane and change her mind, Bailey pressed the digits of Craig's number and before he could speak she blurted out an invitation. After a pause she heard a loud whisper: "Did you talk to a cat? An *orange* one?"

"What?" Maybe she hadn't heard right. "What did you say?"

"Nothing, sorry." Craig stopped whispering. "Whoa! … Egypt! I think I need to go there…"

Unsure of what to make of it, Bailey hung up.

"Well, he's coming so I guess that's settled…"

CHAPTER THREE

1,360BC

Malkata Palace, Waset, Egypt

Aplump man stood sideways in front of a polished gold mirror. His eyes followed the curve of his own body, resting at his bulging belly covered by gold-trimmed linen. He sighed and turned to face the mirror. Amenhotep III held incredible social power. His lengthy reign had established unprecedented prosperity for Egypt and an age of artistic splendor. Politically, Egypt was in the position of top international might. Artistically it had seemed to reach its highest peak. The riches of Egypt were, of course, the riches of its pharaoh. And so Amenhotep III stood as the richest man of his time.

At this particular moment though, he stood in front of the mirror wincing in pain. He quietly moaned and pulled from his mouth a cloth pouch filled with cloves. His teeth had been hurting for a while now, and the mixture he was given just yesterday by his doctor had stopped working already. He took a deep breath and attempted to return to his thoughts of grandeur – "I am the god of Egypt." Amenhotep smiled to himself and grimaced, because stretching his face into a smile pulled on the inflamed gums. "And what kind of god am I if my own body does not seem to listen to my commands! Well, neither does my wife..."

But, he was a pharaoh and so he had to be a living god. Members of his family, the Thutmose pharaohs, had ruled Egypt for over one hundred and fifty years before him. By now Amenhotep III had been given four daughters and two sons by his Chief Royal Wife Tiye. Named after previous generations of pharaohs, his eldest son, Thutmose V, held the title of crown prince of Egypt. Thutmose was also the high priest of Ptah and he seemed more involved with religious matters than matters of state. But Amenhotep knew that Thutmose would be able to rule Egypt well. "With the help of Amun's priests, of course. As long as I leave my son a harmonious, powerful country... I am so blessed by the gods to have lived so long and I will live through many more Sed festivals," mused Amenhotep. "What is my eldest son to do? Wait for me to pass to the Land of the Dead? Of course Thutmose pursued his interest in religion and became the high priest of Ptah, the Overseer of all priests... There is no harm in that, only honor for our family. As is customary, my first born son Thutmose is the Crown Prince. It is my second born son that is meant to become the High Priest of Amun..."

But Amenhotep IV, his younger son, and still only a young boy, so far showed no interest in the priesthood. Amenhotep worried about that fact, but Tiye saw no cause for concern – the prince was young and he had the time to acquire an interest in religion. At least all four daughters were well taken care of. They were the wealthiest women in the land; art was made for them and songs sung in their honor.

He heard his servant's sandals flopping on the polished stone floors as he came into the room. The servant stood there quietly. Amenhotep had noticed him, but chose for a while not to remove his attention from the mirror. A new necklace, a gift from the Mittani kingdom in the north, adorned his fat neck. How did he get so fat? He used to be able to move fast and eat all he wanted. But loving sweet fruits and foods prepared for him only made him desire movement less and less...

Amenhotep finally turned to the servant with an inquiring look. The servant informed him that the principal architect-vizier had arrived to update him on the glorious progress of the construction of his temple. The temple was one of Amenhotep's major undertakings. Its double pylons rose higher than any other temple, and could already be seen from Waset. With the largest foundation of thirty-five *ha*, Amenhotep's temple had no rivals. Representations of his family adorned its walls – his lovely daughters taking a major place next to his wife and sons. Deciding to see the vizier in his chamber, Amenhotep waved to the servant. The architect-vizier entered and bowed deeply, sprawling himself on the floor. Amenhotep waved him up and listened. The vizier's presentation included two papyrus colored renderings of the temple's inner court and the obelisks that would be placed in it. When the vizier fell silent, Amenhotep could not contain his excitement and walked toward the windows. Two servants and an ornate cane materialized next to him.

Amenhotep's brows came together, creating a deep crease on his forehead, but he took the cane. He limped to the wall opening of his Malkata Palace, from where he could see his temple coming into existence on the other side of the Nile. River waters caressed the massive harbor, revealing the darkness beyond the front pylon, the place where Amenhotep was to be worshipped as a god, during his lifetime and afterwards.

Amenhotep entered the adjacent audience chamber and servants ushered him into a large chair. More a throne than a chair, it had been built especially to accommodate his expanding size. He winced again, this time from to the action of sitting down, because his knees and hips hurt. Even with all the special care of the gods, he was still a forty-year-old man – he was old.

Amenhotep took a moment to settle into the chair and recover from the ache. His eyes took in the expansive audience chamber with the massive open windows along the side. Large vases with miniature palm trees stood in front of the wall openings. The light streamed through the leaves into the room, cutting a curious crisscross pattern on the sandstone floor.

Painted plaster walls displayed scenes from the pharaoh's life. An ornate border of repeating figures in precise sequence ran across the ceiling perimeter – these were the gods in procession. Amenhotep himself had insisted on having them painted. He believed that inviting gods into one's life must go beyond going to a palatial chapel; their painted figures brought life and the god's favor into his palace. The human god closed his eyes and settled into his chair. The leaves of the miniature palm trees hung still in the hot air, but right over Amenhotep's body two large fans moved gently up and down, propelled by two Nubian servants, their ebony skin glittering in the sunlight. A massive shallow copper bowl filled with water and pink flower petals was ready for his feet, while on the low table next to his chair were many more smaller engraved copper bowls filled with tasty foods. The smells of fruit and flowers filled the air.

Amenhotep yawned. He was pleased that the quartzite stone had been dragged here, to Waset, from the Nile delta. Not only that, but two colossal statues of himself were already hewn. They would soon be positioned on each side of the temple's entrance, facing east so that he could watch the sun rise for eternity. It was Amenhotep's choice, at his architect's suggestion, to use quartzite instead of granite or limestone – under the sun the quartzite crystals sparkled, giving life to his statues. His Chief Royal Wife Tiye's perfect form was carved onto the right side of his seated figure and his mother Mutemwiya's to the left, so that Amenhotep would feel secure – with them protecting his legacy he could enter eternity confidently.

After the report on the temple construction, an international relations vizier was allowed in. Amenhotep's campaigns reached far and wide, into Assyria, Mittani, Babylon, and Hatti. He had officially married Gilukhepa and Shutarna of the Mittani kingdom, and many others had entered his household. The royal Malkata Palace was a cosmopolitan place, filled with beautiful and powerful women who spoke dozens of different languages, and many viziers and important men from other lands.

Trusting his Principal Wife Tiye was easy – they had been married since he was eleven years of age and she was only a few years younger. He had inherited the throne at that time after the death of his father, Thutmose IV, and a royal marriage was immediately arranged. Oblivious to a huge political underground campaign to arrange the coupling, to Amenhotep's delight he was married to his long-time friend, Tiye, a daughter of a prominent and very wealthy official from Khent-Min. She was not a typical royal wife, but it never occurred to the young Amenhotep to question that fact.

Khent-Min, a town in Upper Egypt, was a strange place of mixed population and desert routes. It was also the seat of the god Horus, and there were many festivals, temples, and statues in his honor. The most prominent town family was that of Vizier Yuya and his wife Thuja. They had three children, sons Anen and Aye, and a daughter Tiye. Offspring not of royal blood traditionally could never be considered for a royal marriage, regardless of how influential or wealthy the parents were. But Vizier Yuya was the brother of Mutemwiya, Amenhotep's mother, a minor wife at court at the time. The family quickly rose in power, so much so that young Amenhotep III was placed to become the next pharaoh of Egypt. Vizier Yuya became well known at the court of Thutmose IV, bringing his children along to play with the royal family. Yuya's son Aye was almost a young man when Thutmose IV died, and Ay's sister was only eight. The influence of the family was paramount because soon after Amenhotep's coronation, Tiye, a wealthy and educated commoner, was maneuvered into the position of Principal Queen of Egypt.

Amenhotep had many women in his harem, all desiring to please him. But he trusted only Tiye. He loved her, more as a friend than a passionate lover – after all, it was a childhood arranged marriage. He hated when they fought. After one of their fights many years back, right when he had married Gilukhepa, the Mittani princess, Tiye refused to talk to him. Their relationship was such that she was not afraid to speak her mind, although officially she had no right to such behavior. That did not matter to Tiye. She kept up appearances, but for almost a year found many other cities to travel to, away from her husband. Amenhotep III did not like being without her counsel, which he valued greatly, just as much as he valued her sense of humor. He was simply bored without her, no matter how many other wives he had! To remedy the situation, Amenhotep elected to make a lake in Khent-Min in Tiye's honor, in a small area of Djakaru, her home. A large artificial pond was excavated and filled with water. Invited onto a barge that smelled of flowers and incense, Amenhotep and Tiye were rowed for hours in the rich opulence by a few dozen men, for all the people to see. Tiye forgave him; it would have been impolite not to.

Amenhotep refocused on the present: "Where is my Wife? She was supposed to have already returned from Ro-Setau, from paying her respects to the Sphinx." Amenhotep thought it was odd that she chose to take three months away from him, and during the preparations for the festival at that, to pay respects at the temples in the delta. She had taken their youngest son with her on the journey – he loved the idea of sailing down the Nile on the royal barge. That boy liked everything that could move – barges, horses, chariots. Chariots scared Amenhotep III, they rode too fast for his comfort. He preferred being carried by servants in his richly decorated litter. He could even envision being slowly rolled in a carriage by the bulls. But horses? Riding should be left to the time of war, and even then only to ones who knew how to do it properly. "Besides, fast speed reeks of indignity!" thought Amenhotep, squinting at the sunlight.

CHAPTER FOUR

Current time
Cairo, Egypt

The flight to Egypt took over eleven hours, and their last-minute seats were in the middle of a huge plane which made comfort impossible. Bailey was exhausted by the time they finally arrived at the Cairo airport. Craig, on the other hand, took in every detail, barely able to contain his excitement. The airport was new, spacious and full of light, with the air-conditioning on full blast. An Egyptian man quickly grabbed their bags, ready to carry them wherever they wanted. Bailey could hardly find her own self, never mind know where to go! Scared to finally face the land that had taken away her parents and returned her sister broken down, she was lost in grief and pain. It was Craig who managed to figure out where the taxis were, and soon they were en route to their hotel.

Their taxi sped through the large open streets of Masr al Gedida, Cairo's northern section, filled with cars, donkeys, trucks, camels, and tourist buses. Noise penetrated everything, even the taxi's closed windows. A large green divider separated their side of the road from the opposite lanes, and on it, in the distance, stood a huge statue of Ramesses II. Neither of them had been to Egypt before, but both felt déjà vu as they stared at the towering Ramesses.

They were dropped off at the Osiris Hotel in the middle of the city. It was a tiny place located entirely on the twelfth floor of a pink colored building. Their room was white walled, had two neatly made beds with a nightstand between them, and two large windows covered by curtains of a deep red color. Sunlight streaming through the curtains gave

36

the room a reddish hue. They were high above the noisy city; the sounds of Cairo were muted, but easily heard. Bailey crossed the room to the windows and shut them. The silence was instantaneous. An electric clock on the nightstand showed the time to be a bit past one in the afternoon. Bailey's whole body ached from the flight, and she wanted a shower and a bed. Craig, on the other hand, welcomed the unknown and was itching to explore.

Walking through the pink hallway, which brought him into a pink lobby, Craig found a few dark Arab-style chairs, a sofa, and a man staring at him. Unsure of what to do, he asked the man about the hotel's restaurant. The entrance was right in front of him, hidden by a column. As Craig peered around the corner, he noticed a man standing next to a small shelf filled with bottles of cheap liquor; he was the barkeep. Perhaps leaving the hotel altogether would be a better idea.

The sounds of the loudly alive city crashed into him as he stepped onto the street. Craig jumped; he was being yelled at by the driver of a car speeding by. He had better pay attention, he realized. Silly little tourist shops surrounded the hotel, filled to overflowing with meaningless statuettes, the wanna-bes of the magnificent ancient statues. He bought a bottle of water and walked on in the afternoon heat. Turning left, turning right, left again... soon he arrived at a large square filled with people and traffic, and overwhelmingly loud horns. Craig had stopped in awe, staring at the commotion, when he was startled by a horse's head materializing over his right shoulder. The head was attached to the body of a horse, which was further attached to a carriage carrying a man holding the reins. "I am your friend! I will show you Cairo, safe and good shopping too!" the man said again and again with intensity. Craig tried to explain that he didn't need to shop or get a carriage ride, but the man refused to listen. Craig walked faster and faster – the horse followed, speeding up to match him. In desperation, he ran into a side alley. When he stopped, two things were clear: one, he had successfully avoided the carriage and two, he was officially lost. As he wandered along the back alleys, a multitude of street cats followed him, hoping for food and company.

*   *   *

Reality had changed remarkably. Bailey and Craig were all of the way across the world in Cairo nonchalantly sipping their morning coffee on the rooftop of a shabby pink building in a not-too-shabby hotel. Bailey sat with her laptop, a gift from a strange friend a year ago, and planned their day. The computer had all of the information that she needed: a list of agencies that she had called from home and a few new ones to check out. She felt ready.

Hopping from taxi to taxi, they had visited one agency after another, but with no results, unless, of course, "nothing" could be considered a result. Now they waited in the offices of the Cairo Council of Antiquities, photocopies in hand. Craig had had the idea to show only the photograph of the locket and the photocopy of the precise drawing made by her father, instead of the locket itself. Bailey showed the papers to someone she had made an appointment with before arriving in Cairo. Pretending to be busy, he made her wait for a long time in his impressive British-style wood paneled office. When he finally returned, he was adamant that the design was not Egyptian at all. Then he proceeded to question her about where she had gotten the locket. Her answers did not satisfy him, and he demanded that she tell him, threatening to charge her with "selling Egyptian treasures illegally." Bailey was baffled. First of all, she was not selling anything, and secondly, she was just told that the locket was *not* Egyptian.

She left the office in confusion, her long time enemy. She knew how to override pain or fear – just push through it – but confusion remained undefeated and she would just have to wait for it to pass. She looked at Craig – they were both alarmed. All they needed was to have some legal action brought against them simply for asking the wrong questions!

Now what? The Cairo Police Headquarters was their next stop. Standing on the busy street looking at the legion of empty tourist buses, Bailey's gaze fell on the police station. Fifteen men in white uniforms were stationed by the square to make tourists feel more comfortable, and they looked around in boredom, fingering their cigarettes and machine guns. After Bailey and Craig had repeated their request three times to three different people, they were finally received in a pompously decorated office. The chief officer of the Cairo police held a photocopy in his hands – it was the same report of her parents' death that Bailey already had in her possession, with another page attached. Ignoring her protests, the police officer silently studied the report, then read it out loud to her. Exasperated, she inhaled sharply and asked if the killers of her parents had ever been found.

"Ma'am, there is no indication here that this was a murder. It is deemed to be an accident. There were no perceptible signs of injury on the Rixsons' bodies. Maybe they were scared to death?"

"What??"

"Ma'am, I am sorry for your misfortune, but this was such a long time ago…who knows what happened…"

"My sister, the child who was found with my parents, had this in her possession. Could this be helpful? Maybe if we know where my father bought this…"

Bailey's voice trailed off, as the police officer silently studied the photograph of the locket.

"This was probably purchased in Khan-El-Khalili… there are hundreds of these."

"No, you don't understand, this is a very ancient unique piece of jewelry. I have consulted the experts and they…"

"Ma'am, this type of information you will find in the Museum Archives. But if this is ancient Egyptian, it was stolen from our museum or an archeological excavation – was your father involved in anything like that?"

"No, no… He must have just bought it at the market… I was mistaken, it's probably not ancient…"

Afraid now that it had been a mistake to visit the police after all, Bailey began to worry – what if the Egyptian authorities accused her of stealing the locket, declaring it to be some national treasure? And since she actually had it in her possession, they could confiscate it and fine her, or worse, imprison her! At this point Bailey could not imagine parting with the locket. Her own freedom seemed less important.

*   *   *

Only one place remained on Bailey's list – the Museum Archives. She reasoned that knowing the correct time period in Egyptian history in which the locket originated would tell her the archeological dig's location, which in turn could shed some light on her father's whereabouts during his trip to Egypt, maybe even leading her to what had killed her parents.

Immediately upon entering the Cairo Museum Craig wandered off. He jumped from case to case and room to room like a kid in a toy store – Bailey could barely keep up with him. Craig was about to say "yes" to a man asking to be their guide, when Bailey pulled him away – "Hey, remember why we came here? We have to talk to the curators first, we can always walk around here later." In truth, she didn't want to walk around the museum at all – all of those large, granite pharaoh statues carried a flavor of death and doom to her. Craig's face contorted into an expression combining disappointment, pain, and pleading, but he sighed

39

and followed Bailey, who dragged him into the "research office." She was on a mission, and the history of Egypt was of less interest to her than the history of her parents. Asking the authorities the same questions, Bailey showed them the same photograph of the locket and the detailed drawing. Nine people in the office looked at the design, and no one recognized it. Sensing that soon they would be asked to leave, Bailey attempted to gain access to the Archives – if she could not get these scholars to look for the required information perhaps she could locate it herself. But of course, access to the Archives was refused.

Suddenly Bailey felt cold, as if she was being watched by a predator, and she turned her head to search for the cause of the sensation. An official looking man stood in a doorway at the end of a long hallway. He was a stocky, but not fat, Egyptian, with a well-trimmed beard, wearing a dark blue suit and a shiny gold colored tie. He was studying them both with his sharp eyes, definitely interested in them, but he didn't move from his position in the doorway to introduce himself. Bailey sensed that he was the real authority in this place, and the only one there who was not thinking of them as "American idiot tourists." She gathered that the man actually felt something for them, but whatever that feeling was, it was not nice at all.

*   *   *

The man with the golden tie retreated into the office. He was alarmed. Who was this young woman, and why was she here, on his doorstep? He had heard of the paper she was showing the curators and had immediately become intrigued. She wouldn't give it to anyone, holding it in her hands as if she were afraid someone would try to make a copy of it for further study. He had recognized the design instantly, from far away, when one of the men had asked her to hold it up to the light.

With the door closed, he made phone calls and waited. He sat in near-total darkness, smoking a cigar, his cavernous office illuminated by a single desk lamp. He knew that he should probably turn on the lights, but like a desert cat stalking its prey in the night, he craved the shadows, the safety of a well-positioned hiding place. After a while his phone began ringing, taking him out of a focused freeze. The background check on the strangers was complete. What he found out, he did not like at all. The woman was the daughter of the two people who had died in Egypt thirty-one years before. The names of these two, who died in the "previous attempt," were etched in his memory. Furious, he could not believe he was being faced with the same thing his father had been faced with! But there was also another feeling, one which he had almost forgotten, a feeling from many years back – fear.

He understood what the Americans' search really meant and his decision was instant: that redheaded woman, and the tall young man with her, could not be allowed to know the truth. How much did she know about the incident that happened thirty-one years ago? No real records had been kept. More wheels were set in motion as he searched. His calls were returned with the information that the young man was a "nobody," and Bailey Rixson seemed to know nothing because her sister Abigail never recovered. He took a deep breath. "Nothing is lost, no need to worry… handle this with care and confidence," he told himself, as he slowly exhaled. He had not realized he was holding his breath…

As a decision formed in his mind, he relaxed. Resolved to politely force the Americans out of their meaningless endeavor, he smiled to himself: "Let's cooperate." The two were to be given access to minor areas of the Archives. "It will do nothing for their search, but it will satisfy enough of their Western curiosity. Americans need immediate satisfaction and do not have the patience to dig beyond what is right in front of them. They will find nothing and they will let it go." Satisfied with himself, the man in the golden tie placed one more call.

*   *   *

Bailey and Craig could not believe their luck – they were allowed into the Museum Archives! After filling out endless numbers of papers and paying a large fee, a guard handed them silly chained cards to hang on their necks. They entered the Archive rooms in the basement of the museum. But their excitement faded as it became clear that access was a way to appease them, if not simply a way to take their money. The Archives were huge, and they had no way of knowing where to go. The person assigned to them, a tall snobbish Egyptian, obstructed them at every turn instead of translating and directing. His tone was one that might be used to speak with little children.

Frustrated, Bailey was prepared to argue with their escort, but one look at him showed that it would be futile. Furiously slamming shut her laptop, she sprang up and moved toward the main Archive exit.

Catching a taxi was easy, considering the number of them in front of the museum. Craig had no problem quickly stuffing Bailey into the one he flagged to the curb. At the hotel, exhaustion overtook Bailey.

She sat on the bed, shoulders slumped, discouraged that her well-thought-out list had borne no results.

"Maybe we should just give up… go home…"

"Oh?" Craig could not believe what he was hearing, as he struggled to divert his focus from the article he was reading on the computer. Changing the subject was always hard for him, because thoughts for Craig were always accompanied by feelings, and feelings were sticky and slow. He dove so deeply into whatever he focused on, that to re-focus on something else meant he had to pull himself out of where he already was and back to the surface again. And that process, understandably, took time. So, he shook his head and stared at Bailey.

"Bailey, it's right here in front of us, it's the opportunity of a lifetime to uncover whatever 'it' might be. We have to try! I bet this locket is really ancient and is worth a lot, and what happened to your parents is somehow connected to it."

"I don't know…" To her embarrassment Bailey was near tears. This was not what she had signed up for!

Knowing that if she wanted to go home there was no way that he could stay behind, Craig's only option was to convince Bailey to continue.

"It's only been a few days – you still have almost two weeks to figure it out. You are already here, you might as well get a vacation out of it – it's not so bad, it's sunny and there are lots of museums to see… and we can still find out something. Maybe we just don't have the right support…"

"We have *no* support!"

"True… but what if we had some other help?"

"Like what? Hire a detective, here, in Cairo? They might just deport us then!"

"Yeah… I meant the *other kind* of help… never mind…" Exhaling, Craig tried a more conventional approach: "Do you know anyone who might be useful in this type of situation? Maybe back in the States?"

"I don't know anyone, Craig!" snapped Bailey. "I've never been in this type of situation before!" But surprisingly, Martin's name popped into Bailey's head. She told Craig about her acquaintance from the past; he, in fact, was the one who had sent her the laptop as a birthday present last year, bragging that it had all sorts of amazing "unofficial" software. It looked just like any other laptop to Bailey, but since her old one had been near death, she welcomed the new one.

A long time ago, while she was still accumulating therapy hours for her final exam, she was assigned to a mental health facility in western Massachusetts. There, she met Martin. She was not allowed to have personal relationships with patients, but Martin somehow magically found a way into her email. At first she thought it was a sexual fixation but then, realizing who Martin was, she figured that it was more of an emotional attachment and a form of control on his side. She was never able to get rid of him. It hadn't become a huge issue, although she did report it. Eventually she stopped worrying about it and he became a curiosity for her – this man, who seemed incapable of living in the normal world, was able to find anything he needed with ease, and he had an uncanny ability to make money. Even during his stay, when at times he was quite heavily medicated, Martin always had some big shot visitors consulting with him about a programming issue, or even demanding that he be taken off of his meds because of their deadline. When important businessmen don't care that their "consultant" is in a mental health facility, you know that he must be some sort of genius.

When Bailey left the facility and began her work in Boston, she and Martin "kept in touch" in an odd sort of way – she received regular emails from him about his life or something he thought she might find interesting, even though she never emailed him back. Martin's emails came about once every month. A year ago or so, Bailey had a bad day and without thinking, she hit reply. She was startled when within a few minutes she heard back from him: "Hello, my dear, glad to know you are alright. How is the weather in Boston? – Your Marty." This began their semi-personal contact. Bailey didn't know what category to put him in. They talked about the weather, clothes, news, and even sometimes medications. Bailey knew Martin had moved to upstate New York and built a fortress for himself – he bragged about how his house had all sorts of alarms. But he never, ever, left it.

Unsure if it was a good idea to involve a man with severe mental problems in this very private matter, Bailey finally decided to email him. The one thing she was sure of was that Martin would be there at the other end of the email – he always was. It gave Bailey the uneasy feeling of being spied on; as if he was near her all the time without her knowing it. Giving up no information, just in case, Bailey requested an urgent reply, yet she was startled when Martin's email appeared in her inbox in just three minutes. It was the usual: "Hello, my dear, how are you doing over there? I see you are in Egypt, how interesting… How is the weather in Cairo? – Your Marty." Bailey didn't give herself the space to freak out – this was Marty's usual behavior. In the few moments that he had before responding to her email, he searched for information about her whereabouts, as if he wanted to shock her with his ability to locate her.

Bailey quickly asked if he could find out why their search was so unsuccessful. Had no relevant information survived, or were they being blocked from finding it? She explained the situation without the particulars, assuming that Marty could probably find the details he required faster than she could type. Marty's reply came in ten minutes: he was unable to find anything the easy way, but promised to go at it the hard way.

Before she finished reading his email, her laptop suddenly shut down. "Damn!" she jumped, startled, but Craig's voice sounded behind her shoulder: "It's only the screen. Look, something is happening..." It was true, the little light on the side was blinking feverishly. After a few long seconds the laptop came back to life, buzzing and chirping; the screen lit up and on it they saw the rapid opening and closing of many files. Both stared at it in disbelief. In a few more seconds it all returned to normal, with her Outlook email the only window left open. There was a new message in Bailey's inbox, and she opened it. "Hello again, sorry for the intrusion, but I needed some files from your hardware, thought you wouldn't mind if I looked in. I see your internal webcam is broken. Dear, please get an external one – it will simplify things, and of course you know I would love to see your beautiful face as soon as possible ☺ - Your Marty."

Bailey was speechless. Before she could react, Craig responded to Marty's actions with "I'll borrow what's in your wallet; I saw a store two blocks down. Be right back" and ran out of the room. Left alone with a computer screen, Bailey felt a bit lost. The "ding" of her Outlook brought her back to reality – it was Martin again – "Hello, my dear, we are alone at last. So tell me, did you miss me? – Your Marty." "Oh, no..." thought Bailey, slowly exhaling. This beginning promised to lead to a difficult and odd interaction. She began to type her response.

Craig returned with a webcam, and to Bailey's surprise he knew what to do with it. Technology had always scared her. She thought she had to spend years studying it, and only after that, maybe she would begin to know. Solutions like "let's plug this in and see" were not an option. Yet in a few seconds the webcam program was uploaded and the camera connected, and Bailey could see her own stressed face right there on the screen. Craig punched buttons for instant communication with Marty on the other end. Soon there was the scarred crooked face of a man of indeterminate age in front of them. Marty was, from the look of it, sitting at his desk, with complete darkness behind him.

Ignoring Bailey's protest, Craig dangled the locket, still attached to her neck, in front of the webcam, so Marty could clearly see it. As Bailey watched in a stupor, Marty's machinations locked her laptop with his security system, and his voice, somewhat disembodied, came from her laptop speakers. It explained that despite the Egyptian filing system being a mess, he was hoping to soon receive responses to his carefully placed inquiries.

Halfway through listening to Marty, Bailey felt the urge to run – away, far and fast. Faining a sudden urgent desire for dinner, Bailey hung up on Marty.

In the hotel's rooftop restaurant, after careful deliberation, Bailey and Craig each ordered a meal of chicken and a glass of wine. But even after the meal and a second glass of wine were finished, Bailey couldn't bring herself to return to the room. She reasoned that she was simply dreading further interaction with Marty. She will have to buy a new computer when she got home because she was sure it wouldn't be possible to kick Marty out of this one! But as she and Craig stepped out of the hotel and began to walk, Bailey knew that it was probably the truth about her parents, her sister, and the damn locket that this connection with Martin's information-gathering abilities would surely bring that was scaring her, and not Martin himself.

As they walked around Cairo, Craig seemed to know the layout and intuitively guided them to points of interest. Hearing the questioning intonation in Craig's voice, she noticed that she had conveniently gone into her self-analyzing again, and had not heard a word Craig said.

Suddenly she felt a rough, sharp pull on her arm as something smashed into the back of her neck. Confused, she began to fall. Craig caught her and yelled, but she couldn't understand the words; they sounded as if they were coming from far away. A carriage raced past them. Then all of the loud noises of the busy city suddenly returned with a rush, and with it came the pain in her neck.

"What's happening to me?" Tears filled her eyes.

"Are you OK? You just got whacked with a whip! He totally aimed at your head, Bailey, if I hadn't pulled on you he would've hit your head!" Bailey heard Craig's voice, and realized he was shouting.

"Where are we?" she mumbled, touching the back of her neck and wincing.

"I hope you mean which street, not which country! Whoa, Bailey, he was aiming at you! It's the same carriage that followed us today, I saw that guy twice…"

"Am I bleeding? Maybe he just doesn't like me…"

"Yeah, he's very familiar with you! I thought I was supposed to be the crazy one here!" Craig's face was right in front of hers, and he held her arms firmly.

"I think I'm OK."

"You aren't bleeding, but it's a hell of a red line! And it's getting redder..."

As Bailey got up from the sidewalk, she rummaged inside her purse for a small tube of pure aloe, and painkillers. She took two pills, and felt a little safer.

"This is insane... Did someone just try to kill me?"

"They probably wanted to scare you. It's hot, Bailey. There's the museum, I think it has some AC'd rooms. And we can get you some cold juice."

Figuring that standing in the middle of the street wouldn't help, Bailey agreed. They crossed the square to the Cairo Museum, bought the entry tickets, and quickly got a very cold glass bottle of mango juice. Bailey held it against her neck to reduce the worsening swelling. The painkillers and aloe had begun to work, and soon she felt better. They walked along the corridors. Hundreds of vitrines filled with thousands of artifacts lined the walls, and tourists and guides crowded around them, talking and pointing. Craig strained to see through the crowds, and Bailey followed him, her thoughts scattered. "Why would someone try to hurt me? This is because of the locket... What does that mean? How does it connect to me? Or Abby? How did daddy get the locket?"

The man with the golden tie looked up and was shocked when he saw the subjects of his ruminations right in front of him. That locket! How could it be? He froze, his gaze following Bailey's odd arm position to the glass bottle pressed against her neck, then he quickly turned into another hall.

*   *   *

The walk back to their hotel was anything but straightforward, as Craig's curiosity constantly diverted them from a direct path and prevented them from noticing the tall man dressed in a long gray caftan and a white turban, following them around the city and making calls on his cell phone.

He was speaking to the man with the golden tie who didn't find the tour of the city interesting at all, and barked into his receiver, "Check their room. Their belongings might hold clues."

"Yes, but that will take time to set up."

"I don't pay you to limp like an injured mule!"

*   *   *

By the time they returned to the Osiris Hotel, it was already dark. Bailey turned on the ceiling fan, and Craig went straight for the laptop. "This is odd... Bailey, you better look at this." When Bailey read the email she turned white – it was a response from her bank, confirming a deposit of ten thousand dollars. She knew it could only have come from one source – Martin Shwabster. While they were away, Marty had wired ten thousand dollars to her bank account and requested that a confirmation of the transaction be sent to her. *How* he had found out her account information was not what scared her most – Bailey could not believe he had done it!

Horrified, her fingers flew over the keyboard. But Marty's reply to her email was that he "simply wants in."

"'Want in' to what? I don't even know what this stuff is, and you are acting like this is some sort of a secret mission, some mysterious assignment!"

"Is it not, my dear? I just want a front row seat, you know, I don't get out much."

Swearing not to touch his money, she soon had to acknowledge that there was no point in arguing with him. So she stopped, and Martin's scarred face grinned with satisfaction. She had been so involved in bickering with Marty that she almost missed it when Craig said: "Didn't we see this man before?"

Looking out of the window, Bailey saw him. The man was sitting at the edge of the rooftop restaurant, the only spot from which someone could see their window. He had binoculars and looked as though he was surveying the Cairo rooftops. He looked familiar. He was the same man who walked past them when Bailey was almost run over by the carriage. The same man who was a few steps behind them in the ticket line in the Cairo Museum. And the same man who they saw mysteriously appearing in the same museum rooms they had been visiting. They had not seen him follow them back to the hotel, but there he was...

"Maybe this is just a coincidence, he might be staying at the same hotel..."

"You are much smarter than that, my dear." Marty's computerized voice reminded them that the microphone had been left on. He could not see, but he could hear.

Returning to her laptop, Bailey faced Marty: "I think we're under surveillance."

"Undoubtably," Marty replied, "This might be a serious business we've gotten ourselves into. It might explain why all my inquiries are diverted and get nowhere... But don't fret, I assure you that you're perfectly safe, my dear. No one can break the encryption I just uploaded into your laptop. You have my word on that."

"So, they can't hack into her computer. But they can steal it! And they can physically hurt us, you know..." Craig said over Bailey's shoulder.

"Your young companion thinks with clarity and speaks with conviction," replied Martin. "I agree that you had better guard that laptop like hell... or heaven, whichever you care more about... and the same of course goes for yourselves, the locket and the papers..."

That night an amazing transformation took place inside of Bailey. She felt angry. Not that being angry was a new emotion for her; she had been feeling angry for as long as she could remember. But this was a bit different – she felt angry more than scared, while earlier it had been the other way around.

She woke from a fitful sleep. The clock showed ten minutes past five in the morning. The sun had not yet risen, but the city was already bustling. She walked out onto their tiny balcony and looked at the traffic-filled streets. There were cars, trucks, and carriages filled with hay or fruit being pulled by donkeys. People were awake and active, and the air was still cool. In a few hours the temperature would be over a hundred degrees Fahrenheit, but right now it was only about seventy five. The air smelled of incense, gasoline, and fruit. Bailey took a breath and realized that she was not ready to give up. Though she was being blocked at every turn, she was not ready to go home, and that was why she was angry. The part of her who wanted to stay was fighting with the part of her who was scared and wanted to go home. As she listened to Cairo's morning noises she remembered her grandma saying that her father went to some place in Giza with her mother and that they had "had an accident." Later on, in her teen years, she had come to believe it was just a nicer way of saying that they had been murdered. Bailey had always assumed that they had been killed in Cairo by robbers. This made sense because witnessing it had freaked Abby out; maybe they even grabbed *her* and daddy had tried to defend her and he and mom got killed. But how, then, had a priceless locket of pure gold stayed on Abby's neck? And why was it on a dirty twine instead of a nice chain? That had never made sense to Bailey. "And then there was this 'Sekhmet," thought Bailey, "The reason why dad had left for Egypt in the first place."

Oh, the word "Sekhmet." Every time Abby said it, Bailey felt like killing her. "Sek-Met"... the word hurt so much. When she was a teenager she had looked it up: "Sekhmet, the Egyptian warrior goddess of destruction, who restores Maat when life gets out of balance..." Knowing what the word meant did not make hearing it any easier. To Bailey the word was less of a name and more of a symbol; a sound code for complete devastation and loss. She flashed back to the kitchen where, as a five year old, she saw her grandma fall to the floor crying, and lie there staring into space in shock. Then her grandma had pulled her close and hugged her, ignoring the leftover chickenpox spots that were not supposed to be touched. No, Sekhmet's name might not mean "death" in Egyptian, but this goddess was no abstraction to Bailey.

By the time Craig woke up, Bailey was already dressed. Martin had convinced her to buy another laptop as a decoy and she was ready to go to the store. While Bailey ordered breakfast in the hotel restaurant, questioning the waiter about the details of her morning coffee, Craig ran out to the store a few doors down. He returned before their food reached the table. Bailey's eyebrows rose when she saw he had no box in his hands. He had dumped it on the way back and the new laptop was nestled safely in his backpack. They ate and hurried back to their room. The new computer was hooked up to the original one and Martin uploaded file after unremarkable file into it. The decoy was left in the room, and the original laptop was securely hidden in Craig's backpack. Now what?

They could do nothing but wait until Martin's research was completed. The Osiris hotel guests had access to the rooftop pool of the neighboring Moon Lotus Hotel and they headed there. The first stop was the Lotus café, where a snack of a little hummus platter and fruit smoothed their frayed nerves. They hoped that swimming would do more of the same. At the pool, Bailey took over two loungers. She checked the tie of her bright yellow swimsuit on the back of her neck and tested the pool water with her foot. It was warm and inviting and, without looking back, she quickly submerged her body. Every muscle ached from tension. Moving as if in slow motion, she imagined that all of the recent events had never happened, and that she had come directly here, to the Moon Lotus Hotel's rooftop pool, and it was somehow, magically, *not* in Cairo. Craig decided to stay out of the water, and guard the laptop that sat in his backpack. As he watched Bailey swim back and forth, he noticed a man who looked out of place – an Egyptian, dressed like a tourist, but too stiff and focused to be one. He caught Craig looking at him, immediately averted his eyes, got up, and left. In a few minutes he was replaced by another, similar man. Bailey finally returned to her lounge chair, cool and more at ease until Craig told her about the surveillance. Further relaxation was out, conversation was now tense, and both Craig and Bailey stared at the surrounding tourists with suspicion.

"We must be paranoid!" reasoned Bailey. But even as she spoke her muscles tensed and the aches returned with a vengeance.

"Do you think Marty found something by now?"

Taking Craig's question as a cue to leave, Bailey bolted upright from her lounger, almost tipping it over. Craig headed for the poolside concierge to return the towels and tip the waiter while Bailey, trying to conceal her desire to run, hurried to the elevators. She exited on the Osiris hotel floor and rushed to the room but was delayed by a group of cleaning personnel crowded in front of her door. Frustrated, she pushed her way into the room, stepping around a young, muscular Egyptian in a cleaning uniform. The man suddenly spoke loudly in Arabic and Bailey almost ran into another uniformed youth coming out of her room. At first she thought that the first man she side-stepped had simply sworn at her in Arabic, but now it was clear that he had told the second man to get out because she was on her way in. The men quickly exited. Nothing was disturbed in the room and everything looked clean, but one look around told Bailey two things: one, the cleaning staff had been there much earlier that morning, because all the smells of their activity were already gone; and two, her suitcase and the drawers in her cabinet had been searched – the intruder hadn't had enough time to put everything back the way it had been. She ran out of the room, unsure what she hoped to accomplish by catching the men. There was no one in the hallway, no one at all. The service cart and the uniformed men had disappeared as if they had never been there.

Bailey walked back into the room and closed the door. She inspected her suitcase and all of the drawers. Even her toiletries had been searched! Who were these people? It was crystal clear that they were not afraid to break into the private property of foreign citizens. Bailey had grown up with the rosy idea of the United States being the best country in the world, and had always innocently assumed that being an American citizen was the strongest protection one could have. How could this have happened? What could she and Craig be looking into, that warranted searching their belongings? "What the hell was my father into?" She took a deep breath, stirring her courage to walk back out into the hallway.

"One more breath and I will be free of my fear," she told herself. She yanked the door open and felt a jolt of fright when she almost ran into Craig – she had forgotten about him.

"You're jumpy!"

"There were men in the hallway, pretending to be the cleaning staff. They searched our room, I caught them..." She sat on the sofa. "What can they possibly be looking for? This is insane! The laptop was right there on the table...what did they hope to find in my toiletries bag?"

"A flash drive..."

"What?"

"A memory card – that's what they're looking for. It's a small stick thing, an external hard drive... that makes sense. They probably wanted the copies of your father's papers, and they searched this laptop and didn't find anything, so they assumed we must have a flash drive to store the information."

"But we don't..." Bailey's fingers massaged her aching neck.

"It doesn't matter; they don't know we have another laptop. They know you use the laptop for recording information because they saw us with it in the hotel and in the museum. So they were looking for that information."

"We haven't done anything to be in any official trouble, right? These people that are after us can't be the police or any other official authority, they would have come with a warrant. They must be criminals... maybe we should go to the police?" As soon as these last words were out she realized, remembering their visit, how ridiculous they sounded. They better go for a walk so she can clear her head!

It was nighttime; the air was cooler, and the loud sounds of Cairo were overwhelming. It seemed that every person who could be out, was out. Thousands of people were on the streets: families walking together, workers returning home, cars, donkeys, camels, tourists browsing in shops, buses. They found themselves on the Nile embankment, watching the cruise ships and their passengers crowding the river, and walked slowly along the water's edge. The sight of people going about their business calmed them.

Bailey began to summarize all the information about her parents in chronological order. But after conversations with the local agencies she felt she knew even less than before she had begun her search! Everything was an assumption now. What the policeman said reflected his belief that Bailey's parents had died during an attempted robbery, perhaps from fright and not by any direct action of the robbers. It was absurd!

"Bailey, even if they were not shot, robbers could have hit them, or poisoned them. So bruises or drugs would have had to show up in the autopsy. Why did they perform an autopsy on the American citizens anyway?"

"I do not know... No marks were reported on their bodies."

"That means that someone was paid off to do the autopsies here in Egypt, and that either there truly were no marks, or there were and the police and even the American Consul were paid off to sign a false autopsy report. Maybe we're looking in the wrong direction. What if this 'robbery' was something much more premeditated? Your father would have been followed and could have been drugged... It must relate to whatever he was doing here in Egypt."

"*He was on the errand of Sekhmet...*" Bailey's eyes grew wide in shock at her own words. "I think I dreamt that..."

As they crossed the street towards a donkey cart filled with bananas, a blue car revved its engine and swerved towards them. Instinctively they leapt out of the way and fell roughly to the ground. They stared in the car's direction as it sped away but it was already a blur, too far to read a license plate. Bailey's arm, clipped by the metal, was scratched along its length, and Craig's hand was bleeding from the rough impact with the sidewalk. His bananas forgotten, the merchant ran towards them, yelling in Arabic, waving his fist at the road.

The taxi ride back to the hotel was surreal. Feeling as if time and space had warped around her, Bailey lagged a few steps behind the current moment – decisions were made and she acted according to them, although she had not yet made them. Was this what it felt like to lose your mind? Changing time zones, sleeping at odd hours, the stress of facing the land that took her parents from her, and now running away from someone who had tried to kill her? The lights of the city spun as the taxi made a wide, fast turn in hopes of avoiding a traffic jam. She had never been in trouble with the police and here, as she sat in the back seat of a speeding taxi, she tried to reassure herself that she was not in trouble now, but the assurances felt like a weak attempt at sanity. She was deeply shaken.

By the time the hotel room door shut behind her, Bailey was emotionally and physically exhausted. She rubbed an antiseptic cream onto her scratched arm and stared into space. One look at her told Craig to check with Martin without her participation. Hopefully Martin had found some solid information. There was mixed news. The only record of the Rixson's misfortune existed in the archives of American Embassy – an obscure report stated that the identities of three American citizens, the Rixsons, were confirmed, and that Abigail Rixson's family was contacted in the States and a plane ticket was issued for her by the Consul. There was no mention of what happened to the bodies of Abigail's parents. In the Embassy's "crime statistics," Martin located the same report Bailey already had – a copy of the one issued by the Cairo police. But after hacking into every possible Egyptian system, he had found no record of Bailey's parents being killed, or having an accident, or even being in Egypt. Marty was sure his translation software had crawled through every possible file. There was no record of Bailey's sister being shipped home to the States, and no hospital records. Marty wasn't surprised. An event of thirty-one years ago was documented by hand, in Arabic, and that book was probably collecting dust somewhere, the information in it having never made it into an electronic data system.

"Marty," Bailey's tired face finally appeared on the screen. "Someone just tried to kill us. A car almost ran us over."

"Oh… are you OK?"

"We're fine, but it could have been much worse! I just don't know how to deal with this situation. The Egyptian authorities are not going to help anymore."

"Err… their 'help' so far seems to have been a big part of the problem, my dear."

"Do you think it's sensible to go to the Embassy?"

"You have no proof to present to them – they will simply advise you to pay better attention, or to leave the country. I can look into getting the satellite records… What was the exact time and location, and what color and type of car was it?"

A visual record of their encounter with a blue car did exist, but the resolution was too low and it could hardly be considered evidence.

When the screen went black, Bailey spoke again: "Martin is very good with computers, but he can't help us here in Cairo if we're faced with real danger. I don't know what to do."

"He said there could be handwritten records, in Arabic. Maybe if we could get our hands on those…" The same thought came to both of them – getting their hands on those papers would involve bribery and probably theft, and neither of them knew anything about such things.

But Simon does, thought Bailey casually of a man from her past. Not that Simon was a thief, but he was really skilled, in an odd sort of way. His skill set might be just the one they needed, but here she goes again, involving some not-even-sure-if-they-are-friends people in this very personal mess!

"I know someone from far back, his name is Simon, maybe he..." – Bailey did not get to finish her sentence because Craig almost fell out of the chair he was sitting on.

"How do you know him?" he whispered, glaring at her.

"It's a long story, we met in Bali years ago."

"Mmm... it's possible, they live a very long time..."

"Who?"

"Tell me something, was he orange back then too?"

"What??"

"Oh... oh! He's a man!" Craig looked so relieved that Bailey immediately forgot how annoying he could be.

"Of course he's a man, what else could he be? He might be able to advise us."

Bailey's story about Simon sounded interesting, but Craig was not convinced that he could possibly comprehend the situation they were in. Chances are he would just dismiss them as lunatics. That is, if he even remembered Bailey. She searched through her Outlook address book and couldn't find an email, but there was a phone number.

She dialed, and a stranger answered. Simon's number was now someone else's. Marty might be the best person to locate him. He came through in less than twenty-four hours. To keep the connection clear of any suspicious listeners, Bailey dialed the number through her laptop.

Beach house, Bali

His stomach turned as if he were on a boat in rough seas. Bailey, dear Bailey, was in trouble, and from the sound of her voice, and the fact of this phone call, big trouble. She thought she had uncovered something about her parents. She was not sure what it was, but others apparently wanted to keep her from finding more and had made attempts at scaring her and even killing her. She was not sure what to do and she needed his advice.

Bailey was not the type to ask for advice – she gave advice, she didn't ask for it. She was scared. She had to be, to have unearthed him! She was not easily scared, being a very logical and measured person. To hear the underlying fear in her voice made his heart hurt. The conversation ended, and he hung up the phone. He wasn't sure what his next move would be, but he sensed that a part of him had already made a decision.

He poured himself a stiff drink and slumped down in a worn armchair, remembering what he did not want to remember. Why did she have to call? Why couldn't these memories stay buried in the deepest part of his unconscious? In spite of himself the images flooded his mind – the very painful moment when he learned of his wife Elona's death, and then the baby's death. His earlier years in Bali, when he was trying to forget it all. By then he had been decommissioned from undercover field operations, and eventually had been retired from MI6, then he moved away from the UK for good. He was trying to escape his feelings, but he only escaped the regimentality of life: the schedules and drills, and the training he once thought he could not live without. He had felt so broken inside that nothing really mattered anymore. He knew that he was not the type to throw himself to the sharks, but living was not a fun alternative.

Simon swallowed deeply, drinking from his heavy crystal glass. He had retired to Bali and successfully "disappeared" himself, but in the end the accomplishment was worth little. He was miserable. He had met Bailey in Bali nearly eight years ago. She was a young woman, traveling alone, celebrating finally getting her psychology license, and divided between hoping to start her own practice and ideas of staying put for a few more years in the hospital she was affiliated with. "Guess she decided to stay with that hospital after all," thought Simon, remembering Bailey say that she had just recently started her own practice. "Life never is what you think it will be..."

There were so many implosions in such a short time back then. No assignment had ever gotten to him this bad. That was when he knew he was done for, he had to get out, he was no good anymore – broken men do not make good agents. Bailey had helped him tremendously then. It was because of her that he was somewhat normal now. If they had not had their long talks, walks, and whatever else it was that they had, he was sure he would have ended up down at the bottom of some reef by now. Hell, if he had really created his reality as the self-help books he read said he had, he was a seriously lousy creator! His wife and baby were dead... and he was not.

He remembered mentioning how long he had been a "living dead" man, and how Bailey had stiffened up. She later told him that the year of his wife's and baby's deaths was also the year that both of her parents had died in an accident. Maybe there were just some very unfortunate years in the universe: some comet passes by or some other stellar shit happens, and wham – everyone's life is messed up for that year! Simon never asked for more information and Bailey never gave any. They had stayed in touch by phone and with the occasional email, but after a while they got busy in their own lives and the connection remained only in their hearts and memories. He went back to doing some secret assignments for private parties who paid well for his expertise, and assumed that she was busy with her new practice.

But here she was calling him, and asking for help. "That year, thirty-one years ago, I can't seem to escape," thought Simon. "Bailey just rang...of all people...and from Cairo, of all places. Bloody hell, she might really be in trouble!" Bailey's voice had sounded so shaken, and Simon felt that there was something else she needed, but she hadn't felt able to tell him on the phone. "I'll contact you tomorrow afternoon," he had said.

He put down the empty glass, stopped by his bedroom to pick up a black duffle bag from the bottom of his closet and walked out of his small house, right onto the beach. The wind was strong, the sand hot and the only sounds were the waves, and the leaves of palm trees scraping against each other. He got into his Land Rover and drove away.

Cairo, Egypt

Bailey looked at her watch for the hundredth time as she paced back and forth in front of her laptop. What if something went wrong and Simon didn't call? He was his usual cryptic self on the phone and she never could tell what he meant. Craig was about to suggest that she relax when their hotel phone rang. Bailey picked up the receiver, relieved to hear Simon's voice.

"Can I come up? The flight was a bitch..."

Bailey hung up the phone, relief on her face replaced by concern. "How did he know which hotel I was staying in? I called him through my laptop..."

"What's wrong, Bailey?" Only now she noticed Craig was studying her face.

"I think he's here..."

Before she could explain, there was a knock on the door. Bailey unlocked it. Dropping a large duffle bag onto the floor, Simon walked straight to her.

"Give me a hug, gorgeous," his tanned face stretched into a smile. Dressed in a white linen shirt and camel colored slacks Simon looked relaxed. "Nice to see you again. Wish it was under different

56

circumstances…" He wrapped his muscular arms around a confused Bailey while his eyes methodically scanned the room. When he finally released her his stare rested on Craig. There was an awkward moment until Bailey remembered to introduce the nervously smiling Craig, as she realized that Simon might not have expected to find him here at all.

They ordered room service. Room service is one of those amazing things that feels as though it can fix anything – it makes odd realities seem normal and realigns timelines. A small folding table was set up and two large trays placed on top of it. Craig cautiously tried *ful medammas*, a bean dish with spices and slices of hard boiled eggs on the side, while Simon hungrily dug into his rice-stuffed pigeon. Bailey spooned her *mulukhiyah*, a spicy soup-like dish – she had tried it before in the rooftop restaurant and now wanted to stick to known foods. Afterwards, as she chewed on her baklava, Bailey told Simon how she and Craig had traveled to Cairo to look for information about her parents, how all records of her parents' deaths seemed to have mysteriously disappeared, and how they were not helped and were even being blocked and intimidated by the local authorities. Simon was unsure how he could be of help to them. Craig explained: "We believe that these records exist, and need to get them somehow, but digital means are not working…"

Simon whistled – a prolonged whistle signifying "bloody hell!" He did agree to help, but on his terms. He walked onto the balcony and made some phone calls from his own cell phone, claiming it to be encrypted. Knowing his previous line of work, Bailey could guess there were probably many things like that at Simon's disposal. When Simon returned to the air-conditioned room from the hot balcony, he was greeted by two pairs of inquisitive eyes.

Instead of responding to them he asked, "Is there a pool in this hotel?"

"Not here, but Moon Lotus has a pool, it's on the next roof. Bailey and I went there yesterday, that's when someone searched the room."

"A swim will do all of us some good. Come on, folks."

Craig dutifully held onto his backpack which contained the laptop, walking after Bailey to the elevators. In her orange and white floral cotton dress and her shiny lip gloss, large sunglasses and bouncy reddish ponytail under a wide-brimmed panama she would have passed for a happy tourist were it not for the tense movements of her body. For his part Simon dragged his entire, if partially emptied, duffle with him.

Plopping himself on the tightly positioned lounge chairs, he acted as if he were on a well-deserved vacation, laughing and chatting loudly. His mood seemed contagious and finally even Bailey began to relax, ignoring the judging tone of the waiters who brought them glasses of wine between their swims. Simon was the only one who remained on a lounger and Bailey wondered if he was actually drinking the wine he ordered. A few hours later Simon suggested dining at one of the Moon Lotus's restaurants, claiming it to be a fantastic place even though earlier in the conversation he mentioned he had never been to Cairo before. They went straight to the restaurant from the pool without returning to the room – in the intense heat their swimsuits dried almost immediately.

Seated in the large Italian-themed restaurant, Bailey and Craig felt safer, especially with Simon next to them. He told one story after another, his loud deep voice easily carrying throughout the restaurant. Bailey tried to keep track of the conversation, but her head began to spin – shit, was it the alcohol? How much wine did she have? She watched Simon look at his phone a few times, quickly reading text messages. After the meal Bailey did not have enough energy to protest when Simon insisted on taking care of the bill. She wasn't sure how they all ended up on the sidewalk in front of the Moon Lotus hotel and it seemed like the next second she was being ushered into a taxi, Craig excitedly saying something about Old Cairo and the Walled City. Dropped off in front of the Khan-El-Khalili Bazaar, one of the oldest markets in the world, they walked past the mosque and under the entry arch. Even though it was nighttime thousands of people were there. Narrow streets were filled with merchants pushing their wares and little café tables belonging to local restaurants. They passed stalls filled with shawls and statuettes and tables stuffed with people laughing as they smoked their apple *hookas*, and all the while uncountable cats ran busily past their feet. The bazaar was alive with locals and tourists, eating, talking, walking, and shopping. They strolled around leisurely, and Bailey even bought herself a few brightly colored shawls and a turquoise necklace.

The incense smells of the bazaar lingered in the warm night air, and Bailey and Craig, engrossed in all the new stimuli almost forgot Simon in a spice shop. That man sure could buy spices! He came out of the shop with a bag almost half the size of his duffle, filled with some odd smelling little paper bags. Turning around they could see the bazaar gate – the exit where taxis waited for potential passengers. This was a perfect end to an imperfect day – they were either drunk or off guard, but everything seemed surreal. Sitting on the back seat of the taxi, Bailey fingered the shawls that she had bought, enjoying Egypt for the first time since she arrived here. Craig stared at the buildings and people passing by the taxi window like a mad kaleidoscope. A chatty driver, speaking with a strong Arabic accent, yet in clearly understandable English, talked about the passing attractions as their taxi raced through the streets to their hotel.

In the room, Simon intently read the information remotely uploaded into his phone. He did not seem a bit inebriated, and Bailey's heart sank when she saw his facial expression change from curiosity to concern, then to an unreadable mask. Apparently Simon's sources had found the thirty-one year old problem to be not just a matter of bad recordkeeping – somebody had intentionally made sure that the incident had not been investigated any further.

Bailey felt hurt, angry and a bit hung over – the alcohol was wearing off but her mood had been tainted by it. Her short escape from reality had ended with Simon's stern face, and another blow came with the announcement that the whole time they were having fun, someone had been following them. Apparently the surveillance was now more elaborate than it had been before, so much so that they had not lost it even at the busy bazaar. Simon had known it all along, and Bailey could now see that he had suggested a trip to the bazaar as a means of testing the skill of that surveillance. She felt so angry she was ready to hit him! Recognizing this as a childish attempt to avoid her pain by blaming him she suppressed it. With all the alcohol in her blood, it was not an easy feat.

As Bailey plopped herself into the armchair with a bottle of water, Simon explained about the people with cell phones and how they constantly changed their position, following at a distance, and even changed cars to follow their taxi around town. Simon had not been sure of the magnitude of this problem before – it may have been just one unfortunate coincidence after another and screw-ups by the authorities. But now he was convinced about the reality of the danger. Something was wrong. Something that Bailey and Craig were digging up was big enough that a very determined party was willing to use scare tactics on them and maybe even kill them to keep it hidden. They had uncovered no information so far yet their attempts had been punished. Simon's face bore an expression of intense concern and looking at him, Bailey felt fear – this was the man she had *never* before seen this concerned about anything.

While Craig took a shower, Simon grabbed Bailey's arm, pulled her out of the armchair and to the balcony. "How serious are you about this, love? It's not too late to just park the whole thing and go home."

The reply was written all over her face – a question in her eyes, a question concerning her whole being. If she did not know what happened to her parents, who was she? There was no way to talk her out of it.

Simon took a deep breath and continued. "Well, you might as well know what you're really getting into… These are not small fish with a little grudge coming after you, these are major people with a major secret to protect."

"I gathered that!" snapped Bailey, touching the back of her neck – it was still sore.

"Was your family connected to the oil market, or diamonds, or some antiquities trade? Or anything political?"

"I don't think so… My father was an architect…"

"Who is this computer mate of yours?" He had to be some kind of genius to have unearthed Simon's unlisted number!

"He's an old friend… well, acquaintance really… he's harmless," added Bailey, seeing Simon's questioning expression. "And he landed me money for all of this. Well, gave me the money… kind of made me use it… he said he 'wants in'…"

Simon listened silently, unsure if Marty was a phenomenal asset or an enemy in their midst with the desire and the means to control them.

"This is what brought me to Egypt." Bailey took the locket off her neck and handed it to him. He studied it carefully. He had looked at it earlier, of course, but somehow it felt important to hold it again. He was sure now that Bailey's parents and this locket were somehow wired into a major undercover operation set up by a private party. The weight of the problem was apparent. If these people were *really* serious about getting this piece of jewelry, they would not hesitate to sever the neck it hung on, and that neck was Bailey's. The only reason it had not happened so far had to be that they needed something. Probably to find out what she knew, or who else she had told.

Simon wanted to see the computer genius for himself. They returned to the room, and he asked Bailey to dial Marty.

"How terrible of you to keep me out of the loop for so long, dear!" began Martin, cutting himself short when he noticed Simon standing behind Bailey's shoulder. The momentary look of fear on Marty's face told Simon that Marty was definitely *not* the enemy. Nevertheless, Marty had an ego to match his fears, and so he and Simon proceeded to have a bizarre "stand down" about Bailey, while she, exhausted, left the room – the balcony seemed to be as good a place as any.

"You folks won't mind if I crash here?" said Simon later on, moving the poofy leg rest next to the large armchair.

"Oh… I'm so sorry, Simon, let me rent you a room, I'll call the desk right now…"

"Don't bother. I might as well be close rather than in another room in case of trouble."

The possibility of trouble did not calm Bailey at all and she lay in bed, staring at the ceiling, for a long time while Simon silently half-sat in the armchair. Was he sleeping? She felt guilty that he did not have a bed, as if somehow it was her personal failing.

She tried to remember her father – maybe if she could make him come alive in her mind, it would help the search. She focused on his face, his kind eyes looking at her, his voice… One of their phone conversations just before they left, when he told her he would go to Egypt without her… He said "*one day you will understand why I have to do it…*" Bailey sat up. "Have to do what??" She had always thought that the trip to Egypt was a tourist thing, but now she recognized there might have been more to it, something she had not known about at all. She had never thought to ask her grandmother about it.

Dragging her laptop into the bathroom so as not to wake anyone up, Bailey dialed Martin and asked him to find any information he could about her father, in the States or elsewhere. She could not believe she had never done this before! All she knew was that he was an architect, and where he and her mother were buried!

"Miss Bailey, do you ever just sleep, dear? But you can count on your friend here – I promise to find out what I can, even if it means I have to turn the earth inside out."

In the morning Bailey felt awake, but not because of a deep sleep. She sensed some danger coming and could not shake off the feeling no matter what.

"I never cared why they went to Egypt… It didn't matter before!"

Marty's face looked excited as he sipped his coffee. He explained that apparently three years before his death Bailey's father, Jonathan Rixson, had come into contact with an Egyptian firm. He was working on a house design in a rare antique Egyptian style for a man in Long Island. This wealthy man flew Jonathan into Egypt to view an estate there and copy it. While he was in Egypt, Jonathan made a connection with a man called Sahed Ashi. He was an engineer and he assisted Jonathan on the project. Later Jonathan even asked to have Mr. Ashi flown to the States, and it was done. Mr. Ashi remained in the States for six months, registered in a long-term residence hotel near Long Island. But it seems that he spent more time at the Rixson home than at the hotel. Bailey did not remember this man at all. She had been only three years old back then... According to Martin, after that project Bailey's father became preoccupied with something. He stopped attending business meetings and his firm's extra-curricular activities and, if the registers were correct, almost disappeared from the books. He did not work on many jobs from that point on.

"Could he have been blocked from jobs? Unofficially fired or something?"

Marty did not think so; he had found some job papers with requests for Jonathan Rixson's designs and expertise, all marked with his own request to be substituted. It was as if he had refused to do the jobs.

"I'm amazed my mother didn't divorce him – she's home with two children, and her husband is refusing jobs? Maybe he was severely depressed? Nobody talked about depression back then so it might have been overlooked," said Bailey.

"Or maybe he had uncovered something in Egypt. And maybe that was why he brought Sahed Ashi with him back to the States, to get more information. Or maybe to repay him for something," ventured Craig.

"It's more likely that your father was used by Sahed to do something in Egypt," said Simon.

"How so?"

"He was solicited by Sahed for some job, something illegal, something that probably had nothing to do with architecture or engineering... and for some reason he agreed. Or maybe he was blackmailed into it. But he had to work out all the details and maybe get some resources. So perhaps bringing Sahed into America was part of the deal, and he couldn't refuse. It's possible that when Sahed left, something was completed. But then your father either had to do 'phase two' of the project, or maybe he just wanted to get something out of it for himself – either way he had to go back to Egypt."

Everyone was silent after Simon spoke.

"Err... one more thing. There is something in the design of that Long Island house that was connected to the private villa in Cairo, something that had elements of the Temple of Sekhmet – you mentioned

Sekhmet before so I thought I'd check to see if that name was mentioned anywhere. But I couldn't find anything on that temple. Sekhmet is an ancient Egyptian war goddess of destruction or something like that – and odd choice for a house theme," said Martin in his computerized voice. "But because information connected to her is rare, your father supposedly went to Egypt to research her."

"You keep saying 'her,' like it's a person!" exploded Bailey. This damn Sekhmet again! Besides, her father was an architect, not a historian or an archeologist!

Small village outside Luxor, Egypt

An old man woke from a dream, tears running down his face. Beloved Sekhmet had visited him again. His wife, who he loved dearly, would understand… but she was not here anymore. She died three years ago. The only thing that held him in this life was his promise to Sekhmet. She, the "one who loves Maat and detests untruth," had visited him this night, reminding him of his mission. He wished he could fulfill it quickly and then join his beloved wife. But he loved Sehkmet as much as he feared her. His children and grandchildren would never understand. They were unaware of Sekhmet; their hearts belonged to Allah. Even though this man had nothing against Allah, he *knew* in his heart that Sekhmet was the powerful one. And nothing could change that belief.

He got up and made himself some food. There was no reason to try to fall asleep again, he knew better. It was early morning and the sun would soon rise. He lived alone, his kids and grandkids had moved to a nicer part of Luxor. His eldest son had opened a tourist firm in the city and operated it with his two brothers. The "Horus Land" was quite successful, even in the current times. His only beloved daughter was married and had just had her first baby.

"Good morning to you, Sahed," said a voice from the street. It was another old man, although much younger than Sahed, who stood there with a milk jug, and many more attached to his donkey.

"Yes, good morning." Sahed took the milk. As the vendor's donkey continued down the street, Sahed smiled to himself – soon he would be able to join his beloved wife. He missed her so much… and his only daughter, Sanura, reminded him of her greatly. She had been so pretty when she was pregnant with her first baby. Sahed did not understand the man she married, but Sanura loved him and he was decent and treated her well, and that was all that mattered. She now had her baby, a boy, and she was happy. Sahed drank his milk, chewed on a flatbread, and wondered what Sekhmet meant by her words. In his mind there was no question – it would be Sanura, he trusted no one else with the secret. If she knew, she would bring her son up in the correct way to carry forward the secret. It would soon be time to tell her… Perhaps tomorrow?

Cairo, Egypt

It was well past midnight. Taking out his medicine bundle, Craig sat on the floor. Inhaling deeply, he unraveled the bundle. There were familiar shells from Lynn beach, a button from his favorite jacket, a seagull's feather, and a wooden stick that looked like a hand. He arranged the pieces in a pattern that made sense to him, and began. Closing his eyes, he asked his spirit guide to come. At first there was nothing, only the sounds of Cairo spilling into the room from the window. He took another breath and tried to focus. He had never done a vision quest in another country, so it might take more than one attempt.

"Maybe it's the candle…" There was no candle. Craig looked around. Then he remembered the lantern that was outside on the balcony, it might have a candle in it – they had never lit it. The candle was quickly extracted, matches found and struck, and everything was repeated.

When Craig opened his eyes and looked around his mind, his heart sank – he was in that scary room again, the one with the cube and the pyramid. He was about to open his eyes to get out of it, when he heard a purr – Simon-the-cat was rubbing against Craig's leg.

"Sit down and stop panicking," said the Cat calmly.

"I'm not panicking! I just don't like this place, that's all. Can we go somewhere else?"

"It's a long way up…"

"Up where?"

"Never mind. By the way, you do know that this candle business is just for looks, right?"

"Oh… you mean I didn't need a candle?"

"Well, I probably shouldn't tell you this, but you didn't need the shells either – or the feather, or the stick, and whatever else you've got there."

"But … oh…" Craig felt flustered now, not that before he began he was sure of anything.

64

"You can focus, can't you?" The Cat sounded annoyed again. Then he began to lecture: "There is an inner flame, light it up through your spine, then anchor down like you'd do with a boat, and open your mind."

"Oh... no candle?"

"Inner flame, you odd child, *inner* flame! The outer flame is a symbol, nothing more."

"OK, I will try without the candle the next time... but I kind of like my medicine bundle." Craig could not help himself.

"I know, I know, it's OK, you can use the damn thing if it suits you." From the Cat's voice it was not clear whether he was being kind or sarcastic. "What did you need?"

"Oh, I almost forgot. I need to find out about this Sekhmet goddess, she is Egyptian."

"No, she is not, actually, but who cares..." replied Simon. "She is from somewhere else, but yes, she probably made the biggest ruckus in Egypt, that much is true."

"What ruckus?" Refocusing, Craig spoke again. "I just need to know if there is something I should know. We're trying to find out about some incident a long time ago."

"Don't toy with Sekhmet, she is a wild cat by nature, and she will pounce and take you apart before you can say 'nice kitty,'" purred Simon, as if remembering something very delicious.

"Ah? You mean she'll *eat* me? Neah," smiled Craig, as if he got the Cat's joke.

"Do as you wish, but I warned you. She is no sweet kitty."

"Why do you keep calling her a cat? She looked like a woman with a lion's head in the pictures."

"Don't believe everything you see! She is not a woman, she is... well, I reckon you can say she is a woman, although that is not correct, but you can say that... She is a hybrid. You know what that means?"

"Like a mix of two somethings, right? She's a woman and a lion?"

"No, she is neither, she is... well, you would not understand. Anyway, you will meet her and that will clarify some things."

"Yes, we're trying to find out if there are any temples to Sekhmet left and go see them, tomorrow actually. Eh... tomorrow as in the day after today..." said Craig, attempting an explanation. "Remember we talked about linear time? Does it mean anything to you?"

"What am I, a vegetable? Of course time means something to me! Just not what it means to you," hissed Simon.

"O-O-OK, Simon." Craig cautiously petted his back and thought to himself: "I'll bet he was also planning to be a mountain lion, but ended up being this cat, that's why he's so frustrated all the time." To the Cat he said: "If you maybe tell me something about Sekhmet… that I need to know…?"

"She is so tired of you people! She tried so hard and still nothing worked. And the few that she entrusted the secret to screwed up anyway! She had to do it all over again." Simon flipped to his side and began to clean his paw. "Well, you are going to fix it."

"Fix what?" Craig jumped to his feet. "I didn't break anything… I am pretty sure…"

"You did not, you are correct. But this is part of your path. You need to remember how to breathe, and others too. And Sekhmet wants this to finally happen, but some idiots are too narrow-minded to realize this…"

Craig sat down and faced the Cat.

"Simon, I think I remember breathing…" He took a deep breath and exhaled, as if to demonstrate.

"That is not what I mean. You'll get it, the queen will probably tell you."

"What queen?" Craig jumped up again.

"Never mind, you'll know. It is all on your path, like this space…"

Craig bent down to look directly into the Cat's eyes: "Are you telling me that Sekhmet's temple is somehow connected to why I see this room over and over?"

"Must I spell it out for you? You are the shaman, right? Well, Sekhmet requested the services of a shaman to get the correct people together to do the work. But there was no one available who was capable enough, or who she hadn't pissed off a while back. So that leaves you, kid."

"Oh." Craig bit his lip. "So, Sekhmet wanted something from people and they didn't do it right, and now I have to fix it?"

"That's right. You are the shaman, aren't you?" Simon flopped on his other side and twisted his neck to stare expectantly at Craig.

"How will I know what to do?" exploded Craig, then whispered down into Simon's face: "Do you think I know how to do it?"

"Oh, the insecurity again... Will you just get over it?" replied Simon sarcastically. Then, in a voice of an annoyed teacher, he proceeded: "You are loved and cherished, you are powerful, you know what to do. Everything is alright."

66

"I know what to do...." Craig sat on the stone floor of that scary place and stared into the darkness.

He woke up because he heard Bailey moving. She was getting up – it was morning already. He had never even gone to bed, he had fallen asleep on the floor next to his medicine bundle. Getting up, dressing, and eating was all jumbled up for Craig. His neck hurt from sleeping on the floor. Simon-the-cat was nowhere to be seen.

Martin reported no new information on the "private villa" Bailey's father was supposed to have copied, and no means of finding it. As for the "Temple of Sekhmet," Internet searches only brought up a small, barely preserved chapel located at Karnak, south of the Great Temple of Amun. The photograph on the website was dated at eight years ago. If there was a Temple of Sekhmet in Egypt, it had not been standing thirty-one years ago, and it was not there today. The chapel was the only thing that remained of Sekhmet's glory...

"There's nothing left to see!" said Craig, unable to hide his disappointment.

"Unless what's there to look at is not in the picture..." said Simon-the-man.

There was an insistent knock on the door and all heads turned. Simon immediately stepped to the side, hidden and ready, and motioned to Bailey to open the door. A sweating hotel manager stood in their doorway, and he pushed a long sealed envelope into Bailey's hand. "Madam, this was hand delivered from the Police Headquarters," he said nervously. "You must read it now. If you need something, I will be in my office. If you are in trouble with police, you cannot stay here, madam. That is hotel policy..." Sharply exhaling, he left, twice glancing suspiciously over his shoulder as he walked away. Bailey noticed that her hands shook; her fingers felt cold and clammy as they attempted to tear open the sealed official-looking envelope. The letter was a directive to leave Cairo. No explanation was given, no charges, yet it was clear that they had outstayed their welcome – an immediate departure was suggested. Unsure of what to do, Bailey looked at Simon.

Suddenly Marty's voice came up over the speakers – once again they had forgotten about his presence. "Did the letter say to 'leave Egypt,' or only to 'leave Cairo'?"

Simon reread the letter.

"Considering there are no charges listed against you and you're still tourists contributing to the Egyptian economy, there is no reason for you to leave the country. If Cairo is not an option, let's go somewhere else."

"Let's go to Luxor, we can see the Chapel of Sekhmet for ourselves," suggested Craig. "We were gonna see it anyway, we might as well... Is it far?"

Martin was way ahead of them. Using previously acquired passport numbers from Bailey and Craig, he booked an evening flight for them and simultaneously searched the hotels. Since they had to be at the Cairo Airport soon, they began to pack.

"I'll take care of my own travel. I'll find you, mates, in Luxor." Picking up his duffle bag, Simon stepped out the door. Bailey watched his departure as if in a stupor – her safety was leaving.

"There are hotel, transfer, and flight confirmations in your mailbox, dear."

"What transfer?" yelled Bailey, stuffing her clothes into the suitcase. The answer was only a beep – Marty had signed off. She heard the ding of her Outlook. Besides their flight and hotel confirmations, there was an automated message from her bank, reporting a transfer of another ten thousand dollars into her account. She was too tired to be furious. They still had to settle their bill downstairs. She had better get back to reality.

∗   ∗   ∗

Their flight to Luxor was short and pleasant, aside from the Egyptian man who looked at them frequently from the corner of his eye, and later deplaned with them. Walking as fast as they could to the carousel, they found Bailey's suitcase and pulled it off.

"Let's lose him," whispered Craig, his eyes shining with ideas for this new game. "He'd expect us to go out right there... where else can we go?"

They came out of the small airport and darted to the right, away from the crowds waiting for taxis. This was an unexpected move since the other tourists were waiting at the taxi stand with their luggage. Keeping up a fast pace they ran back into the airport building from the side exit and waited. Through the glass they could clearly see the man from the plane zig-zagging in front of the taxi stand, looking for them. He swore and pulled out his cell phone. While he was talking, Bailey and Craig jumped into a taxi that had just dropped people off and was getting ready to pull up to the taxi stand. The surprised driver, seeing dollars in Bailey's hand, made a quick adjustment in his manner and happily obliged them. They ducked as the taxi slowly passed right by the man, who was too busy talking on his cell to notice them.

When they stepped into the cool green marble lobby of the St. George Hotel, they visibly relaxed. The place was magnificent. Bailey remembered to check in under Bailey Shwabster instead of Bailey Rixson – a little white lie Marty had made up. Since he paid for the room from his account, he thought Bailey could play the role of his niece to make herself less traceable. "Well, dear, you are always welcome to be my wife, but something tells me you wouldn't like the role. So if the closest I can get to you is to pretend to be your uncle, I am all for it, dear niece."

The desk clerk was confused for a moment by Bailey's passport because it had a different last name, but then he saw "uncle" on the reservation, and handed her the key. Not wanting to leave the hotel, they ate chicken salads in the lobby café. Craig scanned the place for anyone who could be paying extra attention to them, while Bailey stared at the huge, sparkling chandelier and attacked her grilled chicken.

"Relax, will you," she finally said, hungrily chewing on lettuce. "We've lost that guy in the airport and no one knows about us here. I have the key and I was watching the clerk, he never called anyone after I stepped aside, I'm sure of it."

The elevator was covered in green marble and gold Egyptian designs. It resembled a museum exhibit, as did everything in the hotel. The elevator opened on the seventh floor, and they saw their reflections in a huge mirror with two sphinxes on either side. When they opened the door to their room, both were speechless. It was a Nile view suite, spacious, with a plush sofa and an arm chair by large open doors leading onto a balcony. The huge balcony had two lounge chairs and a table with flowers on it. They stepped out onto it and were mesmerized by the view – in front of them lay the Nile, with clusters of felucca boats and a few cruise ships, and underneath them was a pool in the shape of a lotus flower, with lounge chairs arranged around it.

Craig took the bed in the main room. Bailey pulled her suitcase through the door on the left leading to another large room, which also had a balcony and full bathroom. The stress of the last few days had felt unbearable at times, and in this new comfort and luxury Craig could see that Bailey did not want to think about her family's death. She wanted to forget it all and have a vacation.

"You're happier," smiled Craig.

"No one died in Luxor," she reasoned. "Look at this place!" She pulled the swimsuit out of her suitcase and headed to her bathroom.

Craig decided that he would be better off taking a nap, since now he had a bed and last night he didn't. "Wish Simon could see this." Craig always felt this compulsion to share his experiences with his guide, forgetting that the Cat was probably around somewhere anyway, unseen, and being a non-physical entity he surely could not appreciate matter-type comforts. Coming out onto his balcony, Craig inhaled – the air was warm, and had a slight scent of flowers and incense. A light breeze caressed his face and blew his unbraided black hair into his eyes, and he brushed it away. His hair was almost to his waist in length, and it seemed to grow faster in Egypt. Contemplating this mystery, Craig looked down and noticed Bailey coming out at the poolside. He didn't want to worry her because she finally looked relaxed, yet he was not so sure that their troubles were over.

And so instead of going for a nap, he watched. Bailey walked to a lounge chair covered with a striped yellow and white towel. She had taken off her flowery sundress and stood next to the lounger, her orange hair fiery under the sunlight. It was the hottest time of day, close to mid-day, and not many people were by the pool. Bailey stood out, with her red hair and yellow swimsuit against the green carpeted ground and bright blue pool. She jumped into deep end of the lotus pool. Craig began to relax, and was about to tell himself that he was just being paranoid and he should go back into the room and sleep, when he noticed two Egyptians with tight movements talking among themselves as they looked in Bailey's direction. They were not behaving like tourists and they were not dressed like the hotel staff. One of them stationed himself where he could see Bailey's lounger, while the other went back inside. Craig was too far away to see the men's eyes, but if he could have he was sure they would be cold and calculating, like a crocodile's. Unsure of what to do, he raced out of the room and into the elevator, arriving downstairs in time to see the second man leaving the front desk – he undoubtedly had been asking about them!

"Where the hell is Simon?" thought Craig tensely, hoping his guide's namesake would appear. "Right about now I could totally use that man!" Craig was sure Simon said he would "check in" with them. "That doesn't even mean he is here in Luxor! He might have stayed back in Cairo for some reason and just plans to call us!" Nervously walking through the hotel's indoor avenue of shops, Craig stepped out towards the pool. "Could these guys rough Bailey up? Or kidnap her?" The man by her lounger seemed settled, sitting with his newspaper, choosing to simply keep an eye on his target and in no hurry to leave. Craig returned to the elevators. "No need to worry Bailey at this point, she might as well swim."

Discouraged that they had not lost whoever had followed them after all, Craig thought the sphinxes on the seventh floor were giving him a look of disdain, he was sure of it. Caught in his thoughts, he fumbled with the room key and pushed the door without thinking – there in the armchair by the balcony sat Simon-the-man, looking right at him. Craig jumped, startled. Somehow Simon had gotten into the room undetected.

"Don't look so shocked to see me. I told you I would check in soon, didn't I?"

Craig quickly told Simon about the two men who followed them.

"Incorrect. There are three men – one followed you in the taxi from the airport, while the other two came straight to the hotel. And they are definitely not locals, they came to Luxor from Cairo."

"Impossible, we lost the guy from the plane!" protested Craig.

"Yeah, that was very smooth how you ran around the building and took the side taxi," a Cheshire cat smile appeared on Simon's face. "You did lose that man, but he was nothing, perhaps a decoy."

"A decoy...?" Craig's voice trailed off in discouragement. He had been proud of his ingenuity and now felt foolish.

"And from the look of it, at least one of the men is a professional," continued Simon.

"A professional what?!"

At that instant Bailey arrived, her hair wrapped in a towel. She was relieved to see Simon, then her smile faded as she looked at Craig's face. They had been followed after all...

Luxor, Egypt

The morning came fast, as though the night had never happened, but Luxor was definitely not Cairo – there were no gasoline smells or loud traffic horns; in fact, no commotion at all. Craig had opened the balcony door and Bailey woke up to the sounds of children laughing, silverware clinking in the patio downstairs, and water splashing in the pool.

It was only seven in the morning, but clearly other tourists had had the same idea – to rise early and avoid the heat. After a quick breakfast in the lobby café they flagged down a taxi to take them to Karnak. It was a short ride, less than twenty minutes. Simon kept himself separate from them; it was the best way to control the situation in case they were being followed.

The Temple of Amun was impressive and, as they waited in line for the entry passes, their eyes were drawn again and again to the sixty-foot-tall front pylon – remains of Amun's past glory. Guides, constantly offering tours, stood in the pylon's shade and a few feral dogs lay near their feet. They had passes, but Bailey and Craig still had to go through two check points, a test for their nerves, but the security guards, their oily black guns shining in the sunlight, were more interested in chatting with each other than looking at tourists.

It was a relief to get into the temple complex. Bailey took comfort from the flat, swept ground – her sandals were finally free of sand. Leading up to the pylon was an avenue of ram-headed sphinxes, a remnant of a processional path that had once been two miles long. They were pushed through the temple pylon by an excited group of Japanese tourists. Inside the temple walls everything was huge and impressive – there was the massive colonnade, the enormous sitting pharaohs and the six standing ones in one of the major courtyards, the ruin of a mosque almost on top of it all – the layers of history mingled together. Which was more important – the ancient past, or the recent past? They overheard an English-speaking guide commenting on the attempts to preserve the crumbling mosque, which was apparently one of the oldest in the area. Frenzied tourists were taking pictures as though they were afraid to lose the moment, switching between the ancient and Muslim past, their tour guides talking over each other in a dozen different languages. It all seemed insane – fast-moving, modern people attempting to trap the past with their cameras.

Walking through the temple, they searched for anything connected to Sekhmet, but they saw nothing. No statues in her honor, no bas-reliefs. They came to the very end of the central temple path, which stopped at the temple's Holy of Holies. All that remained of this room – behind the ancient altar was a large block of granite set in the middle of the room and a fragment of a blue ceiling mosaic – the sky, filled with stars...

"There is nothing here about Sekhmet!" whispered Bailey.

"Can you believe it? This is all that's left of this temple's most important place." Craig was near tears. He could feel the pain of the temple's disintegration as if he were watching something very personal and precious to him being destroyed. "I think I've been here before... I know what this looked like when it was all... the way it was, you know?"

72

"We have to go, come on," Bailey pulled on his arm, seeing a tour group ready to enter.

They stood in full sun in a plaza-like square, the place where the main ceremonial procession would have ended. Craig took a breath and shook his head, trying to shake off the images of people carrying golden trays of food and laying them in front of the Holy of Holies, and of shaven-headed priests taking these trays into the room behind the main wall, where the gold statue of Amun stood in its grandeur.

"Amun was a fake…"

"What?"

"He was not a real god, but I believed he was… I was misled… I believed…"

"Craig, what are you talking about?!" said an exasperated Bailey as she held Craig to prevent him from swaying into the tour group rushing by. He was looking somewhere far away, eyes open but unseeing.

Finally Craig returned to the current time and looked around.

"We have to go off the central walkway into the south exit. It's there, all the way back to the front of the temple, behind the columns." He moved forward with sure steps, Bailey following closely, but when he came to the place where he knew the Chapel of Sekhmet had been, there was nothing there but dirt. Craig stared at the emptiness in disbelief – the image in his mind was of a colonnade which led to another temple, the courtyard, more steps and passages… Yet there was nothing there – the Temple of Amun ended at the edge of its own columns. *Nothing* stood to the south of it. He stood still and listened, as if a sound might give him a clue as to why he was not seeing what he knew was supposed to be there. Taking a breath he whisked Bailey away from the melee of tourists into a roped-off area. Hiding behind the massive temple columns they saw an upward sloping dirt path leading away from the temple to the south.

"This is the way," Craig whispered, pointing. It had to be.

A uniformed guard passed by them, looking with suspicion.

"Damn!" Bailey looked in the direction Craig pointed. It looked like the path only led to more dirt. Running down it could get them noticed. They looked at each other, and then ran out and ducked as soon as they were over the hump of the path. At the top of that little hill was a tree – a "thousand-year-old sycamore" – a direct descendant of the ancient temple trees. Craig had read about it online, and now he also seemed to have a strange recollection that it used to grow inside the courtyard of the smaller temple which wasn't there anymore. He tried to point out the tree to Bailey, but she unfortunately was too scared about "breaking the law" to care.

There was no one there, only a feral dog. The dog gave them one serious look and trotted away.

"Now what?" asked Bailey, finally able to look around.

They were inside a small enclosure with only the southern wall still standing. Craig looked at the walls to orient himself, then replied with conviction: "This way."

They went farther down the path, and it ended in a small courtyard. The buildings surrounding the courtyard were half-buried.

There were voices behind them. Could someone have seen them? They slipped into the darkness of the closest doorway, and the voices soon disappeared. Inside there was a damaged statue of a typical pharaoh on a throne. But no Sekhmet. Relieved and disappointed, Bailey realized that she had hoped to "meet" Sekhmet, and she was afraid of seeing in person the goddess who had whipped the rug out from under her when she was five years old.

"It's in there," said Craig, pointing to the right. They walked through a narrow doorway and entered an even smaller room made of large plain stone bricks. It was dark, with only one beam of light coming from somewhere in the ceiling. At first the room looked empty. But underneath the beam of light was a dark granite statue of Sekhmet. Bailey halted – she had not expected Sekhmet to look this real. The statue had an incredible presence; it looked as if the next second Sekhmet would take a breath. Bailey walked towards the statue and stopped a few feet in front of it. Her hand unconsciously grasped the locket. The feeling of déjà vu was strong again, and the space around her seemed to float like a thick substance, not air. Bailey was there, in the room, and yet not there. Time stopped and all sounds disappeared. Something was happening in her being, her heart; she couldn't think, but she did not fight the feeling. Then a wave-like motion went through the room, as if Sekhmet had released her.

Bailey wasn't sure how long she had stood in front of the statue. Disoriented, she looked for Craig – he stood next to her, staring at the statue. When they finally came out, Craig walked across the small yard and sat down on the stone steps, while Bailey stood in the doorway in shock, the locket a gleaming speck of gold on her chest.

*   *   *

Simon watched them go into the restricted area on the south side of the Temple through his large camera lens, but by the time he was able to position himself by the south exit, they were gone. "Where the hell did they go?"

Inching between the columns, he saw the path and quickly covered the distance between the temple and the sycamore tree, noticing that the area was an archeological dig. "What the devil are they doing?" He swore under his breath. "This is a sure way to be noticed!"

He quickly located Craig. Craig was sitting on stone steps, disheveled, his fingers in his long hair. Still choosing to stay away, Simon pretended to study designs on the wall outside of the courtyard Bailey and Craig were in. Looking intently and with reverence at wall hieroglyphs always created an aura of comfort for temple guards – they would still remove you if you were in the wrong place, but they would not worry about you because you love the art of their heritage. In the worst-case scenario, Simon, dressed in a pale blue short sleeved shirt and a khaki panama, could always claim to be a tourist who had wandered off the path. And so he stared at the wall with all the passionate curiosity he could summon.

*   *   *

Craig attempted to collect his thoughts. He never thought that an encounter with a Sekhmet statue would shake him up this much. That nagging feeling of a memory close to the surface, yet still unavailable to the conscious mind... the déjà vu, which began inside the Holy of Holies of Amun Temple, continued inside the chapel. "I think my Simon was talking about this... how she is so... Sekhmet needs our help..." he tried to focus. "Why can't Simon ever be clear!" The next moment Craig quickly looked around his own mind, afraid that he had offended the spirit guide. "Sorry, you are as clear as you can be, I know."

It was getting very hot – the midday heat had caught up with them. As Craig moved to stand, he noticed an old man in a long gray robe and a white turban staring at Bailey with fear and shock. As he followed the man's gaze, he realized that he was not staring at Bailey's face, but at her neck. It must be the locket. The old man was just on the other side of the courtyard, less than five feet away, close enough to see the locket. Craig struggled to find himself, unable to believe how out of it he felt. The déjà vu felt incredibly disorienting!

As his eyes roamed around, they finally fell on Simon-the-man, who was watching him intently from farther away. Simon could not see Bailey, or the old man, but he looked at Craig with questioning eyes. Using his eyeballs, Craig pointed in the direction of the old man. Simon disappeared behind the wall, and Craig forced himself to look back at Bailey – she was standing in the same state of semi-shock, the black rectangle of the doorway behind her.

"How long has it been?" Craig felt as though he was stuck in molasses. The old man must have heard him and, as if he had finally noticed Craig, disappeared behind the wall. Craig had not heard his own words – had he said them out loud? When he looked in the old man's direction again, there was no one there. Not only that – all sound was gone; he felt deaf. The strong, constant heat was penetrating, insisting that Craig find shade, but he could not move. "Was the man real? Or was it a vision… I swear an old man was just standing over there…"

Craig struggled to get up. Finally he stood and stumbled towards Bailey. Only then did she notice him. Craig took her by the elbow and pulled her – they had to get out of the heat, they had to get back to the main temple. As they passed the sycamore tree Craig's thoughts wobbled like jelly. He looked for Simon-the-cat, mentally calling for his support, but the Cat did not appear. There were only two physically present cats, both gray, napping high over a doorway in the shade of the Temple of Amun, not even moving their ears as Craig and Bailey rushed under them. "Where is Simon? When you need this guy, he's never there!" Craig thought in frustration, this time about Simon-the-man. "What's the point of having him around?" Bailey followed Craig with her eyes half-closed. "Whoa. She's never like this. What is happening?" He felt groggy, and all his remaining sensible thoughts were about Sekhmet. "The statue is a symbol, but it's also alive, it means something… *she* means something… Simon said I would meet her… Did I meet her?

"Are you feeling it? This déjà vu?" mumbled Bailey.

"Yeah, the whole time!"

"Why would we feel this *off* from looking at some piece of rock?"

"She was so real… I mean *it* was… Whoa, Simon was right! And she is huge, somehow… I think I saw more of her than just the statue…" He suddenly remembered that it was Bailey he was speaking to, and stopped before he said something he wasn't supposed to. She believed she was on a mission to find out about her father, so why confuse her with the rest of the story? It wasn't her fault that she didn't know the real meaning behind their being here… well, neither did Craig, really. But he was a shaman and the Cat said that Sekhmet needed him.

Sekhmet was the destroyer of her life! Bailey struggled to regain control over her overwhelming emotions. She would not give her feelings the satisfaction of getting the better of her! Crying was not an option, defeat was not an option! Bailey was the master and feelings were slaves, they had no rights and no voices. As she suppressed the feelings, she was ready for a fight – she refused to see any power in any temples or symbols, only the history of the civilization that killed her parents. Her pain would not be denied its righteous place!

Leaving Bailey to her rage, Craig stood in the temple shade, as if in suspension, staring at the kaleidoscope of walls, people, and cats. Everything around him began to swim a little, then more than a little. Bailey's face, the temple walls, even the two napping cats disappeared, and were replaced by the oh-so-familiar darkness of the room with the cube and the pyramid.

"Oh, no…" whispered Craig, as darkness overtook him.

*　　*　　*

A tour group had just passed them, and they were alone in between two massive columns of the Temple of Amun. Bailey had broken Craig's fall and struggled for a moment with his dead weight until he slid to the stone floor. She frantically looked around for help as she propped him against a column. She was standing in an ancient temple halfway across the world with a semi-conscious young man at her feet. Bailey felt the panic raising up inside her. "Everything has a reasonable explanation!" she scolded herself. "Spirit? There is no such thing! Everything comes down to traumatic childhood experiences and chemical imbalances, and those things can be fixed with therapy and medication!" The appeal to "normality" had been her survival mechanism since childhood, why change now? But still she felt as though her emotional lid had been loosened. She felt all alone in the land that took away her parents. Traitor tears began to well up in Bailey's eyes. Like a five-year-old child again, she felt helpless.

Craig opened his eyes, looking as if he had just seen a ghost. "Oh, yeah… he doesn't see those," she reminded herself. Still frightened, she couldn't believe that this had happened again! She should have asked him why he fainted in Boston, to find out if he had a medical condition – why hadn't she? And thus she pummeled him with her words until Craig promised to tell her – as soon as he got some water and could lie down.

Bailey elected to get out of the temple and get a taxi back to the hotel. She slowly guided Craig to the main road where there were a few taxis behind a line of tour buses. As if from nowhere a little black taxi jumped out, and the driver invited them in. What a godsend, they avoided having to walk farther! The taxi driver was an Egyptian in his late forties or early fifties, he made conversation in broken English, saying that the "young man must have overheated, happens often with tourists, make sure he has water and some rest, so he can view more of the treasures of this wondrous country..."

The driver was happy to receive the US dollars, and he kept up his lecturing about "water for the Mister." Walking towards the hotel steps, Bailey was too occupied with Craig and her thoughts to notice that, even though the taxi pulled away from the curb, it had stopped again after just a few feet and the driver was scrutinizing her in his rear view mirror. Then he sped forward heading back into town. The St. George's bell captain helped Craig to the elevators. "Heat can be very strong, he is dehydrated." The sphinxes on the seventh floor looked sad. Bailey finally sat Craig down on the sofa and got him a cold bottle of water from the mini-bar. The AC aided their recovery; both of them felt safer in a colder room.

As Craig lay on the sofa by the balcony door, his long legs hanging off the sofa's arm, he began his tale. He told her about the childhood dreams that caused him to wake up startled. In those dreams there was a room made of yellowish stone walls, and in an adjoining room, a perfect cube pedestal with a pyramid on top of it. And how he was always drawn to the second room, towards the pyramid, but as he got closer something happened... everything would become very bright for a moment, like a huge explosion, he would be hit by a kind of wave and... then he could never remember what happened next, because that was when he usually woke up. His bladder would often let go, and his body would shake and ache all over, as if he had been electrocuted. His grandma was kind and accepted the dreams without trying to stop them because she didn't believe in drugs or doctors, but the dreams continued into his later years and he was laughed at about it many times over by the other kids in the foster families. One foster mother took him to a psychiatrist, who prescribed drugs for him. The drugs made him feel slow and groggy and he was laughed at even more. But the dreams went away. The disappearance of the dreams was supposed to be a comfort, but with them went all the other fun things, like talking to his spirit guide and having visions, and he felt physically unwell. So in Craig's young mind this was proof that grandma Betty had been right, that drugs were poison. The next family he lived with did not take him back to the psychiatrist for more drugs, and he felt better. The spirit guide reappeared, and so did the visions. But the dreams began again, even

78

though his body handled them better. The dreams were always the same; it was really one recurrent dream.

One day, when he was placed with his last foster family, he was walking in the corridor at school, he suddenly was *inside* that room again and then, just like the dream, there was an explosion-like flash, and then he was lying on the floor. He hit his head hard when he fell, enough to have to stay home. But he didn't want to go back on the little pills and so he lied and said that he "just fell," not mentioning the "waking dream" at all. Craig worried that something was really wrong with him, because he had been awake when that "dream" happened. His spirit guide told him it was because he was getting closer to the truth of what his path was about.

Since then, the awake-dreams had been happening about once every two or three months. But after he met Bailey, they begin to happen very often. And now he would even meet his spirit guide there, in that room.

"What do you mean, 'in that room'?"

"When I'm on a vision quest, I have to be somewhere and it's usually... not that room. But lately it's always the room, and he meets me there..."

"Your spirit guide?"

"Yeah... Like he's mocking my fear a little..." smiled Craig.

Bailey felt the hairs on her neck stand up. She remembered her own childhood "visions" and the "voices." Did she project onto herself her twin's experiences or were these her own memories? She could not remember clearly, but she had a very strong feeling that what Craig was telling her was familiar because she had seen it too! She suddenly felt dizzy and afraid.

*   *   *

They talked well into the night. Simon did not return until two in the morning, looking dirty and tired.

"What happened?" said Bailey, exhaling as she let him in.

"You were followed, I followed them."

"Jesus! Where, when?"

"We both noticed that old man looking at you, Bailey, at the chapel," said Craig.

"Yeah, he didn't only look, he called a taxi for you, folks, and you took it."

"What taxi? The one we were in? It just came up to the curb and Craig needed to sit down... Oh, my god..."

"I followed the taxi. It belongs to a man named Axil Narmy. He's around fifty, married with six children, is a licensed taxi driver and has been for twenty-five years. It's a legitimate setup, he clearly loves his family and he works very long hours to support them on the income from his taxi. From the look of it he doesn't have much time for anything else."

"How do you know all this?"

"I have sources. And expertise. I believe that's why you wanted me here, isn't it?"

"Simon, that means that the men here at the hotel saw us leave, and told that man at the temple to follow us. Then they got us a taxi, right?"

"No, not right. They are two separate groups. The men here at the hotel are trained; one is very well trained. They are from Cairo. They are not interested in harming you here, I am quite sure about that."

"Well, that's a relief! What the hell, these were the same people who probably tried to kill us in Cairo!"

"They probably tried to scare you. From what I can see, if they wanted to kill you, you would be dead by now."

"Great! Even better! So these men in the hotel are just *watching* us and *following* us everywhere we go?"

"Yes. But they don't always follow you. They are confident that you are going to stay in Luxor. They saw you set out on the road to Karnak and they saw where you went. They didn't seem interested in any more particulars."

"Well, they told the old man at the temple to call us a taxi. Why would they need to do that? If they know where we are and where we are staying..."

"No, Bailey, I saw that old man looking at you – he wasn't expecting us, he was definitely shocked to see you in front of the chapel," said Craig.

"But the old man could not have known me. Why would he be scared of me, or shocked to see me?"

"I agree with Craig. The old man is not connected to the blokes in the lobby at all. He actually made them nervous when he whisked you away in an unauthorized taxi." There was a smirk on Simon's face.

"What do you mean, *unauthorized?* You just said yourself that this Axil guy is a bona-fide cab driver."

"Yeah, but he was unauthorized. If you remember, he came from the direction of the exit, the opposite side from where the rest of the taxis were, and because of that he had to turn to get you guys out. Didn't you hear the horns?"

"Yes, I remember. I was so focused on Craig... I thought it was just something outside, or maybe he turned too quickly and pissed someone off... He did speed off, didn't he?"

"Yes, he did, so quickly that the hotel men lost you. Oh, boy, were they ticked off!"

"So who was the man at the chapel then?" asked Bailey.

"Oh, you don't want to know who these friendly blokes downstairs are?"

"You know??"

"I do. They each have at least two guns, I checked. Don't ask... And they kept up the surveillance from Cairo. That tells me that they have connections. At first I thought it was the government or the military. But when I investigated I found that they aren't, but their employer has quite a bit of influence in the government. They are connected to..." – Simon glanced at the tiny notebook in his hand – "...the Supreme Council of Antiquities of Egypt."

"What? You mean like their private police or something? Why do they care about us? They think we stole the locket??"

"I don't know, but I'm really itching to find out. I'm not sure why the Council of Antiquities would need its own security force, so I don't know if it's just a cover, but that is the official authority they are 'attached' to."

"And who's the old man from the chapel? And this Axil guy?"

"I don't know... yet."

*   *   *

Bailey suddenly woke from an intense dream. In it her father was telling her something in his warm voice, something about that statue in the chapel, something about *talking to Sekhmet*. Bailey was about to dismiss the dream as her mind's twisted recollection of recent events when she noticed that in the large room opposite hers Craig was also sitting up on his bed, and so was Simon, alert in his chair, and both of them were staring at her through the open door.

"What are you doing? What happened?" Bailey could hear her voice shaking.

After a moment Simon spoke.

"Well, your friend here woke up, with tears on his face and shaking, telling me to not worry when I asked for an explanation, and then seconds later you bolted up, all freaked out. Would anyone care to tell me what's bloody going on?"

At that instant Bailey had an inner moment of truth. It was one of those moments when you just know something really big is happening even if you have no clue what it is; when many unconnected things suddenly come together and make sense. Her father had just told her: *I have to go talk to Sekhmet, people are waiting for me in Egypt, we have to do it so the world can be all better for little girls like you...* As the memory materialized in her awareness with profound clarity, tears began to stream down her cheeks. Maybe he was not as guilty as she made him out to be. Maybe she had suppressed this memory because it was so much easier to simply hate him. Just like she convinced herself that her childhood visions were only the product of her overactive imagination. Now she remembered her last vision – the only one she had when her family was in Egypt, when she was already recovering from chickenpox. She had wanted so much to share it with her twin sister! Bailey had believed that the pox had stopped all her visions permanently. But there was this one... It was about a tall woman showing her a glowing pyramid, and the woman told her that she, Bailey, was her *other option*. At the time Bailey had not known what the words meant and had pushed the memory into the recesses of her mind, and with her parents dead and Abby unwell, she had never had any reason to dig it up. Could this woman be Sekhmet, and the glowing pyramid the same one that Craig had dreams about?

CHAPTER FIVE

4,122BC

Edfu, Egypt

Being corporeal was difficult enough; existing under the limitation of a linear perception was a whole other challenge. It had been her choice to enter the Earth Experiment. She desired involvement, and her heart was leading her to explore the newly discovered sister world. Facing any difficultly was pleasurable, because on her Sirian world difficultly was almost nonexistent. Her Sirian form was not one, but two. This of course could not fit into any corporeal existence and she had had to choose only one. This choice seemed impossible – how does one choose to have only half of oneself? Which half would be chosen? If she embodied her woman form, would she miss stretching her feline body or pouncing? But on the other hand, her feline form might not have been able to communicate with the people of Earth if they did not yet have telepathic abilities. They might not know how to interact with a large cat anyway. It all pointed to a humanoid form. That form was better for her assignment, and so she chose it.

Squeezing her multidimensional self into a corporeal form was painful, but Sekhmet endured – she desired some difficulty after all!

She could not wait to see the child of the thirty-two beings, who had come to Earth before her. "Before" was such a strange concept, so very linear, but she had to get used to this limitation. The thirty-two had come to Earth thousands of years before her, measured in the time of the third dimension, even though she knew it to be almost an instant birth in her own dimensional perception. The thirty-two could not create a child on their Sirian home. They required another participant, who would make their number thirty-three – unheard of on Sirius. This thirty-third entity was the being of Earth, the sister world. Earth's first mission was motherhood. Sekhmet's passion for meeting this new child of the thirty-two and Earth was burning so brightly that the whole crystalline pyramid radiated ruby red light as it materialized in Earth's orbit.

That was such a long time ago, thought Sekhmet, sitting on a large chair. The house was devoid of people. She had not allowed visitors for a long time now. She liked it this way. The visitors reminded her of how disastrous was her affair on this miserable planet, and she could not allow any more pain. She had been so naïve, so young, so hopeful back then…
    Sekhmet flexed her fingers – her knuckles still hurt from being recently broken. She no longer healed instantaneously, and the pain had taken a toll on her. "This planet might just be my death," sighed Sekhmet. She was the only one of her kind here, the only one who didn't leave when the energy became denser. The cycle of unconsciousness was threatening to begin, promising a long sleep, even though eventually the awakening was expected. But they all felt the limitation of density, the pain of being squeezed by this reality, and so the others decided it was best to go home, to abandon this world to its own path. But Sekhmet knew the truth: they were afraid. "For all their expanded consciousness and enlightened teachings, they were simply cowards!" She slammed her fist on the arm of her chair and winced in pain. She remembered when physical pain had been such a novel experience – it was fascinating to become so fused to this corporeal form that it hurt. She could heal instantaneously, so no harm was done. As the energy of Earth became denser and denser, her matter-body became less and less connected to the rest of her multidimensional self. And so every move she made had to be calculated more carefully because the damage to her form now required regeneration time. Of course her form healed eventually, but it seemed to take longer and longer.
    Sekhmet smiled and purposefully smashed her fist on her chair again. A large lioness, which lay by Sekhmet's feet, lifted its head and stared at her. The chair's wooden arm flew off and Sekhmet looked again at her hand. There was blood on her fist and the pain was strong. "Good," she thought with satisfaction. Physical pain took her focus away from the internal anguish she felt.
    She was the only one. This in itself was painful – she had no support. A long time ago she had watched the transparent pyramid disappear, vibrating itself out of this damned dimension. She was alone,

alone with the children of Earth. Oh, she loved them so very much. They were her students, her playmates, her friends.

What she had not realized was that the density would eventually become stronger than her. Sekhmet had never before encountered anything she could not conquer with her intellect, passion, or consciousness. She thought she would be stronger than this intermediate issue of lesser consciousness. She was wrong.

Slowly squeezed by a python of time, Sekhmet endured. She thought that the period of density would be short. Back then, she had still been able to revert to her feline form. That helped tremendously to relieve the pressure of density.

Sekhmet smiled again, a sad and angry smile that had no laughter in it at all. Standing up, she slowly walked to a shelf, picked up a jar and smelled its contents. The mixture was designed to help her battered body heal. It had stopped working a while back, but she liked the smell and so she scooped some of it up with a finger and spread it over her hurt hand. She had come to hate that hand, and the whole body with it!

Returning to her chair, she sank into it and again stared into space. Another large cat, not a lioness but comparable in size, jumped off the windowsill it was resting on. Lately Sekhmet had surrounded herself with Earth felines – these creatures were drawn to her and she allowed them free access to her house. They were more honest than people.

It was getting dark and the wind was picking up. She could hear the large green leaves outside her window scraping the side of the house. "Maybe it will rain," she thought, without enthusiasm. Her body only hurt more from the wetness.

She remembered celebrating the rain; it was such a novel concept to have water molecules fall from the sky! That was so long ago... She had been eager to help then, to educate and to involve herself in human life. Working tirelessly with many other Sirian entities in corporeal forms, she studied the planet, people, nature. But if others were focused on the process of study itself, Sekhmet's passion was about human nature. She was bored with methodical calculations, preferring the active engagement of life. Her inner fire shone brightly and she fearlessly engaged the people of Earth. Being the only hybrid among her Sirian colleagues, she was capable of deep feeling and emotion, much more than any of them. Human people loved her; she was almost one of them.

"Was I?" thought Sekhmet, staring at the window. It had begun to rain after all, and she could smell the water in the air.

She had thought she was one of the people. They accepted her and loved her. She taught them everything she knew and they still asked for more, hungry for knowledge and depth. People forwarded her knowledge to their children. Sekhmet loved watching these children grow up, generation after generation. So many people, and so much expansion. There was peace and cooperation.

The Sirian mission was not to lead humans, but to be with them, to simply experience their half-siblings. They shared their knowledge freely, but only with the ones who wanted it. Sekhmet was excited to see people flocking to her – fascinated with her hybrid nature, they loved her stories of multidimensional existence. She taught in her female form, but when she could, she always reverted to her feline self. Her golden fur and soft paws felt like home, even if they could not actually touch the ground. Her feline body was multidimensional, not corporeal, meaning it existed only in higher vibrational frequencies and did not touch matter. Sekhmet was so proud when her advanced students were able to see her as a feline – when they achieved the ability to see other-dimensional aspects of reality.

She remembered trying to explain being both corporeal and matterless to her students. The concept was alien to them – the best they could do was to think of her as "really a cat but looking like a woman." That was not true, because she really was both at the same time, even if the two existed in different dimensions which were parallel to each other. Sekhmet could not tolerate untruth. Like a sword blade cutting the edge of her soul, it literally hurt her. She spent countless hours clarifying details – in this reality, everything seemed to be either saved or lost in the details!

Those were good times, when people were growing and learning. Sekhmet was pleased with their progress and proud of their achievements. She showed them how to dive into the unknown, how to be brave, how to know the illusion of fear and respectfully decline its invitation. The truth was above all; it required not only knowledge but passion. The fire of truth burned brightly in Sekhmet's heart then, so brightly that people felt the vibration all around them when she spoke. They used to tell her that they felt her truth in their skin. In their language there was a word for this experience – Maat. Sekhmet began to be called Maat, the Lover of Truth, the Detester of Untruth…

She smiled to herself. The wind was blowing the rain water through the window right into her house but she did not care. She was remembering…

86

Convinced she could change things, she had stayed behind in density – it was her own choice, of course. She knew she could not change the entire course of human history, but at least she could help some people maintain their consciousness, help these few remember who they really are so that they can lead the others into awakening...

The polar shift came when the planet reversed her magnetic polarity. Earth was preparing for the second phase of her mission: to learn power, she had chosen to experience powerlessness and victimhood. The devastation to all corporeal life was incredible. Instead of fascination, Sekhmet felt pain. She loved the people and now she had to watch them die. The most advanced in consciousness knew what was coming and they survived. There were a few small groups of them all over the world. Sekhmet could feel them. In the land of Egypt her students survived in very small numbers, but they were alive and ready. And she was ready – ready to rebuild.

That time had seemed so hard to her. Now Sekhmet knew what pain really was and the memories of her difficulties seemed almost good. She had worked tirelessly to help the people of Egypt rebuild their civilization. At first it was on a much smaller scale, but she knew that people would multiply and all would be restored. She was wrong. Soon it became apparent that all of the survivors outside of her little enclave had succumbed to animal-like behavior. What had happened to her beautiful, powerful, brave, and conscious children? They were lost, asleep, trapped in survival fear. In just a few generations even language skills had deteriorated – Sekhmet could no longer recognize her half-siblings, could not communicate with them. They had become like animals, hunting each other, fighting for domination, ruled by fear.

Horrified, Sekhmet poured all her love, energy, and knowledge into preserving the small enclaves of people who had retained civilization. She even attempted to rehabilitate the animal-like creatures the rest of humanity had become, with no success. But at least her enclaves grew into large communities. These people were trying to stay awake, to remain untouched by the changes, to rebuild. Small towns and villages sprung up all over Egypt, and Sekhmet patiently taught generation after generation about who they really were. But unfortunately each generation could only understand Sekhmet when they were children. When they matured, they could no longer comprehend her words, the truth, even though they loved her nonetheless.

That was when the imposters came. Just when it seemed things could get no worse, the people of Earth were given one more temptation – gods! The imposters were powerful and they were not of the third dimensional Earth. Sekhmet did not know much about them and she did not care to know. She quickly saw the result of their involvement in human affairs – they wanted to use the people of Earth to serve their own needs. Her beautiful, powerful children were becoming sheep eager for a shepherd! The imposters were aware of Sekhmet's existence on Earth, although they did not understand why she had stayed behind while the rest of her kind had gone home. They knew that she was very powerful, but they also knew she was the only one on the planet and that she could not derail their plans. And so they left her alone.

It was not her fight; it was up to the people of Earth to choose which path to follow. All she could do was educate, pour her soul into them, and hope. But her students were reduced to a handful, and were soon so few that she had to go into villages to introduce herself again and again. Few remembered who she was. People even stopped caring about what she was saying. It was easier to give their power to someone else in the hope that they would be taken care of.

Witnessing generation after generation falling further into fear, Sekhmet fought to preserve life. She failed. Her soul was bleeding as she burned inside her own pain. Reverting to her feline form became harder and harder as the planet continued its downward spin. Cut off from the comfort of the rest of herself, Sekhmet only hurt more. Her love was spent; there was nothing left inside, even for herself. She was falling apart as the life bled out of her. No one knew her pain. She was alone.

How was this possible? Was it not the truth that these people were the inheritors of Sirian wisdom, initiators of change, and creators of their own destiny? Yet they were choosing to be sheep, led by abusive shepherds! They were becoming ignorant and dumb, devolving to their animal nature. Yet they *still had* free will! The density had not taken it away from them! They did not *have to* become slaves to anyone; they *chose* it. Oh, Sekhmet was angry, not with the imposters who took the names of her Sirian comrades, but with the people. The imposters were power-hungry manipulators, but the people of Earth were divine. They had not become slaves because they were overpowered, but because it was convenient! This Sekhmet could not reconcile inside herself. Her rage spilled outwards, onto the people of Earth.

Joining with the imposters in their schemes was beneath her; they were irrelevant. Her struggle was with the people. Such betrayal! In Maat she knew they had betrayed themselves, choosing the path of slavery and false gods. She and her Sirian friends were never worshipped; they could never have allowed that. But the imposters encouraged it. People were scared and gave in to these bullies, elevating them to the position of gods. The imposters were now worshipped everywhere, and people's lives given away in everything from sacrifice to warfare. The people of Earth had betrayed their divinity, and Sekhmet's rage was all-consuming. Yet all her rage accomplished was to inspire fear in people. They began to fear her, and made her into another of their gods. How humiliating! She, the multidimensional being sworn to educate and support the people was neither respected nor loved, but feared and worshipped!

People saw her pain but they could not understand why she hurt and what they needed to change to help it. They told stories about "fierce Sekhmet, the goddess of war, destruction and death" and even created a holiday dedicated to her. Unfortunately, Sekhmet knew it was not to honor her – people had lost the ability to honor themselves, so how could they honor her? No, it was to appease her, to celebrate her scary, fiery power in hopes that she would spare their not-too-conscious lives. Thus it was that each fall at the end of October, they gathered together wearing scary masks and carrying fiery dolls, and covered the Nile with small ships lit with fiery lanterns – and, of course, the altars of her temples overflowed with offerings, sacrifices, and lit torches. It all was so pathetic that Sekhmet wept. The silly people thought that they had secured the survival of their crops and children by appeasing her.

Misunderstood by her Sirian comrades and the people of Earth, she had to stand alone in her truth and passion. But now even her passion was spent. She felt hurt and broken; her heart was shattered by this insane human drama. She raged at the universe that had allowed them to become slaves. As a human mother might rage at god for taking her child, Sekhmet raged until her fire was extinguished. She felt depleted. She sat in a stupor, knowing that if she allowed herself to feel anything again she would be consumed by pain. And that would be the end of her for sure. People feared her because they were not sure how to appease her – and if you cannot appease a god, you are in trouble! An unhappy god would not help a person, and might even inflict harm. Sekhmet was unpredictable, for what she was asking of people they seemed to have lost the ability to give.

She had overworked herself to the point of exhaustion with no result. People were still slaves; they preferred that condition to divinity, and in their eyes she remained a fierce goddess of destruction. Was her belief in human divinity an illusion? She stood on the edge of life and death and bravely looked into the face of oblivion. It seemed that the only way to resolve the pain was self-annihilation. Sekhmet was trapped in her corporeal form. She could not revert to her multidimensional existence. Tortured by her own pain, she was suicidal, homicidal, and almost insane.

Her house was hidden by the lush vegetation of the nearby Nile river. She used to be visited by her beloved students. They would come on a small boat and she would welcome them at the dock, leading them into this very house. She smiled again, sadness apparent on her tired face. She used to wear a lioness mask when people were around, true to her own multidimensional feline form. Gold was a fitting material. She never realized how heavy and uncomfortable the mask was... until this density happened. Her face began to bruise from the mask and because regeneration now took time, it was unwise to continue wearing it. She had another mask made by one of her students, hiding the previous one in the underground vault. The new mask was thinner and much lighter, and also fit better. She used to wear the mask all the time because it reminded her of her feline component. Now it hung on the wall. Sekhmet looked at it and had to blink. She had not realized that tears were streaming down her face. She missed that time when the mask was as much a part of her as the rest of her feline self. Now it was useless. No one was coming to her hidden house and she was sick of wearing the mask, pretending she was not as alone as she really was. And so the mask hung on a crude nail on one of the walls of this prison Sekhmet called home. She was slowly dying, numb without her fiery passion. The golden mask reminded her of the days when she was alive and shiny in her Maat.
"This world is cruel to shiny things," she thought with an absent smile.
And then it happened – Sekhmet heard a voice. At first she was not sure if she had really heard it, but it repeated itself. Confused, she looked around her small house – she was sure she was the only one there. Even though her essence was trapped in a corporeal body, her perceptions were not, at least not all of them. She was still the most advanced being on planet Earth, more capable than any imposter god. But her pain had worn down any desire to perceive life – why do it? It would only hurt more... However, now she refocused her inner vision and hearing, scanned her surroundings, and followed the voice.
Let them go, said the voice. It was familiar, but in her numbness Sekhmet could not place it at first. Then she recognized it – it was the voice of one of the beings she had known, her mentor and the one who had inspired her to come to Earth in the first place. As if waking up from a nightmare, Sekhmet focused on the memory.

The voice was that of a feline, a full feline, not a hybrid like Sekhmet, and a very influential one. A long time ago, before the current Earth Experiment, that entity had facilitated the activation of the feline genes on Earth. Because of her this wretched planet had multitudes of cats of every possible shape and size. Sekhmet smiled as she looked at the lioness and the other spotted large cat lying at her feet. Without these cats she would have gone insane or died a long time ago. They reminded her of her own feline component, and kept her alive in this density.

Let them go, the voice repeated. It sounded as if it had to go through water to get to her. Her mentor must have had to do a lot of work to locate her here, in the density of linear time on Earth. Sekhmet shook her head – she was so numb, half asleep in her pain, she could barely focus! Images began to pour into her mind – people with all their troubles, the Solar Council and her Sirian friends, the entity of Earth and her new learning choice, this feline mentor…

The avalanche of perception stopped and Sekhmet looked around the room. It was morning already – how long had she been in contact with her mentor? The large cats were gone, and so was the rain. Walking up to the window, she took a deep breath, trying to process the information. The air smelled moist and warm, fresh somehow with a new sense of hope, hope that she had not felt in a very long time. She had not visited people for almost a thousand Earth years by now. What was she hiding from in this small house? Her pain? Her guilt for becoming a goddess to humans? Her fate was merged with that of people and she had bled silently for them for a thousand years, alone. Were the people of Earth even aware anymore of her presence on the planet? It was likely that they were not.

"How did she find me?" wondered Sekhmet. Over the thousands of years of density, Sekhmet had lost contact with everyone from other dimensions. If back and forth communication was not possible anymore because of this damn density, perhaps a tunnel could be opened, a message delivered… And so it was done – she had not been forgotten.

"I am not to blame for the fall of human consciousness." Sekhmet spoke out loud, as if testing Maat. "I am not a god, I am a passionate, fiery Sekhmet, and I do not apologize for my existence!"

Sekhmet took the gold lioness mask off the wall and put it on. It felt cold on her skin. Taking another deep breath she walked out of her small house. The path to the Nile was no more – she had to push aside branches and leaves with her hands. The dock had disintegrated, as if it had never been. She realized that from the river no one would have known that there was a stone house hidden in the trees.

Two women were singing, their boat slowly moving down the Nile. Sekhmet yelled to them, waving her hand. After a moment of confusion, they paddled her way.

*　　*　　*

As she slowly walked through the main avenue of the city of Edfu, people froze. There were quiet whispers, and they were in obvious terror for their lives – the goddess of destruction herself had returned! Moving aside, they stared at her with shock, forgetting to fall to the ground. Sekhmet was still the tallest among humans. Her bright blue-white skin and her gold face shone, her dark amber eyes glowed. She had returned to avenge consciousness!

Walking straight to her temple, which was still standing after a thousand years, she was met by the priests. These men were ignorant idiots and Sekhmet dismissed them. Looking around with her higher vision, she was determined to find the worthy ones – the people who still had divinity in them. There were none. But she was not going to give up so easily. She had given thousands of years to numbness and she was through. If people misunderstood her, so be it. She would find the worthy ones and teach Maat only to them. Eventually she would let go – if she could only figure out how!

After inspecting her temple, she decided to stay there. Edfu was where she had her previous human community, and this temple had been built by her students as a house of learning. When consciousness fell, people came to associate the large stone structure with Sekhmet herself – she remembered watching it being turned into a temple to her, the goddess. Now she sat on the throne in the temple's Holy of Holies. Something was missing... How could she let go? She had tried the wine once before and her corporeal body had felt relaxed from drinking it. This was more than three thousand years ago – but people still knew how to make wine and she had to allow herself to feel... Sekhmet could not let herself feel the pain – one more drop would surely kill her. But by staying numb she would not be able do what she planned. Unfortunately, feeling was unavoidable.

She asked for wine to be brought to her temple – food was easily available from the overflowing altars. And so barrels and barrels of red wine were delivered to Sekhmet's temple.

That year her holiday, which she found out still existed, was the most lavish in the history of Egypt. Her temples and statues throughout the land were decorated with red and orange flowers, and fires burned through the night. She was passionately worshipped and passionately feared. Sekhmet laughed, watching the people. "Well, at least they are passionate about something!" She ate the food off the altars, she drank the wine and she even came out of her *Per-Sekhmet*, "house of the goddess," to bless people. "How silly," she thought. "They think that somehow I can make all their troubles go away..." She knew she could not do that, but she was finished with apologies! No more would she worry how her actions would affect them – they were already so "affected" that nothing could make them worse! She knew she was in Maat and that was enough. It had to be...

She had reclaimed her fire. Her pleasure in being alive was back, her heart almost mended, and she began to feel herself again. One night, focusing on her feline form, she was able to revert to it again after over six thousand years of being trapped in her corporeal female body – for a week she joyfully roamed the temple as a golden lioness. No one could see her because people's vision no longer extended to the faster frequencies. Then a young woman, no more than fifteen years of age, entered the temple and stopped, staring at her. Sekhmet roared and the woman made a step back. She could see Sekhmet's feline form and she was not afraid, simply cautious. Sekhmet immediately reverted to her humanoid female body – the young woman fell to her knees, seeing the goddess. Sekhmet knew then she had found her first recruit – this young woman had a destiny to fulfill!

It took more than decade of human years for Sekhmet to find other people who she felt could carry her knowledge. She found only twelve more. Rivers of wine were consumed and people made up songs and tales about the "fiery, fierce goddess who was so dangerous that, to save his people from her, a pharaoh had come up with the idea of giving her wine instead of the human blood she loved so much, and she drank and the people were safe"... Sekhmet refused to be horrified by this. She drank the wine that she herself requested and she refused to acknowledge any pharaoh, or anyone else for that matter, as a god. She laughed in the face of human unconsciousness.

The thirteen people she had chosen were special, each of them had a quality most people had lost – they were not afraid! Thirteen people in the whole of Egypt... But if these were to be the odds of her success, Sekhmet would not be scared off by them. She spent countless hours training these thirteen in consciousness alchemy, until they were able to perceive Maat. Sekhmet traveled with them throughout Egypt, showing them the special places above and below the ground. This was Sekhmet's last gift to humans – now that she could revert to her feline form she knew she would have to leave Earth soon because the density was only getting stronger. The first girl she had found at her temple, the one with her middle eye open, knew the most and so Sekhmet made her the High Priestess of her secret school. She called them the Shenu.

CHAPTER SIX

Current time
Cairo, Egypt

"They did what? You are hired to report to me every move they make, not to inform me that you cannot account for two hours! Two hours! Where did they go?" he yelled into the phone, exasperated at the incompetence of his men. The man on the phone was sweating despite the air conditioning. He wore a tailored shirt, open at the collar, in a light yellow similar to the colors of Cairo outside his window. His tie was loosened around his neck and his neatly trimmed beard was, like his wavy hair, mostly gray. Last month he had celebrated his fifty-eighth birthday. But thoughts of a peaceful year ahead of him had vanished.

He had done something he could later regret, and it was not paying off. As undersecretary of the government-run Supreme Council of Antiquities he had dispatched the Council's security only a few days ago to follow the two Westerners, and his men were already having problems!

He slammed the phone down. Two hours! They could have gone anywhere, Luxor is huge! And if they had lost his men they had probably done so intentionally, and had already gone to Sekhmet's only chapel at Karnak. It was beginning all over again!

He went to the foyer of his large house and grabbed his jacket from the chair. His wife was in Europe visiting his youngest daughter and son-in-law. He was alone at home, which was good, because he needed space to handle this mini-crisis. "Mini-crisis!" Who was he kidding, this was developing into a serious problem! He had to handle it, and it was essential that he handle it by himself. He did not want to inform the Shenu. He climbed into his black Mercedes Benz and slowly backed out of the driveway.

It all began thirty-one years ago, when his father, on his deathbed, told him to come to this very neighborhood to see the Shenu… He had driven here and knocked on the door. He was allowed in. He remembered feeling surprised and somewhat alarmed about that because he had been so sure his father had been mistaken or delusional in sending him there. But he was expected. He spoke the words his father had him say: "I am Mahmoud Mukhtar Halib, Sharif's son, the chosen one, and I am here to tell you 'they know and they must be stopped'." He was asked many questions by a man of his father's age, most of which he could not answer. The man, Faruq Bashir, wanted to know how his father had died but he had no answer even to that; he had seen what looked like wounds made by bullets but he did not know for sure. He had been so innocent! Allah! He could not imagine why someone would want to hurt his dear old father!

He was asked to stay there, in small guest quarters on the other side of the courtyard. It seemed like the old man was studying him. Imagine – being watched like a little child! Nevertheless, he did not complain, just went along with all that the old man asked of him; he was bound to honor his father's last words. He telephoned his brother-in-law's shop, telling him about the dark events: the death of his father and his needing time to take care of things. Of course, his brother-in-law understood. "Don't worry, call if you need anything, may Allah be with you…" His brother-in-law was always kind…

Mahmoud pulled onto the highway. Traffic was light, he could make it to his office and back in time. Thoughts of the past kept coming… He remembered how frustrating and hard it had been when Faruq Bashir asked him to study subject after subject – the history of Egypt nearly brought him to tears. It was insulting to be asked to pick up books again, and hard to do at twenty-seven. High school he had finished, but he had never gone to college; he married young, and had chosen to work and make money for his family. His father always said that it was what was in the heart that was important, the mind could always catch up later.

Faruq Bashir was strict and insisted on the studies, for reasons unclear to Mahmoud. But he had promised his father. Faruq allowed him to return home as long as he continued his studies. Studying at home, with his wife and children, was uncomfortable. His wife did not understand; she just assumed it was one of his new interests and left him alone so long as he performed his duties as a husband and father. After a while Faruq Bashir asked him to take specified courses at the University of Cairo. Everything was paid for by Faruq, and Mahmoud was even given a monthly allowance, which was explained as "compensation for the time he was not spending with his family." He was told that the money was repayment of a debt to his father who had wanted his son to be educated in the event of his untimely death, but Mahmoud doubted that. What could his family have ever given someone like Faruq Bashir?

Mahmoud's wife saw how persistently he struggled with his studies and began to pay more attention. Soon she enjoyed listening to the new things he was learning and hearing about his new experiences. And the money was there. The early difficulties passed and learning finally became interesting, and so he learned. He studied history, languages such as English, French and ancient Egyptian; the tourist industry, more history… Archeology was easy for him. Before long he was sent to England to study for five months, while his family was moved to a much nicer house in Cairo with everything paid for, including the two men guarding it, so that his wife would feel comfortable and safe without her husband. She did not understand why he had to go but it was good for the children to be in a better neighborhood, so she did not complain. The guards stayed in front of the new house day and night, and Mahmoud wondered if they were there for his family's safety or to guard him. Was he really lucky, or a hostage?

Instead of coming home from the UK, Mahmoud was "asked" if he would go to the United States. As with England it was clear that "no" was not an acceptable answer, so Mahmoud telephoned his wife to tell her he was being sent to America. To his surprise, before he could say anything, she happily congratulated him on his new position in America and told him how much she appreciated his thoughtfulness in making sure she and the kids were well taken care of by sending the girls to an exclusive private school, and getting them a car with a private driver! All Mahmoud could do was take a deep breath and play the part.

But that was so long ago… Over the last thirty years he had risen to a very high position of power. He was smart, confident and knowledgeable, spoke English well, had two higher degrees, and plenty of connections all over the world. It was he who now lived in Faruq Bashir's house.

A car swerved in front of him just as he was about to exit the highway. Mahmoud sounded his horn. "Can't you see this is an official vehicle! Look at the plates! Kids are so disrespectful today," he thought, glancing at the young man at the wheel as he passed the car. He turned onto the exit and off the highway. He was almost at his office now...

Faruq Bashir died fifteen years ago. Mahmoud had learned to trust that man as he trusted his own father, if not more. He wished now that Faruq was here.

Near the end of his life Faruq had finally told Mahmoud what his father's words meant. He was chosen alright! His father Sharif Halib had carried a great burden, and he had selected his son to continue shouldering it. He was chosen to be part of the Shenu... The word was ancient Egyptian, and it meant a loop of rope protecting whatever was inside it. That was why the royal names were written in a cartouche, a form of "shenu." The hieroglyph for "shen", a circular form of "shenu", often seen being held in a talon on Horus, representing eternity and protection simultaneously. The Shenu were powerful and very discreet. It always had thirteen members, connected like a rope, protecting the secret. Only five of those members at any given time were available to the outside world. Today he was one of those people. Being the Undersecretary of the Supreme Council of Antiquities, he knew them all personally. There was a Minister of Aviation, Minister of Culture, Minister of Social Solidarity, and of course, the Council of Foreign Affairs and International Cooperation, a position set up by the influence of the Shenu.

He walked speedily through the lobby and was almost at his desk now, his mind filled with ideas presenting themselves and being rejected. How could this matter be resolved without contacting the Shenu? There was only one more thing he could try...

Luxor, Egypt

Falling asleep well past midnight, Craig and Bailey woke up close to noon. Simon was already fully dressed – he had ventured out to check up on the men in the lobby. Bailey, busy ordering from room service, shot him a questioning look.

"The gentlemen are still here."

"Do you think we should go back to Sekhmet's chapel and talk to that old man?"

"I don't think he will be very forthcoming..." yawned Simon. "Besides, since we decided he's not affiliated with our friendly blokes downstairs, we might not want to introduce *them* to *him*."

"You mean they don't know he exists? That he got us a taxi?"

"I am sure of it."

"But Bailey has a point, Simon," interjected Craig. "We need more information, right? Why was he so scared? And he did get us a taxi? He wanted something... Maybe he wanted to listen to our conversation. Not that we were talking..." Craig looked at Bailey apologetically, remembering that he passed out yesterday. "But anyway, he knows something. Maybe if we isolate him, he'll tell us."

"*Isolate* him? You sound like a special ops agent in a movie! But it is a sound idea..."

The taxi carrying Bailey and Craig pulled away from the hotel and in the direction of the neighboring temple complex in Luxor. From the lobby café Simon watched the surveillance team follow them. Then he got into the next taxi in front of the hotel and traveled to Karnak. Looking like any other tourist, he snuck out over the dirt hill, Sekhmet's chapel in his sights. Simon was sure that the old man was close by. His eyes scanned the area... The old man was sitting behind the chapel's south wall on a large fallen stone, lost in thought as he petted a feral dog. Simon checked out the surroundings – there was no one there besides himself, the old man, and the she-dog.

Making sure he remained unseen, he approached the man and asked if he spoke English. The man was startled and said that he did, thinking Simon was a tourist looking for a tour of the temple. "I will show you the great temple of the god Amun. But not here, you can't be here, we go over there, where the large obelisks are..." he mumbled as he walked in front of Simon, leading him toward the main temple. The old man had begun to recite the temple's history when Simon quietly extended his hand and pinched his neck. Instantly the man's body relaxed as if he was nodding off, and Simon, supporting him by the elbow, guided him out of the temple. They looked like old friends, or a satisfied tourist thanking an old guide. A promise of dollars had kept a taxi idling at the curb, and Simon quickly stuffed the man into it. As the old man recovered from the pinched nerve he opened his mouth to protest, but the gun Simon pressed to his ribs kept him silent. The driver, unaware of the drama happening in the back seat, wondered why his Egyptian passenger was not chatting with him. There must be some strange business going on between the tourist and the old man, the driver concluded, and decided that perhaps it was better to not pay any attention. The taxi dropped them off right in front of the hotel, behind a tour bus. A large, loud crowd of overweight women and men, most in light blue or pink colored clothes and with cameras on their necks and panamas on their silver-haired heads, were disembarking from the bus. Under cover of this commotion Simon shuffled the old man into the hotel lobby, his eyes sweeping the area for Council men. There were none. The surveillance team was still tracking Bailey and Craig around town, unaware of Simon's existence.

Once in the room he led the old man to the armchair and indicated that he should sit in it. Simon sank into the sofa facing him, pointing the gun his way. "Who are you?"

The old man began to plead in heavily accented English that he was just a poor local interested only in "introducing Egyptian beautiful heritage to the tourists," and what was Simon talking about?

*   *   *

Bailey and Craig entered their room cautiously, remembering Simon's warning that he might "bring a guest." The old man gasped in shock the moment he saw Bailey. She stared back at him, not understanding. Craig gave Simon a questioning look.

"Hello. How was the Luxor Temple? I trust it was at least as magnificent as the Karnak one. My old friend and I are getting acquainted, but it's rather a slow process. We've been chatting for nearly an hour and, oh, he swears that he knows nothing. Somehow I just don't believe that…" Simon's voice was calm, no trace of frustration.

The old man looked unharmed. He sat tensely in the armchair, his hand at his neck.

"Who are you? Do you know me?" exclaimed Bailey, stepping closer to the old man. "Please tell me… we are not going to hurt you…"

"Speak for yourself," mumbled Simon.

"Please talk to me… Do you know me? Why did you get us a taxi yesterday? Please, tell me… we are being followed by some men…"

"You are?" this was the first time the old man had spoken truthfully and in surprisingly good British English. Gone were the strong accent and the timid look. Simon let out a long whistle.

"Yes, some people from Cairo, from the Council of Antiquities, but they are not scholars, they're more like security or militia of some sort… Do you know why they are after us?"

"They probably think you are looking into the death of your father. And mother and sister…"

"My sister is not dead!" Bailey shouted at the old man. "How do you know about my parents? Tell me!"

"I knew him, your father…"

"What?" Suddenly disarmed, Bailey slumped onto the sofa. This man in his simple gray caftan was not an educated man who her father might have associated with in Egypt.

"I am Sahed Ashi. I worked on the project with your father, Jonathan Rixson."

"Sahed? The engineer…?"

"I know that I do not look like one to you. I never really was… But that was the only way to officially maintain contact with Jonathan."

"I don't understand…" Bailey suddenly felt exhausted, and she sank farther into the cushions next to Simon, aware that if she were not sitting she might fall down.

"Could I please see that gold locket on your neck?" The old man's voice was clear.

Bailey took the locket off her neck and allowed Sahed to take it in his trembling hand. Closing his eyes, he began to moan. Bailey again felt a powerful sense of déjà vu. The moment seemed important somehow, even though she did not understand why. Simon stayed alert, making sure that there was no route of escape for the old man. He didn't want him to run off with the locket… or throw himself off the balcony, for that matter…

When the old man opened his eyes, they were filled with tears. He smiled at Bailey as a grandfather would, and gave the locket back to her. "Do you know what this is?" he asked.

"I think it's made of gold, my father gave it to Abby, my sister… It's Egyptian."

"It is not Egyptian, it is Sirian," said the old man calmly.

"From Syria? I don't think so, it looks more Egyptian than Arabic…"

"It is from Sekhmet, the One who loves the Truth and detests the Untruth…"

"Well, you contradicted yourself, Sekhmet is an Egyptian goddess," said Bailey, satisfied that she had caught him in a lie, "… so the locket has to be Egyptian too."

"No, it does not have to be… There is so much you do not know, child… I think I have to tell you, while there is still time…"

"Tell me what?? ... Tell me!" She sat forward on the edge of the sofa and glared at the old man.

Cairo, Egypt

Mahmoud Halib hung up the phone. His last option had also failed. The top computer specialist in Egyptian security had been given the task of finding out who Bailey Rixson was talking to through her computer. The last search of the Americans' hotel room and computer brought no useful information, only basic tourist junk turned up – but Mahmoud knew there had to be more. So he hired the specialist and stationed him in the room next door to the girl to intercept her wi-fi communications. Mahmoud couldn't travel to Luxor himself to follow the girl, but he had hoped that the information the specialist acquired would be enough. It was not.

The news was grimmer than Mahmoud could have imagined. The specialist informed him that the computer that his men had "searched" was not her only laptop. Apparently there was another one, a much more powerful machine.

Mahmoud had to stop pacing and sit down. He had not believed what he was hearing. The other laptop was not "talking" with someone through wi-fi, but via a satellite! It got worse. The signal was bouncing between so many satellites from different countries and locations around the globe, that it was impossible to trace the signal's origin. Plus, the signal itself was solidly encrypted, so solid that even after working on it nonstop for twenty-six hours, the specialist had been unable to touch it. The specialist's last question was "Mr. Halib, would you like me to involve my European and American colleagues in deciphering this encryption? You specified that this endeavor was highly sensitive... If this is connected to terrorism, I have to involve the authorities..."

Mahmoud had not been able to answer. His thoughts were spinning. Satellites? Highly encrypted? Who is this girl? Who is she talking to?

"Mr. Halib...? Are you still there?" the specialist said, interrupting his thoughts.

"Yes, yes, sorry... you have done well. No, definitely not a terrorism issue, no... This woman is one of the art collectors perhaps connected to the black market trafficking our artifacts, we were investigating her connections... There is nothing conclusive then, we must have been mistaken. No need to involve anyone else. We assume you were handsomely compensated for your time and efforts?"

Mahmoud sat at his desk, staring into space. The situation was much worse than he had thought. Oh, sons of the pharaohs, so much worse! This girl, the daughter of Jonathan Rixson, was apparently not as naïve as he thought. She had led him to believe she was unaware of the real situation. But her communicating with someone through a complex set of satellites and her use of rare encryptions... She was aware of the well. She had to be. This was *very* bad.

At this point he had to contact the Shenu. The council of thirteen had to convene and Bailey Rixson was to be its main agenda. He could no longer hide the situation in hopes of a swift resolution.

He reached for the phone and made a call to a no-name village, the kind where the only phone was at the main militia office. Mahmoud's voice was tired: "I am inquiring about Assanwy Bahgrat, I was told her health is worsening."

"Did you say 'worsening' sir?" replied the uncaring voice at the other end of the line.

"Yes, I was told she has not been feeling well since Tuesday." Mahmoud hung up the phone. The code had been activated. Within twenty-four hours all thirteen of them would do everything they could to meet in Cairo, or call if they were not able to come. It had begun.

Mahmoud felt fear and shame. Fear of the gods. And shame that he had been the one, just like his father Sharif, to convene the Shenu again. And it was he, like Sharif, who was bringing bad news, the same news actually... almost about the same person! The daughter of that man, anyway. Mahmoud's chest felt crushed, and he struggled to breathe.

He sat like that for almost an hour, immobile. But he had to go home. His secretary's soft face, wrapped in a white shawl, looked at him through the door's glass panels, questioning. She had looked twice already...

"It must be late, the office building is closing." Of course no one would dare to ask him to leave, and security would keep the building open for him as long as he had to be in his office. But this was not the right way. It attracted far too much attention he did not need right now.

He took a deep breath and stood up.

Climbing into his black Mercedes, he mentally went through the things he had to take care of. His was the last car left in the video-monitored lot. He knew he had to tell his wife to stay in Europe. She might not even protest, since she was happy visiting the children. He had to have an empty house, it was absolutely necessary. He also might have to take leave from his job. Nothing official of course, perhaps he would invent some special business or expedition requiring urgent travel...

At his house, Mahmoud sat in the study for a few minutes holding a bottle of scotch. He opened it and poured himself a glass. Leaning back in the soft brown leather chair, he took a large sip. It was going to be a very long night.

How would he present this mess to the others? Would they blame him? Despite his accomplishments Mahmoud always secretly felt inadequate. His father had not had the wealth to give him the kind of education he had had and the position he had in life... It was all given to him by the Shenu. Faruq Bashir had told him that the wealth of the Shenu was available to all members, and it was up to them to use it as needed. His father Sharif *chose* not to use it. It was agreed that he could better serve in the position he was in. Sharif was an educated man, but that was not obvious to an external observer.

Mahmoud thought of the promise made to the gods. Again he felt fear; it ran like electricity through his nerves, making him jump. Outwardly Mahmoud was a liberal Muslim. He talked about the gods of Egypt all the time but that was seen as natural, he was a historian and an archeologist. No one expected him to actually believe in the ancient gods. Educated people would see such belief as ignorant.

Mahmoud believed. He knew the gods of ancient Egypt were real. At least, some of them were. He had "met" one of them, Sekhmet, and he still felt a chill down his spine every time he thought of her name. If he had had any doubts about the things Faruq Bashir told him, that meeting erased them all. By then he was no longer a young nobody but a well-educated and respected man, a scholar and a professional. He had to have been smart to get this far, right? He was told about the Shenu and the importance of their mission to protect the gods. He understood that his father Sharif fully believed in that mission. He knew what was required of him as one of the Shenu: it ranged from protecting the written records of the gods and the Shenu to influencing political decisions to prevent excavations in particular areas of Egypt. The ancient records had been shown to Mahmoud and he knew the power of history when he saw it. But even then, there had been a part of him that did not believe the gods were really *gods*. He didn't dispute the reality of the history in front of him – the documents were obviously ancient, so they had value. But the gods... he just did not know.

Now, sitting in his study, another glass of scotch in his hand, he remembered how incredible it had been to see a first-hand record of the generational lines of the Shenu and corresponding pharaohs, and the connection to particular gods, including records of the gods and their actions. He remembered how he had thought it would be priceless information for historians, because many of the records did not correlate with what he knew from his education. There were no records of the gods themselves that were in Egyptian writing. What was known about the gods and their actions was based on Greek copies of the original texts which were made thousands of years later. There were clear distortions in the copies, but these, these were actual true records of the gods! After he had studied those records, he was shown more. In his normal scholarly life he would have dismissed these as nonsense, but... there they were, ancient and obviously not forgeries.

The list of Egyptian pharaohs began in approximately 3,100BC with the Scorpion King, then there was king Narmer who united Upper and Lower Egypt. The only pharaohs before that were minor kings of the Lower or Upper kingdoms, often rivals of each other. This is what he had spent his life studying. But the records in his hands contained information about the gods written as though the gods were people, and they showed a very different truth. The "reign of the gods" listing Ptah, Ra, and Thoth was copied by the Greek philosopher Monetto from ancient Egyptian texts that had burned in Alexandria. No one had ever taken these lists seriously. They were seen only as a magnificent piece of Egyptian folklore, metaphorical stories. No self-respecting Egyptologist would ever confess to thinking the gods in those lists were real beings...

The period of the reign of the gods went well back in time, beyond anything historically acceptable to Mahmoud. Thoth reigned for seven hundred years starting from 8,000BC; before him Horus reigned, before Horus, Seth, before Seth was Osiris, Geb, Shu; before them Ra had reigned for one thousand years, and before that Ptah reigned for eons... But there was more. There were other names, unknown to Mahmoud, and all of them extended well beyond the "era of Ptah" which started at 9,800BC, well before the time of the biblical Flood, before the last ice age ended in 10,800BC; as far back as 30,000BC, with references to the period even before that! It was impossible, insane! The scholar in him had panicked... If there had been no civilization in Egypt before the pharaohs of 3,100BC, why would they have invented events so far back in time? These measures of time could not even have been comprehensible to ancient people!

There were records of detailed human anatomy and what looked like the transcripts of complicated surgeries, regeneration techniques, and healing medicines. Records of internal alchemical transformation – using detailed energy anatomy adjustments and something called "shem-anna" the white powder made into a conical bread which was gold and bread, and powder all at the same time, and the exact changes in the brain all of this awakened. Mahmoud was in awe: there were astronomical records going back not even thousands of years, but hundreds of thousands! There were detailed diagrams of the solar system, and other stars and their systems, unknown vegetation and animals...

Oh, how naïve Mahmoud had been. He remembered how he felt... All this secret information collected and protected by the Shenu looked like priceless history to him. He was unsure why it had to be hidden. He would never let the other Shenu notice it, but he was not convinced they were correct. This was definitely highly controversial information, but it would only benefit the world to expose it. After all, it was only history, no great secret... How incredible to have such an ancient, well-preserved record of civilization and its knowledge – it made his country the most ancient culture on the planet, or at least it set an amazing example of preservation of material evidence. It could be cross referenced with other texts and copies of the god lists, new timelines would have to be officially stated in Egyptology... People would know that they had not become civilized a few thousand years ago, but tens of thousands of years back! It would be incredible to expose the records!

He never expressed any of his opinions to Faruq Bashir of course, but the old man must have sensed Mahmoud's attitude because before he died, he arranged for Mahmoud to go into the well.

And there he had met Sekhmet. Nothing was the same after that. The gods on the papyrus, in paintings, in stone; he suddenly saw them in a very different light. Oh yes, Mahmoud believed. After that encounter with Sekhmet he met with Faruq Bashir for one last time, and the old man told him: "Now you know the truth. Protect it!"

He took another large sip of scotch – another non-Muslim action, which he never did in public. But here, at his house, facing the largest crisis of his life, Mahmoud had no problem with his drink. The glass was empty but he felt nothing, adrenalin was quickly burning up the alcohol. His heart was pounding...

It had begun. Again...

CHAPTER SIX

Martin Shwabster sat at his desk, his palms sweating. In all the excitement he had forgotten to take his medicine, and now he was feeling a mixture of exhilaration and terror. He had to stop what he was doing and take the pills. Oh, and eat, it had been almost nine hours since he last ate. He made himself stop. Rolling his wheelchair to the kitchen, his mind raced with thoughts of the research he was doing. He had just spent nine hours looking for information about Jonathan Rixson. What he found was strange and alarming. It was nighttime in Egypt so he would wait to tell Bailey, and he might as well eat something and maybe sleep. Sleep? Who was he kidding? That would never happen, he was way too wired up. Unless he took some sleeping pills... Maybe...

He rolled his wheelchair into the kitchen. It was gloomy and somewhat messy there. From the décor no one would ever have been able to tell that Marty was a multimillionaire. For the last ten years he had a person come to cook every day, and clean his whole house once a week. Her name was Larisa. She was a fifty-four year old Ukrainian woman who refused to be labeled a maid. She spoke heavily-accented English, was a great cook, and she cleaned and ran errands for him. Marty paid her well. His only requirement was that he be her only client. That way he could trust her to be available when he needed her. He hated people coming into his space and Larisa was the only one that he allowed in, but only after he had scanned her with the detector installed in his doorway. This machine was more elaborate than the metal detectors at airports – in addition to metal it also swept for listening devices. Larisa was always "clean" and after ten years he could probably forego the ritual, but they had both grown to like it. Marty was lucky that Larisa had a good sense of humor. But now it had already been four days since Larisa last came. He had told her to take this week off because he was too busy to have anyone around. She was surprised, then suspicious – he had never given her a paid vacation. "Where will I go? I don't need vacation, Marty, I only know you here and I will come, take care of you, OK?" But he didn't want to be interrupted, even for food, while he was working on the project – the project being helping Bailey with research that only he could do. He eventually convinced Larisa not to come, and gave her a handsome check, which she tore up in front of him, and then walked out of the house. Martin did not understand her actions. She looked near tears as if he had offended her. How? He was too busy thinking about the project though... But this left Marty with a messy kitchen and an almost empty fridge. He didn't do his own shopping, that was also Larisa's job. He made himself a sandwich with bologna and Swiss cheese. It was dry and a little stale, but it would have to do.

So, Jonathan Rixson apparently didn't take on any major jobs after his trip to Egypt. The house he was doing all that research for, the one he brought in an Egyptian engineer for, was never built. This was puzzling, because the man who financed the construction "changed his mind" – he didn't run out of money or anything of the sort, but after spending a fortune on designs and sending his architect to Egypt he had just decided to not build. Furthermore, Jonathan had taken *another* project involving Egyptian architecture and that was why he had gone to Egypt a second time. An old lady in Baltimore, Jonathan's secretary at the time, told Martin on the phone that Mary, Jonathan's wife, suspected he was having an affair because of his long nights at the office. When Marty asked about the project that Jonathan was so busy working on, the lady only said that it was with no firm she saw a contract for. Her answer to the question of infidelity was much more definite: "Jonathan? No, he would never cheat on his Mary. She had just spent too many lonely nights at home thinking. No way was he having an affair! He adored her and the girls! He only took them to Egypt because of Mary's insistence, you know? She put her foot down on his travel, saying that either she went with him or he didn't go, and if he dared to go without her, she would divorce him. Can you believe that? He couldn't bear to lose his girls and he probably couldn't convince her that her suspicions were unfounded. Oh, it was all so unfortunate. If she had not insisted, Mr. Rixson might still be alive, all that tourist business they had gotten into might not have even happened if he had been alone! And Mary would be alive now too, of course, if she hadn't gone. If you ask me, she didn't deserve him..." – Marty had not asked, and did not care to hear the rest, that was more than enough!

Sleep eluded him, and the sleeping pill only made him feel groggy. In his dozy state Martin imagined Jonathan Rixson talking to his wife Mary, fighting with her about his trip to Egypt. His second trip...

"If you have nothing to hide, then you won't mind your family traveling with you!" yelled Mary.

"I don't think it is such a good idea, darling."

"Either we come with you, Jonathan Rixson, or we are through! I'm sick of your lies!"

"Don't say that, I don't know what you have invented in your head, but there is nothing, nothing going on! You've got to believe me! Besides it'll only be for a month, there won't even be time for you girls to get settled..."

"It's summer, they aren't in school anyway, and this is a perfect time for all of us to see where you work... if Egypt is really where you're planning on going!"

Martin bolted upright from his pillow. He had been dreaming about Jonathan's conversation with Mary when he realized something. Now that he was awake again, he could not remember, but something had startled him out of his semi-sleep. Ohhhhh, his head hurt... He shouldn't have missed his medication, or taken two pills at once, or taken the sleeping pills... Shit! What was it?

He pulled himself into the wheelchair. In the kitchen he got some water, drank it fast, put the glass back on the counter and rolled into the bathroom. While slowly urinating, seated on the toilet, he debated taking a painkiller. No, he probably shouldn't add even more meds to the mix...

He was about to get himself up when he remembered it – what woke him up was something he had missed in the conversation with the secretary. She had told him that Jonathan Rixson was "doing some job that involved Egypt"... That was why Marty just dreamed of Jonathan telling his wife that it would only be a month, and that there wouldn't be time for them to get settled. That was what the secretary had mentioned. The second trip to Egypt that Jonathan Rixson took with his family was not holiday travel, but a business venture! Bailey had *never* mentioned that... She must not know. She was told that her parents died in an accident. What accident? The assumption had always been that they were tourists, and were killed in a robbery attempt, something of the sort. But if they were not tourists... Why did Jonathan Rixson go to Egypt? What was the "job" he could not refuse, even after being threatened with divorce, so that he elected to appease his wife by taking his family with him, instead of staying home?

These questions had no answers, at least, not yet. Marty looked at his watch. It was only 8:30pm; Jonathan's old secretary was probably still awake. "I am sorry to bother you again, but I realized there was something else you might be able to help me with. Do you know, by any chance, how long Jonathan was supposed to be in Egypt that second time?"

"Five weeks. I remember clearly. I was to hold all his mail and calls, and he promised me a vacation once he returned. I was going to see my sister, it would have been right around her birthday when Mr. Rixson returned... Such a tragedy..."

109

"One more question: do you maybe know where Jonathan was staying in Cairo? If he was there on business, he must have organized where he was going to stay, especially with his family?'

"Oh, I don't know that. I think his Egyptian colleague arranged that for him…"

"Do you happen to remember who that was?" Marty held his breath.

"No, not the name… It was that same engineer that came here before, to work with Mr. Rixson on the previous Egyptian project."

Thanking the old lady, Marty hung up the phone. A very different picture of Jonathan Rixson was emerging. He had worked on the Egyptian-style property design, was sent to Egypt to view the "original architecture," and there he had met with Sahed Ashi, the engineer. Then this Sahed had come into the US for five months, and even though he had been set up at a hotel, had spent most of his time at the Rixsons. When Sahed left, Jonathan began working a lot more, much of the time late at night, on some unknown project that was also connected to Egypt. It was not a continuation of the Egyptian design project, because the client had changed his mind and the house was never built. Mary, Jonathan's wife, suspected he had a mistress because he was showing signs of having a mistress: he was withdrawn, secretive, and spent long nights at the office. But if the secretary was to be believed, there was no mistress. What the hell was Rixson doing?

Whatever it was, he had to travel to Egypt again and meet with Sahed. But Mary didn't trust him and tagged along with Abby. If Bailey had not gotten chickenpox at that moment, she would have gone too. So Jonathan probably told Sahed that he was now bringing his whole family, and had to have a place for them to stay for five weeks. Had he been planning to stay with Sahed before his family decided to come along? Why would he do that? This had to be connected to the new design project he was working on… whatever that was!

"All this new information and we still don't know anything about how Jonathan and Mary Rixson were killed. Or how Abby survived whoever it was that killed them," thought Marty. If Sahed had booked the Rixsons into a hotel, he would have to have known that they were killed. When Abby was flown back to US along with the bodies of her parents, Sahed had to have been contacted by the US Council in Cairo – yet there was no record of that. Sahed was a major mystery, because no agency in Egypt had any record of him, not even of his birth. There was a US record of someone called Sahed Ashi traveling from Cairo into the States, and five months later traveling back to Cairo. Sahed

Ashi was also on two official pieces of paperwork in Jonathan's firm – he was "the Egyptian engineer." But there was no record of this Sahed having ever traveling outside of Egypt before this trip to work with Jonathan. That meant he had to have gotten his engineering degree in Egypt. Yet there were no records of him graduating from any Egyptian university. So was he an engineer, or not? Mr. Sahed Ashi seemed to have never existed in the periods before and after his trip to the States.

Cairo, Egypt

It was already almost six in morning, and bright sunshine warred with the heavy burgundy curtains on his windows. Mahmoud Halib had spent the whole night in the chair in his study, sleeping on and off. The members of the Shenu would be gathering in just a few hours. Mahmoud got up and went to his bedroom to undress. He would take a shower and prepare his thoughts.

The Shenu did not come together often; he almost never had the opportunity to be in the same room with the others. Having all of them together was very dangerous, reserved only for the direst of circumstances. And yet it was already the second time in his lifetime that it was happening!

Mahmoud took a last look at himself in the full length mirror. He liked what he saw, even though he did not feel himself to be the man he was looking at. The man in the reflection looked confident and established, a merchant proud of his business, while Mahmoud the Egyptologist felt lost, scared, and ashamed.

Transformation complete, he got into his security guard's beat up truck, leaving his own shiny Mercedes in the garage. He had to keep reminding himself that this was not his fault. This meeting had to be convened, and he had not made a mistake in requesting it. The situation was such that to ignore it was potentially deadly.

Early morning traffic was already filling the roads to Cairo; people were hurrying to markets and their jobs in the city. But Mahmoud would not be affected by that traffic – his dirty truck was heading away from Cairo.

His thoughts returned to Sekhmet. He always sensed she disapproved of them, the Shenu, as if she thought they were not doing a good job. Or maybe it was he who had failed her somehow. The Shenu, the protectors of the gods... They had two vaults in Egypt, both very deep underground, both created eons ago and not by men. The vaults held many material artifacts, most of them of the sort that Egyptologists had never even dreamed existed. Feelings of fear and shame didn't prevent Mahmoud from comprehending three things: first, he was fortunate to know the truth and serve the living gods by being chosen to be one of the Shenu; second, he was grateful beyond measure that he was allowed to see many of the artifacts in the vaults; and third, he had been very lucky to be given the unique chance to actually "meet" Sekhmet.

Mahmoud wished he could spend years, his entire life, studying the artifacts in the vaults. At the same time he feared that opportunity, unsure about how much he was willing to really know. Knowing what he was told seemed to be already more than enough, even though the scientist inside him fought to find out more details. Mahmoud knew that most of the Shenu were never allowed into the vaults at all, they were only told about them. The few who were allowed were never able to spend any time studying and researching the artifacts. Being an Egyptologist by profession, Mahmoud was in a unique position. He was not only allowed to look at the records in the vaults, but to do so again and again, to study the material. He had had to swear to not take anything out: no small notes on paper, no photographs. But the scholar in him had to do something. At home Mahmoud had a highly encrypted file on his computer filled with information he had gathered and cross referenced. He wasn't sure why he had made that file in the first place and where his research was going, because he was already convinced that the material was true. What was the reason for research at that point? He knew he couldn't publish it, but he couldn't help himself, and so the encrypted file got bigger and bigger. He was a man possessed, in the worst possible position – to know an incredible secret beyond any doubt, yet have absolutely no one to share it with!

The drive was almost peaceful. No one on the road was headed in his direction. Mahmoud tried to allow his mind to relax, and he reflected on his meeting with Sekhmet. Were it not for Faruq Bashir, he would have never met her. Of the current Shenu, Mahmoud was the only one besides Faruq Bashir who had met Sekhmet, and Faruq was now dead. It was said that until Faruq Bashir, she had not shown herself for fourteen generations. Sharif, Mahmoud's father, was there with Faruq when it happened, but he fell unconscious. By the time Faruq thought Mahmoud was ready to go into the well he was already very old and near death. He wanted to take Mahmoud to the well himself, to this place where he had encountered Sekhmet, but he could not. Mahmoud was instead accompanied by two other Shenu. No one expected Sekhmet to show herself, but she did. The other two Shenu fell unconscious, as

Mahmoud's father had, but Mahmoud stayed awake. It was the most terrifying experience of his life.

Mahmoud pulled off the highway onto a small road then turned onto another road. The roads led away from the Nile, into the desert. Soon he came to the ruins of an old marketplace. The village it had once served had water at one time, but no more. And so it had been abandoned: no water, no people. There were still roads leading to this place, but they were not on any map.

Mahmoud thought about the Shenu, realizing that Sekhmet scared him much more than the circle of twelve men. This whole mess had started when an American, Jonathan Rixson, somehow found out about the sacred well... Mahmoud was told that before the ancient planetary Flood, which he figured was a reference to the end of the last ice age in 10,800BC, there was no need for the Shenu, but after the Flood there was. And so it began. There were men and women in the Shenu, with the top position always being reserved for a female. That was how Sekhmet wanted it. But women had betrayed the Shenu by showing a piece of Sirian technology, the locket of Sekhmet herself, to one of the pharaohs – the heretic Akhenaten of the eighteenth dynasty! After that Sekhmet took back the locket, making the well lifeless. The Shenu regrouped, and the top position became male. Over the years fewer and fewer women were allowed in, until there were none at all. Mahmoud felt this was right, because no woman could handle this amount of knowledge and responsibility. Women were not weak, but they were soft. Men were guided by passion and reason, but in this situation, a man could learn to curb his passion for loyalty to the oath.

Mahmoud pulled up and parked next to the six cars that were already in the dusty marketplace. The cars were all occupied, with engines kept idling to run the air conditioners. It was already hot despite the early hour; this was the desert after all. He sat in his car and prepared to wait for the others.

St. George Hotel, Luxor

Bailey and Craig sat on the sofa in their plush hotel room. Across from them, on a chair, was sitting a tired old man who called himself Sahed. Small beads of sweat were apparent on his face despite the AC. Simon stood by the window, his gun shoved into his pants at the small of his back. No one moved as Bailey repeated with urgency and conviction: "Tell me now!"

Sahed began his tale.

He was a part of an organization called the Shenu, the True Shenu... A very long time ago, before the ancient Flood, there were living gods in Egypt. They were from the star Sirius, and one of them was Sekhmet, the Lover of Truth, the Detester of Untruth. The star gods left Egypt before the Flood, and only Sekhmet remained. She initiated a small group of Egyptians who were to become the priests and priestesses of the Shenu, the protectors of the secrets.

The Shenu were always thirteen, with a woman, the High Priestess of Sekhmet, as the head of the circle of twelve. When someone was about to die, they gave their place in the Shenu to one whom they trusted, an inheritor. That person could be a family member, a close friend, or even a trustworthy stranger. People were tested in many ways before the rest of the Shenu deemed them acceptable. Then they were told the secret of the Shenu's existence.

"You're talking about these 'gods' as if they were people! I get it, they are part of your cultural heritage, and it is all a very nice *story*, but what does it have to do with me?!" This was madness. Some secret "order" called Shenu, and "gods"? Bailey fought back tears.

Sahed took a long tired breath: "Dear child, truth is always bigger than any history. You were a part of this story, from the beginning. Your father, Jonathan, was supposed to... do something... that might be yours to do now."

"What are you talking about? Weren't you and my father involved in an architectural project together? You came to see us in the States, I kind of remember you... I think..."

"Oh, you and your sister were very little then... both so sweet and smart... I thought then that if your father failed, either one of you might be the next one in line."

"In line for what?!" Bailey exhaled, outraged. She felt bolts of electricity shooting uncontrollably through her spine and she couldn't sit still; she desperately tried to calm herself. It was maddening; this man was telling her a completely irrelevant story about some Shenu group and "star gods"... And he was probably the only person alive who knew how her father and mother had died! She drew in a breath and asked bravely: "Tell me how my father died."

"That is a complicated issue... You need to understand more."

"Right, well, you'd better get on with it then, hadn't you?" said Simon, his voice unexpectedly coming from behind Bailey.

"After the Flood, there were other gods; these gods came into Egypt and took the names of the star gods. They were not from the Sirius star..." Sahed took a breath. "Can I have some water? – I don't know where they were from, I only know they were not the beloved star-gods of the Shenu." Craig gave him a bottle of water from the mini-bar.

"...There were two groups of gods," Sahed continued. "Some were real gods; they didn't want to be worshipped and they were loved. The others were imposters who wanted to be worshipped, and they were feared."

The AC in the room suddenly felt freezing. Bailey shivered. This Sahed knew something very important. She didn't know why it was important; she desperately wanted this strange Shenu, the "gods" and this Sekhmet to not be important at all. She didn't want this stuff in her life. She felt as though her mind was slipping from her control. It felt like when she was a child, seeing the tall beings and hearing them talk, and then getting so scared when her twin sister went insane from hearing voices! Maybe it wasn't major stress that had caused Abby to lose her mind, maybe this was some genetic weakness, something that she, Bailey, actually shared... and this was the beginning of it...

Bailey's thoughts were interrupted by loud sounds and a commotion – Craig laid on the floor with Sahed holding his head and Simon pulling on his arm to sit him up. "What happened?" said Bailey.

"He is sick, yes?" Sahed looked into Bailey's eyes, his eyebrows raised.

"He just collapsed. Bailey, give me a hand," Simon's concern barely covered up his frustration. They raised Craig back up onto the sofa, and Bailey checked his eyes and pulse.

"What is it with him?" Simon tensely whispered to Bailey. If Craig kept fainting there was no controlling this situation!

Craig finally came to.

"I saw something... I don't know, I got so cold and then it happened again..." Craig's voice was a barely audible whisper, his wide eyes were also looking at Bailey.

"Did you see Sekhmet?" Sahed quietly asked him.

"Listen, old man, stay out of this," snapped Simon.

"I did, I think... I felt someone, it got so cold... What you said about those people... gods... I don't know, sounded true somehow, and it scared me like hell!"

Bailey gave Craig a bottle of water. She also had that feeling, strongly, and it terrified her too. Were they all beginning to imagine things now? Was this contagious? Some shared psychosis?

"It is all true. The temples you see in Egypt were made for the worship of the imposter gods, they were houses for these gods. But most temples had statues and symbols, made by priests who knew the truth, replicas of the true star gods. The truth was preserved; the true statues and symbols were worshipped as if they were images of the imposters, that way they were kept hidden. People squandered their power, spent it on the imposter gods. The True Shenu kept the secret… For many generations, the false line continued. The people from the Council of Antiquities are part of that line. And I am part of another Shenu line, as was your father, child," said Sahed, exhaling.

"My father…?" Bailey felt the floor tilting under her feet. "My father was part of this Shenu?"

"Yes, he was."

"But if those blokes downstairs are the Shenu, why are they after Bailey? Shouldn't that mean that they are the 'good guys'?" interjected Simon.

"They are not the Shenu, although probably hired by them. They are after her because they think she knows about the well, I hope…"

"You *hope?*

"I hope they are not after her because of what she *has*," said Sahed quietly.

"The locket…" whispered Craig from the sofa.

"The Shenu hold, in their secret vaults throughout Egypt, many artifacts and relics of both true and imposter gods. Of course the gods are not called the 'imposters' by the Shenu. They are all seen as real gods by them, the beloved star-gods and the others… One of the most precious relics was the locket of Sekhmet. Sekhmet wore the locket before the Great Flood, when the ice melted, and after… She *gave* it to the High Priestess of the Shenu, as a means of reaching her if necessary. The locket is the key to the well, to the portal in time and space…"

"Hold on, 'gave' as in *personally handed* it to some priestess? And she *wore* it *before* the Flood? I am new to Egyptology here, but all your literature says that Egypt began in something like 3,100BC with the pharaoh Narmer. Was this way after the biblical Flood? Are you talking about some other 'flood' we are all supposed to know about?" Bailey was attempting to cover up her trembling by sarcasm, but she failed – she *felt* something and she knew that what this strange old man, this man who had known her father, was saying, was true…

"The Egypt you were told about is an echo of the True Egypt. The star-gods walked freely among us here, in this land. They were not worshipped, feared, or asked for favors. The star-gods were *people*, but from the stars. They were here before the Great Flood. The Flood in your Christian Bible is not really that old. That story is a copy from the records of the Hebrews, who themselves did not write it… they copied it from the records of ancient Sumer. I believe that flood to have occurred less than a thousand years before the official beginning of the Egyptian civilization, when the Mesopotamian Valley, today's Iraq and the home of ancient Sumer, was flooded and Sumer was destroyed. But there were other floods before that one... The Great Flood came in 10,800BC, when all of Earth's ice melted. There were many small floods after that, and some of them are in recorded history, but the story itself always goes back to the Great Flood, the one from ice... The Nile Valley was flooded and most people died. The few who survived lost everything, and couldn't rebuild without the help of the other gods, the imposters who came from somewhere else. Those were not the star gods, but people needed some guidance, they were scared. The new gods comforted the people, teaching them how to rebuild, and taking the names and attributes of the star-gods. You see, these new gods wanted to be as powerful as the star-gods, but they were not. They fought among themselves, which the star gods never did. The new gods took over Egypt as a battlefield, even though some, like Ptah, were very honorable and wise... These new gods did not see themselves as powerful enough, they were always competing for more power, each one wanted to be superior. So they pretended to be the star-gods in front of the people, and demanded worship. They wanted to be praised and feared and they were willing to control to get the status of gods. People were lost and weak, they fell for it. After the devastation of their entire civilization and the departure of their beloved star-gods, people were lost and they wanted to *believe*, you see? They needed to believe that they were not alone, not lost, not abandoned by the loving star-gods... And the imposter-gods became seen as The Gods."

"Wait a minute. Before the Flood? There was a civilization and some star-people here, in Egypt, before *another* flood, the Great Flood that came from an ice melt?" repeated Bailey, mesmerized. She felt dizzy. Was he talking about ice in Egypt? Or the ice age maybe?

"Yes. Many thousands of people, living peacefully, the true Egyptian civilization along the Nile. The Nile was more of a lake than a river back then and the delta was much wider... The star-gods and the people lived harmoniously. The star-gods taught them skills, sciences, and arts. But they never imposed their knowledge; they were fascinated with people, their ability to feel, to create, to learn. They didn't want to make people into something else, give them rules or laws... Instead they just taught them what they knew, what people were interested in, and people agreed with their words, choosing to be peaceful. There was harmony in Egypt. I know this as the Shenu, we were taught this truth…"

"Old man, I ask you again – why is it, then, that these Shenu blokes are after Bailey? She doesn't have any artifacts except for the locket on her neck. Is that what they want?" Simon's voice was solid, he seemed to be completely unaffected by the emotional wave that Bailey and Craig were experiencing.

"I pray to Sekhmet that the Shenu do not know she has it! They are powerful and they will stop at nothing!" Sahed explained quietly.

"You keep saying 'the Shenu' as if they are someone else, while just before that you said you were part of that… organization," said Craig, who after drinking an entire bottle of water could think clearly again. "That doesn't add up."

"The Shenu had lost their way. The imposter-gods were in Egypt, the people were worshipping them. But at some point the imposter-gods withdrew, went into hidden abodes in Egypt and other lands…"

"The pharaohs were the imposter-gods then?" Bailey was confused.

"No. The pharaohs were not the imposter-gods, although originally many were appointed by the new gods, and in contact with them. Actually the queens had the power… The pharaohs started to believe they were 'gods' only after the new gods left Egypt. Before that they were just people, privileged and genetically enhanced, but manipulated by the new gods. They had powers, but as a consequence of their genetics and "external technology", as Sekhmet would have said, the shem-anna. They were not able to be awake like the true Shenu. After the imposter-gods left Egypt, the pharaohs became increasingly selfish in their belief that they were gods too and had to be worshipped. Without true gods or imposters, the pharaoh's lines gained more and more power over people, who worshipped them as if they were real gods. The Shenu became political, favoring one pharaoh's dynasty over another, manipulating who was going to be raised to power and who would be crushed. The secret of the Shenu's existence was a legend known to all pharaohs and most had searched for the Shenu, but it was meant to stay hidden. The Shenu had broken their oath – they began revealing themselves, one member or two, to the pharaohs they favored. This was reasoned away by their withholding real knowledge. They thought: 'What was the harm in some political strategizing, if no real secret information was revealed?' This thinking was shameful! The Shenu thought they were in control, scheming and manipulating their way into false power, as if they were above Sekhmet herself! It continued until three of the Shenu decided to change all that. They saw what the others did not. They understood that revealing the Shenu knowledge for political favors would set humankind far back in its development, for people were not awake enough to comprehend the information, not ready for the technologies of the gods. The pharaohs were only going to become more and more hungry for the Shenu's secrets, since they had started thinking they were gods and wanted to acquire the power of the gods... and one day the Shenu would make a mistake, be followed, or tortured, or something else, and then outsiders would have access to the Shenu's knowledge – and they would squander it in foolish human power games! The three Shenu initiated the True Shenu then. They revealed their existence to pharaoh Akhenaten, and they gave the locket of Sekhmet to him."

"The famous Akhenaten? We saw his statue in the Cairo Museum... He must have looked very strange... You mean this whole thing you are talking about is actually real? This very locket, this actual thing," – Bailey held the locket out with her hand – "was given by the Shenu to Akhenaten??"

"Yes. And he used it well. The Shenu were furious. The locket is the key to the well, and without it their power was significantly diminished. And to these Shenu the power of the human world was everything."

"There you go again, *these* Shenu, *those* Shenu, *True* Shenu... You *are* the Shenu, the Council of Antiquities is part of the Shenu! If it was *given* to Akhenaten, how did my father get the locket?" Bailey screamed, finally losing her patience.

"I gave it to him."

Desert, outside of Cairo

Mahmoud Halib came out of the truck and silently walked into an abandoned building. As he proceeded down the squeaky, dusty steps, to the basement, he felt himself perspire. He exited into a large underground room, it was cool down there, almost cold in comparison with the heat on the surface. "Sons of the pharaohs," swore Mahmoud. "Why am I sweating?!"

Two vents reached down from the surface to the underground chamber, and through them came light. Furniture was scarce: three old dusty chairs, a table with crooked legs, and a few boxes lying around. There was nothing dignified about this room, this arrangement, for a special meeting of the highest of the highest and the most influential of the influential. But no one cared. This was the way of things. In regular life they played their prominent roles, but here they were all equal members bound by an ancient oath. Seven of the thirteen Shenu had been able to make it; Mahmoud was the eighth. Eight was enough to vote on a course of action.

Mahmoud was not the high priest of the Shenu, not even close. He was the eleventh one down. But because he had called them together, it was he who was expected to speak. As everyone settled onto a chair or box, Mahmoud took a deep breath. Seven pairs of eyes looked at him expectantly, and he felt like they were examining him. He squeezed his fists inside his pockets, exhaled and began to speak.

He told them everything: about the girl, Bailey, the daughter of the man they had had to deal with thirty-one years before, and her quest; how even though she looked like a typical shameless American tourist (she had even brought a boyfriend half her age!), she was not; about the communication through satellites and the highly encrypted messages that even his top specialists could not break; about her frantic visits to agencies, the Cairo Museum, and even the Cairo police; about her travel from Cairo to Luxor. Mahmoud concluded in this way: "She is following some hidden path – we must find out what it is so we can be a few steps ahead of her, or she might become even more of a problem than her father was…"

"I doubt some American woman will ever be more of a problem than a man…" mused a heavyset man with a large round belly, his voice was filled with confidence, his forehead bruised from bowing to Allah. "Jonathan Rixson was a serious issue, but it was handled." The High Priest knew exactly *how* it had been handled.

Everything was on the proverbial table, all words were eventually spoken. They acted as masters of life and death, they were the Shenu after all. Not having the supernatural special powers of the gods did not mean they did not have "special powers" of their own. Each member was confident that taking a life in the course of protecting the secret of the Shenu was justified; more than that, it was noble. Erasing Bailey Rixson might not be as complicated as it seemed, some well-placed forgeries and rumors would do it – even the Americans, with all their technology, would find only evidence of an unfortunate accident. But for now, they decided to spare Bailey's life. They wanted to know what she knew, and to whom she might have told it to.

It was early afternoon when the first of them emerged from the dusty basement, and it was hot. The first man walked to his car and started the engine. The others followed at a distance, as before. Mahmoud was the last to leave. He sat for a long moment, staring at the dust raised into the heated air by the departing vehicles' tires. He heard no sounds, as if he had abruptly fallen deaf.

"What have I done?" He knew that this meeting had ushered them all into a new era, and he was no longer sure that things would end well for them.

St. George Hotel, Luxor

His head felt better, clearer. But the feeling of déjà vu had returned. Craig had never felt it so intensely and so often in his entire life! He carefully looked around his mind for his spirit guide, but the Cat was nowhere to be found. Oh, well, he would have to ask him about this déjà vu later. Afraid to miss anything, he listened closely to Sahed's story. As strange as it was, it made sense. Much of the information Craig had found about Egypt seemed to point in the direction of exactly what Sahed was talking about. It was, most of it, either pure speculation or new-age stuff, but this was real. Sahed was not a new-age type man, and he wasn't trying to confuse them – he was telling what he believed was the truth. Sahed's last statement had been said with the calm confidence of one who was stating the obvious, yet it felt like a lightning bolt to Bailey. Craig could see how it affected her from the blank look on her face.

"Dad got this thing from you?" she whispered to herself, staring at the locket, struggling to make sense of things. "And you seem to believe you're part of some secret organization... This gold locket was in the hands of the pharaoh Akhenaten? Are you sure...?"

"There is so much to explain... I understand that this is probably very hard for you to believe. Most of the history you know is not true. It was set in motion by people interested only in control and social influence. It is this way everywhere, I imagine, but I *know* it is this way in Egypt. The True Shenu is the line I come from, not the other Shenu who betrayed truth for political power. They call us the 'traitors' and they are the ones after you."

"Do you know why? You said it's because of something they think she knows." Craig turned to face Bailey. "Bailey doesn't know anything about things like that..." Bailey was smart, but she definitely didn't know anything about secret organizations, star-gods or magical lockets!

Over on the kitchen counter, Bailey's computer beeped. Everyone was startled. Craig raced to the laptop and opened it. Marty's concerned, tired face was in a small screen in the corner.

Bailey stared at it, a bit shocked, and mumbled, "Oh, my god, Marty, you look like you haven't slept in years! Does the medication still work? I can ask your doctor to increase the dosage if you need to…"

Martin looked uncomfortable with Bailey's announcement about his sleeping issues. All he needed was for this Simon character to conclude that he is crazy, and he would be excluded. And Marty did not want to be excluded. For the first time in a very long while he felt purpose, and he was needed not as a programming brain but in a real, human, tangible sort of way. Here was the mystery of a lifetime, Martin could feel it. "Every puzzle has a solution," he had said to himself many times, but lately there had been no formidable puzzles left, at least until now. He would not let Simon take this one away from him!

"I am fine," replied Marty forcefully. "Which is more than I can say for your father."

"What? He is dead, Marty." She said it gently, as if she were speaking to a child. "Did you find out something new about my father?"

Biting his fingernails, Marty reported his findings and was about to confess that he had hit a dead end, when he looked again at the screen. Bailey and Craig were in view, but they didn't look surprised, puzzled, or even frustrated after listening to the story related by Jonathan's secretary about him and Mr. Ashi. Why? He stopped mid-sentence and stared.

"You might as well tell him, before he bites all his nails off," declared Simon. He was still standing next to Sahed, who sat with his back straight in the main room, a few feet away from the laptop.

"Yes, I might as well know what you are all talking about!" replied Marty, flustered. "I thought you left…"

"No, still here," came Simon's low voice.

"Marty, we…erh…found…Sahed Ashi," said Craig, sensing the tension build-up.

There was a moment of silence, and then Marty's voice, barely audible, came through the speakers: "How did you do it?" He was so ashamed he could barely breathe.

"He found us," started Craig. "Well, he noticed Bailey and then Simon found him."

Martin's lungs constricted and his words came out as a tense whisper: "Where is he?"

CHAPTER SIX

*   *   *

Sahed couldn't see the computer screen. Who was this other person? How many people had they told? How many more were involved? What had these Americans done?

"I am here," replied Sahed, startling Bailey and Craig, who quickly turned from the screen to face him. Sahed came closer to the laptop. He saw himself now in the little window on the screen, moving. He stopped and moved to the left, as if to test the camera.

"This is called a webcam, it's right there," said Craig, pointing.

"I know what a webcam looks like, young man, do not let my age fool you," said Sahed, studying Marty's face. Everyone was dead silent, including Marty, but Marty, unable to hold it, was the first one to break the tension.

"Hi, you must be the famous Mr. Sahed Ashi I spent the whole damn night looking for! Do you mind telling me how you have managed an engineering degree without ever attending school?"

"Don't be rude, Marty," scolded Bailey, her face appearing next to Sahed's on the screen.

"I did not complete university and I do not have an engineering degree. I have some higher education from London, actually, from a private tutor. But that information could not be available to you. You must have been looking into, how do you say it, my *cover*," smiled Sahed tiredly.

"London, eh?" said Simon. "You've *lived* in the UK then?"

"On several occasions, and I do not choose to speak of it," Sahed said, closing the subject.

*   *   *

Having Marty in the mix made Simon uneasy. He knew now that Shwabster was harmless, but advertising his presence had laid open one more card to Sahed. And Simon was still not sure what to think of Sahed.

As the situation settled, Sahed returned to his story.

"The Shenu have political power. They can manipulate the Egyptian government and any other major system in the Middle East if they need to. We, the True Shenu, have worked very hard to stay hidden from them. My father sent me to London to learn about life and the religions and history of the world. It was a private matter. I lived unseen in a man's house and he educated me in many subjects. I did not know then how my family could afford to send me abroad to study, but it was not my place to ask. My father made it clear that it was a private wish of his and that even my mother was not to know where I was or what I was doing. Everyone was told I lived in Cairo and was studying engineering there. When I returned to my family an educated man, no one was surprised, since most of them had never been to Cairo," smiled Sahed.

He paused, and finished his bottle of water.

"The True Shenu were never involved in politics, only truth… I know the names of everyone in our Shenu line, but I only personally know a few generations. There was my father, Naram; his dear friend, a woman called Omickh; and young Salam," smiled Sahed gently. "Naram and Omickh each were married and had children. Salam was not so blessed. He was a consular staff member, the first one of the True Shenu in such a high position in the government. My father and Omickh had very high hopes for him – they wanted him to find out the identities of the other Shenu, the political ones. But then the Second World War began and he was sent to France… There was nothing we could do. He wrote us letters. Egypt was politically more and more in favor of the Nazis, and the government was satisfying its anti-semitic feelings by flirting with Mussolini and the Germans." Sahed paused again, remembering the past.

"Naram and Omickh received many letters from Salam, delivered secretly through many hidden channels. Then the last letter came… My father was fifty-nine years old then, and I was just over forty, but I was not yet part of the Shenu. He had not yet told me the secret…

In his last letter Salam wrote that he had contracted hepatitis and was dying. He wrote from the hospital. France was under a lot of strain politically and militarily, the country was full of soldiers. The Egyptian Embassy had been watching Salam very closely, but when he got sick they dumped him into a public hospital like some useless garbage.

As a Shenu, it was his right to pick his inheritor. Salam was forty-two years of age and he was not married; he had no children and no true friends besides us. Friends were dangerous in his position, he could not allow himself that luxury.

Salam met a man in the hospital. He was an American, a chemist I think… He was helping with the chemical weapon damage that many of the soldiers were recovering from. I am not sure how this worked out exactly, but he was stationed in the hospital for a month and Salam got to know him very well. His name was Michael Rixson."

"Oh, my god! My grandfather!" said Bailey, exhaling. She had not expected this turn in Sahed's tale.

"He told Salam he had a child who had been born since he had left America, his young wife was alone at home with his son."

"My father... he was born in 1942. My grandfather was killed soon after, in '44. He never saw his son."

"We did not know that. All we knew was what was in the letters – that Salam had picked an inheritor, Michael Rixson, an American. He had told him the truth, and he had initiated him into the Shenu. There must have been something amazing about Michael Rixson, because Salam had picked him, a foreigner. That was all we knew..."

"My grandmother, his wife, told me that grandpa Michael from his school years was really interested in everything Egyptian... He read books... Oh my god. He had a small statue of Sekhmet on his desk! A gold one, or gold plated, but he loved that thing..."

"Michael Rixson must have been a man of great integrity, and he must have known a lot about Egypt. Salam would have never picked him if he hadn't thought that he was capable of being a Shenu.

After the war the political situation in Egypt was difficult. Most information channels were dangerous; it was a time of surveillance and espionage. To begin asking about some American in Europe was not a very good idea. Naram and Omickh were family people and they were not equipped for such a search. Nevertheless, they looked. As the time passed, my father Naram retired and I came into the Shenu. Right around the time he died Omickh was ill, and she picked her son, Omar, to be her inheritor. And so Omar and I began the search for Michael Rixson. Imagine our shock when we finally found him, and discovered what had happened to him – he had been killed in the war and had never made it home...

We did not know if Michael Rixson had picked an inheritor for himself before he died, or not. We could not leave to chance that he had – this would mean that there was a person out there with full knowledge about the existence of the Shenu! We had to find that inheritor if he or she existed. And so we found his son, Jonathan Rixson, and attempted to contact him. I knew some important and wealthy Egyptians who had immigrated to America – I met them in London years ago. We convinced one of them to approach the firm Jonathan worked in with a project for an architectural design of a unique private home."

"Why didn't you just come to the States and meet my father?"

"Neither Omar nor I could risk going out of the country, especially to America. It would have been very strange. You see, Omar was a minor merchant, and I was hidden almost completely. My beloved wife..." – here Sahed was silent for a moment and his eyes wandered up the wall to the ceiling, as if he was remembering something very potent, very important. Finally he looked at them again and continued "...My beloved wife and I lived in a very small town. I was someone you might call a judge – people came to me to resolve disputes. We lived far away from the cities in a small desert oasis, hidden in the quiet of village life. If I or Omar had suddenly bought tickets to New York, the government, and the Shenu, would have become extremely interested. You see...?

So instead your father flew here, to Cairo first, then to Luxor, which was where I moved eventually. We met here. I asked him here without exposing any information. I was discreet. But apparently I was not as good as I thought, perhaps I was too old..." Sahed smiled his sad tired smile, then took another drink of water. "In any case, Jonathan recognized that there was something else I wanted. I knew some things about his father that I should not have known and no matter how well I explained them, he did not believe me. He was a man who wanted to know, it was as simple as that. He just would not let it go. Maybe it is an American trait, you see? Assuming that every desire man has can, and should be, fulfilled? He had to know and he was going to find out no matter what, I could sense that in him. After a while I decided to explain a small part of the story. After all, I needed to find out if he knew anything..."

Covering up her fear, Bailey almost growled, her face contorted into a grimace of suspicion. This old man obviously played her father somehow, maybe even killed him!

But Sahed continued, his sad eyes now looking directly into hers: "Bailey, did you know that your grandfather had picked his son, your father, as the next one in line for the True Shenu?"

"What...?" For a moment, Bailey looked lost. Then anger began to well up inside her. "My grandfather believed all the stuff this total stranger told him? My grandfather had a scientific mind, he was not religious... He was in his early twenties then... Your Salam was forty-two, right? And grandpa Michael believed him? And told my father? But grandpa died, he never came home, he never even saw my father! My father was two years old then anyway! Nothing could be told to him! This is nuts!" Bailey could not calm down.

"He wrote his wife a letter. Your grandmother, Michael's wife, received many letters from her husband with the help of his American and British friends. And in the last one he sent her a letter for their son. She gave him that letter when he turned twenty-five. Of course, Jonathan did not know what to make of it, he was not really interested in Egypt and most of the information in the letter was unfamiliar to him. But he

126

was interested in anything about his father since he had never known him. And he knew that his father loved everything Egyptian. He even researched some of what his father wrote, so very American of him – no discretion whatsoever! But of course it went nowhere, since there are no official records of the Shenu. Thank the true gods of Egypt that his inquiries never raised any alarms. I assume his requests never made it to the Egyptian authorities, otherwise…"

"So when my father was in Egypt, you told him what this Shenu meant?"

"Yes, and he believed me. He was a man who knew the truth when it was in front of him. He wanted to become an active part of it. But I had to be sure. I had to see if he was true, if we could trust him. So we arranged many things, including my official degree in engineering," smiled Sahed, extending a hand for the water bottle that Craig was handing him. He continued: "I flew to the States under the guise of the architectural project and stayed there for almost six months, studying Jonathan. By the time I left, I was convinced."

"What did you need him for? I mean, why did he come to Egypt again?"

Sahed sighed deeply. "There is one more thing the imposter Shenu never knew. They assumed that the locket of Sekhmet, the key to the well, was lost forever, returned by Akhenaten to Sekhmet herself. But they were wrong."

On the highway outside of Cairo

Mahmoud Halib inched along in his guard's beat up truck. The highway looked more like a swarm of scarabs than a road. He had spent the rest of the day visiting places and leaving requests or commands. Now, driving slowly in the traffic, he stared at the orange sunset. His mind was blank. He felt lost. Just a few days before, maybe a week, he had been fine, one might say on top of his world. He smiled tentatively, thinking of his scheduled television appearance and the banquet that was to follow it. He would not be able to attend either event. "I must reschedule," he thought absently. His truck slowly passed a walking camel, barely visible underneath the hay piled on top of it. Everything seemed to be in slow motion. His eyes looked ahead, dazed.

"Follow the beloved… You are the beginning of the end…" – the words appeared in Mahmoud's mind as if from nowhere, a voice not his own.

He stiffened, startled by it. "What in the name of Allah is wrong with me? I'm doing everything as I should."

But his intuition would not shut up. He *remembered*, and almost crashed his truck into the car in front of him. Loud horns erupted from all sides and he had to bring his focus to the road, if only for a moment. He yanked the steering wheel to the right, as far as it could go, pulling off the road into the dirt of the desert. Shaking and gripping the wheel, he struggled to stay blank, to not allow the memory to return. He was afraid to allow himself a path back to the voice he had just heard.

For almost an hour Mahmoud sat white-knuckled – he could not allow himself to relax, or surely he would remember... But when the soul wants something to be known, there is no way to hide from it, no matter how much you want to or how much self-control you think you have.

Something hit the roof of his truck, jarring Mahmoud back to reality. He jerked to the left, toward the highway, immediately regretting the sharp movement – he was not so young anymore, and the twist hurt his tense body. There were three men next to his truck, picking up wooden trays and refilling them with the bananas that had fallen off the back of their truck. Their vehicle had sped up to pass another hay-covered camel, and the sudden acceleration had knocked the banana baskets from the truck's roof. Some of them had fallen right on top of Mahmoud's parked truck. The men were fast, and most of the bananas were back on their truck in no time. One of the men knocked at the truck's window, but seeing Mahmoud's blank stare, he shrugged his shoulders and put a large bundle of bananas on the hood of Mahmoud's truck. They moved back into traffic, leaving him alone.

"She said *follow the beloved... do not stray from Maat... you are the beginning of the end...*" whispered Mahmoud. He was back in the sacred well, remembering with terror how the two men with him had fallen to the floor unconscious while he stood there, staring at the transparent apparition. Her features soon became clearer and he saw her head, covered by a gold lioness mask. Her eyes, he had been told, were amber, but they were not, they seemed bright red, like two rubies on fire, and they stared at him through the holes in the mask as if she could see straight into his soul. Mahmoud had never experienced fear like the fear of that day. He was unable to move, he wished to simply be unconscious, like the others. And then he heard her voice inside his head saying *do not stray from Maat... you are the beginning of the end*. That was when he lost consciousness. When he revived, the other men's faces were above his and they were blathering, fear in their eyes. They were Shenu, like him, but they had not seen Sekhmet. No one had expected her to show up;

the well was thought to be dormant. When Mahmoud sat up, they stared at him in silence. The experience had turned his hair gray. They knew then that he had seen something incredibly intense and frightening. Oh, Mahmoud wanted very much to convince himself that he had seen nothing. But he could not. He knew he had met Sekhmet, he had stood in front of her. He remembered what she looked like, especially the red eyes, which he had many nightmares about, those eyes of ruby with the semi-vertical pupils like a cat should have... He didn't remember what Sekhmet told him, but he knew she had said something. He told the High Priest of Shenu what had happened and since then he had become known as "chosen by Sekhmet." The trouble was that he did not know what he had been chosen for. All he knew was that the prospect of being chosen for anything that was outside his control terrified him. He had political and cultural power and the financial standing to match; he had his desired "controllable" power. Anything else, he did not want.

And now, hearing his own whisper, Mahmoud began to shudder. He was sweating under his clothes even though he felt very cold. This memory cut straight to the bone. He was the chosen one, but he had been chosen to begin the end. "The end of what?" whispered Mahmoud, as if hearing the sound of his own voice would make him feel safer.

A loud horn blared right next to his truck, shaking Mahmoud back to the current moment. He suddenly became aware of the cacophony around him. Looking at the road, while his hand searched the bag on the passenger seat, he produced a pocket-size bottle of whisky. He shook his head and gulped from the bottle, then took a deep breath and opened the truck door. Grabbing the large bundle of bananas from the hood of his truck, he fixed his gaze on them for a moment. It was almost dark – how long had he sat there?

Frustrated with his own impotence, he tossed the bananas onto the passenger seat and climbed back into the truck. The drive back to Cairo would be long, but he would get there. He started the truck and pulled back onto the road.

St. George Hotel, Luxor

Leaving his position by the window, Simon put away the gun. The old man was making at least some sense, and he spoke with sincerity. Yet nothing he said really *should* have made any sense, so bizarre was his tale. Simon did not care much for the mystery of a secret sect, but he saw clearly the signs of a well-protected, well-trained and wealthy covert organization muscling its way around. He didn't want Bailey to get hurt. She seemed to be completely oblivious to the danger of the situation, pushing through the information and her feelings with tenacity. "I guess all her unanswered questions caught up with her," he thought, glancing at Bailey's concerned face. She appeared to be studying the gurgling electric kettle on the counter. "She is so wrapped up in these issues with her parents that she doesn't notice she's scared breathless..."

And she was scared. Simon had noticed her getting confused on more than one occasion, and that was not the Bailey he knew. The woman he knew did not get confused. Angry, maybe, or lost in reams of analysis, but not disoriented. The fact that her father was not such a bad fellow after all had her seriously rattled.

"I'll go check on the blokes downstairs," said Simon to Bailey on the way out of the hotel room.

Bailey nodded, then emptied the packets of instant coffee into the electric kettle, and stirred. "I guess he doesn't think Sahed is dangerous anymore. Or that he will try to escape..." She felt unnerved without Simon. But she would have been lying to herself if she decided her nerves were screaming right now only because Simon had left the room. She was overwhelmed and a little numb. So much had occurred in such a short time! Holding the lid to the kettle, she paused, forgetting what she wanted to do with it. After all these years, now that she was finally so close to the answer, why was she back-pedaling? Shouldn't she *want* to find out the truth? She had spent such a long time judging her parents as irresponsible and self-centered that she was ashamed to find out that perhaps they weren't... Perhaps their trip to Egypt had a meaning, a much deeper meaning, than a tourist excursion. It would mean that her blame had been misguided.

Realizing that she had been staring at the coffee, she finally placed the lid back onto the kettle and prepared to pour the hot brown liquid into the small cups next to it. She could not figure out what she felt. How do you react to finding out the truth about your parents, especially a truth that is practically opposite from what you thought you knew? How do you cope with the years wasted on hating? She had always felt betrayed by her parents, especially her father. She had believed it had been his idea to go to Egypt and that it was he who had dragged the family there, he who had refused to let go of the trip when his child came down with chickenpox. He was a selfish man! That had to be the truth! "But," she said bravely to herself, "just because I'm so used to believing it doesn't necessarily make it the truth, does it?" She hated her reasoning, it felt like her own mind was against her! "No, this insane story is only that – an insane story, told by some senile Egyptian, right? Why am I buying this stuff...?"

She jumped; she had spilled hot coffee right on her hand. She could hear Craig and Sahed's voices coming from the suite's main area but she couldn't pay attention to what they were saying, her thoughts brought her back to the pain she felt in her heart. The pain about her father, *daddy*...

She had grown to resent him for his decision to travel to Egypt. Yet she was tired of hating him. She had been so lost all these years! Life had become about being safe, being comfortable, getting enough hours to get her therapy license, then getting enough money to open her own practice, always getting enough of something... But it never seemed to be enough. And then what had happened once she reached the goals she set for herself? She found that her life was empty, instead of being filled with satisfaction. "I thought being safe would make up for everything..." thought Bailey. "I thought I would be satisfied with being comfortable." She had not been satisfied; she had felt as if she had extinguished a little flame inside her being. When Bailey thought back to her childhood, the flame had been there – she was alive then. Now she had a life, but she was not alive... The thought made her feel faint. Holding onto the counter, she again studied the locket.

What she experienced then was unexpected: the more she stared at the locket, the more reality was slip-sliding from her grasp. Then there were voices, spinning lights, darkness with strange whitish ribbon-like swirls, and suddenly a bright light, blue like liquid sapphire; and then a tall woman was in front of her. The same tall woman she used to see as a child. This was not a dream, and not material reality; it was something in between... Like an awake-dream, or a live memory... Bailey could not see the face of the woman. As she looked closer, straining, she saw that the woman was wearing a mask, a gold cat mask. "Or maybe not a cat, the nose is too wide for a cat.... What the hell am I doing?" thought Bailey. How could she be inside this strange experience and still get stuck on arguing with herself about the size of the apparition's nose? Meanwhile the tall woman was still there, seemingly unaware of Bailey's inner debate. She was extending her transparent hand toward Bailey. She occupied a strange space, so far away and yet right here, in front of Bailey. As the hand got closer, Bailey focused on the face – the mask was of a lioness, and through it shiny amber eyes with semi-vertical pupils looked at her. Hypnotized by the eyes, Bailey didn't notice the hand again until she felt her heart ache. Tearing her focus away from the amber eyes,

Bailey looked down at her own chest. The extended finger of the tall woman's hand was so close to the locket that the two were almost touching!

But as soon as Bailey thought about the hand, everything disappeared. There was no more blue light, white spiraling mist or masked woman – only Bailey standing in front of the coffee pot and four small cups on the tray, her own fingers still grasping the locket. She froze for a moment, unable to reconcile what she had just seen with the present picture of the coffee pot and cups. The vision of the woman was too real... Her mind shouted a suitable explanation: she had hallucinated, a condition which could be brought on by extreme stress, exhaustion or perhaps a serious mental illness... Bailey felt she might be slipping into insanity. That brought her mind to Abby: "What if Abby saw the same things... the same person in a mask?" Bailey shook her head a few times. It made her feel disoriented, but in a reassuring, physical kind of way. Her fingers were still clutching the locket, joints white from tension. "So, this thing was in the hands of real pharaohs whose mummies are in museums now?" she thought, numbly. "And some other important people had it too... Never mind this stuff about Sekhmet, who I think I just saw... Am I having an acute psychotic break? This isn't happening! It must not be..." Bailey desperately tried to convince herself that this was too absurd to actually exist – not in her measured life. Yet more and more of the inner flame she had suppressed for all these years was awakening, that little courageous, adventurous and stubborn girl was coming out – and she knew the truth when she saw it, just like her father had.

Simon had returned from his reconnaissance.

"Our friends are still there in the lobby, one's reading the Cairo Times, and the other one really likes his sweets, I've not seen him once without them," Simon explained to Bailey, giving her a questioning look. "They look relaxed, so there's no cause for alarm. Not yet, anyway," he added with a satisfied smile.

Picking up two coffee cups, she carried them into the main area, trying to hide the shaking of her hands. Relieved of the cups, Bailey returned to the counter for her own cup, and noticed a blinking light on her laptop screen. She quietly took the laptop into her bedroom, ignoring Simon's raised eyebrow as he watched her go.

Of course it was Marty. He had news, and it was logarithmic. He had gone over the design on the locket again and again, trying to figure out what it meant. There was nothing quite like it in Egyptian history; in fact, as far as he could tell the design was barely Egyptian. It had a clear pictorial representation of someone, like an Egyptian god with a staff, in the center, but even with his precise technology Martin could not match it to any god known in Egypt. There were many symbols which at first looked like Egyptian hieroglyphs, but on closer examination he had found they were perhaps hieroglyphs but not Egyptian, or any other historically known type. There were also some geometric figures – a triangle, a circle, a smaller upside down triangle. And in between all of these shapes were tiny, barely noticeable dots. On Jonathan's drawing these dots were actually little star-like contours and Martin had to trust they really were that shape, since Jonathan was precise. The dots were of varying sizes and they looked like a background, as if they were placed all over the design at random. Martin ran the picture through a pattern-recognition program and the pattern appeared, clear as day, on his computer screen.

Excitedly, Marty whispered into the monitor: "I've got it! My dear, I've got it! The dots are not just the background, they're a hidden logarithm. There are four sizes of these dots all over the place, and I found four separate patterns, you know, if you connect the dots the right way. One is a formula for *pi*, the other is a very complicated mathematical formula related to electrons and space/time which I barely understand, the third one I can't even guess at what it is, and the fourth one is an exact geometric representation of a Fibonacci logarithm." Martin picked up a sheet of paper and held it up in front of his face so Bailey could see it. A strange pattern was drawn on it. He moved the sheet away and replaced it with another, and then another, and then another. The last pattern looked like an unfolding spiral.

"*Pi*, time-space, a logarithm? What are you talking about?" Groggy from the recent incident, Bailey's mind couldn't immediately grasp what Martin was saying. "I thought it was ancient, they didn't know anything like that back then."

"Well, apparently they did, and very well, I might say, this is perfection!" Marty whispered with fascination, breathing into the microphone.

"Why are you whispering?"

"Oh…" Marty cleared his throat, he had no idea why he was whispering. "Anyway, it is *pi* and a Fibonacci spiral for sure. The other patterns are also formulas. Something I have never seen before – and believe me, I've spent the night looking." Marty swallowed. "One I still know nothing about; the other one is a formula that allows for the separation of electrons from their atomic bonds, a sort of "electron pairing" that shifts part of the atomic mass out of this material dimension... err... elsewhere..."

"What?"

"I know, I know, it's strange... But I've discreetly contacted three scientists I know, really smart guys, and all three told me this: if that formula was applied to matter through some sort of a wave pattern, at high temperature – really high, like in the sun – it could cause a rip through space/time... or something like that... And if applied to biomatter, it could theoretically "translate" one into another dimension... well, if it doesn't vaporize him, I mean... They said that the math is sound – which I could have told you myself, mind you, but quantum physics is not my area... so... They said that even if it is correct, we can't apply it, because a component is missing, which is probably in the fourth formula we don't understand – I mean, we can't tear any time or space without that other 'something' – but unfortunately I don't know what that is..." Marty sounded crazed yet focused; his eyes shone with excitement and almost fear, but in a good sort of way.

"What does *that* mean?" Bailey's voice was tired.

"Err... I am not sure..." swallowed Marty. He really needed some sleep. "I will call you back later..." – and his face disappeared from the screen.

Bailey sighed, and closed her laptop. Many thoughts competed for her attention. Distracted by these thoughts she returned to the main room and placed her computer back on the counter. Martin's information about the logarithmic spiral, *Pi* and some "magic formulas" was really absurd. She trusted he would have checked and rechecked all his information before calling her, so he definitely was sure about what he said. And if Marty was sure, it meant he was right, unless he had lost it from excitement and exhaustion. But if it was true... Lowering her aching body onto the sofa and staring at Sahed, trance-like, Bailey tiredly demanded: "Tell me more about this locket."

"The locket... As I have said, the Shenu were wrong in thinking that the locket was lost. The True Shenu had possession of the locket at that time, well after the other Shenu thought that Akhenaten had given it back to Sekhmet." Sahed inhaled sharply. He seemed frustrated with having to condense the information to accommodate the attention span he was presented with. "I was the one who gave the locket to Jonathan Rixson. And he attempted to enter the well."

"Why would he do that? What well?" Her semi-hypnotized voice surprised her.

"Oh, my darling child, this is a very long story. There was a prophecy…"

"No! No prophecy stuff! I want to hear the real reason why my father climbed down some obscure well. He would never have done it because of some prophecy!"

"Don't be so sure, my child. If you do not like the word prophecy, think of it as a message. A message was given to one of our priestesses. It came from Sekhmet herself. The priestess lived a long time ago, but the message given to her was passed along for many generations, until it reached ours. Your father and I were to be the two Shenu to descend into the well and meet Sekhmet again, after all those years… But something went wrong. I am not sure what, but it was beyond our control. Your father was killed. And so was your mother, as I later learned when I climbed out of the well. I am so very sorry, dear child. Your sister, Abigail, must have survived. Jonathan somehow hid the locket on her, but I did not know… I assumed that the locket was lost there, I mean, back in time. I could not stay, I had to leave. When I did not see the locket on your father's neck or anywhere else on his dead body, I assumed that Sekhmet had taken it. I only touched your darling little sister to see if she was alive to carry her out, but she was not, her heart was not beating. I had to leave, I chose to leave her dead body next to your father's, in the well. It was the hardest day of my life, harder perhaps than the day my beloved wife died. I was sure that all three members of your family had died and that I was the only survivor. I researched you, Bailey… I studied your life and your actions, I even have your picture in my house. I sent my love to you every day, knowing that I had inadvertently caused your family's death. I am very sorry, and I will have to take that to my grave. But I believed the words to be true and that Jonathan and I were the two Shenu to open the gate… I must have been wrong, I do not understand… That is why I was shocked to see you, dear child, in the Chapel of Sekhmet, with the locket on your neck. I did not know that the locket was still here, in this time, and I did not know that Abigail had survived."

"Sahed," said Craig, "Abby's survival, and the locket, and now Bailey coming back here with the locket – doesn't it prove that you were wrong? That you and her father weren't the two "chosen" Shenu?"

"Yes. It means we were wrong. Jonathan was as convinced as I was, though. But if the locket is still here, there must be two other Shenu. It has to be true!"

"Sahed, we need to know why you and Jonathan believed that you had to go into that well." Craig spoke in a low voice, and although he was asking he looked like he already knew the answer.

"You know, that very night, before I saw you at Karnak, I talked to Sekhmet... She told me that the story is almost complete. I did not know what she meant, but when I saw you in front of the chapel doorway with this locket..."

"What do you mean *talked* to Sekhmet?" interrupted Bailey.

"She came to me... in my dream," said Sahed softly. He got up, looked around, and started for the washroom.

There was a long moment of silence. No one knew how to react to what they had just heard. On an assumption, following a strange prophecy, Jonathan Rixson and this old man, Sahed, and apparently a five year old Abby, had voluntarily climbed into an old well, and this action had later caused the death of Jonathan in the well, and his wife on the surface. Abby had survived, magically reappearing in the States with the locket on her neck. It was all too much to believe. Even if Jonathan Rixson had become obsessed with some secret organization in Egypt because of his father, what they had just heard was a long step away from anything reasonable.

When Sahed returned, Simon broke the silence: "What did you say before all that, earlier? Something like 'the locket is the key'? What kind of key?"

"It is the key to the well," replied Sahed.

"Wells do not need keys..." mumbled Bailey.

"Oh? This one does need a key," said Sahed with a grim look on his tired face. "This well was built a very long time ago. It is a part of a large system, from the times of the star-gods..."

There was a loud beep – Bailey's laptop had received a download. As they watched, the screen turned on and small windows opened one after the other; something was installed, and the computer automatically began to restart.

"Are you expecting something?" Simon looked quizzically at Bailey, remembering her disappearance into the bedroom.

"I gave Martin access."

"Like he didn't have it before," Craig chimed in, well aware that Martin was pretty much in charge of their computer through his remote access – the only thing he could not do was turn the camera!

Caught in the lie, Bailey was embarrassed. "Yes, it looks like he's downloading a large file..."

"Actually," Marty's face had appeared on the screen in the corner, "I've downloaded a whole program so you can see for yourself – it is quite remarkable... Have you told them?"

"*Told them* what, Bailey...?" Craig looked hurt.

Sahed got up and stood behind them. Simon's training prompted him to hang back so he could keep a close eye on Sahed.

"Ah... While you were talking, Marty figured out what the symbols on the locket mean."

"What is it?" The pinch of betrayal forgotten, Craig excitedly looked at Bailey and then Marty, and at Bailey again.

Sahed's expression had changed. He suddenly looked older, and somehow defeated.

"I just uploaded a satellite program into your laptop. It's live, so you can see for yourself." On the screen a window opened up with a view of the planetary surface, and the ground grew closer and closer as the satellite camera zoomed in. They were over Africa, then closer to the Nile Delta, then right on top of Cairo and Giza; now they were looking at the pyramids from high above. They could see the three pyramids, the Sphinx and all the modern structures like buildings and roads, even the parking lots crammed with cars and tour buses.

"The *pi* formula is obvious, and the other one for shaking electrons loose, the quantum physics stuff... I don't know anything new about that yet," Marty mumbled, embarrassed. "But this one..." In the lower right corner of the screen there opened a small window containing a computerized drawing of the design that was on Bailey's locket; the drawing was detailed and precise. "This one is a geometric representation of a Fibonacci logarithm." Marty's voice was confident, lecturing.

"Now watch this." And he made some of the lines on the drawing change color. Green lines now stood out from black ones, and it became apparent that the green lines represented a partial grid, and the spiraling curve expanded over it.

"We have to do it now – so watch carefully." Marty's voice was tense. "The satellite will move away in another fifteen minutes and we won't get another chance until tomorrow."

The green lines of the drawing magically lifted off the little window and floated over the satellite picture, expanding to match the scale. Everybody stopped breathing. They were looking at the three pyramids and the Sphinx, which perfectly fit into the grid of the green lines. Around the four structures, expanding, was the large curve of the spiral.

"This is what I was talking about!" Marty's excited voice took them out of shock. "See the spiral? That is the Fibonacci logarithm. It starts at this point, at those small buildings, and expands from there out, passing through the right shoulder of the Sphinx and smack through the apex points of the pyramids."

"What does it mean?" whispered Bailey.

Everyone turned to look at Sahed.

"You have uncovered the ancient secret," said Sahed, as he slowly backed away. Suddenly looking unstable on his feet, he let himself drop into the sofa. "Perhaps it was bound to happen with all this technology around..."

No one broke the silence, but collectively their thinking was nearly audible. This ancient locket bore an encoded design of the Giza complex, which apparently related directly to the "modern" Fibonacci formula. Craig's eyes were still glued to the screen, while Bailey's face showed exhaustion as she pulled mercilessly at her red hair.

Finally Simon spoke. "Not much of a secret, I am sure people figured this out before from looking at a map. The question is, my friends, how does this relate to our situation here?"

Sahed was expected to answer, and so he spoke: "The answer you are looking for is in the beginning of the spiral. That is the location of the well."

Stunned, Bailey could not respond. This was that actual well that her parents had died in? That little dot on the screen? She stared at it in disbelief, as if something that was so horrific could not be reduced to this trivial dot.

"Watch this," came Marty's voice from behind. As everyone turned back to the computer screen they saw the core of the spiral magnify as the satellite camera zoomed into it. "I can't bring you any closer, sorry, guys."

"What is this?" Craig pointed at the line around it.

"It looks like a fence..." suggested Marty in his computerized voice.

"It is a fence, and this is a guard station right here," said Simon, touching the screen with his finger.

"Yes, you are correct." Sahed did not look at the screen. "The area of the well is under government protection now. The Shenu are in control of the guards and they stationed them not far from the well. There is a small building covering the entrance."

"We have to go back to Cairo," said Craig matter-of-factly. He was like a wild creature on the hunt; he had just caught the smell he had been searching for and he was not about to lose it. The Fibonacci logarithm, *pi*, and formulas about electrons connected to time/space – all this could be figured out right there, in that spot. Bailey gave Craig a long look, and no one spoke. Finally, she returned her attention to the screen, as if confirming to Marty the decision to leave.

"I will get the tickets," said Marty. "Is Simon traveling with you this time?"

Deciding it was best to leave right way, Marty signed off. Simon would be on the same flight but sitting separately.

Sahed sat on the sofa, silent. His posture was perfect despite his age.

"Are you going to come with us?" asked Bailey quietly.

"It is not what I want to do. But I am obliged to help you. I will meet my friend, another True Shenu, and we will come to Cairo."

"How will we meet?" asked Craig, excited about the adventure.

"Leave that to me. I will contact you tonight in Cairo," replied Sahed. Then, looking at Simon, he added: "Am I free to leave this room?"

Cairo, Egypt

Their evening flight was on time. It was later in the day, and the city had cooled. There were people everywhere. Bailey stared out the window of their taxi as it weaved its way through traffic. The lights were merging into smudges each time the taxi made a turn and soon Bailey realized that she was crying. She didn't want Craig to see her tears so she turned farther away from him into the cab's window.

Craig was making sure he didn't miss anything. He stared at his handwritten copy of the information Marty had given them and went over it again, including his own additions. He had already spent the whole flight studying it. Craig was on the path, he could feel it – he meant to do his job well, whatever it was he had to do.

The taxi stopped in front of the Cleopatra Palace. The grand name was a bit much for the little two-star hotel. But as they checked in and walked into their room, it became clear that it had been a good choice. The hotel was on the side street leading to Tahrir Square, almost directly facing the Cairo Museum. They could see the police station, the one they visited the last time they were there, its white lights ablaze on the rooftop as if to proclaim its powers.

Not feeling up to talking, Bailey opened her suitcase. She took out her pajamas and walked into the bathroom, hastily shutting the door.

*   *   *

Turning on the laptop, comfortably sitting on his legs in the large armchair, Craig opened up the satellite picture, itching to see it again.

There was a knock on the door. A cold wave of fear ran through him. But he reasoned that it was probably overeager hotel staff looking for tips, perhaps wanting to know if they needed anything. As he walked to the door he noticed there was no peephole.

"Who is it?" he asked, worrying that maybe answering the knock was not the correct course of action.

"Your *old* friend," was the reply. "And I brought one more."

Craig immediately recognized the voice of Sahed. How did he get here so soon? He would have had to have been on the same flight.

Opening the door, Craig was surprised to see that the "friend" Sahed mentioned was the taxi driver from Luxor. "Whoa…" he jumped back, staring at the man. "Simon was right, everyone is a message on the path," thought Craig, remembering what his spirit guide had told him. The newcomers walked into the room, and Sahed sat down. He looked tired.

"This is Axil Narmy," explained Sahed, pointing at the cabby.

"I know."

"You do?" Sahed was surprised.

"Yeah, Simon, the one… you know," said Craig, attempting to differentiate his guide from the man. He soon realized he was the only one in the room who thought there were two Simons and he shook his head and continued: "Err… I think Simon said you have six children and you're a family man, something like that…"

Axil laughed. "You I like. Glad that you are feeling much better, young mister. Last time we met you were sick."

"Yeah…" Craig hated the subject, but before he could try to change it there was another knock at the door. Sahed's eyes met Craig's as his shoulders went up.

"Who is it?" Craig asked, without moving towards the door.

"Do you need some towels, sir?" The speaker's voice was muffled, but it had a definite British accent.

Smiling, Craig walked back to the door and opened it. Simon spilled in, his large duffle bag on his shoulder and a bag in his hand.

"Where's..." he began, his head turning sharply toward the sound of the shower. "Never mind."

When Bailey, in pajamas and with a white towel on her head, finally came out of the bathroom, all four men were sharing beer – the contents of Simon's bag. She gasped in surprise.

"Sahed, why did my father go into that well?" The question Bailey had been going over in the shower finally materialized on her lips. It was the same question that Craig had asked earlier, but somehow it never got answered.

"Because of the prophecy."

"I thought we agreed on a no-prophecy policy?"

"You are free to think of it as a message."

"Tell me." Bailey was committed. She had found her resolve while standing under the hot water. She was through running; it was time to face the problem. She had to know, and she was not afraid anymore.

Simon noticed the change and one of his eyebrows raised as he gulped his beer.

"A long time ago, many centuries back, one of our high priestesses met Sekhmet in the well. She had used the key to open it and Sekhmet came through. This was not the priestess's intent; she was only trying to send a message to the other side, but instead she was met by Sekhmet. This was very rare, you see. Sekhmet did not visit us often, and almost never anymore. Sekhmet showed herself to the priestess of the True Shenu, and she gave her a message to carry over many generations. She said – and Sahed, closing his eyes, began to recite: *When the metal birds fly in the sky and people walk on the Earth's little sister, the end of time will be near. Two will enter the well and open the gate, initiating the beginning of the end. The key will return to me, as there will be no need for it any longer. The people of Earth will remember how to breathe.*"

Everyone was silent for a moment.

"Whoa...! This makes so much sense!" said Craig, exhaling. Looking around the room he could see that he was the only one to whom it made sense.

"And my father believed he was one of those two people, in the message?"

"Yes, and I believed that I was the other one of the two," replied Sahed.

"Hold on, this means that now is 'the end' or whatever it is you just said..."

"Yes, I believe it is the beginning of the end already," added Sahed quietly.

"This is insane! What, you believe that the world will come to an end and somehow you convinced my father of it and it got him killed?"

"I do not believe that the world will come to an end. But time will. This is what Sekhmet said, and I have no reason to doubt her," smiled Sahed.

"You believe that *time* will end..." repeated Bailey absently. "This is absurd..."

"It's not so absurd, Bailey," said Craig softly behind her. "The Mayans talked of the end of time, and other Native American cultures too. And Christianity talks about the Apocalypse. All religions have some 'end' in there. Or at least a re-start?"

"So the Apocalypse is a *good thing* now?" flared Bailey.

"Dear child, do not doubt Sekhmet. She is a lot of things, but she is always in Maat. If she told the priestess that the end of time will come, it will come," said Sahed with urgency. "She revealed that people *will* remember how to breathe. This is very good news!"

Bailey rolled her eyes. "I know how to breathe, so do you or you wouldn't be sitting here!"

Her sarcastic movement distracted Sahed for a moment and he frowned.

"There is breathing of air, and there is breathing of life. Sekhmet talked about breathing life. People have forgotten, and we need to remember."

"Go back to the previous point please," interjected Simon, taking the discussion away from the metaphysical to the physical. "What made you think that you were one of the two? Or that Jonathan Rixson was, for that matter?"

"Oh, that is complicated..." sighed Sahed. "The planes began to fly widely in my lifetime, the metal birds in the skies. And astronauts walked on the Moon, the Earth's little sister. It had to be the right time... The previous generation of us, the True Shenu, had not witnessed people on the moon. Besides me, there was Omar and Narim, my father. Both went into the well and nothing happened. You see, the gate had not been opened since that time many centuries ago when Sekhmet gave the message to the high priestess. No one had been able to open it since then, even though we had the key – this locket. And your grandfather, Michael, was killed. We had not had the chance of having him try..."

142

"You speak of this with such ease," choked Bailey. "*Try...* as if his life was not at stake!"

"We did not know what was supposed to happen when the gate opened; this information had not survived the passage of time... All I know is that we felt we had to try. We thought that without the right person nothing would happen, as nothing had happened for my father or Omar. And with the right person there would be nothing to fear, since it is foretold."

"Did you say you were the last one to see Sekhmet?" Craig blurted out suddenly.

"Yes, she came to me."

"But not in a dream, like before you met Bailey, right?" he pressed, intuitively knowing the answer already.

"She came to me in the well. I went there alone, looking for signs, clues. There were none. And when I was about to leave, the gate opened and Sekhmet was standing there in front of me. She was not solid, like you or I, she was a transparent vapor..." Sahed's eyes looked somewhere past their faces, back in time.

"Did she say anything?" Craig moved toward the edge of his seat as if Sekhmet's words were a matter of life or death.

"She said that *the time is near, it is almost here*," whispered Sahed. "And then she dissolved."

"What do you mean 'dissolved'? Like disappeared?"

"Yes, you might call it that. I assume the gate closed, and she was gone."

"Do you know how to operate that gate? How it works?" asked Simon.

"No. I know that people and star-gods can walk through it with their forms intact. But it has not been done for a very long time. Even when the message was delivered by Sekhmet, people did not walk through the gate. Before the time of the pharaohs the gate was used, but as ancient Egypt gained power, going through the gate was hardly ever attempted."

"But you just said that Sekhmet came into the well, so did she go through it then or not?" Craig was confused.

"I do not believe so. There is a way, I am told, to open the gate by standing near it without going through. If you know how to breathe, you can preserve your awareness and be able to see what is on the other side, as if you were looking into the window of time. From the other side of the gate it would probably look as if you were made of transparent vapor. I think Sekhmet opened the gate from her side, but we are too slow, too dark for her. Probably, she cannot come here anymore without causing pain to herself. And so she spoke to me through the open gate."

Bailey was sure that everyone must have been able to hear her heart beating, because that was the only thing she could hear!

"I know you said there are soldiers, but I want to look around the area where my parents died."

No one spoke.

"Maybe we can try an official tourist route?" she continued with urgency. "There are temple ruins everywhere in Egypt, there must be some near by this well site, right?" She turned to Sahed.

"Yes, a temple from the later Roman period... But it is closed to tourists."

"Why not just ask the Council of Antiquities for permission to see the site of this Roman temple, for a generous fee?" It seemed that in Egypt large sums did open large doors – and, thanks to Marty, she had access to these large sums.

Simon was sure that route would go absolutely nowhere – the authorities were not idiots. Craig shared his assessment. Sahed and Axil were quiet, both frightened of Bailey's audacity. She was the only one who held the hope that the Council of Antiquities would actually let them into the protected enclosure, but there might be something to poking the bee's nest.

Bailey's hair had dried and she exchanged her pajamas for a sundress and grabbed her purse. Perhaps she can make her way in, even though it was well past the business hours... Flagging a taxi, Bailey and Craig hurried to the office of the Council, leaving the others back at the hotel.

*   *   *

The Undersecretary of the Council of Antiquities of Egypt stared at the visitors through the glass paneled doors. They were here, he almost refused to believe it. This woman had the nerve to come to him directly now? Was she taunting him? He had to meet her. His secretary would be surprised that he agreed to the meeting, but so be it. He must know what she knows. A lot might depend on it.

The Americans walked in, she awkwardly holding her purse and he tugging his long hair as if he was retarded. "They have no idea what they've gotten themselves into! Or do they? She is so young looking...

They told me she was thirty-six years old, but she looks ten years younger... and this man with her, he is an overgrown boy, so immature, thin and awkward," he thought with disgust.

They took the chairs on the other side of his desk, and Mahmoud shook their hands as he sat down. The visitors were both perspiring. Mahmoud noticed how they became more and more relaxed as the ice cold air in his office cooled them. "Good, let them think we are friends, let them get very comfortable..."

They voiced their request.

Internally he was shocked, but Mahmoud appeared to listen with a look of concern and care about their wishes – to study the heritage of his people and the Romans of the later period. Unfortunately they must be disappointed: it was not possible at this time. Of course, in the near future, when the territory was available to the public, they would be welcomed... Besides, in that particular area there was nothing at all to see, it was simply the desert with a few ancient stones... they would be much happier exploring the major temples. He offered them a map of temple locations around Giza. Unbelievably, the woman mentioned money; sweat pricked at Mahmoud's neck and he delivered a well-practiced lecture about the importance of protecting the antiquities of Egypt. He was clearly understood – the area they wanted to see was not available, even with the help of a bribe.

To his surprise, the Westerners got up. He had been fully prepared for a tantrum, but no, they left quietly. They even thanked him for his time, and told him they would leave their information with his secretary in case in the future there was an opportunity to see the requested area.

He was sure that somehow he just got played, but he couldn't pinpoint how. He closed the door and stood there with his hand on the door frame. "She wants to descend into the well. Oh Allah, help us!"

Giza Plateau, Egypt

Bailey, with Craig behind her, entered the hotel room. Three pairs of expectant eyes greeted them, but her gaze found Sahed and she started talking right from the door: "You said that the locket is the key. It has all this logarithmic information on it... Do you stick it into a door in the little building over the well, like a physical key, or is it something else, like a code?"

"There is no door. The well has a cover, but it was made by men in recent years. The gate itself is deep below and it has no door, so yes, I suppose the locket is a code... I do not know precisely how it works. The locket was worn by Sekhmet herself; then it was given to the high priestess of the Shenu who always wore it and could open the gate."

"It has to transmit some kind of coded signal then that the systems of the gate recognize," said Simon.

"My grandmother thought it gave her headaches, and one of the Egyptologists I showed it to in Boston had blisters on his hands from holding it briefly," added Bailey.

"You showed it to an Egyptologist!" said Sahed, horrified, but before he could continue, Simon spoke again. "It might be radioactive – headaches and blisters are symptoms of radioactive poisoning. Or it might be an electromagnetic pattern that makes electrons spin differently to code the signal, something based on that "electron pairing" formula..."

Everyone turned to Sahed.

"The locket remembers the other side, that is all I know," sighed Sahed. "It has a memory of the life breath of Sirius, and somehow this memory is the key which opens the gate."

Craig attempted another approach.

"What does the gate look like?"

"It is like a window, I am told. But I have never seen it open."

"What about when you saw Sekhmet, the transparent image of her? What did the gate look like then?" pressed Craig.

"I do not know... I do not remember the gate at all. I was in the same space, but in front of me was Sekhmet. She was very tall, and I could hear her voice inside my head. I was not looking at anything but her. I listened."

"Did she speak to you telepathically?" continued Craig.

"Oh, come on, Craig! Telepathy?" scorned Bailey.

"Dear child," said Sahed patiently. "I cannot imagine how difficult this must be for you. I am very sorry that it had to happen this way. Maybe it did not have to, but it did. The only consolation I can give you is that no one forced your father to do anything, he went voluntarily."

"I have to take your word for it, don't I? There are no records of *anything*!" Bailey felt her anger imploding. She was near tears.

"Bailey, we have to look at the information Mr. Ashi gives us as real, it's all we have to go on." Craig stood up and put his hand on her shoulder to comfort her. He knew that Sahed was telling the truth, his

146

spirit guide had alluded to the "breathing" and the "meeting." He had to know more, he was the shaman chosen to help Sekhmet, as Simon-the-cat said, so he must keep this process going!

"Maybe we should go and check it out anyway?" suggested Simon. It was his way of soothing Bailey. "Just because they won't give us permission to see the structure doesn't mean we can't."

"There are guards there…" Axil pointed out.

"Of course there are, it's their job to be there, right? But we can find a way around them, they have to take a leak sometime, haven't they?"

Everyone smiled, somewhat relieved.

"Can you get us inside?" asked Craig.

"You're eager, aren't you! I had more of a fly-by mission in mind, not a full scale infiltration, mate!"

"The young mister is right," said Axil suddenly. "If we can get around the guards, we might as well go in."

It was so simple. No one actually noticed the moment the decision was made, yet it suddenly became apparent to all that they would descend into the well.

*　　　*　　　*

Night came quickly, and with the cool darkness the sounds of the city grew louder. Bailey sat alone on the balcony cradling her fifth cup of bad coffee. She was tired of worrying, but she could not release herself into sleep. The men had gone out – Craig to clear his head, the rest to check on the surveillance and to prepare for the "mission." Staring at the cityscape, Bailey's thoughts were of Abby, her poor twin. What time was it in the States? She stalked back into the room and, using the encrypted laptop, called Abby's medical facility. After four rings the nurse picked up, and after a few more moments Abby was put on the phone.

Assisted Psychiatric Facility
Outside of Boston, United States

The room with the white walls was not her favorite room. It was the common room, and it was always crowded with people. Abby hated the common room, but it was where she was expected to be, or they

147

would suspect something. She had skipped her meds again and was on the verge of remembering... But it was her third day without medication, and Abby knew that she was usually not well by the end of the third day. The second day was the best. On the first day without meds she did not remember much and her head hurt from all the noises, but by the second day, even if she had a nightmare, things were clearer and made more sense. Unfortunately, by the third day her fear and anxiety would begin to take over. She could still remember things and try to place them in order, but her emotions interfered instead of helping.

Abby sat in her favorite armchair. It was large and dark red in color, like her blood. She saw her blood often, when the nurse took it from her arm. For some reason blood had never scared Abby, even though most things in this world did.

Abby's hair was loose and she twirled a lock of it as usual. Her fingers moved much faster than they had to, but Abby did not notice. She was inside the beaded necklace of memories that she had been constructing. Yesterday, on the second day without medication, Abby had, as usual, remembered more of what that tall cat-woman said. As the memories came, she called Bailey and left messages. She had called over and over until the mechanical voice on the other end of the line told her that the machine was full. Then last night she had a dream, similar to all the others, but this one did not scare her, so Abby decided it was not a nightmare, just a weird dream. In the dream she was in her bedroom, and she walked up to the window. But instead of the tree outside that she looked at every day, she saw the tall white people, the ones from her nightmares. Yet here they were not so scary, they just hovered in front of the window. They spoke, again sounding like a voice in her head, and they told her *Bailey is in Egypt*. Before Abby could say anything they dissolved, and she could see the familiar tree again. Then she woke up. Sitting up in bed Abby stopped to think for a moment. Two things had happened. The first was that she was not afraid even though she had seen and heard the tall white people – that was really a first! The second thing was that Bailey was in Egypt. That explained why she wasn't answering the phone or calling her back. She was in Egypt. There was no doubt at all in Abby's mind.

A nurse walked into the common room and looked around until her eyes rested on Abby. Abby felt a mild panic, thinking she might have been caught and they had found out she skipped her medication. But the nurse smiled and walked towards her chair. The smile meant she didn't know. Abby could barely hold down her excitement at the news that

Bailey was on the phone and she hopped out of the armchair, running to answer the phone in the nurse's office.

"Where are you?" Abby asked with a huge conspiratorial smile – she wanted to tell her twin that she knew where she was.

"I am at home, Abby. How are you? Is everything alright?"

Abby was shocked that her dear sister lied to her.

"You are not home, they told me."

"Who are *they*, Abby?" asked Bailey, and Abby could hear the tension in her voice. Abby knew she should not talk about "them" with Bailey because it worried Bailey, and she did not understand. Abby hoped that if she could only remember enough, put enough together, then Bailey would get it.

"The people from the Council," Abby whispered quickly. "The Solar Council is here to protect us, they know about the locket. They told me, *they* told me!"

"What do you know about the locket?" This was the first time Bailey had asked her anything about the locket.

Abby was confused. "I know about the locket, I know about it," she replied.

"What is it, Abby? What do you know?" insisted Bailey on the other end of the line.

"It is the key. Sek-Met told me, she told daddy too. She is like a cat, you know…"

"Sekhmet…?" Bailey's voice sounded lost and faint.

Abby was reassured – her sister finally understood! They would be together again, they would! Abby had known about this all along, something about their father and Sek-Met. Why, why was Bailey so stubborn, why had she *never* listened to her before?

Realizing there is silence on the phone, she whispered: "Bailey? Bailey?"

With great effort, words finally came: "What did Sekhmet tell daddy?"

"Oh, she… she…" Abby stopped talking and breathed heavily.

"It's OK, Abby, it's OK, relax. Everything is OK. We don't have to talk about it anymore, it's OK," soothed Bailey, sounding apologetic.

"Sek-Met told me *you are not the one*, and *must let go, must let go*, and that there are *two people who will begin the end*, and that *your enemy is here*," said Abby proudly.

There was a long, heavy silence on the other end of the line. Abby's excitement was wearing off and she was beginning to feel confused and scared again. Why was Bailey quiet? She should not be quiet, Abby had just remembered, Bailey should not be quiet!

"Bailey? Are you there?" Abby asked. Had she done something wrong? Had she done something bad to Bailey? She started to tremble.

"Yes, Abby, I'm here," replied Bailey. "Can you please repeat what you just said?"

With a joy Abby had not felt in years, perhaps since she was a little girl, she repeated her words to Bailey, almost choking on them with excitement.

"What do you mean 'must let go'? Did Sekhmet tell *you* that, or daddy? You said that she told daddy…"

"I don't know, I don't know, she just said 'must let go' and then again 'must let go,' and then again…"

"I got that," interrupted Bailey. "But did she say that to you or to daddy, Abby?"

"I don't know, she just said 'must let go' and then again…"

"When was this? When did Sekhmet speak to you? How long ago?"

"I don't know, Bailey… It was a few days before we…" Abby felt herself spin. Then she realized she was not spinning, but the floor was, and she was now sitting on it. The phone was still in her hand. She could hear Bailey's voice screaming her name, but she could not answer. Someone was lifting her into a chair and someone else was checking her pulse. The room kept spinning as Abby saw her daddy in the bright light and then on the ground, and her head hurt really bad, as if it was going to blow up.

Cleopatra Hotel, Cairo

Bailey exhaled. She couldn't believe what just happened. Her sister repeated almost verbatim what Sahed had told them earlier. From what seemed like a great distance she heard the nurse on the phone saying that Abby fainted, but she would be OK. "She must be off her medication again," thought Bailey absently. This time the thought that Abby had skipped her medication did not interfere with her acceptance of what Abby said.

"What did she say? She told daddy, or… Sekhmet told daddy…?" Bailey's mind was looping. She opened up a Word document and began to type, fearing she might forget something.

"Letting go...'must let go' she said. Then she told daddy, or Sekhmet told her this *for* daddy? 'You are not the one, must let go'... Oh my god..." She stopped breathing and sat staring at the screen. "Abby was communicating somehow with Sekhmet... Am I saying Sekhmet is a person? Someone who can talk? I must've lost my mind... What if it's true? What if she's not a hallucination in Abby's mind? What if she's real, this whole thing is real? And Abby has known it all along... She was so little back then, my poor sister, she must've not been able to handle this, her mind gave out..." Tears were streaming down Bailey's face. She wiped them off with the back of her hand, which did no good and she sobbed, and sobbed, and sobbed.

But even the most insistent tears run out at some point. Bailey took a deep breath, got a tissue to blow her nose, and began to type again.

"What else did Abby say? She said 'there are two people'... no, she said 'the two people will begin the end'..." Bailey stopped, staring at the words. "This is the prophecy that Sahed told us about, a message that Sekhmet supposedly gave to the high priestess a long time ago. Why the hell was I so dumb? So selfish! I should've asked Abby more, talked to her about this before..." Guilt overwhelmed her. The tears came again and this time there was no stopping them.

"Abby actually *heard* Sekhmet." Bailey said the words out loud, as if she was testing a theory. "She was 'talked to' by Sekhmet, the star-god, and we all thought she was insane." Bailey felt lost and numb with guilt and fear. Knowing what she knew, she could not allow things to be "as is." She had to change it, but in her emotional overwhelm she was unsure of which reality to call real. Not trusting her mind, Bailey typed.

"Abby said that Sekhmet told her 'you are not the one, must let go' and that there are two people to begin the end, and something else...what was it?... Oh, something about the enemy..." Bailey forced herself to stop feeling and think instead. "Yes, she said 'your enemy is here.'"

She stopped, hypnotized by the words she just typed. "Ok, so let's assume for a moment that this is true, that Sekhmet actually talked to my sister. How? When? In the well? So far I know of two ways this communication can happen – one is in the well, and the other one seems to be in dreams..." A dark cloud crossed Bailey's mind. "Oh, my god, could it be? Abby was *in* that damned well!"

Bailey immediately contradicted herself: "No, that's not possible, my father would never have taken her inside the well." At the same moment she realized that Sahed had already told her that Abby *was* in the well. "What's wrong with me? I should have remembered that, should have connected the dots, asked him more… How could I have missed that?" Bailey felt as if her mind was playing tricks on her. "Sahed said that he checked Abby's pulse but she was dead, and my parents were dead, and all he could do was leave…" The tears flowed freely.

It was some time before her face was dry again, and she felt exhausted. When Craig returned from his night walk, she felt relief in being able to share the content of Abby's conversation with him. "He seems to have more insight, his mind unafraid of where the information leads him… He is not personally connected to this entire drama, so he can afford to think clearly… Or maybe because he is a shaman, whatever the hell that is!"

"She said 'you are not the one,' those were the words, right?" Craig asked.

"Yes, that's what Abby told me."

"Maybe it was a message she got in her dream, and it was for your father."

"No, she got it from Sekhmet, in the well – Sahed said she was in the well, remember?"

"Yes, I do, but that doesn't mean that was when she got the message…"

"Maybe," thought Bailey aloud, "that was why she is the only one alive, she was in the well and something happened, but she could hear Sekhmet and she didn't die in the end. For all we know, maybe she did die and somehow Sekhmet went through the gate and resurrected her! Listen to me, I sound like some religious maniac…"

"No, you're just thinking… All the visions of events of this nature need to be decoded. They come from… somewhere else, so they are not on the same wavelength as we are, so we kind of have to figure out what they mean. It's never clear, usually… True, Sekhmet could have come through the gate after something malfunctioned, which killed your parents and Abby. But then why would she save only Abby? If she could do it at all, I mean bring people back to life, she would've saved everyone, right?"

"You sound so sure of what she would or would not do." A sad smile appeared on Bailey's face. "I'm not even sure that Sekhmet is real, never mind the star-god idea…"

"Oh, she is real alright, I know it."

"Your spirit guide told you?" responded Bailey. She was too emotionally exhausted for sarcasm. Craig stared at her with rounded eyes.

"How did you know?" Then he realized she wasn't serious. "Bailey, we're in the middle of this story and we're the ones playing the parts in it, so we must let go and trust…"

"What did you say? We must let go… Maybe Sekhmet didn't mean that for Abby…" A realization blossomed. "You're right, she meant it for my father! She was telling him that he was not the one meant to open the gate and that he must let go! And he missed the message and went anyway, and got himself killed…"

"…because of his 'enemy,' his enemy was there – someone who killed him, either the gate system itself, or those Shenu people," finished Craig with satisfaction.

They both were silent for a moment. A very different picture of events began to emerge. For one thing, Abby was not delusional. Or at least she had not made up the stories about Sekhmet. That meant that the rest of it, about the Solar Council, was probably also true. When she was a little girl in Egypt with her parents, Sekhmet gave Abby a message. If Abby did tell her father, he must have misinterpreted it. Instead of reading her words as a warning that he should not go to the well, he thought that "must let go" meant he had to trust the prophecy, as in "relax and let go." He probably assumed that the enemy part of the message was about the authorities they had to hide from anyway. It was easy to imagine Jonathan believing he really ought to go into the well, because Abby repeated the same message that Sahed had given him from Sekhmet: two people were to enter the well and somehow begin the end.

Bailey spoke. "Why did my father take Abby into the well?"

"He probably thought that since Abby could communicate with Sekhmet, she should come, and considering that the authorities could stop them, exploring an archeological site with a child was even better…" replied Craig. "And your mother probably didn't like the idea, and insisted she go at least to the mouth of the well, since she couldn't change your father's mind about leaving Abby with her at the hotel. She did the same thing at home, remember? She couldn't convince him to stay, so she made him take her and Abby to Egypt."

Exhausted, there was no more room left for thoughts or feelings. They finally went to bed, but Bailey's mind refused to turn off. When she did fall asleep, she was greeted by the same tall woman in the gold mask, but this time she heard the same words that Abby just relayed to her: *two people will begin the end, your enemy is here.* Bailey bolted upright, almost bumping heads with Craig. He was bent over her bed, his arms on her shoulders and his face, framed by the long black hair, concerned.

"Are you OK? You were screaming, I tried to wake you."

Bailey did not remember herself screaming, but as she swallowed, she realized that her throat was sore. "I just had a dream... I saw Sekhmet..."

"Did she say anything?"

"She said the same thing that Abby told me – two people and the enemy... I'm so tired! My mind probably made up a story about it, with Sekhmet and everything."

"What if this was a message?" Craig's eyes were serious.

"Yeah, exactly the same one! Sekhmet must not be very imaginative if she can't come up with anything else," smiled Bailey, still feeling silly for screaming.

*   *   *

In the morning Simon arrived, followed by Sahed and Axil, and announced that he was ready – they should try tonight. There was a nervous silence in the room as the magnitude of the enterprise sank in. They were going to break human laws in the hopes of following the message of a star-god. Yet no one doubted that this was the right course of action. The déjà vu feeling returned, signifying they were on track.

Axil borrowed a taxi from a friend in town and got himself counterfeit cab papers and a half dozen license plates. The plan was that Axil would pick up Bailey and Craig and drive them away from the hotel. Simon would follow them in another taxi and "take care" of the surveillance team – Bailey was afraid to ask how. Axil was to follow a complex route of turns and lane changes for the entire day, until Simon was sure they weren't being watched. Then Axil would change license plates, Simon would join Bailey and Craig in Axil's taxi, and together they would drive to the site of the well. Sahed would join them just before midnight. Axil would wait for them in the cab.

In the middle of the Giza desert, under the starry night sky, stood two armed and uniformed men, smoking cigarettes and talking quietly. They looked bored. In the far distance by a broken-down wall sat four other soldiers, their machine guns resting on a bench. Their cautious laughter could be heard between the slaps of the cards on the box between them, serving as a table. None of them was looking around.

It was amazing: here they were, hiding in the desert behind a derelict building and in front of a wire fence, just one short jaunt away from their target. Simon motioned everyone to be quiet and to get low to the ground. In a few moments a small sound penetrated the air – a barely audible beeping. One of the two men said something into his radio, and they began to walk away from the fence.

Simon approached the fence with wire cutters.

"They are exchanging positions," he clarified, bending the loosened wires. "In. Now!" he commanded quietly, and soon they were all crouching next to some large granite stones. Bailey touched the rough edges of the rock with her fingers.

"It was meant to be a statue, but it broke and they left the pieces here," whispered Sahed, watching her hand.

The unfortunate statue lay half buried in the sand, away from the path of the soldiers. Two of the men who had been playing cards were now approaching the position by the fence, red cigarette dots accompanied them.

"Now we wait," stated Simon. "They will soon get bored."

In about half an hour Simon must have thought the soldiers were sufficiently bored, because he led everyone farther into the enclosure. To Bailey's surprise there was another structure in the distance – part of a stone wall. She had not seen it at all in the darkness. They hid behind it, and as soon as they did the beeps began again and the soldiers wandered off slowly along the fence.

"Now!" whispered Simon, disappearing into the darkness. There was a new moon, and it gave limited illumination. Following his shape, Bailey, Craig and Sahed sprinted ahead. In less than a minute they were crouching next to a large granite rock – probably the other end of the unfortunate statue. They could hear the hum of a generator somewhere nearby.

"This is the building with the well inside," pointed Sahed.

Simon motioned for everyone to remain hidden. Like a shadow he disappeared in the direction of the sound. Another half an hour passed and Bailey realized that she had never entertained the idea that something might happen to Simon. Now that there was no sight of him, she suddenly felt seriously worried.

As if to relieve her worry, Simon silently appeared from the darkness.

"They had a live wire wrapped around the structure and the door's metal, so anyone who attempted entry would be toast. Simple but effective. These guys aren't playing... But for some reason the contact was off on the door... we'll just have to step over the wire. Let's go."

In a few seconds all four were inside the small structure. It was made of cement blocks with one window covered by metal bars, and was obviously a recent addition. There was a square, wooden box on the ground, aged and dusty, with a rusty metal frame. The frame had a metal grill, in similar condition, bolted onto it, and the grill was fastened with a large chain and a padlock. Sahed slipped a pair of wire cutters from his bag. He had been expecting the lock. Together, he and Simon worked to cut the chain. They took care to sever it at the end farthest from the lock, so that afterwards they could pull the ends of the chain back, preserving the look of an uncut chain and unopened lock.

Simon turned on a tiny flashlight. The chain gave way and he lay it down, slowly pushing the heavy grill. It was noisy work – the metal was old and rusted, and had probably not been opened for years. Then, just as Simon pulled out a small can of oil to grease the hinges, the gate quietly swung open. Surprised, he focused his flashlight on the hinges. There were oil stains on them.

"Interesting... They keep it oiled so it doesn't seize up on them..."

All four stared into the darkness – they were at the mouth of the well. Simon quickly distributed leather belts, linked the three of them together with rope, and attached the end of the rope by carabiner to the metal frame. It was rusty, but looked solid enough to hold their combined weight. Sahed took the flashlight and stepped onto an old wooden ladder. Craig hurried after him. With one last glance at Simon, Bailey joined the men. Closing the metal grill after them, Simon parked himself on the inside of the little structure. There were no electric lights outside; in his black clothes he visually merged with the wall.

The well was five or six feet in diameter, and made of large stones precisely cut and fit together. Unexpectedly, the air inside it was warm and humid, and it got progressively hotter as they descended. Bailey carefully placed her feet and hands on the ladder, unsure of its stability. She was grateful for Simon's foresight. He was waiting for them to give him a signal that all was well, and then he would pull up the rope. Or, if nothing happened when they were down there, they would just climb right back up.

"There are footprints here," whispered Sahed in surprise.

"What do you mean? Someone has been here *recently*?" whispered Bailey in response.

"It appears so..." Sahed carefully placed his foot on the next rung. The dust on the rungs was old, but footprint smudges were clearly visible.

"Something must be wrong," said Bailey, embarrassed by her own fear. "Maybe we should go back."

"We've gotten this far, Bailey, now is not the time to turn back!" whispered Craig passionately, and they continued their climb down the old wooden ladder.

CHAPTER SEVEN

Over five thousand years ago
The Multidimensional Space of the Solar Council

Agartha, a space between slow matter and fast energy, deep inside the Earth and yet beyond it. Filled with iridescent light, a Crystalline Sphere – a place for the meetings of the Solar Council – is alive with conscious resonance, nevertheless the silence is all-penetrating.

The Solar Council is about to begin its meeting. It is a special meeting, much like the one they had a very long time ago, at the beginning of the material Experiment. Many thousands of years have passed on Earth, but in this Crystalline Sphere time is irrelevant – there is only eternity. Council members view the Experiment from inside this place, where they are capable of witnessing any timeline.

The thirty-two beings from the Sirius star are welcomed by the conscious entity of Earth. They have been her guests for centuries now, sleeping deep inside her body. Their dreams have guided the Experiment. Here, on Earth, they were able to create an ovum, an egg to contain new life. This life was given to one of the Earth's new species, humans. The humans' matter-body is made of the Earth, their finer energy bodies are constructed in ingenious detail by many conscious entities, but the link between the matter and energy, the etheric form itself, is given to them by the Sirian thirty-two. In essence they are a merger of Earth and Sirius. They have been given the means to awaken and join the galactic multidimensional family – but in the end the process is up to them.

Despite the multidimensional tear which their first visit caused, three times entities from the Sirius star came to visit the humans, to

158

support them in their development, to guide them and to love them. Even though the tear was sealed long ago, it affected human evolution more than anyone supposed it might. It set the children of Earth on a traitorous path. They fell many times, forgetting their connection to the galactic family, but always they managed to get up again and start walking, always their sleep has been temporary.

This meeting is pivotal. Humans have vibrationally fallen again, but this time their remembering is being delayed indefinitely; the effects of the tear have now caught up with them. Action has to be taken to support their awakening, but there are no timelines available from which to choose. It is assumed that this might be the end of the Experiment – humans will not wake up again.

It is time for reassessment. But no matter how many timelines are scanned, no solution is found, and the end of the Experiment is proposed – perhaps it is best to complete this one and review the knowledge gained from it. Shiny orbs one by one change shape into a unique form, each a separate being expressing their will. A consensus seems to be reached – opalescent orbs begin to pulse in unison. Nearly the entire space is engulfed in rhythmic resonance…

But then there is one different note – a red-orange glow with a completely different rhythm has appeared and is moving to the center of the space. Soon the bright, fiery sphere changes into a large golden cat. But not all members of the Council see this cat; some see a humanoid figure. There is a moment of confusion, until the fiery one introduces herself: she is Sekhmet, the Lover of Truth, the Detester of Untruth. The bright pulsing stops and the space opens for Sekhmet to express her will.

Securing a telepathic connection with the space, Sekhmet reveals her passion: fiery flames, orange fog, blue freedom, and the black-red pain of entrapment. Like a kaleidoscope she spins all her experiences, showing the Council that this Experiment cannot be allowed to die; it has to be completed. The children of Earth had at one time arrived at a very high level of truth, following their innate capacity, but then they forgot… Forgot everything! If only they remember their Light Body breath, they will awaken, and the Experiment will be completed correctly – their biology will be modified by their advancing consciousness. It will bring the children of Earth to the next level of their existence, freeing them from the confines of the Experiment itself. This is a very high honor, rarely achieved by any species, and Sekhmet is sure they can do it.

As her fiery sphere pulses, her golden cat roars while her person's eyes glow. She herself can feel the red blaze in her amber eyes.

The rhythm of her fire is convincing – more and more opalescent orbs begin to have a reddish tint, matching her pulse. The impossible has just occurred – one being has changed the entire Council's decision.

As the room proceeds to resonate with Sekhmet, the red-orange glow radiates through the Crystalline Sphere of the Council, announcing to all Agartha that something incredible is taking place.

Now the question is how to help people remember…

And so the Solar Council, the Earth, and the thirty-two contemplate, looking through all the feasible scenarios, all the trajectories so that the impossible might be achieved. A solution is proposed: if no existent timeline is available then they must create a new timeline. The change will have to generate gravity and be so drastic and obvious that time itself will naturally want to flow into it, attracting the expansion of space, and hopefully, awakening humans.

Can this be done? Can a new timeline be so strong that it will change the course of human history?

It is understood that even if the timeline can be artificially created, it will probably collapse as soon as it is activated. But exactly how soon would it collapse? How much time, in human terms, is necessary to anchor the energy and change the history of the human race? Will a thousand years in the new timeline be enough? A hundred years? Ten years?

The debate goes on, entities flashing in and out of form, telepathically relaying to the rest their wisdom. Finally a decision is made: as long as the timeline is highly visible, and is maintained for at least fifteen Earth years, it will be enough to infuse human consciousness with the required upgraded codes. After that its collapse is fully anticipated; the artificially created timeline will be no more. It may even be erased from human memory. But its mission will have been accomplished, and human beings will be walking again, if ever so slowly…

Now that the outline, the direction, has been created, someone or something must anchor it in form. The Solar Council is aware of the anchor quandary. Timelines are created multidimensionally, but in order to make a difference on material Earth, there has to be an anchor, a form on the planet, to hold the timeline in place. This form can be stationary, like a temple built on the site of a vortex. But this version is soon dismissed, since there are not enough conscious humans to desire such a project, nor have expertize to build it. It has to be a person, or a group of people. But this version of anchor is even more complicated than the previous one. A person who has the power to anchor the timeline has to have the energy range to match what she or he is anchoring, and the absence of humans who have such wide ranging multidimensional access is the reason for generating a new timeline in the first place...

There are no more forms or flashes – only silence as the luminescent orbs float in space. The Council members are experiencing the weight of their current predicament. Sekhmet, the original thirty-two, and other Sirian entities request to enter the anchoring matter-body – but their requests are quickly rejected – the energy range available on Earth at the current moment in time is too narrow for any of them to fit into.

If the anchor cannot be a structure, and it cannot be the non-material multidimensional entity, how can this be done? The lights begin to pulse, all in different rhythms – the entities are not in agreement. Suddenly there is a strong emerald-colored surge originated by the Earth entity herself, and others begin to match it, one by one.

A decision is finally made. Not many, but only one entity will enter the Earth's realm. It is a Sirian entity that will take on a human body. The genetic matrix of a human form will be modified to hold the Sirian blueprint, making this being capable of the multidimensional access required to anchor the artificial timeline. It is seen that the life of this hybrid will be extremely difficult, for he or she will have to break apart all that is already built, because what is built will only lead to a further fall. Additionally, that being, because of its human component, will not be able to have full access to multidimensional knowledge, although the Sirian element will know what to do.

It is decided to place that being into the land where it all began, in Egypt. The entity would have had an easier time seeing the truth in a female body, but considering the current culture it is decided to place the entity into a male body instead. He will be able to have more social influence in a male form.

The Crystalline Sphere is now shimmering, as the Solar Council entities are coming in and out of form, desiring involvement. It is understood that this Sirian-human hybrid will require a lot of help. Someone will need to awaken in him his Sirian heritage. Someone will need to support him on his path.

The plan for a new and short, but powerful timeline is complete, all the roles are distributed among the members and the visiting entities. Without this artificially inserted timeline's fleeting existence the human race will not wake up and the Experiment would be lost permanently. And even though humans might not recollect this brief timeline after the restoration of the Experiment path, it is of paramount importance to the Solar Council and all other entities involved.

The lights pulsate in unison – the design for human awakening is complete. The Earth's Experiment is the recombined code of a Universal compressed holographic fractal, and the total resolution of cosmic expansion into contraction, its next breath, fully depends on what occurs on Earth.

CHAPTER EIGHT

Current time
Giza Plateau, Egypt

Mahmoud released the door knob. He had not moved since the Westerners left. It was astonishing – he could not believe that woman had asked him for permission to visit the site. "There is nothing of interest to tourists there. She *must* know about the well!" He desperately tried to collect his thoughts. "This means she might try the same thing, might try to go there like her father did... If she tries anything...There is round-the-clock security, and it won't be easy for the woman to go around them, unless of course she has some hidden talents I am unaware of... Either way, she will need a few days to prepare. She is a woman and she is not trained to do this sort of thing, neither is the boy. Maybe she won't dare... Oh, who am I kidding, she is sure to try! I wonder how she will do it? Walk there at night, chat up the guards, bribe them... Since she tried to bribe me she must have the money. Oh, this is bad! I need to re-enforce security, make it hard for her to even try."

The drive home was uneventful. Mahmoud pulled into the garage and went directly from there to his study. En route to his favorite chair he picked up an almost empty bottle of scotch. "No, I shouldn't..." he thought vacantly, as he poured himself a drink. He fell asleep in his armchair, drink untouched, and was jolted awake by a ringing phone. It was his wife calling from Europe, checking to make sure everything was OK, wanting to tell him all about their son-in-law's speech at a conference, and how happy their daughter was, and that they got themselves a new poodle. He undressed, barely listening to his wife's voice filling the room through the speakerphone. Finally she came to the end of what she had to say; he could cease being polite. He wished her well – she had always been good to him. After a quick shower Mahmoud crawled into bed.

Heavy sleep overtook him, but it was not restful. He was enveloped in a thick cloak of darkness and he could not find his way out of it. He felt the presence of someone next to him, someone large and powerful, and terrifying. He struggled to move away from that presence, but his legs were like logs and he could not move. He heard a voice in his head, the same voice he feared – it was Sekhmet. She was saying *you are the beginning of the end*; she said it over and over, until Mahmoud finally woke up, drenched in sweat.

The next morning he was not himself. He went through the motions of showering and dressing, and he ate his breakfast, an elaborate affair prepared by a maid, but he did not notice the taste. Returning to his study, he called the Shenu line. Feeling hypnotized by the magnitude of what he was about to do, he reported that all was well, everything was under control. It was a lie, but how could he say otherwise? He couldn't bring himself to reconvene the group, to tell them the truth about his personal failure – their anger might just result in his death! All he had to do was stop Bailey from entering the well and there would be nothing to report. Preventing her entry would resolve it all, wouldn't it? He turned over in his mind the idea of calling the site's security, to alert them to the possibility of a break in. But why make such a big deal of it? He could stop a woman by himself.

He stayed home and searched his encrypted computer files, diving into the information he had copied from the vaults of the Shenu, for any mention of the "end," or even the beginning... Yes, it was time. He was finally ready to know the meaning of Sekhmet's words – he had run from this message long enough. Morning changed into day and day became evening. He searched first in likely places, then everywhere, every folder, every file: nothing. He felt defeated. Now what? He could not lose face in front of the Shenu! In desperation a new decision was made – he would go and explore the well himself. "Am I mad?... Perhaps being at the location will help me remember something." He had sworn to himself that he would never set foot in that well again – it had brought him the most terrifying experience of his life. Yet now, sitting in front of his computer, his eyes tired from staring at the screen for hours, he knew he had to go back there. His mind tried to come up with a few arguments against the idea, but was too tired to fight the decision with logic.

CHAPTER EIGHT

*   *   *

Mahmoud approached the guards at the site' gate. The one in charge instantly recognized him, and Mahmoud quickly came up with an explanation for his presence there: a measurement is required, it is urgent, that is why he came at night, he is sure that others will screw it up, so he needs to do it himself.

"Now!" barked Mahmoud Halib.

The guard hurried off in the direction of the generator to deactivate the current protecting the fence. He returned in just a minute, holding a key in his hand.

"Reactivate all of the electric fence again, just keep the little building's door turned off for me."

The guard was surprised, but he took the hundred dollar bill from the head of the Council of Antiquities, shut his mouth, and stepped aside.

Taking the key from the guard, Mahmoud walked to the structure. It was far from the guard station, about a five minute walk. The electric contact was off the door, and Mahmoud stepped over the live wire. Everything was as they had left it the last time. He took out a small flashlight and set it on a rock while he undid the chain and opened the padlock. The metal grill was heavy. He felt a chill run down his spine. "What am I doing? I should never have come back here!" But even as his mind told him to turn back, he climbed onto the wooden ladder. He was soon reminded that he was not as young as he once was: his back muscles ached from the strain as he closed the grill over his head – not an easy task while standing on the ladder.

Wrapping the chain through the bars of the grill, he pulled and secured it, then turned the key in the lock. He reasoned with himself that he must do this, he must lock it, but now, feeling trapped, he was not sure if it was so smart. His original thinking was that if the woman came to the site, the entrance would be locked and the guards would discover they did not have the key – because, of course, they had given it to him. They would assume that he had left and forgotten to return the key, and they would take the woman's bribe but give her no entry.

Standing on the dusty ladder, Mahmoud's heart pounded – he had just cut off the only escape he had – the metal grill was shut over his head.

"Stop it!" he snapped at himself. "You have climbed into enough tombs in your life; this is just another damn tomb!" His gut sank as he realized it just might be *his* tomb if he was not careful. As he slowly

165

climbed down, he became more and more certain that it was all a bad idea. His fingers found it difficult to grip the ladder and he began to feel terrified. It was a long climb down, very long…

He willed himself to keep going, to breathe. When half an hour later Mahmoud finally reached the bottom, he was exhausted and almost mad with fear. It was very hot and moist down there; he unbuttoned the neck of his shirt then ripped the whole front open, but it didn't help to cool him. Perspiring heavily and breathing with difficulty, his mind told him that it was just the lack of oxygen in the well and exhaustion from the climb and that he would soon adjust and feel fine. But he did not feel fine; he was near panic, barely able to get a hold of himself.

Shining his flashlight around, he took in the room. It was exactly as he remembered. It was a large, almost circular, space with small niches in the walls. Opposite to where he stood by the ladder was a doorway into a smaller room with a domed ceiling. Inside that room the beam of his flashlight could pick out a cube with a pyramid resting on top of it. Mahmoud didn't want to go any closer to that room, he remembered what happened in there before.

When he came here with the two other Shenu, they showed him that room and told him that entry was impossible. They told him the doorway had a key, but traitors had given it away. The Shenu had been betrayed. Akhenaten, the heretic pharaoh, had the key, and he had left it on the other side of the gate. Without the key anyone who went through the doorway would die. Mahmoud did not see any gadgetry, no scanner or laser embedded in the doorway, but he had no reason to doubt the other Shenu. They had incidents before, so they knew.

Besides, when the – he was not sure what to call it – incident happened the last time, he was sure it had nothing to do with the doorway. It was the pyramid. That pyramid on top of the cube pedestal looked like it was made of stone, but then it had glowed bright white. He had not realized it was a pyramid then, but he remembered afterwards. There was a very bright light and a piercing sound, and the two men screamed and fell over, covering their ears. Mahmoud did too, but then the sound stopped, as if he had gone deaf. He tried to see, but it was too bright. Then the brightness began to subside and Mahmoud could see the doorway to the smaller room – the light was definitely coming from there. He could also see the two men lying on the ground, dead. He was so terrified, he couldn't think. And although he was trying to say something, to call the other men's names, he still heard no sounds at all.

He shuddered again, looking in the direction of the doorway, but not moving an inch closer. Mentally locating the spot on the floor where he had lain, he shone the light on it, to the right of the doorway. The other two men had been in the middle of the room. And then he had seen her, Sekhmet. It was the most terrifying moment imaginable. She was transparent, but she was real, and she had stood there, and she had spoken inside his head.

His breath erratic, Mahmoud wiped the sweat off his face. This was a hard memory to deal with. When she disappeared, so did the light. The last thing Mahmoud remembered was the pyramid in the smaller room, glowing as if it retained remnants of light. Then everything went dark; he had finally fainted.

The men, it turned out, were not dead. Hours passed before he and the others regained consciousness. All three had horrible headaches and felt sick to their stomachs. The other men looked at Mahmoud and realized he had spoken with Sekhmet, because his hair had turned gray.

Mahmoud pressed a little closer to the ladder, and ran his fingers through his hair.

Then he heard a sound. His heart began pounding so hard he thought he would have a heart attack. The sound was of squeaking metal. Still inside his fear, he didn't at first realize where it came from, and stared at the doorway on the other side of the room. His flashlight revealed nothing, but it had to be coming from somewhere.

Very slowly he took a breath, and his heart hammered a little less loudly inside his head. He inhaled and exhaled silently, afraid to make a noise himself, and remained rooted to the spot right next to the ladder, the spot where he had been standing since he got there. What was that sound?

And then he heard some other sounds, very faint and muffled. Thinking a little clearer this time, he soon located the direction from where they were coming and his face turned white. It became clear that what he had heard first was the sound of the metal grill opening all the way up at the surface, and that what he was hearing now were whispers, voices… "Why is the guard looking for me? I haven't been here that long, and anyway I didn't give him any time limit…"

The realization went through Mahmoud like lightning – it wasn't the guards, it was that woman! Bailey Rixson had somehow managed to make it to the well!

Holding his breath now, Mahmoud listened. The acoustics were distorted and no words could be deciphered, and he was very far away from the top. Hoping that she, and probably that overgrown boy, had come to simply look at the well, he listened closely. He heard them pulling on the chain to see if it was solid. "It is solid, and it is locked," now Mahmoud was glad he had locked the grill. "This will prevent her from even thinking of climbing down."

Just then he heard another sound and saw a faint flash of light. The light was so faint he was almost not sure he had seen it, but the sound repeated itself – it was wood squeaking!

"Oh, Allah! Are those two climbing down?"

He couldn't digest it, it was too preposterous. They must have looked into the well with their flashlight and seen how deep it was. There was no way they would attempt to climb in!

But in the next few minutes he heard more sounds, this time the unmistakable creaking of wooden steps. Mahmoud swore under his breath. Fully realizing what was happening, he did the only thing he could do – he took out his gun. At home he had thought of taking it for protection, an odd thought and an illegal one at that, but after some consideration Mahmoud had decided that the power that came from having a gun was well worth the extra weight in his bag. What he was going to do with that gun, he was not sure. He could shoot, of course, he had taken basic training. But shoot whom? Sekhmet? Because it was her that he might really need protection from; the others were irrelevant. But what good would a gun do against Sekhmet? Mahmoud had to remind himself that he was doing her bidding and so she would not hurt him. That reasoning did not lessen his feelings of dread, and so the gun was removed from the locked drawer of his desk and placed in his bag.

There were more sounds now, occasionally accompanied by a faint beam of light dully illuminating the falling dust. Mahmoud listened silently, mentally trying to generate a plan. His head was not cooperating...

*   *   *

Sahed kept quiet, focusing on the climb. Craig, on the other hand, had to use all his will to not talk. The environment of the well was somehow familiar to him. It was the kind of place you wouldn't want to wake up in, because you would feel like you didn't know how you got there... Yet this was exactly the feeling Craig had, like he had been in this place before but had no memory of how he had arrived. And there was that damned déjà vu again! He was feeling trapped in the enclosed space, so he focused on the excitement of what he was attempting. He was going to see this ancient place, to "open the gate," to really do the "shaman thing" – he was not sure what that meant, but Simon-the-cat had said Sekhmet had chosen him for this mission because he was a shaman, so acting like a shaman was what he looked forward to. Craig had no idea what the opening of the gate actually meant. In his mind he fully believed that there was a gate and that it could be opened, but he did not know what this process involved. He thought of it as a metaphor for transformation, something that a person would feel because they were so far under the ground, perhaps a solicited vision similar to a quest. But at the same time, the anxiety he was experiencing was strong enough, and he knew it was as much about claustrophobia as the waking dream he kept having. The dream... Craig remembered very well how real it felt. It was the same dream or vision that he always had, yet somehow here it almost made sense. Craig could not quite put his finger on it. "Why am I thinking about it now? This is not the time, we are going to open this thing and hopefully I will know what to do... Simon seems to think I know..." He struggled to keep his hold on the ladder. The images of the dream were etched in his memory, and at this moment they were beginning to flood his conscious mind. "No! Not now!" he screamed inside his head. He wasn't about to faint in the middle of the climb – not only would it be super embarrassing, it would also put Sahed and Bailey in danger, since they were all connected to the same rope!

Craig bumped his foot on Sahed's turban. "Sorry! I wasn't watching..."

"We are almost there," came Sahed's whisper.

In a few moments Sahed was standing on the ground.

Such excitement was running through Craig's mind and body that he did not sense the man until he was standing in front of him. It was the same man he and Bailey had met earlier in the Council of Antiquities building, the man who had refused to give them access to this very site. Mr. Halib was here, many feet underground, pointing a gun at Craig and Sahed.

"Whoa..." was all Craig could say. This was exactly the type of thing his spirit guide would keep him in the dark about, just so he could see Craig's face when it happened! The Cat had known this would happen, he had to! "So, if he knew and didn't tell me, there must be a reason why I had to not know," reasoned Craig. "...Unless he was just being mean... Nah!" He dismissed the thought and was brought out of his conversation with himself by Bailey's annoyed and tired voice from above him. She was on the last rungs of the ladder.

"Craig, shine the light over here, will you, please." When nobody answered and the light did not come to her, she finally descended to the ground and turned around. And faced the same gun.

"Mr. Halib," started Craig. "What are you doing in here?"

"I was going to ask you the same thing. You are trespassing on Egyptian property!"

"And you, of course, are here to protect it, personally," suggested Sahed.

"Shut up, you old fool! I will have you thrown in prison! How much did they pay you to break the law? To be their guide?"

Mahmoud sounded in control. Craig could tell that this was not true; Mr. Halib was not in control as he wanted them to believe, and his shaking hand proved it. "He thinks Sahed is just a guide, so he has no idea that we know there is a gate in here... Does he himself know?" Craig could not stop wondering; thankfully he wondered silently. He wished Simon-the-cat was here.

No one said a word and the silence began to feel uncomfortable. The man held his gun in his right hand and the flashlight in his left, and he did not look stable. "Can we overpower him? Take the gun from him?" Craig immediately rejected the idea. "It's too dangerous, he could shoot us in here and no one would find the bodies for years! He has nothing to lose."

The man with the gun stood there, staring at them. He was sweating and his eyes looked a bit crazy to Craig. "It is so hot in here..." That was Bailey's quiet non sequitur he was hearing. All Craig knew was that they should not leave. If they tried to leave, this man would either shoot them as they made their attempt – and it was a very long climb up! – or he would have them killed later. Either way, they wouldn't make it out of Egypt. So what were their other options? "Pretend we are dumb tourists, same line we were selling him earlier – he obviously bought it."

And so Craig started talking: "We are very sorry, mister Halib, but we were just so curious about this place!" he said, inching away from the ladder and the well, farther into the cavernous room. "What are you doing?" whispered Bailey, terrified, as she saw him moving deeper in. As Craig slowly moved away, Sahed shone his flashlight around in a nonthreatening way, gliding the beam on the floor, but Craig knew he was looking for others in the room besides the man with the gun. There was no one else! Craig was amazed at how large the room was – it was a huge round hall, not the small "bottom of a well" one would expect. The walls were carved out of stone, as was the floor, and the space was dusty, hot, and very humid. It also smelled bad, like old sweat or urine. The air was stale; obviously it did not circulate much in the well. Sahed's beam found the doorway and Craig noticed it. Forgetting the gun, his natural curiosity made him take a step towards the doorway.

"Don't move or I *will* kill you. You have no business being here in the first place…" Craig did not hear the end of Mahmoud's statement, because his eyes were riveted to the doorway. Beyond it, the beam of Sahed's flashlight had revealed a stone cube with a pyramid on top of it.

"No, not again," thought Craig, as his whole body suddenly became very cold. He could not take his eyes off the cube with the pyramid – it was his waking dream, right there in front of him. The next moment the room got brighter and brighter, and the pyramid began to glow. "Am I dreaming? Is this really happening?" His own questions dragged him out of the beginnings of a vision. Disoriented, he stared around. The room was still dark, nothing was glowing. His eyes wandered back to the doorway and the pyramid, and the brightness and the glowing restarted… Somewhere in there was Simon-the-cat, sitting by the cube on the floor, and he was saying something. "Why is he here? This is not a quest…"

Opening his eyes, Craig saw Bailey's concerned face right over his, with a very bright light shining onto them both. He turned his head, realizing he was lying down. "Where is Simon? Is he gone?" Craig looked up at the man with the gun, who was confused and not so much in control as he had hoped to be. "What happened?" thought Craig. He felt deaf; he heard no sounds at all, he could see that the man with the gun was saying something, even yelling, but he heard nothing. Bailey's face was staring right at him, her eyes intense and pleading. As a few more moments passed, Craig's sense of reality returned to the current moment. His fainting had confused the hell out of Mr. Halib. He didn't know how to handle this – no doubt he had expected very different behavior. Craig's head hurt very badly, and he shook it gently in an attempt to rid himself of the pain. It helped him to focus, but it didn't kill the pain. Sounds suddenly assaulted him all at once – the man with the gun was yelling at Sahed in Arabic, and Sahed was saying something back to him.

Getting up, Craig felt the floor dip low to the right, so much that he almost slid over. "No, I'm just dizzy, the floor is fine," he told himself. He managed to stand up and, holding on to a wall, began to walk towards the doorway. Bailey, holding his arm, ended up following him. They were barely five feet from the doorway when the man with the gun noticed. He spun around, waving the weapon and screaming: "Get away from there!!" There was a warning in his voice, but somehow Craig knew that this man was at least as scared as he was angry and threatening.

"You, come over here!" the man commanded, pointing his gun at Craig. Craig walked back to the specified spot by the ladder, and sat down. He was too tired and hurt to be afraid of the man. His body

171

slouched by the wall, Craig suddenly heard the Cat's voice: "So, what do you think of the doorway? Not the gate you had in mind, eh?" Simon-the-cat was close by, he was sure of it. Craig looked around...

It all happened so fast, Craig barely noticed. Maybe it was because his head was pounding, or maybe it was for some other reason, but the speed of events seemed really erratic – first too slow, then too fast, alternating randomly... Somehow Sahed grabbed Bailey's arm and propelled her to the doorway, so fast she almost fell over. For a moment they were both out of the beam of the flashlight, completely concealed by the darkness. Sahed's voice whispered something loudly to Bailey, but Craig could not understand the words. The next second the beam of light caught them – Mr. Halib had spun around, searching for them. Bailey's shining eyes, stared intently at Craig, as if she was saying something to him, then she spun around too. The beam of light lost her again, and it swerved around to find her.

"The doorway *is* the gate! That is what Simon meant!" Suddenly it all became clear to Craig. Then he realized what was happening around him – Sahed had made a mad dash for the doorway to the room with the pyramid. He was thinking that Craig had passed out and couldn't come anyway, but he and Bailey still had a chance to make it to the doorway. If they could open the gate, Mr. Halib would probably just freak out, or more likely pass out – records of previous attempts stated that anyone who was not the "right person" would lose consciousness. So since Craig was already unconscious, or so Sahed thought, opening the gate might be a way to knock out Mr. Halib. "How clever," smiled Craig, still unsure of what was real to everyone and what was real only to him.

But then nothing happened. Instead, the beam of Mahmoud's flashlight finally found Sahed and Bailey – they were standing in front of the doorway. To Craig's surprise Mr. Halib said nothing. Craig could barely see the man's face, and it was clear that he was smiling – an evil smile, as if he had now gained power. Craig's stomach spasmed: "This is wrong." The smirk on Mahmoud's face was important; it signified that something else was going on. His expression was more devious than someone who had simply trapped two defenseless people on the other side of a dark room. They were certainly trapped there and Mahmoud had an obvious advantage – the gun. Yet he looked like he had understood something that was much more powerful than the weapon he held in his hand.

The next thing that happened was even more bizarre. Sahed grabbed Bailey's arm and pulled her to the doorway – as it was they stood only inches away from it. "They will open the gate!" thought Craig excitedly. But nothing happened. Instead, in the long beam of light that stretched across the dusty room, Craig saw both Bailey and Sahed collapse onto the ground, their legs folding beneath them. Craig was not sure what he had expected, but it was definitely not this. Sahed had mentioned that entering the room could kill you if you were not "the right one." When they had all descended into this large round hall and no one died, Craig thought that Sahed had been speaking metaphorically. But now Craig thought: "Oh, my god! Are they dead?"

He had actually spoken the words out loud, and Mahmoud spun toward him as if he had just remembered that Craig was there and realized that his back was exposed. Before Craig could react, he was hit on the side of his head with the gun. Craig's head snapped back and hit the wall. Then there was nothing but blackness, but it felt good, almost comforting.

Simon-the-Cat came up and rubbed his cheek on Craig's neck. Opening his eyes, Craig was confused for a moment. Then, moaning, he remembered the man and the gun.

"You might want to stay conscious, you can do more that way," purred Simon.

"Am I inside a vision quest? This is the place you brought me the last time and before that..."

"Well, you are here, and yes, you are there too."

"Ehh... Are they dead?"

"I don't think so. It would mean so many changes! They have to walk their path, they can't leave now, that would be irresponsible!"

"But they didn't do this to themselves, it's the gate..."

"And who tried to open it?"

"Oh... you know about the gate?"

"It is a window, like a hole between here and somewhere else. There are many somewhere elses, you know. There is more than one of everything."

"What? I thought this went back to Sekhmet, wherever she is."

"Yes, that too. You'll find out."

"You mean we will open it?" Craig suddenly felt awake.

"Well, that is up to you, I have no idea." Simon began to walk away.

"Wait, where are you going? What about the gate?"

"She needs your help."

"Who? Bailey? Sekhmet?"

"Obviously the woman can figure out her own way back to the land of the living," noted the spirit guide sarcastically. "I meant Sekhmet.

She tried to be helpful herself, but people kept messing up. What's a girl to do?" Simon returned and was now lying on his left side next to Craig. "You know what her problem is?" – not waiting for an answer, he continued, "she is too independent. She never delegates. Everything is her job. But she couldn't do it, and mind you not due to her shortcomings, there were no trained personnel, so to speak, to do the job."

"What are you taking about, what trained personnel? What job?"

"You are the shaman, right? Well, figure it out then!" snapped Simon in response. He licked his curled paw, and said, "The breathing, remember?"

Craig didn't really remember. It was something about "breathing life" – both his spirit guide and Sahed had mentioned it. Well, both of them had said that Sekhmet talked about it.

"It's time for you to go back." Simon sat up.

"But I have more questions…" There was nothing Craig could do. He felt himself opening his eyes again…

His head hurt even more, but now at least only in two places. He remembered being hit, and there was a salty taste in his mouth. Craig struggled to think of salty things he might have eaten… and soon realized he was tasting blood. Was there blood on his face? Did it somehow get into his mouth, or did he bite his tongue? It was reassuring to feel the localized pain – he could deal with that. He was still in the same room, by the wall. In the darkness Simon-the-Cat was nowhere to be found.

*   *   *

"This should have worked," mumbled Sahed. "This is the right time, the beginning of the end…"

"What did you say?" Mahmoud's loud whisper sounded menacing and at the same time disoriented.

Sahed stared defiantly at Mahmoud. Now both were silent.

A million calculations flew through Mahmoud's head, his eyes jumping back and forth between Sahed and Bailey, until they finally stopped at Bailey's neck. He noticed the gold locket for the first time – it had fallen out of her shirt and now hung over her clothes.

"Give that to me!" he demanded, his hand extended.

Bailey was terrified and near tears. She had failed miserably in everything, in her attempt to find the truth about her parents, in helping her sister, even in holding onto the only thing that connected her to her father. The thing that seemed to have some huge importance to so many people... Terrified and defeated, she extended a shaking hand with the locket to the man with the gun.

He stared at it – it was the locket of Sekhmet. There could be no mistake. He had studied the records for years. He could not conceive of it – it was simply not possible! The words he had just heard from the old guide, the "beginning of the end"... and now he was holding in his shaking hand the locket of Sekhmet... The puzzle began to come together in his mind, just under the surface of his conscious awareness. He walked toward the doorway as if he was hypnotized, his body already in action, his mind still processing the data. "I am the one who is to open the gate again." His thoughts were odd, revealing themselves one by one to his conscious mind. "The locket that was lost for all these centuries was not lost... somehow it was in the possession of this ignorant woman..." Mahmoud could not grasp the reasoning behind his logic, but he sensed it was sound. "This is what Sekhmet was telling me – I am the one to open the gate. This is her message, I am the one..."

But as Mahmoud, like a zombie, walked into the doorway, his legs buckled and he lost consciousness, falling onto the floor in slow motion.

Craig jumped up, so fast that he almost fell over from dizziness. Scrambling on all fours towards the doorway, he grabbed Mahmoud's gun. Next, together they pulled Mr. Halib away from the doorway. Sahed uncurled Mahmoud's fingers and took the locket back. By silent agreement they used the extra rope that Simon had given them "just in case" to bind the man's feet at the ankles. Then, rolling his heavy body to the side, they bound his hands behind his back. He was still unconscious, but definitely alive.

"Did you see anything? Did something happen?" Craig's questions spilled out as fast as he could think. "When you were knocked out, did you see Sekhmet?"

"No, Craig. It was only the blackness of my own mind." Sahed's voice sounded sad and disappointed. Sahed and Craig looked at each other, then at Bailey. She understood – neither of them knew what it meant to have this gate open, but they wanted to try again.

"Maybe we shouldn't do this," she said. "Didn't you say it could kill us? If it doesn't work..." Nervous and reluctant to try anything, she met the two pairs of expectant eyes and knew she would give in.

Sahed walked to the doorway and stood a foot in front of it. The doorway was a simple opening. The walls were about two feet thick, and there were no signs of a device or technological components, there was only the rock. "We are the ones chosen by the star-gods centuries ago, dear child, we have to do this..."

Bailey put the locket back on her neck and walked up to Sahed. Clasping each other's hands, they stepped closer to the doorway. No one breathed, expecting anything from space exploding to annihilation.

A few seconds elapsed. There was no flash of light or sound, only two bodies yet again slowly collapsing to the floor.

Craig cautiously approached the doorway. His two companions seemed to be alive, just unconscious. Unsure if the black outs might have some kind of cumulative effect, he pulled them away from the gate towards the middle of the room. "If they lie down, they can't fall," he reasoned. He avoided the doorway. Looking through it was dangerous, and Craig did not want to restart his waking dream and end up losing consciousness himself! He looked at Bailey's face and was reassured – blank, it did not reflect pain. She had a pulse, too, a very faint one, but a pulse. Sahed also had a pulse. Craig shone the flashlight in his face and noticed that, unlike Bailey's, it looked like he was in pain, or had been in pain.

Exhausted from pulling the bodies, Craig rubbed his throbbing head. He moved to the wall and sat down – the heat was getting to him, and the walls were cold. Feeling too dizzy and tired to stand up, he crawled to the wall near Mr. Halib. Resting his back on the cool wall, his mind busied itself with silly puzzles in an attempt to prevent itself from shattering: "How can it be this hot, while the walls are so cold? Where is the Cat – he must be hiding somewhere... but there is nothing here to hide behind... unless he is in *that* room..."

"You will regret this..." Mahmoud's hoarse voice came from somewhere behind Craig. Turning his head, Craig pointed the flashlight in the direction of the voice. The man was awake and staring at him. But instead of hatred or anger, there was overt fear in his eyes. Craig knew a lot about fear and he could easily recognize it. "Why is this man afraid? Does he think we will leave him here to die? Probably... Or he knows something, that smirk he had earlier, when he saw Sahed and Bailey by the doorway the first time..."

"You do not know what you are doing!" insisted the man. "How did you get that piece of jewelry? Did you steal it? Who sold it to you?"

Not telling him would not do them any good now. The man would definitely not let the whole thing drop – he would report the locket to the authorities, or take matters into his own hands, and either way they would be in trouble. Obviously they wouldn't leave Mr. Halib here to die. They would climb back up and probably tell the guards that they had seen a man "fall in" or some such story. But this man knew something, and it might be far more important to find out what he knew, than to play dumb.

This was one of those moments when you know you have to stop hiding and start acting. Everything you thought you knew turns out not to be really so, and things are not working out as you had planned. A piece of a puzzle is missing, and the only way to get it is by finding more pieces.

Summoning his courage, Craig spoke. "We didn't steal it. It's a family heirloom; it was given to Bailey by her father."

"Jonathan Rixson *had* it?"

"Whoa! You know about her father? You know his name! How?"

After a brief pause Mahmoud feigned an outrage: "I researched it, what do you think? You think I wouldn't? You came to my office looking to enter a government-restricted archeological area!"

"Why is this place a restricted area?"

"Because it is an archeological project, a dig, and it is dangerous to tourists!"

"The only thing dangerous about this place is you, with a gun."

"I was checking on the progress of an archeological discovery, and I always carry a gun with me!" lied Mahmoud.

*   *   *

"He must be the Shenu…" from the darkness came Sahed's strained voice.

Mahmoud's heart hurt and he felt it might explode out of his chest. Did he hear what he thought he heard? The sacred name of Shenu was spoken by this old Egyptian guide. "He is not a guide…" Sluggishly, the realization crawled into Mahmoud's mind. "He is not a guide at all, he knows the sacred name of the Shenu! Someone betrayed the oath, someone told a relative, or was careless with information…" As Mahmoud examined the ways this old man could have found out about the existence of the Shenu, he went through the members in his mind, one by one. He knew them all. None of them would be so stupid as to reveal even a glimmer of information to an outsider. Yet this old man had just accused Mahmoud of being one of the Shenu!

Mahmoud stared into space, glassy eyed, shocked. Thoughts whirled around in his head until his mind went blank from the pressure. Craig continued: "If Mr. Halib" – the sound of his name cut into Mahmoud's thoughts – "is from the Shenu, he knows about the gate and the key, and he believes he is the right person to open the gate, right?" Craig turned to Mahmoud and again shone the light at him.

Craig's words pained Mahmoud. Pure hatred rose up inside of him – how dare this arrogant American mosquito question him! How dare he know any of this! He is nobody, an insignificant little nothing! He stared at Craig with venom. But even as his eyes confidently bored into Craig, he knew that his hatred was only a defensive posture – there was terror underneath it. The age-old secret was known by this group of people. How far did the knowledge go? How many more were involved? How much of this was his fault?

"You thought the Shenu weren't known outside of your circle," guessed Craig.

Mahmoud swallowed hard and continued to stare.

"Why do you think you are the right person to open the gate? Did Sekhmet talk to you, too?"

Mahmoud felt like he was ready to faint. All the blood drained from his face, again. There was only one question in his mind: "How do they know about Sekhmet?" Gathering all the mental strength he had, he spoke up: "Sekhmet is an ancient goddess of Egypt, she is a myth. If I had talked to her, I would have put myself in a hospital."

"I don't think so!" Craig got on his knees to face Mahmoud. "I think you know very well that she's real, you know because you know people who talked to her, maybe even you yourself talked to her."

"No! You idiots! She does not exist!" Mahmoud yelled out with all the conviction he could muster.

"She talked to me…" Sahed's quiet voice filled the room. "What did she tell you, false Shenu?"

Mahmoud tried to process the information. He needed time to think! Not only do they know about the gate, they know that the locket is the key, and they know about Sekhmet herself being a real goddess… and they had just accused him, Mahmoud, of being part of the *false* Shenu! Why false? What did he mean by false? The Shenu are true to Sekhmet! She talked to him… Mahmoud felt a lump in his throat, the tears welling up. He was so tired. Was Sekhmet toying with him? Did she guide him into a trap for her own entertainment? He swallowed hard again to stifle the tears.

"What I'm saying is that if Sekhmet talked to Mr. Halib here, and he believes he's the right person to open the gate, then maybe it's him and one of you... Bailey maybe?" finished Craig.

Mahmoud held his breath. From what he was gathering, there had to be *two* people to open the gate. Why? If they had the key, they should have been able to open it... But it didn't work. And he is the chosen one, but when he had the key it didn't work either... "Oh, Allah! This young mosquito might be right!" Mahmoud was immediately ashamed of his thought. "He can't be right!"

Then he heard the tired voice of the old guide. "If you are right, it has to be Bailey and this man, she is the right one, not me..."

"No! Why would you think so? It has to be you! You even said Sekhmet talked to *you*. She doesn't talk to me, so it has to be you..." The young woman was babbling, she was scared.

Inside his own thoughts Mahmoud tried to reconcile his previous knowledge with this new reality, when he felt himself moving. Suddenly he realized what was happening – Craig and Sahed were dragging his body across the floor towards the doorway, while Bailey stood and watched.

"You... idiots! You will regret this!" he sputtered, as he understood their goal. They wanted to place him by the doorway, hoping that the presence of the three correct ingredients, the locket, himself, and this insolent woman, would open the gate. "How dare they!" He thrashed around, outraged, but his body was tightly bound, and his protests were getting him nowhere. Would he die in this well?

They propped Mahmoud's body right by the doorway. He felt a curious combination of anger and fear. The old guide was convincing the stubborn woman, and she fought with him. With a minute to reassess the situation, Mahmoud realized that he now knew another piece of the puzzle – these people said Sekhmet told them that there were supposed to be two people. All might not be lost, he might still be the chosen one! It shouldn't be so important; his own life was meaningless next to the Shenu secret being exposed, but he had thought it for so long that his mind circled back to it from every possible angle: he might still be the one.

And if he was the chosen one, he, Mahmoud, would be one of the two people. But – and here was the place Mahmoud's mind stumbled – "The stupid woman, the daughter of the one who had tried, couldn't be the other person!" Mahmoud was not sure why he was so adamant about this. It might be the fact that she was a young woman with no apparent knowledge of Egyptian antiquities; or that she was an American tourist, which was probably more damning.

Now they would find out: The woman seemed to finally make up her mind. Clasping the locket with her fingers, she walked up to the gate.

For a moment nothing happened, though everyone remained conscious. Then there was a sound. The sound built up from inside Mahmoud's head and interpenetrated everything around him. If he had been able to run, he probably would have attempted it, but his legs were bound. Then bright light exploded into the space, so bright that instead of illuminating the room, the light almost blinded him. The fear inside his being completely won over his anger, making him feel paralyzed, like a tiny mouse in front of a cobra. This was almost exactly the experience he had tried for a long time to forget – the time when, after a very bright light he had seen Sekhmet materialize in front of him, a goddess made of transparent vapor, her voice echoing inside his head. Mahmoud did not ever want to revisit that experience. A wild recognition ran through his mind – only a few moments ago he was assuming he was the chosen one and wanted to open the gate! What was he thinking? That was the worst thing anyone could do! His inner terror magnified Mahmoud's insignificance. He felt so small next to this experience that all he could do was fight to end it – fighting was a way for his ego to survive.

He could hear voices, people speaking in English. It took a while inside this blinded state for him to realize that these were the voices of the woman and the young man with her. They were talking to each other. They seemed to have a better grasp of the situation; the young man was pushing her, the woman, to step in, and he was saying he would push "him." "Oh, no, he is talking about me…" – understanding finally caught up with Mahmoud, and he was on the verge of protesting when he grasped that he was already being pushed.

Then the sound became so loud that Mahmoud almost lost consciousness. Feeling breathless, he opened his eyes – it had been so bright he had not even known they were closed. What he saw was complete darkness. Where was the light? What was happening? On top of the blackness there were also no sounds, he felt like a deaf man. He called out in English: "Hello…? Anyone…?"

"Yeah…" – was the reluctant response. This was the young man. "Bailey, are you OK? Sahed…?"

Both Bailey and Sahed answered at the same time. It appeared that all four of them were still conscious. For a moment, while their eyes adjusted to the darkness, no one moved. The old man turned on the flashlight and slowly guided it around the room. Everything was the same, only it was not; something was different. Some things had "materialized" in the room. Inside the stone indentations in the walls were unlit fire torches, where before there had been none. There were also some wooden pieces of furniture scattered around – small stools and a long, low table with three jars on it. None of this had been in the room earlier. The nasty smell of sweat and urine was also gone, and the air was suddenly musky and moist. Mahmoud struggled to believe his eyes as he stared at the new objects. How did they get here?

*   *   *

Oh, blessed Sekhmet had granted them passage! Sahed felt the tears on his face as his flashlight illuminated the room. "This is not the same room!" his spirit sang. Waves of gratitude washed over him. Sahed was in the presence of a Miracle. His lips formed a smile as he allowed himself to exhale. For a moment he was oblivious to his companions, and only suddenly heard them talking again. Bailey was asking something, and Craig was attempting to answer her question. Mahmoud remained silent. Finally Sahed tore his eyes away from the room and looked at his companions. Bailey's upper body turned back to look at the large room, while the lower part of her still turned towards the room with the cube and pyramid on top of it, as if she were afraid to move her feet from that spot. Craig had walked into the large room and was looking around, touching the furniture to check that it was really there. Sahed's gaze traveled to Mahmoud. The man's eyes were wide, transfixed. "He does not understand..." thought Sahed, and he bent over to touch the man's shoulder. "We are not in the same time anymore."

The man looked at Sahed with utter terror in his eyes. "I wonder why he is this scared, if he is the Shenu, he had to know this gate was genuine... Perhaps he was as arrogant and pretentious as all the false Shenu, playing the role, as if the oath to Sekhmet was a membership to some prestigious club... He probably never thought *this* could be a reality..." Then he took his first step into the large room, unafraid.

"Sahed, where are we?" asked Craig, without turning.

"I do not know. But I am sure this is a different time from the one we started in. A more accurate question is probably *when* are we?"

"… a different time?" Sahed heard Bailey's whisper echo his words.

But before anyone could come up with an answer, they heard sounds and fell silent. The sounds were voices, and footsteps. The voices sounded strange and barely distinguishable, but soon they became louder, clearer. The words were in ancient Egyptian, a language that had not been spoken for thousands of years.

CHAPTER NINE

1,360BC
Giza Plateau, Egypt

"**W**e have to be there when they arrive!" exclaimed the woman's voice, authoritarian and confident.

"We are not even sure if it is true, if they will come!" returned a male whisper.

There were other voices but Sahed could not understand them all. As all Shenu, he had been taught the basics of the ancient language. He struggled to listen, and was caught off guard when Bailey pulled on his arm. "What is this?" There was alarm in her voice.

"We are in the past, my dear child," said Sahed with an ache in his heart. "These voices speak the ancient Egyptian language. And they are coming here to meet us."

"Whoa! You can understand ancient Egyptian!" Craig's amazement was obvious.

"They know we are here?" There was disbelief in Bailey's eyes as she spoke over Craig.

"They appear to know of our arrival. I believe they are coming here to greet us," Sahed said, straining to decipher more words. But he could not understand anything else. The people were talking over each other in the well shaft, and their voices echoed. He turned off the flashlight – they were now in the dark.

Bailey grabbed his arm tighter as she stared at the base of the ladder, waiting for people to come down. They could smell the incense and the tar or oils from the lamps that these people carried. The light from the lamps flickered, illuminating the smoke they were giving off.

A man stepped down first. His dark skin contrasted with his white clothing: a sleeveless top and a long kilt that covered him to below the knees. His slightly protruding belly was tied over with a sash. The man did not look back at Sahed and the others; instead he positioned himself to help the next person come off the ladder. It was a woman, apparently a wealthy one, for she was wearing a large necklace on top of her white sheath. The necklace covered her chest and shoulders entirely, gold pieces intermixed with bright blue turquoise, glimmering and shining in the light of the lamp that the man held. The man helped the woman to step to the side as one more person descended.

The woman bent over and fixed her shoe – a strappy sandal of sorts, with a gold scarab on the front. She wore a black shoulder length wig adorned with a gold circle with two cobras and a sun disk in the middle. The headdress looked heavy, and the woman took care not to tilt her head as she attended to her shoe.

Sahed held his breath, tears in his eyes, as he stared at the woman – she looked remarkably like his beloved wife, who had recently died. Sahed would do anything to join her in the afterlife, but Sekhmet had forbidden his departure, prolonging his life to fulfill the prophecy. Bailey's fingers dug into his arm. No one said a word.

A third person descended from the ladder. It was an old man, much older than the first one. His body was thin, and he limped slightly as he came off the ladder. There were more people coming down, much faster now that the old man had finished his climb. The old man sat down on one of the small wooden stools next to the well's shaft. The lady stood, with her back straight. She said something to the younger man who had descended first. Sahed only understood the word "fire," and in the next moment his assumption was proven correct when he saw the man fiddling with a lamp.

He lit up one of the torches fixed to the walls, the one closest to the well's shaft. The woman in the gold necklace turned around and gasped. She could now see four people at the other end of the large room, and although they were in the shadows, they were clearly there.

Sahed's gaze was fixed on the lady. She was about forty years of age. With her small tight frame she commanded attention, displaying an uncanny, strong presence. She looked tough and hard to please. Her intense eyes, beautifully framed by arching eyebrows, were further apart than usual, and they were almond shaped and dark in color. She looked like an Egyptian, but at the same time there obviously was some other blood in her, perhaps Lebanese, for her skin was an olive brown lighter color and it remained smooth despite her age. Her cheekbones were high, her nose straight and her chin chiseled, giving her a stunning statue-like appearance. Her perfectly outlined, full lips were parted as she stared in silence at Sahed.

The next second she said something that Sahed did not understand, her voice commanding. Everyone who was already on the ground turned and looked at Sahed and the others.

She made a step forward: "In honor of Sekhmet, the Bringer of Truth, the Detester of Untruth."

Sahed repeated her words back to her, speaking ancient Egyptian out loud as best he could.

"Your arrival was foretold," said the lady, as the others hastily came down the ladder. Now the room was filled, there were thirteen of them – "The entire Shenu…" thought Sahed as he finished counting them.

The woman gave another command with the only discernable word being "fire," and the other torches were lit. No one came near the newcomers.

"I am Tiye, the High Priestess of Shenu. Do you come on the errand of Sekhmet?"

Sahed thought for a moment of his response, desperately trying to remember the ancient words, enough to explain what he needed to say. "We are of the future. We honor Sekhmet, the great star-god. I am the true Shenu."

His words came out awkwardly, and he was afraid to be misunderstood. Unsure of which time period they were in, he did not know if the Shenu were one here or if they were already divided.

Before Sahed could finish his thought a coarse voice spoke up behind him: "The Shenu is the will of Sekhmet. We pledge our lives to serve the cause." Sahed turned and saw Mahmoud staring at the woman. He had spoken in ancient Egyptian. There was no more doubt in Sahed's mind that Mahmoud was one of the false Shenu. Only the Shenu still possessed the knowledge of spoken ancient Egyptian. The spoken version had been lost, even though the hieroglyphs had been translated from the Rosetta Stone in the beginning of the nineteenth century. If Mahmoud Halib knew how to speak this language, he had been trained by the Shenu. And it was not the true Shenu, since Sahed knew them all.

"I am Tiye," repeated the lady. "I am the High Priestess of the Shenu and I am trained by Sekhmet. I am also the Chief Royal Wife of Amenhotep the Third."

There was silence as Sahed retraced the past. This beautiful woman was Amenhotep's wife, and not just any wife – his main wife, the queen! The queen of Amenhotep was the High Priestess of the Shenu! He had never suspected that. "Her first title is 'priestess,' not 'queen' – she honors her allegiances…" noticed Sahed. "Her oath to Sekhmet is above her position as a queen."

This also meant that in the current time there was still one Shenu and all the tensions had just begun. "Why did Sekhmet choose to place us here, in this turbulent time?" wondered Sahed.

"Speak and explain your presence," commanded the queen.

"I am the chosen one. They have bound me to use my power!" Mahmoud blurted out, in words broken and odd in ancient Egyptian. But Sahed clearly understood their meaning.

The lady took a step forward. The man who had come down the ladder first jumped in front of her with a lamp, and one more man came to her right, his hand on the handle of the large knife on his belt. But the queen continued walking towards the group of newcomers, taking the light and protection without notice, as something expected. She stopped in the middle of the room – she was less than ten feet away from Sahed. But she looked at Mahmoud instead, the one who had last spoken. No one breathed; awaiting her next act.

"If Sekhmet gave you the power to open the gate, she must have been drunk at the time…" she said confidently but slowly. "They bound you, the chosen one, so they must also have some power – do they not?" The high priestess stared at Mahmoud, and the look on her face was that of outrage.

"She does not think that someone who claims to be powerful should whine," quietly whispered Sahed in Arabic to Mahmoud. Mahmoud stared at him in frustration, obviously aware that the queen was annoyed at him.

"Did you bind him?" asked Tiye, looking at Sahed.

"I and this young man did," answered Sahed, pointing at Craig. "This woman was also chosen, she has the key to the gate."

"*I* have the only key," stated the queen. She placed her hand on her chest and Sahed could see for the first time the locket hanging on a tiny beaded necklace, hidden under her large golden collar – it was the locket of Sekhmet.

Next to Sahed, Bailey gasped, staring at it. Her hand immediately grasped at the locket on her neck – it wasn't there! There was only the empty gold chain, no locket. She looked at Sahed in panic, whispering loudly, "It isn't here, the locket isn't here!" Sahed's arm forgotten, she frantically looked around the floor, then at Craig, who by then had comprehended what was going on and started to scan the floor too.

"High Priestess," began Sahed. "This woman had the locket of Sekhmet: it was given to me, I gave it to her father, and it came to her. She and I are the Shenu. We are not of your time; we are from what has not yet come to pass.'

"Sekhmet told us that reformation would be initiated by the arrival of the Shenu who had seen the future..." the high priestess quietly replied.

"That does not mean they are the Shenu she talked about!" interjected one of the men. "They could be imposters!"

"Imposters?" replied Tiye, eyes ablaze as she looked at the man. "Be ashamed of your thoughtless head! They came through the gate, did they not?"

But he was not easily quieted. "Being a queen has made you arrogant! They could have climbed down here earlier!"

Both Sahed and Mahmoud were shocked by the tone of voice and the words the man was using – he was talking down to the queen! At the time of Amenhotep, the pharaoh was seen as god, and his wife was surely a divine being. But here he was telling her that being a queen had gone to her head!

"I have the guards at the gate at all times and no one came down here besides us," replied Tiye. "As for arrogance, no one is guiltier of that than you!" She raised one eyebrow and stared at the man triumphantly.

"Guards can be bribed, that is the nature of things, your head is too high in royal life!"

"My head is on my shoulders, where is yours?" was Tiye's response. Her last comment elicited a few smiles from the other men and women. She redirected her attention back to the newcomers. "Why have you bound this man?"

"He is also the Shenu, but he is..." – Sahed struggled with the ancient words, – "He was angry with us for opening the gate. He had a weapon and he tried to use it."

"You used a weapon on the other Shenu?" The queen looked outraged again. She now stood only a few feet from Mahmoud, who was still half-lying on the floor.

"They had no right to…" choked Mahmoud in broken ancient Egyptian, unsure how he could explain it all. "They are not the Shenu!"

The queen stopped and looked at the newcomers. She spent a long time looking at Bailey's face. "You were given the key?"

Bailey looked at Sahed – she understood that the woman had just said something to her, but she was not sure what was happening, who these people were and who was saying what, since she did not speak ancient Egyptian, or any other language but English, for that matter.

"I will explain to her what you said," Sahed told Tiye, "she does not speak Egyptian." Tiye's left eyebrow went up in surprise but she said nothing.

Summarizing the events, Sahed translated Tiye's question.

"Tell her that you gave me the locket," Bailey said. He repeated what she said in Egyptian to the priestess.

"You are one of the Shenu, but you know no Egyptian words…" Tiye said, as if to herself. She was visibly puzzled. Sahed translated her words into English.

"You said that you and she are the Shenu. He said he is the Shenu… And who is he?" Tiye pointed at Craig.

"He is … a supporter of Bailey," replied Sahed, pointing at Bailey. "His name is Craig."

"What is your name?" she asked Sahed.

He answered.

"What is the name of the bound one?"

"I am Mahmoud Mukhtar Halib. I am of the Shenu…" he said nervously.

Tiye repeated their names, her tongue mispronouncing the sounds. Then she made a command to the others. Sahed did not understand what she said, but the next moment it became clear – one of the women stepped forward and took Bailey's arm, pulling her away from the spot she was standing on towards the well shaft. The men did the same with Sahed and Craig, while other men patted down Mahmoud as if they might be in search of a weapon. Then they began to untie him.

CHAPTER NINE

*　　　*　　　*

"Are you sure this is a good idea?" Bailey nervously asked Sahed, realizing they were being asked to climb up to the surface. "She wants us to come out of the well! Out there, in this... time! How will we get back?"

"Bailey, you are in the *past!* Get it? The past! We *have* to go up!" said Craig, shushing her.

Bailey focused on grasping the ladder with her fingers as tightly and securely as she could – it was the only way she could keep herself from losing it. They are in the past? She must be dreaming or something... Or had she lost her mind like Abby? "Stop it!" she yelled, reminding herself that she had already decided that Abby was not crazy.

Bailey was grasping the same ladder she had used a short while ago but it was not the same ladder; it was impossible to simultaneously be the same and not the same, yet she understood that that was the truth. The ladder was centuries old, but it actually looked "younger," newer somehow; it even had paint on it... "There was no paint on it when I climbed down... Abby must have climbed down this very same ladder as a little five-year-old kid ... No wait, not *this* ladder..."

"Oh my god!" Bailey whispered the words out loud as a realization blasted through Bailey's mind. "Abby said '*the enemy is here*'! She was talking about that man, Mr. Halib! She knew he would be waiting for *us* in the well!"

When they all finally surfaced, they came up inside a tent. It was a large tent, with off-white canvas stretched over a small frame of wooden posts painted red. Cautiously peering out, Bailey was almost run over by Craig, who couldn't wait to see the outside. It was warm, bordering on hot, and clearly night. They spilled out of the tent and Bailey's sneakers immediately sank into the warm sand. The sky was enormous and there were thousands of stars all over it – it stretched endlessly in all directions. There were no city lights, no lights at all.

They were met by a group of servants who emerged quite suddenly from the darkness. Dressed in almost nothing, their arms and legs bare, their hips wrapped in a white knee-length cloth, they quickly made their way towards the tent. Bailey counted seventeen of them. All wore similar short wigs – black and thick, with wide straight bangs covering their foreheads.

Bailey was unsure of what to think of all this – would she wake up any second now? Her pulse was fast, hammering inside her head. She began to regret that she had not thought to take her anti-anxiety medication on this trip.

"What am I thinking? I forgot to take my meds into the past?" She couldn't form a straight thought, the words in her head all seemed to be running in a million directions. She felt her arm being grasped by someone's insistent fingers. Instinctively she recoiled, and saw that her action had scared a young woman. The woman was a servant, about seventeen or twenty years old. She was obviously Egyptian, but her skin was much darker than the others, almost black. She jumped back from Bailey and lay on the ground at her feet.

"Oh my god..." The woman did not move. Bailey nervously looked around, unable to make a choice inside this unreal reality. But Sahed was far back speaking with one of the men, and Craig was far ahead, his face lifted up at the sky. Bailey looked back at the woman at her feet, who remained motionless as if awaiting instruction.

"Err... Hello...? Please get up," she began in English, finally bending down and lightly touching the woman's shoulder. The woman turned her head, her body unmoving, looked at Bailey for a second, then quickly looked down at the sand again, saying something in Egyptian. "I don't know what you're saying... Sorry... It's OK..." said Bailey in a reassuring voice. The woman stopped talking and looked at Bailey again. Their eyes met. "Please get up," – and Bailey stretched both arms toward the woman, preparing to help her up. But the young woman quickly moved away from Bailey's hands, face down at the sand again.

"Jesus... Ah... it's OK... I will just go get some help." Bailey got up, prepared to walk to Sahed, but the same second the woman jumped up almost in front of her, stopping Bailey in her tracks. Unable to help herself, Bailey stared at the woman's bare breasts.

The young woman bowed her head and stepped to the side, but Bailey did not move, she just watched what was happening. The woman ran to a large low table with jars laid out all over it. She quickly grasped one of the jars and returned to Bailey. The young servant poured the liquid from the jar onto Bailey's sneakers. Bailey attempted to stop her, but as she looked out for help, she saw that most servants were busy doing the same thing – they were washing the feet of the people who had come out of the well. Bare feet! "Oh, damn!" swore Bailey, looking down at her wet sneakers.

The young woman lifted her face up to Bailey and asked something. Then she repeated it.

"I don't know what you're saying... I'm sorry..." mumbled Bailey, feeling deficient. "What's your name?" It was the only thing Bailey could think of asking. Of course, the woman did not understand. Bailey looked for Craig, but he was nowhere to be seen. There were many people around her now, all busy and quietly talking.

The next moment Bailey felt her left hand being grasped – it was the woman again, but this time she had a small jar of oil, and she poured the oil onto Bailey's hand and gently massaged it in. The scent of the oil was just divine. "I have got to find out what this is…" thought Bailey fleetingly. Her hands hurt from grasping the ladder and the body ached everywhere, reminding her that this was very much real.

After both hands were anointed, the servant did the same with Bailey's ankles. The jar was returned to the low table, and the servant moved to stand a little behind Bailey, to her left, her eyes scanning the other people. When Bailey turned to her, she started to stand back. "No, it's OK, hi!" said Bailey, trying to catch the woman's eye. The woman froze, staring at the ground. Then she slowly lifted her eyes and looked right at Bailey's face. Her eyes were beautiful, but it was too dark to see what color they were. "I am Bailey" – Bailey pointed at her chest, the spot where the painful memory that the locket was not on her neck still stabbed her. She repeated this action a few times, until she finally got a response: "Neburetjutwiya."

"Oh…?"

As if understanding Bailey's difficulty, the woman added: "Nab," and smiled.

"Ok, her name is Nab," thought Bailey with a sense of accomplishment. "Now what?"

People formed a caravan, the line of people a twisted thread between the desert dunes. There were the people from the well and others Bailey did not know, servants walking among them, carrying small lit lamps, jars, boxes, carved wooden folding chairs and other such things. Bailey could not see where Tiye was, she was probably at the beginning of the long procession. The pace seemed normal: not slow, but not fast by any means. Nab pulled on Bailey's arm again, indicating it was time to join. And so they walked.

Taking in the surroundings, Bailey felt mesmerized by the beauty of it all. In the darkness she could see only tiny dots of lamps here and there, bobbing in a line. The only real light was from the stars, which there were plenty of, and a sliver of the moon. The only sounds were whispers and the desert wind.

Suddenly Bailey saw a glow coming from behind one of the dunes and, as the caravan turned, she could see lit torches far in the distance. After half an hour of walking they arrived at camp. There were four tents there, one large and three small. Fire – oil burning in large bowls and torches – was everywhere. This was the first "normal" bright light Bailey had seen since they came through the gate.

Nab pulled on Bailey's arm once more, indicating that she was to go into the large tent. At its entrance a white cloth was lifted and tied back with a red ribbon. Nab stepped back. Bailey stopped, waiting for her. When Nab did not come, Bailey turned around to look for her, and their eyes met. Baffled, Bailey realized that Nab had stood to the side of the entrance because she could not go into the tent.

During the walk Bailey had gotten used to Nab's presence, and walking in without her seemed dangerous. She feared she would not know what to do. The brightly lit tent was already filled with people, both men and women. Some were sitting, others stood and talked. Their appearance indicated they were all obviously Egyptian, but facial features differed widely and skin colors varied greatly from light olive to a very dark chocolate color. The center of the tent was occupied by a large tray the size of a conference table, and on it were many small clay cups filled with liquid. Bailey looked around – most people were holding these cups and drinking from them. She walked to the tray, feeling brave, and took a cup. "Hey, I just got transported to hell-knows-where, or when… What do I have to lose?" She put her lips to the cup. It was water. "I probably shouldn't have this," she decided the next second. "In hotels we only drank bottled water… this one might not be clean…" Unsure of what to do with the cup, she held it in her hand.

Craig walked into the tent and practically ran towards Bailey. "Did you see this? Wow, this is real! These people… they are real ancient Egyptians! We are back in time! Can you believe it!"

"Yes, I'm here too, remember?" replied Bailey quietly.

"Sorry… I forgot – you're nervous. It's all so weird…" – but the next moment his concern was forgotten. "But this is real, it's amazing! I've got to talk to the queen…" And he was gone again.

Queen Tiye was seated on a large armchair. She sipped her water and was silent. As Bailey's eyes found the queen, she realized that Tiye had been looking at her the whole time. Tiye beckoned Bailey towards where she sat with a finger.

A childhood feeling of being in trouble passed through Bailey's body. "Jesus, what the hell is wrong with me? This woman is probably only five or so years older than I am! Oh… more than that, I guess…" At the same time Bailey felt drawn to this formidable woman. Although they were only a few years apart, she was a queen and acted like one, and

Bailey surely did not feel royal. In fact, she often felt lost and scared, while this woman radiated confidence and had an intense powerful presence.

Tiye was tiny by current American standards. "She's probably only four and a half feet tall... well, a little taller than that, but not by much... There is no way she is even five feet!" mused Bailey. She didn't realize that as she was thinking about Tiye, she was also walking towards her. It was too late to stop now...

The eyes of the queen were dark brown and there was strength in them, and warmth. These eyes of intelligence, confidence and humor carefully studied Bailey as she approached.

"Great, I meet the queen and we can't even talk!" thought Bailey, angry at herself for not knowing the ancient language. "Why would I know it?" retorted the defensive thought in her mind. "It's not like I knew I would be going back in time, and in Egypt of all places, and that I would meet the queen there!"

Queen Tiye spoke, and Bailey was startled. She intuitively began to look around for help. Then she felt a tight squeeze at her wrist – looking at it she saw that the queen was holding her wrist, very tightly. Bailey's gaze followed the hand up the arm and her eyes met the queen's. There was an uneasy feeling in Bailey's stomach, the childhood sense of being in trouble again...

And then Queen Tiye smiled.

She smiled with more than her mouth, her eyes smiled too. Bailey immediately relaxed, baffled at how she could possibly have been afraid of this woman a moment earlier. Bailey smiled back and they just looked at each other, silently.

A man materialized at the queen's side. He was the only other person, besides the queen, who had spoken in the well. He was a bit heavyset and he looked well taken care of, his biceps adorned with large gold bracelets. His eyes were also almond shaped and similar to the queen's, and his skin was the same color as hers – both of them looked different from the rest of the people Bailey had seen so far. There were light- and dark-skinned Egyptians, black Nubians, and then there was the queen and this man... He seemed to disapprove of Tiye's behavior – holding the stranger's wrist, smiling? What is she thinking!

He began to speak, surely expressing his discontent, and Tiye ignored him. But Bailey could not; she broke her eye lock with the queen and looked at the man, mumbling "I am sorry, I was just..."

The next second the queen's eyes snapped at the man – not one word was said but he stopped talking immediately. She then looked back at Bailey, not letting go of her wrist, and waved the man off with her other hand as if he was an annoying fly. He growled, but retreated.

"It is an honor to meet you…" Bailey refocused on the queen, and attempted a bow. Tiye stifled a laugh at Bailey's awkward attempt at a curtsy, and released her wrist.

Another woman came up to them, a noble judging from her beautiful wig, bright white sheath, and copious amounts of shiny jewelry. Tiye actively engaged her in conversation, switching her attention away from Bailey. There was a large square thing with short lion-like legs next to her, and Bailey absently sat down on it. She was not sure if it was really a low stool, or a table, but no one complained so she remained seated. The stool was lower than the one queen Tiye was sitting on, but it stood next to hers. The queen's chair was of a different design: it was a folding, wooden carved frame with dark red material attached over it. The queen looked comfortable in it, as if it had been made for her. "Of course it was made for her! She is the queen…"

*   *   *

Conversations in the large tent continued through the night. Tiye seemed to be able to talk to everyone and at the same time remain separate, royal. A horn sounded and everyone fell silent, only birdsong could be heard. Queen Tiye stood up and, accompanied by the others in procession, walked out of the tent. Bailey followed, but soon could no longer see the queen, there were too many people in front of her. Looking at the ground so as not to step on anyone's foot, Bailey felt a light tug on her arm – it was Nab again. Her eyes met Bailey's just for a moment, while her other hand pointed up and outward. It was light, an amazing light! Light pink and a little orange, it was huge. Bailey was so mesmerized by it – the sunrise!

It was still somewhat dark. She looked around the huge open expanse of space, taking in the three enormous pyramids standing farther in the distance on the left, the profile of the Sphinx, a few trees on the right, and a road in the middle. The road was made of large stones and adorned with flowers and smaller statues, and was at that moment being swept of morning sand by what seemed like thousands of servants. It was very clean. Bailey climbed onto a large block of stone at the edge of the path so that she could see ahead.

"Wow, it leads to an embankment,' she observed. "The Nile is right there on the right, behind the trees. We must have walked directly to it in the dark… I didn't realize it was so close."

Nab pulled Bailey by the wrist, trying to get her off the rock.

"Bailey, come here, Bailey!" It was Craig, shouting.

She jumped off the rock and walked toward the sound of Craig's voice, but not seeing him, she ended up in the crowd of people. No one seemed to pay any attention to her, except, of course, Nab, who was hurrying behind her. Soon she noticed Sahed all the way at the front of the procession; he was talking with the queen as they walked.

"Where is Mr. Halib?" worried Bailey. "Jesus, hope he didn't run back into the well – what if he was able to open it and go home… and we were stranded here forever?" Frantically she turned her head around, scanning from side to side until she finally located him – Mahmoud Halib was also walking and talking, with the man who had spoken somewhat harshly and overly familiarly to the queen. Both these men made Bailey nervous.

Soon Craig appeared on her right. "This is Harry" – he pointed at the black, mostly naked older man next to him, and patted him on the shoulder. The servant did not seem to mind, he smiled, showing all his existing teeth.

Bailey was perplexed for a moment. "Harry?"

"Well, something like it, Hurrawie I think, but I can't say it right…"

Both of them saw Nab hiding a smile – maybe Craig's mispronunciation of Hurrawie's name meant something else in their language?

The people continued walking and Bailey was swept along with them. She soon found herself looking at the silhouette of the Sphinx. There was a temple in front of it, a large one, but the light was still too dim to discern any details. She did not remember the temple being there when they visited the Sphinx less than a week ago. Following the Sphinx's gaze towards the sunrise, Bailey noticed a glistening pool of water. Seeing the water in front of the Sphinx's temple disoriented her – there was no water in the time she had come from. She struggled to remember what Craig had told her about the area. The Nile had been right in front of all the temples for a long time, then it had moved to its current position, leaving the temples in the desert.

By the time they arrived at the embankment, the sun, reflected in the Nile waters, was bright enough to allow them to see details, not just silhouettes. The crowd halted. Bailey turned to her left and gasped. The pyramids stood like mountains in the distance. They were not brown in color, but glistening bright white in the sunlight! "They look almost... wet. The stone must be shiny... or maybe it is the heat?" She could see a large tunnel-like path leading to the middle pyramid, made of the same bright white stone she was walking on, adorned with flags at the far end. "This must be the processional way that Craig told me about... The covered tunnel..." recalled Bailey from their earlier tourist explorations.

All around her people were hurrying, everyone seemed to have some duty to perform. The servants ran with jars of smoking incense and baskets of flowers. Then a large metal bowl was carried past Bailey by four black men. Swiveling on her toes, barely able to breathe, Bailey looked over people's heads at the Temple of the Sphinx on her left. High above the temple, behind it, she could clearly see the shoulders and head of the Sphinx. It was painted, painted! The bright blue and white stripes of a headdress circled its red face, and there was gold eye shadow over the blue-black eyes... and a white braided beard.

Suddenly the noise all around Bailey became muted, everyone started whispering to each other. Bailey listened carefully, and was surprised she could hear the Nile waters. A soft breeze flapped the flags on the tall posts in front of the Temple of the Sphinx, and carried a gong-like sound to Bailey. She looked, but could not see where the gong sound was coming from. She rose up on her toes, and looked over the heads of the people at what lay in front of her. She was standing on the Nile embankment among what must have been thousands of people.

Nab grasped at her arm again and Bailey gave in. Too many things were happening, too fast. She let herself be pushed and pulled by Nab until she finally ended up in the front row of the assembly. The next second Nab disappeared into the crowd. Looking around, Bailey saw that she was standing among the people who had been in the tent, she recognized a few faces. The others in the crowd, wealthy nobles covered by beautiful jewelry and commoners wearing only simple kilts, all eagerly watched the unfolding sight.

Bailey blinked. In front of her lay a wide area of paved stone, as wide as a few city blocks, with steps descending into the Nile. The river's waters lapped gently against the long embankment steps on the right, but no one in the crowd stood directly between the temple and the waters. A large man-made pool of water, rimmed in stone, formed an enormous harbor directly in front of the temple. Small boats cluttered its surface,

196

with one massive vessel towering over them all. The huge vessel was covered in gold, and red and white flags and tents were mounted on it – it was the royal barge.

The queen moved regally forward into the middle of the open temple plaza. In front of her walked a man with a leopard skin over his naked shoulders, performing a ceremonial rite. On either side of them shuffled priests in long white kilts, their bald heads shining like polished brass in the sun. The priests carried jars of incense and heavy trays with offerings. Birds careened down to snatch at the bounty of food on the large trays.

Queen Tiye had changed her headdress. This one, made of a large gold ring fitted around her thick black wig, was as heavy as her last. At its front were two snakes surrounding a sun disk, and at the back of the headdress protruded two tall Maat feathers, giving her the illusion of height. Bailey smiled, thinking that the feathers also made the tiny queen look like a rabbit. Tiye moved carefully as she went through the motions of the ritual, repeating in a loud voice all that the leopard-robed priest said. A large bowl of water was brought to him and he sang something over it in a surprisingly high voice. Then bare-breasted priestesses in golden necklaces and bracelets, hips wrapped in short white kilts, joined the central group. The women wore the same wigs and gold headdress as the queen, but their Maat feathers were shorter than Tiye's. In each hand they held a shiny golden rattle, a sistrum, which made a delightfully light "dinging" sound as they shook it.

The priest in the leopard robe raised his voice to a dramatic crescendo, and the other priests did the same. Then they were quiet, and the priestesses stopped shaking their sistrums, and for a moment there was silence. Young boys with shorn heads and holding thick candles emerged from the large temple entrance. Young girls came towards them from the side, each bearing a large white flower held against their loose white robes. The priests took the large bowl of water and carried it into the temple, and the queen and priestesses followed behind them.

People whispered to each other, but no one spoke loudly. Bailey felt a strange impulse to clap because she felt as if she had just seen a beautiful "period" performance. Only this was no performance: this was a real ritual performed by a real queen.

She had lost her English-speaking companions. Normally this would have been cause for alarm, but her mind refused to add any more elements of stress to the situation and just ignored the fact.

In about ten minutes Craig came up beside her. "This is amazing! I wonder what's next," he exclaimed, anticipation in his voice.

Sounds of singing came from inside the temple. Then the priests and priestesses spilled out into the temple plaza, baskets on their arms. They moved around the edge of the crowd and gave away the contents of the baskets. Some carried jars of oil and touched fingers to foreheads and hearts. Shoved to the side, all Bailey could see was that the queen was not among them. People were pushing to the front; the crowd erupted in noise and commotion. Soon there was another gong sound, this one deeper than previous ones. The priestesses and priests, still holding the baskets and jars, made two lines stretched between the temple entrance and the embankment. The queen walked out of the temple between the lines of priests and priestesses, still wearing the gold headdress, which glimmered in the bright sunlight. She and a small entourage walked up a long decorated bridge onto the royal barge.

"Isn't that the guy from the well? The one who spoke to Tiye?" pointed Craig.

Bailey saw the man, too. He was the only one from the well besides the queen who went onto the boat. He was one of the last people to go into the barge. A man in a short white kilt and a leather top raised his hand and yelled – immediately the men at the barge's sides began to row, slowly pushing the vessel out of port.

"Let's find Sahed," suggested Craig.

To their surprise, that proved to be very easy. Nab and Hurrawie materialized right next to them, with Sahed and his servant in tow. Another man, richly dressed and official looking, came up behind Sahed.

"We go with him," said Sahed, answering their unspoken question.

A smaller boat with a white sail awaited them. Some of the people from the tent were already on board, as was Mahmoud Halib. He looked a bit more dignified now, as if he had found his footing again and had begun to rebuild his shattered ego.

The boat was released from the dock and began its journey up the Nile, maneuvering between small feluccas. They could see the royal barge up ahead. From the water the view of the embankment was even more impressive. There were many temples, each one larger than the other, with crowds of singing people in front of them, the Sphinx behind them, and the pyramids towering in the distance. As their boat moved along the bank the scenery changed to smaller houses and rolling green and yellow fields.

"Where are we going?" nervously whispered Bailey.

Nab, seated on the floor by her feet, looked up as though she understood the question and answered, "Men-Nefer."

Searching around for a translation Bailey's eye met these of Mr. Halib. With an exasperated roll of his eyes he answered, "Memphis. Men-Nefer is the ancient Egyptian name for Memphis, twenty kilometers outside of Cairo."

Bailey felt like a school girl failing a surprise-test. She shrank farther into the bench. The wooden pillow-covered benches were not comfortable, but she was too stressed to care. Mr. Halib sat on the bench in front of Bailey, luckily facing away from her, while Sahed was somewhere farther behind. The servants sat on the floor between the benches. Craig stood at the front of the boat, next to the man who was yelling commands to the rowers. Bailey counted twelve men, six on each side. With the sail bulging above them, and the help of the rowers, the boat practically flew over the water.

1,360BC

Men-Nefer, Egypt

Soon the scenery changed again. The fields were replaced with teeming warehouses where hundreds of men moved back and forth between buildings, carrying packages, pushing rolling carts, and yelling at donkeys. Sahed came to sit next to Bailey and soon Craig joined them.

Bailey and Craig stared at the panorama with mouths agape. They sailed past one temple after another and many markets, the noise of the markets and the calls of the port officials directing the boats in the harbor rolling over them. Then their boat slowed as it was gliding past the steps leading up to a huge temple. Behind the temple, in the distance, rose an even taller building, its golden roof ablaze under the sun.

"These steps probably lead to the Temple of Amun," said Sahed quietly.

From behind them Mahmoud almost shouted, "Yes, of course they do, magnificent! And those gold roofs behind it – that is the Temple of Ptah. We are in the capital of Lower Egypt!" It was the first time Mr. Halib didn't sound annoyed, he was overtaken by the same feeling of wonder that they all were.

Between the loud calls of merchants unloading the boats they could hardly gather how their captain knew where to lead their vessel. Yet he confidently navigated it, coordinating the people on the embankment. The queen's barge was already parked at the harbor, with a foot bridge placed at its side. They watched Tiye as she came off the barge and her servants helped her into a litter. She was carried away in it.

Their smaller boat waited for the barge to finish its business, then also came into port. An official was waiting for them, a well-dressed man of indecipherable age, accompanied by four guards. The guards were handsome, muscular men in their early twenties. Craig nudged Bailey, and with his eyes pointed to the large knives sheathed at the guards' leather belts. Soon it became apparent why the guards were needed. Crowds awaited them, hundreds of people screaming, singing, waving flowers and raising little children above their heads. Apparently, in Men-Nefer, anyone from the royal court was of extreme interest, even though most spectators were trying to follow the queen's litter. Tightening their ranks and flanked by the four guards, Bailey and the others began to advance along the large street, boring deeper and deeper into the city. People looked at them with mild confusion, unsure of what to think of their strange clothes. Nevertheless women pushed their children forward at them, and men stretched out their arms in attempts to touch the newcomers, but were immediately held back by the guards.

The road ended at a courtyard surrounded by tall white walls. Next to it was the palace, and next to the palace towered the Temple of Ptah with its golden roofs. In front of the palace entrance stood four guards, bright red, yellow, blue, and white flags flapping over their heads. The official who was in front of their party quickly led them inside through a very large hall with lotus-headed, brightly painted columns and into a smaller inner courtyard. They were joined by the people who had come over on the queen's barge and led through the left wall entrance into a huge temple.

Bailey and Craig stared around them, speechless. The lotus-topped gold-clad columns rose well over forty feet, and they in turn were topped by a curved "molding" that was at least another ten feet. The molding was also gold, inlaid with brightly colored ornaments. Many niches and side halls extended from the main space. At the far end of the temple was a large, shallow copper bowl filled with water, at the feet of three statues that stood side by side, each one twenty feet tall. Their red granite heads were in the shadows but it was clear that one of them had a lion's face.

"Yes. It is Sekhmet, the Lover of Truth on the left, and Ptah, the Builder, on the right. The one in the middle is a pharaoh… Considering the time period, it is probably Amenhotep the third, but I cannot be sure," said Sahed quietly in response to Bailey's unspoken question.

Queen Tiye emerged from the side entrance, dressed in a beautiful gown that seemed to be sown from air. It was held together with black thread, and covered with beading of blue turquoise and lapis interpenetrated by thousands of gold threads and a few gold beads.

"Wow, she looks so pretty! She changed her wig," said Craig, craning his neck to see. The queen's wig was longer and had gold threads braided into it.

Next to the queen stood two men, one of whom they had already met in the well. They didn't recognize the other one. The men looked official and wealthy, with more gold on their arms than could probably be found at a bank in modern times. They stood silently, sweating under their thick wigs.

"Which one is the pharaoh?" asked Bailey. Both men made way for the queen and a boy that was walking next to her.

"I don't think either one is," Craig whispered back. "They let Tiye go in front of them."

The queen, with a boy by her side, walked up to the three large statues – the immortal gods of Egypt. The altar, decorated with flowers, was flanked by jars filled with smoking incense.

Tiye spoke, and only then did they see a priest emerging from the altar area – everything was so big it was easy to miss him. He wore white robes, and Bailey and Craig couldn't tell whether or not it was the same leopard-robed priest they had seen earlier. He sang incantations for a while, then made some movements over the water. Tiye and the boy began to speak, repeating his words. The boy was a bit odd looking. His skin was olive colored, similar to Tiye's but perhaps a little lighter. And although his eyes were almond shaped and framed by arching eye brows, and his nose was straight, he did not look like her. He was tall, yet his face betrayed his young age – somewhere between eight and ten years old. His head was shaved and he wore a necklace of pure gold and many gold bracelets, and the jewelry and his head shone in the beam of sunlight hitting the temple floor where he stood. He was allowed to walk between the queen and the high priest into the middle of the open space. As tall as he was his head still didn't reach as high as the top of the statues' feet. He spoke, raising his hands to the sky, his movements graceful and feminine. Then he pointed to the queen. Queen Tiye bowed to the statues, then to the boy as the boy bowed to her. After that, nobles and officials parted to let the queen and the boy walk out of the temple. Everyone then followed them through the open doorway into the courtyard. For a moment Bailey and Craig were disoriented – it appeared that there were many courtyards, and they had walked out into some other one.

"OK, there's the white wall, you can see the flags behind it. We're on the inside of it," said Craig, looking around. Apparently, the Temple of Ptah was not a building but a district – a large, multi-temple complex enclosed within the white walls. It was a busy place – they had to step aside to let hurrying people go past them.

*　　*　　*

As he watched the ceremony Mahmoud couldn't stop thinking. He had to prevent whatever disaster that he was sure was about to happen. But since he could not figure out the nature of the disaster, he could not come up with an appropriate strategy to handle it. Frustrated and positively exhausted, he exhaled. The palace servant was talking to him. This was a nightmare! He could see the others, the old man with the two Americans, on the other side of the courtyard as everyone exited the temple. Addressed by a palace official, they nodded their heads as the guide translated. But before Mahmoud could dash across the yard towards them so as not to miss anything (he was the Shenu after all!) he was forcefully pulled away by two men. Looking back over his shoulder Mahmoud could see that the Americans were split up and also led away. As his body relaxed, so did the hands of the servants. The servants led him through a hallway into a smaller courtyard and then through a side door into a room. Mahmoud paused, examining the designs carved into the wooden door – it was a protective prayer to Ptah, Sekhmet, and their "son" Nebneter. The room was a clean ten by ten space with two low tables and a bed. Mahmoud tore his eyes away from the door, scanned the trays of fruit on the tables and stopped his inspection at the bed.

"They want me to sleep?" Mahmoud just could not believe this. He was the chosen one destined to open the gate, who had arrived from the future so that he could complete a major mission, he wasn't sure what, to begin some end or other, and he was expected to sleep? Sleep was out of the question.

His natural curiosity paired with the anxiety over the events of the last twenty hours pushed him: he had to leave that room. The servant protested, but Mahmoud simply stepped around him.

"I have to do something! I have to find out…" – Mahmoud was not sure what he was looking for, but it had to be important if Sekhmet had sent him all the way back here. He felt new anxiety rising inside him and his stomach began to do somersaults. "What if I can't figure it out?" he thought in panic. "What if I fail Sekhmet! Oh, Allah, help me!" The next second Mahmoud almost fell over in pain and panic. "What Allah?! What am I saying? I will anger her and fail, and ruin everything! I am not worthy… Oh, I have to be, I must be, I must! The future depends on me…"

That thought only made him sicker, so much so that he had to stop running and sit down. The servant almost ran into him – in his haste, Mahmoud had forgotten about that man. He had been running sporadically through the palace hallways, paths, and courtyards while the servant ran after him, trying to keep up. Mahmoud had spent most of his life dealing with uneducated people, and he could easily recognize when someone was intelligent, and when they were not. This man might be a great servant, but he was not an intelligent man, not someone that Mahmoud could put questions to or ever trust… And so he had to be dealt with. How else could Mahmoud walk around freely, without being followed? No matter how many times Mahmoud told the man to go away and leave him alone, he did not leave. So, taking another approach, Mahmoud asked the servant to bring to him some rope and a cloth. Unsure of what this might mean, the servant followed the instructions… and was soon bound and gagged by Mahmoud. The man stared at Mahmoud in terror as he dragged him to a small side niche, and left him there.

"I am the chosen one, I opened the gate…" he repeated to himself, attempting to collect his thoughts. "Then why was this ignorant American woman allowed in?" Mahmoud's stomach growled and, passing by one of the side niches containing yet another statue of Ptah, he grabbed some orange-colored fruit from an altar overflowing with it. "There was a prophecy… about two people opening the gate… at the beginning of the end…" He tried to remember as he hungrily bit into the fruit. "I am the beginning of the end… What end?" Mahmoud immediately corrected himself: "The end of what?"

In his mindless wandering Mahmoud almost collided with two servants carrying a tray. They immediately fell to the ground. Enjoying being treated as a noble, Mahmoud glared down at the servants to enhance his feeling of superiority. "Everything is as it is supposed to be," he proclaimed to himself. He told the prostrate servants that they must watch where they are going, and slowly walked away. He couldn't prevent a satisfied smile.

Rounding a corner, Mahmoud finally located a large side doorway into the massive Temple of Ptah, where the ceremony had taken place. He went in. Most of the people had already left, and Mahmoud was about to leave too so as to not call attention to himself, when he saw the man from the well. The man's name was Ay – Mahmoud had been able to talk to him earlier. He was the Shenu who had spoken in the well, and he seemed trustworthy. On the walk to the temple Ay had told Mahmoud that he felt uneasy with the decisions Tiye was making.

1,360BC
Nab, the Master Body Servant in Men-Nefer Palace

The Servant Overseer of the Royal Palace came towards them. Nab made eye contact with him, as was the custom – no one wanted dumb servants! – then looked down.

The Overseer told Sahed, the oldest of the Newcomers, that it was time to rest, as it would become even hotter under the pharaoh's sun as the day progressed, to clean themselves up and sleep. They would be summoned in the evening.

Nab knew what that meant – each of the Newcomers would be graciously given a room, food and drink, and a bed, along with entertainment.

Nab was one of the top body servants, a Master Servant selected by the queen herself, may she live. Nab adored the queen – she was a living god, an amazing, powerful woman and an honest, fair person. Queen Tiye was never unjust. She picked Nab from her own home town of Khent-Min. Nab had not served in Tiye's household before Tiye became a queen, it was too long ago, before Nab was born. But on one of her visits home, queen Tiye noticed young Nab, then fifteen years of age, and took her to Waset, to the royal Malkata palace. Nab was trained in all the servant duties and in painting to the highest level, and could substitute for the Royal Servant if she fell ill. This time she was supposed to assist the queen on a most important journey, and serve some important person. This important person, apparently, was the Newcomer woman.

More of the palace servants arrived at the courtyard. Nab was part of the entourage of the queen, may she live, and so she had the power to choose palace servants to perform ancillary duties. She picked the ones she wanted and returned to her female Newcomer. The palace servants impolitely stared at the Newcomers, and did not move. This was breaking protocol; they had no right to look at people of such high standing! Nab verbally reprimanded the girls for staring at her female Newcomer, and they looked down.

This Newcomer woman was very strange. She did nothing that a royal guest was supposed to, yet she was indeed a royal guest. Nab did not know where she came from, she had not been there in the evening, and then she and the others had appeared. But the Newcomer was doubtlessly important because not only had she talked to the queen, the queen had held her hand! Nab had seen it clearly through the space between the tent's folds. She was prepared to do her duty when she was given the job of taking care of the uncooperative Newcomer woman, but after seeing her being that intimate with the queen… Nab knew that this was the chance of a lifetime – she had been given one of the most important positions there was – to serve a foreigner of very high status!

The old man called Sahed translated what the Overseer said into their strange language. The sound of it was so odd to Nab's ear – like little rocks, one after the other, thrown onto the floor. After that Nab assumed that the Newcomers knew what to do. But seeing them not move from where they stood, she began ushering her woman in the direction of the room she was given. Nab was told – well, really, the Newcomer was told but did not understand – that she had been given the garden room with the Sekhmet statues in front of it. Nab wanted to have her guest behave correctly. But the woman did not move. Pulling her was undignified, and so instead Nab pulled at her garment, then let it go, then pulled again. This intermittent pulling was supposed to help the Newcomer know the correct action – the accepted practice at court. Yet her Newcomer woman was as stubborn as always, and she resisted such simple corrections. "I have to think of some other way of telling her what is required of her," thought Nab quickly. "She does not seem to think that pulling at her is acceptable." That puzzled Nab, because she was taught that pulling on the guest's arm or wrist was the most polite way of telling them how they should act. Yet her Newcomer became frightened when Nab had done it in the desert, telling her something in her odd language. "Well, wherever she is from, she is now at the center of the world, in the place where gods live, and so she cannot embarrass herself and act inappropriately, and it is my job to help her, and by the gods I will do it well!" Before the woman could protest, Nab pushed her hard, whisking her away into the garden, palace servants in tow.

When they entered the garden, the Newcomer woman slowed down. She seemed to want to look at every flower, every statue hidden by the plant leaves. "She must be from the desert or something," thought Nab. "Maybe she has never seen flowers… Oh, I should let her gaze at them longer then…"

Allowing all the time they could afford on the busy palace schedule, Nab let the Newcomer woman look at the garden plants. Finally they arrived at the right room – there were two statues of Sekhmet on either side of the doorway. "She must be very important," thought Nab. "Guests rarely were placed in this room, only ones that the queen wants to test, or ones she already fully and totally trusts…"

To Nab's surprise, the woman gasped and jumped. For some reason she held a hand at her mouth, her eyes wide in terror as she stared at the room entrance.

"Oh, blessed Isis, I cannot have this!" mumbled Nab, frustrated. She grabbed the Newcomer's arm, forgetting that she did not like it, and stood between the entrance to the room and the woman. Looking at her, the Newcomer calmed down and breathed again. Relieved, Nab let go of her arm. She watched the woman carefully, as she peered over her shoulder at the entrance.

"Why is she scared?" wondered Nab. "Maybe she did something wrong, something against Sekhmet, and is afraid that she will be punished?" Nab reasoned that if this was true, then her queen was just testing the assumption and the Newcomer would be dead soon enough, taken by the avenging Sekhmet. Or if it was not true, then this odd woman was just permanently nervous.

Since grabbing the Newcomer's arms only scared the woman further, Nab decided to talk. She knew that the woman would not understand her, but repeating the same inviting sentence over and over might calm her down. And perhaps also appease Sekhmet, so she would not kill her guest.

Finally, the woman calmed down. Nab was relieved when the Newcomer walked to the entrance and – to everyone's surprise – proceeded to *touch* the Sekhmet statues! Nab was horrified. She would not be surprised if the Newcomer woman was stricken dead right there on the spot where she stood! Only the palace priests were allowed to touch, to clean, to adorn the statues…

All the palace servants following them froze in shock, staring at the odd Newcomer. Nab was embarrassed – it was her job to keep the Newcomer woman acting correctly! What kind of a servant was she, if she allowed her woman to get *killed* by an avenging goddess?

And so Nab decided to risk everything, including her life. She grabbed the Newcomer woman and pulled her off the Sekhmet statue, touching the statue herself to get the woman away. Forcefully propelling the Newcomer woman away from Sekhmet, Nab momentarily shut her eyes and lowered her head as much as possible to show Sekhmet that she was not the disrespectful one. As soon as the woman was away from the statue, Nab grabbed a handful of petals from the tray that the palace servant was holding and threw them at the Sekhmet statue, falling to her knees.

"Dear Highest Goddess, Sekhmet, the Detester of Untruth! It is all my fault for not holding the foreigner back, punish me, not her!"

After a while, when nothing happened, Nab stood up. Sekhmet must have been wise and seen that Nab corrected her mistake of allowing the woman to touch the sacred stone flesh. She had spared her. Nab took a breath and swallowed heavily. It was not every day that you faced Sekhmet and were left to stand unharmed.

Nervously she looked in the direction she pushed the Newcomer woman, fully expecting her to be dead. But she was not dead. She stood at the spot she had been pushed to, for some reason held on both sides by the palace servants, and was staring at Nab. The Newcomer was saying something, loudly, almost screaming. Nab felt she was failing. She had been given this most respected and trusted position by the beloved queen Tiye and she was failing!

She commanded the palace servants to release the Newcomer woman. To Nab's total surprise, the woman ran to her full speed and hugged her. *Hugged* her! Now, that was wrong on so many levels. She could really get in trouble for that. She had failed so far to make sure the Newcomer's behavior was appropriate! Nab was terrified, unsure of what to do. She tolerated the hug until the woman finally released her. The Newcomer was saying something, fast, using many words…

Attempting to remedy the situation, Nab fell to the ground. Maybe by lying on the floor her behavior would appear correct to the Newcomer, and she would finally stop embarrassing herself! But immediately Nab realized that was also a wrong move – she felt the woman's hands trying to lift her up as she repeated the same words she had said many times in the desert, "itsh okeye, itsh okeye…" There was no way to know what those words mean…

"Should I resist? Stay down?" mused Nab, feeling the insistent hands prying her from the stone floor. "Oh, she won't let go, she is determined to be inappropriate! I might as well…"

Nab got up and, without speaking, grabbed the Newcomer and forcefully pulled her into the doorway between the two Sekhmets.

Nab tried to make the Newcomer sit down. The woman wouldn't move.

"What land does she come from?" thought frustrated Nab, pointing again at the chair. "Don't they have chairs?"

The palace servants looked mortified. They were afraid to get in trouble because of Nab's rude action – how dare she push, then pull the Newcomer like that! "Oh, it is better than letting her embarrass herself any further!" snapped Nab out loud at their shocked faces.

Finally the Newcomer woman sat down on a low chair. Nab allowed herself a breath. She had finally been able to get the woman to cooperate a little.

While the Newcomer looked around, turning her head wildly, Nab reappeared with a bowl of liquid. It was time to wash the woman's feet. Nab was not sure what those odd attachments to her feet were, but she was prepared to clean them too.

The woman saw her activity and, to Nab's amazement, took the things off. Inside them were normal feet, but with red, bright red, coloring on the toe nails!

Nab washed her feet, paying extra attention to the colored toenails – she had never seen such bright shiny red enamel! Only the queen and her daughters wore color on their toes, she herself knew how to apply henna to make the red-orange color. But even royal henna was not this shiny! The other royals of the court had some toe coloring, but no one dared to make theirs brighter than the queen's or her daughters. One could be put out of favor for such a frivolity, yet this Newcomer's toes were colored brighter than the queen's! "She must be a princess or maybe even a queen in her own land somewhere… At least she had the sense to wear these contraptions on her feet to hide the fact. Perhaps not all sense of appropriateness is lost on this woman!" mused Nab. "How embarrassing it would be if the queen and everyone else saw that her toe coloring was brighter than the queen's!" It was a shocking thought and Nab shivered.

The woman's feet were washed and another bowl of water was brought into the room by the palace servants. "At least these girls are trained well," thought Nab appreciatively.

Two Nubian servant girls were holding a white sheet of cloth and whispering to each other, hiding smiles. Their blue-black skin, covered by shiny lotus oil, sparkled in the sunlight, and the tiny white kilts on their hips acted as a bright contrast. From the look of it, they were about fourteen or so. Nab hushed them and they froze. How dare they laugh at the odd garment the Newcomer was wearing!

Nab saw a strange look in the Newcomer's eyes. The woman looked like she had realized that Nab was not a lowly servant, but a special servant. The men who brought in the trays of food just moments ago, and these two Nubian girls – all were under her, Nab's, command. "I guess she finally understood," thought Nab, "that we are treating her with the highest respect. Why else would the Queen give me to her as a servant?" Nab finally felt in control, if not a bit frustrated with the Newcomer's inability to "do the right thing." But Nab was a patient person and she was prepared to spend thousands of years, if that's what it took, to make sure that her mistress did not embarrass herself any further.

Yet, strangely, the mistress did not feel embarrassed, but somewhat amused and nervous. "She is obviously curious about our culture," thought Nab, "and wants to find out the proper way to behave." This was a balsam to Nab's heart – finally the Newcomer woman was being more cooperative! She did not want to get Nab in trouble, and that was good. Her initial anxiety in the desert had finally quieted down, she felt safe for the time being. She looked hungrily at the tray of food. "That is a good sign," thought Nab. "No one who is hungry is going to make trouble if you give them food!" Nab immediately waved the men with the food trays to come closer. They placed the trays on the two low tables next to the woman's chair, and she looked at the food with desire in her eyes. "This is a very good sign indeed," thought Nab with satisfaction. "If I can feed her well, maybe we can find a way to connect!"

More servants came in. This time it was a palace fanner, a large Egyptian man with a huge fan, and a tiny Egyptian masseuse. The man was about her age, twenty, Nab guessed, but the tiny woman could have been a whole hundred. She had a shaved head – the only person, besides the priests, that she had seen on this trip from Waset without a wig in public. "I guess when you are that old, you just don't care," thought Nab.

The man began to move his fan over the Newcomer's head and she looked like she had just now noticed how hot she was. Nab was used to the heat, she originally came from Nubia and at home it was much hotter than this. But this woman's skin looked as if it was painted white, white like the plaster on the walls... "She might not find the heat comfortable," thought Nab, trying to assess her Newcomer's comforts.

"Jesjus, it musht be oveh hundred dekrees ine hereh…" Nab heard the woman mumble.

Nab did not know what the words meant, but seeing how gratefully the woman had accepted the fan, she told the man to wave it more often. At least something was working!

Somewhat relieved, Nab looked around the room – she had been to the Men-Nefer palace before, but never in the Sekhmet room. The walls were artistically decorated with paintings of large leopards and panthers hunting birds between flowers, and under her feet fish swam among the reeds on the painted tiles. Two large windows looked at the garden enclosure, and through them one could see slivers of the Sekhmet statues and flowering trees, and hear the water running somewhere in the garden. There were sounds of water and birds, but no voices – all the palace servants were busy with meal preparations.

Nab noticed her Newcomer's gaze directed at the opposite garden wall. Following it, Nab saw the third small wall opening positioned in the opposite wall close to the ceiling. "That is for air circulation," explained Nab tiredly, knowing the woman would not understand. "If only there was some wind, my Newcomer might enjoy it…" Perhaps he had heard her thoughts, because the man with the fan began to wave it faster.

Now that the woman had cooled down – the last thing Nab wanted was for her Newcomer to have heat sickness! – it was time to wash the rest of her skin. Nab pulled at the woman's top garment, then at her short pants. "What odd clothes they wear in her kingdom," thought Nab, tugging at the clothes. "These things wrap so tightly no wonder she is in anxiety!"

Nab had seen women in pants before, even though this was not an Egyptian or Nubian custom. The princesses from the Syrian or Mitanni cultures, especially, always wore brightly colored, loose, thin cloth pants. This Newcomer, though, had thick, tight pants on, too short for a woman of any culture. It did not cover her leg, ending a little above her knee, and it was not brightly colored, but resembled the color of the desert sand. Her upper garment was separate, and it was also odd – it had two layers: something tight over her breasts and torso, and a loose, larger thing over it, with pockets, loops and little round things sewn onto it. Nab had never seen anything like it before. "These things might be amulets?" silently wondered Nab, still tugging on it.

Noticing the woman's nervous look at the man with the fan, Nab immediately told him to go away, and he disappeared. He was replaced by one of the fourteen year old girls. The Newcomer understood Nab's message and took off her clothes. There was an audible "ahh!" in the room when they all saw her undergarments.

Nab was the only one who had the decency to keep her emotions in check. "Who are we to judge? Maybe this is what she has to wear for her husband. Maybe he demands that she have her breasts lifted into these cones and her hips hidden inside this…whatever it is!"

The Newcomer looked like she was finished undressing, refusing to take off the undergarments. Nab reasoned that the woman could just get washed in them. "Maybe she is not allowed to take these off, poor thing…"

Nab moved a wet cloth over the woman's skin and she seemed to appreciate it.

The older servant woman moved toward the Newcomer, ready for her task. Nab allowed her to approach her mistress with a jar of oil. She poured some on the Newcomer's feet and legs and began massaging them. Nab could take a breath. Finally her mistress was feeling comfortable!

Two large trays had been brought in, both filled with food. There were morsels of honeyed duck, and lots of fruit. Nab noticed that at first her Newcomer stuck to eating fruit, but she was so obviously hungry and stressed that she ended up also trying the bird.

Then the Newcomer woman did something very odd yet again – she invited Nab to eat with her! This was so inappropriate that Nab felt lost for a moment, unsure of how to respond. "Maybe I misunderstood and she did not mean for me to eat off her tray…" hoped Nab. But to her horror, the Newcomer woman was insistent and even stopped eating, waiting for Nab to join her!

Nab had to make a decision. "If she falls ill from emotion, or is somehow dissatisfied with me… It is wise then to do what she asks," she reasoned. And so Nab sent all the servants away. She even had to sacrifice the girl with the fan, knowing how much the Newcomer liked the fan. When everyone had left the room, Nab sat down on the floor mat on the opposite side of the food tray, took a piece of fruit, and put it in her mouth.

This was a huge violation of the norm, completely unacceptable. But this was what her mistress demanded and Nab's job was to keep her safe, appropriate, and happy. At this point she was still not behaving correctly, but she might feel happier…

The Newcomer woman smiled. "Oh, her teeth are the whitest pearls!" noticed Nab. They ate. The woman tasted dates and other fruits and dishes cautiously, as though she were afraid of being poisoned. "In her kingdom people must be very rude," mused Nab, watching her. "They poison guests?" The Newcomer kept inviting Nab to eat more. "Maybe she is having me test the food, to make sure it is not poisoned?" wondered Nab.

Once the woman had been fed, the tray was removed, and Nab gave her a cup of water to drink. The servant girls quickly brought in small cups of oil and rubbed the woman's hands with it. She seemed too tired to resist and she looked sleepy.

"Finally, she is well now, and after that meal she will sleep!" Nab mentally celebrated.

There was a bed in the room and Nab pointed it out to the woman. To Nab's surprise, the Newcomer stared at the bed as if it was something odd looking, not like the bed she expected. "Don't they have beds?" wondered Nab. But her job was to be alert and aware of all her guest's needs, no matter how odd. "In her kingdom the nobles must sleep on the floor then, like commoners," concluded Nab. The bed the Newcomer was offered was one of the best in the palace; it was similar to the one the Queen herself slept on. Low to the ground, with beautiful lion feet and Bes, the dwarf god of protection, carved into it, a cow hide stretched over the frame, a skillfully carved ebony headrest, the bed was covered with the softest feathered cushion and a thin layer of finest white cotton. Nab was determined to educate the Newcomer that sleeping on a bed was much better than sleeping on a floor!

The woman walked to the bed but only stared at it, as if it was a table or some other piece of furniture, not a bed. Nab, determined to help, pulled on the woman's arm, inviting her to sit down on the bed. Pointing at the carvings of Bes, Nab calmly explained that there is nothing to worry about, that he would keep the dream demons away. Finally, reluctantly, the Newcomer sat on the bed. The next step was to get her to lie down. Nab put the palms of her hands together and touched her own left cheek and closed her eyes for a moment, making sure that the woman was watching her. The woman understood! She definitely understood!

But she looked around as if she was missing something. "What is missing, what could possibly be missing?" wondered Nab, nervously following her gaze. The Newcomer's eyes rested on the piece of white cotton, a long cloth that could be used to cover her body if she decided to not wear her odd clothes anymore. "Does she want to put this on now?" Confused, Nab picked up the white cloth, but tried to explain that it was time to sleep, not to dress, and that the mistress should surely not sleep in clothes anyway. To Nab's shock, the Newcomer woman took the white cloth from her hands, made a ball of it and stuck it under her head, laying on the bed in the opposite direction! But Nab was the only one in the room and no one had seen this violation. "I am sure my mistress did not mean to insult the queen…" Nab told herself. "I will just keep this secret, so no one talks about it. That's the right thing to do. When she gets up, I will quickly unfold the cloth and offer it to her to wear. No one will know how she slept."

1,360BC

Queen Tiye in Men-Nefer Palace

After sleeping for five hours the queen was awake. She had needed the rest for what was to come. She sighed, watching Ibi, her body servant, stand ready with her clothes. Ibi was an intelligent woman of twenty six years, her perfect eye kohl reflecting her skill with the paints, but above all she was loyal. Tiye knew she would be told about any relevant gossip because Ibi, forever listening, knew it all.

"What did you hear of the Newcomers?" Tiye asked, extending her arms so Ibi could slide a tight sheath over her small body.

"There was talk about the disturbance in the garden court," said Ibi, straightening the sheath and putting a short rounded cloak over the queen's shoulders. She bent to fasten the sandals on Tiye's feet. "The Newcomer lady touched Sekhmet's statue and was spared by the goddess."

Tiye's lips pulled into a smile, which she quickly hid when Ibi got up from the floor. "Was there anything else?"

Ibi rubbed small pellets of incense underneath Tiye's arms. "There was a bad-doing…" she looked directly into Tiye's eyes and whispered, "but no one knows what occurred… Jatarhe, the servant you gave to the other man, not the very old one and not the very young…" Ibi pulled out a stool for the queen to sit down in front of a make-up table, "Jatarhe was found."

"Found?" Tiye was about to look at her face in the polished brass mirror, but her hand stopped midway and she looked at Ibi.

"Yes, my lady, he was found bound, with linen in his mouth!"

"Who did this?" demanded Tiye.

"Huy is attempting to find out, but he is sure it is the work of the Newcomer," said Ibi as she opened the jars of lotus perfume, kohl and ground lapis. "The talk is that Huy's face was stern and we know this means he had decided who to blame."

Huy was the High Steward of the Men-Nefer palace, and a well connected person – his father Heby was the mayor of Men-Nefer city itself, and his brother Ramose, who Tiye could not stand to be in the presence of, was a vizier to her husband Amenhotep III and the Governor of Waset city. If Huy was to make more of the disturbance, it could be very bad. Huy was one of the most dangerous men at court. Tiye was sure she did not want this bad-doing to continue but she also knew she could not reveal the identities of her "foreign guests." In the wrong hands, the information could lead to anything!

Ibi began her work, applying oil onto Tiye's upper eyelids, then the paste of ground lapis. Queen's eyes appeared larger and now gained a blue tint in addition to their natural dark color. Ibi drew precise lines with kohl, the mixture of soot and palm oil, onto Tiye's eyes. She then added golden sparkle from a small, brightly glazed jar. Pulling the queen's hair back with a golden band, she skillfully placed the heavy wig over it. The tiny braids of the wig were finished with beads of lapis, further highlighting Tiye's blue eyelids.

"Detain the servant." As the queen turned her head to face Ibi, the beads in her wig made a clicking sound. "Tell my bodyguards to find the Newcomer responsible before Huy does."

Ibi quickly bowed her head only, and ran out of the room. The large men at the entry to the queen's chamber repositioned themselves, feeling the weight of their responsibility – the queen was now alone.

Tiye stood up, and looked around. She sort of liked her Men-Nefer chambers, but not as much as her rooms in Malkata palace in Waset. It was here, in Men-Nefer, that all of her husband's unwanted wives lived. It was "the second royal harem," as the servants called it. Amenhotep III married many women, mostly for political purposes, and many lived here, never seeing their royal husband. Tiye did not enjoy being looked at with jealous eyes when she moved through the gardens of the harem. She had her own shady palace here, a separate place away from the rest of the women, and even though normally she would have been ready to leave this place, for the moment she found its seclusion useful. Amenhotep III was uncomfortable with the strangeness of his youngest son Amenhotep IV, and did not care much for the boy. Because of this the boy spent months at a time in Men-Nefer. But Tiye always went with him for at least part if not for the entire duration of his stay. Of course Amenhotep III did not miss her in the bed chamber, but he did miss her – Tiye was his friend and only ally. If he wanted her back from Men-Nefer, the prince came too. It was a gamble on Tiye's part, it could all turn out very wrong – but it felt right, and she always followed her intuition.

Tiye picked a date from the tray and sat down – Ibi would soon return with news. A bird flew into the room and Tiye watched it absentmindedly. It flew around the lotus bloomed columns and rested on one of the stone cornices resembling a petal. The air was sweetened by lavender and myrrh, and Tiye took a deep breath. What if they couldn't find the Newcomer? Was he dangerous? Why had he been bound by the others in the first place? Tiye's eyes mindlessly glided from the bird to the blue and red cushions on her bed, to the beautifully carved wig chests on the floor and the vases inlaid with ivory and black obsidian. She focused on the obsidian, then stood up and walked to one of the private chests she had brought with her on her barge from Waset. She opened it quickly, her hand searching inside. Looking back at the door to make sure the guards were not watching her, she pulled out a small knife. Its blade, made of sharpened obsidian stone, was deep black, and its golden handle glimmered momentarily in the sunlight. "I don't know what to expect. Sekhmet would not want me to die right now, and even though I trust her completely, she would not be pleased with unpreparedness," reasoned Tiye. She quickly sheathed the knife and hid it between her breasts under her short cloak. The tight wrap of her tunic, which came up underneath her breasts, would hold the knife in place.

Tiye heard footfalls on the stone floor and turned towards the door. The clicking sound of bracelets made her reasonably sure it was Ibi.

"Vizier Ay is with the Newcomer now, he took him away, out of the palace, before Huy found him."

"Where are they now?"

Ibi looked over her shoulder as if to make sure the guards were not paying any attention to their conversation, and whispered, "They were seen walking the Royal Road to the wharf."

"Good." Tiye fell silent for a moment, and Ibi knew better than to disturb her.

"I will meet the Newcomers alone," commanded the queen, and Ibi quickly bowed her head. "Vizier Ay, and the others, are not to be informed."

"Yes, my lady. How do you want me to arrange the meeting?"

"After the sunset ceremony in the Temple of Ptah, bring them into the Audience Chamber – they are foreign guests and I will see them properly." Tiye frowned at the thought of having to hide. So far everyone in the palace assumed the Newcomers were simply guests from a foreign land, and she must preserve that perception. Meeting them in any other place would only instigate more gossip, and that she did not want. Over the years Tiye had learned that gossip could be used to her advantage. If properly supplied, it could cover up Maat – but only for the sake of keeping to Maat in the first place!

Meeting the Newcomers without the other Shenu present was a tricky business – it could create an impression of conspiring. Yet this is exactly what Tiye was doing. According to tradition she should have brought a few of the Shenu into the Audience Chamber to speak with the Newcomers. They, as were any people important to Sekhmet, were to be heard by the entire thirteen, if possible. Most Shenu were prominent people at court, but even then Tiye would never dream of summoning them all to Men-Nefer palace – it was way too dangerous, they would be exposed. They were sought after by the people in power: the pharaohs, nobles and the priests of Amun, so preserving their anonymity was essential. But she held no illusions about her decision. Tiye wanted to be alone with the Newcomers, and that was the real reason for the private meeting. It was not for the protection of the Shenu.

"All these politics!" thought Tiye with frustration. Her father Yuya, conveniently considered to be a commoner by the current establishment, was of Phoenician decent through the Hyksos kings of the Delta – they were removed from power in Lower Egypt by the pharaoh Seqenenre Tao two centuries earlier. Many generations removed, Yuya was still of a princely descent and a very inventive and intelligent man. "He was so many things…" mused Tiye, "such an influential man, a Senior Overseer of Horses – a high military position, the Superintendent of Herds, and a Priest of Min in Khent-Min. He could have been a general if he had lived longer…" In death he had been given another high honor – his tomb was to the west of the Nile, in the hill next to the tombs of the pharaohs. This was an unheard of privilege for a commoner! "But mostly, he was a master politician. Who else could have orchestrated the marriage of his daughter, officially also a commoner, to a pharaoh?" smiled Tiye to herself, "and as the Principal Wife at that!" He had done exactly what his father did before him. Yuya's sister Mutemwiya was married into the royal harem of the pharaoh at the time, Thutmose IV, as one of many minor wives. But through Yuya's and his father's cunning, Mutemwiya's son, a minor half-royal offspring, was made a pharaoh after Thutmose's death. He took the royal name of Amenhotep III – and he was now Tiye's husband.

Tiye smiled, thinking of her aunt Mutemwiya – Amenhotep III elevated her to the status of a Great Royal Wife of Thutmose IV, no doubt to legitimize his claim to the throne, making Tiye's family even more influential.

Tiye's elder brother Anen held the position of Chancellor of Lower Egypt and the Second Prophet of Amun. Two of his elder daughters were now in Tiye's husband's harem as minor wives, and his son was climbing the ladder of the priesthood, while two of his younger daughters remained unmarried. Tiye had never trusted Anen – he was pretentious and fanatical when it came to worshipping Amun. Now Anen resided in Men-Nefer only part of the time. He spent most of his time in Waset, positioning himself to become the High Priest of Amun. But Tiye knew he was ill and, with a sigh, she thought that Anubis might come for her elder brother before he could achieve his dream.

But Tiye's other brother, Ay, was strong and no less powerful than Anen, only he followed their father's military path, becoming Overseer of the Horses. Tiye guessed that Ay would not stop until he became the Senior Overseer of the elite charioteering division of the army. Tiye knew that in Maat Ay cared even less about the military than about Amun. Ay cared only for political power, he despised actual combat. His titles were political, but his association with the military allowed the family to keep their fingers in all areas of power.

Tiye's mother, Thuja, when she was alive, did not share Anen's priestly obsessions, although she would never have let it show. She trusted Ay and Tiye more than she ever would Anen. "Father married well," thought Tiye. Her mother was a noblewoman, destined to hold high positions at court. She was a descendant of queen Ahmose-Nefertari, and through her, of queen and a female pharaoh Sobekneferu. Everyone knew that queen Ahmose-Nefertari was a daughter of pharaoh Seqenenre Tao and queen Ahhotep, both of whom fought the Hyksos kings. The marriage of Thuja, their descendant, to Yuya, the descendant of the Hyksos, closed the centuries old rift.

Thuja had been Superintendent of the Royal Harem, first at Khent-Min and later in Waset, and also the Chief of Entertainers of

Amun and Min; she was always at the front of the processions. Everyone knew her, and the title of Singer of Hathor was not honorary – she had an amazing voice! But she had passed to the Land of the Dead a long time ago, laid to rest next to her husband in the Valley of the Kings. Tiye missed them.

*   *   *

"My lady, it is time." Ibi held a sheer golden cloth in her hands, ready to wrap it around the queen's waist as a sash.

A trumpet sounded three times, taking Tiye out of her thoughts, and she stood up. The golden sash was wrapped around her body, and a large collar of beads placed around her neck by Ibi's expert hands. The heavy royal headdress now adorned her head. Tiye was ready.

She walked out of the room carefully so as not to disturb her headdress, Ibi following her closely. The guards parted at the door, then followed the two women a few steps behind. As she exited her private quarters, Tiye was met by a dozen of Men-Nefer's noblewomen who bowed deeply to her and praised her health and her dress. Tiye made small talk with them, then resumed her walk to the courtyard. Amenhotep IV, her eight-year-old son, was waiting there for her. He was dressed in a white cloth, and a large gold collar on his shoulders glittered in the light of the setting sun.

They were led to two small palanquins, both ornately decorated with gold-encrusted images offering praises to the gods. Tiye was helped into the first one, while her son climbed into the second. As she felt the ornate box being lifted, she settled back onto the bright orange cushion and looked outside. Although she would have preferred to put the shades down she made herself keep them open, and smiled at nobles and commoners alike as the men carried her litter out of the palace and onto the Royal Road. Participating in the Temple of Ptah ceremony was her duty as queen, and Tiye would not disappoint the people.

But once they had left the main crowd and people were not as close to her palanquin, Tiye returned to her thoughts, staring mindlessly ahead.

Her thoughts returned to the Shenu as she attempted to put recent events in perspective. Tiye had been initiated into the Shenu by her parents and Ay. Anen had never suspected, he was too obsessed with the godhood of Amun to understand.

Ay was a man of twenty years when their beloved parents initiated him into the Shenu. He was their father's inheritor and Tiye was to become their mother's. Tiye was already Chief Queen by then, successfully married to her cousin, Mutemwiya's son, Amenhotep III. Strangely, Tiye had never thought of Amenhotep, or his father Thutmose IV, as gods. She knew they were important people, burdened with the responsibility for the most powerful country in the world, and also privileged beyond measure. But living gods? No. So when her parents and her brother told her the truth about the real star-gods and the promise to Sekhmet, it had all made sense to Tiye. It was logical, and she valued reason greatly. The secret of the Shenu felt like no secret at all, but like something she had already known.

It came as no surprise that her mother Thuja held the position of the High Priestess in the Shenu – she had always been much more interested in the "why" than the "how" and "what." Her mother saw Tiye as the chosen one, predicting that she would eventually lead the Shenu as well. Even though this was an elected position, not an inherited one, everyone agreed that Tiye would be Thuja's successor. She had always shown qualities that would serve her well as High Priestess: strength of character, independent thinking, wisdom, and the ability to be unseen when needed. Her inner light was strong, and her passion for truth led her forward.

A young woman threw lotus flowers at the palanquin and two of the blooms landed right on Tiye's lap. She smiled and pronounced a blessing for the woman's happiness, loud enough for her to hear. As the palanquin moved on Tiye saw the woman fall to the ground, proclaiming thanks to the gods and the queen.

Tiye remembered her Shenu training – she had been just a little older than this woman at the time. All those long hours of studying, reading, thinking… She was taught three other languages in addition to official Lower Egyptian and her home town Upper Egyptian dialects, and she could speak and write them fluently. She was also educated, much more thoroughly than her husband the pharaoh, in mathematics, astronomy, architecture and medicine. As Chief Queen she had access to the latest discoveries of science in Egypt and any country it dealt with, and as a Shenu she had access to the sacred vaults. Tiye had descended into these vaults sixteen times in her forty years – more than any other living Shenu. She was fascinated with the truth; she had to know all she could, as her passion to serve Sekhmet was strong. Her brother Ay also had a sharp mind, but he was more talented at understanding societal power struggles and international politics than the path of human consciousness. He followed the teachings of their father, the master politician, while Tiye walked in the footsteps of their mother, the mystic. She became special to the Shenu, and not only because of her education and skills. Tiye was the only Shenu in many generations who had gone through the gate and met Sekhmet on the other side.

*   *   *

Tiye sat up a little straighter on her cushion, and her eyes, glass-like and still, stared into the past as she summoned into her mind the memory with heightened excitement, yet deep sorrow. Many would have been terrified and perhaps died of fright, but Tiye was exhilarated and she did not feel fear. All thirteen Shenu were in the well that time, yet all but she fell to the ground unconscious when the gate had opened. The next moment Tiye was the only one in the well. At first she was disoriented, but then she decided that if this was her destiny, she could not be harmed by it. "Even if I am struck dead, that must be my destiny, so there is no harm in it." She waited and waited, and when nothing else happened, she elected to climb out of the well to the surface. It was nighttime. To her surprise all the stars looked different. At home she spent hours looking at the sky, studying the ancient texts about the stars, and she knew her sky well – this sky was not her sky! Looking around she saw more discrepancies. Only one of the massive pyramids was visible, it looked different and it had something else over it, Tiye was not sure what. When she felt the presence of Sekhmet behind her, young Tiye turned around, without fear. She met the amber eyes of the goddess.

Sekhmet was incredibly tall. Tiye never imagined anyone could be so tall, she felt like a child next to her. It never occurred to Tiye to contemplate what Sekhmet really looked like – the statues of her had been enough, and in them she was small, sturdy but feminine, with the head of a lioness. The real Sekhmet looked completely different. Her tall body appeared almost weightless. She had a thin waist and a long neck, resembling more a cat than a woman, and she moved strangely when she walked. Her skin seemed shiny under the starlight, blue-white with gold sparkles – nothing Tiye had ever seen. But her most amazing feature was her face – Tiye could not see it because it was covered by a gold mask, the thick, beautiful mask of a lioness. The mask was attached to the

220

goddess' head with a shiny gold-red woven ribbon, and Tiye couldn't imagine how something that looked so heavy could so easily stay on someone's face. There were openings in the mask for her eyes and mouth, and Tiye wondered if the goddess needed to breathe air or not. Sekhmet's eyes had a reflective shine like a cat's eyes, yet the deep orange amber color was brighter than the carnelians in the pharaoh's crown under the sunlight! Sekhmet wore her dark hair down, and straight. Tiye suspected that the color might be blue-black, matching her blue-white skin tone. Her hair somehow seemed to be an extension of her being, so Tiye assumed it was not a wig. As Sekhmet motioned with her arm to follow her, she turned her head, and Tiye gasped – she had a pointed ear! Sekhmet's mask also had ears, rounded ones like a lioness would have, yet her own ears were set farther back and the pointed tips poked through the flowing hair. Walking on the lush green field behind Sekhmet, Tiye wondered with a smile, was there also a tail under that long, gold-red skirt of the goddess?

Tiye followed the goddess into what resembled a town. There were many people, hundreds – but they were all silent, looking at Sekhmet as she walked. Sekhmet's footfalls were also silent, like a cat's, and all Tiye could hear was the sound of her own sandals slapping the stone. Tiye began to feel uncomfortable – she had never seen a crowd being this quiet. And she was the only one walking behind Sekhmet; everyone else stood motionless. Soon they met two women, who said something to Sekhmet, and then looked at Tiye. The people all around her, including these two women, were a little taller than most people Tiye knew. There was no hostility in their eyes, but neither was there curiosity – it was sadness that was all permeating. But Tiye was not afraid. If this was her destiny, she must face it.

They walked towards a strange, large structure that had neither walls nor ceiling, only vertical and horizontal columns and beams. The building was illuminated by fires in large stone pits, and its shape could easily be discerned. Beyond it, to the east, Tiye could see in the starlight an outline of the shore sloping towards glistening waters. When she turned to the west, she gasped – a whitish light was coming from what seemed to be the ground. It was a localized light and didn't seem to be illuminating anything.

"How could there be sunlight in the west? What else can produce a white light?" thought Tiye, when she felt someone pulling her arm – it was one of the women who had come to greet Sekhmet. She led Tiye east, to the structure's entrance. Purple and yellow flowers whose likeness Tiye had never seen, decorated the path. Mesmerized by the flowers, Tiye swiveled her head to take in everything – the columns were made of wood and were intricately decorated with carvings, and the horizontal beams were wrapped in red and yellow cloth and small stone lamps were hanging on them. A gentle breeze swirled the smoke of the lamps, filling the air with an intoxicating bouquet of smells. Tiye felt a soft push to keep walking. Apparently the goddess was already inside the structure – Tiye could see her tall figure farther ahead between the carved columns, and she followed her in.

People silently moved west through the structure and soon Tiye saw what lay ahead. It was a building of enormous size, bigger than the Temple of Amun in Waset. This structure had walls and a ceiling, and it was painted a very dark color, black or dark blue. It was not illuminated from the outside, and its shape stood dark against the black night sky. On the floor in the center of it was a pool of white fire, and Tiye blinked, unable to believe it. As her eyes adjusted to the brightness, she understood that the central part of the floor in this cavernous temple was covered with small shallow bowls. In them some oil burned, but not with red-orange or yellow flames – instead it the flames were white, creating the illusion of a blazing white sea. Sekhmet stood on a stone block in the middle of these lamps, her shape wavering in the fire's heat. A group of men and women formed a rectangle around her and the fiery floor. They were priestesses and priests of the ancient mystery schools – Tiye recognized the necklaces they wore. Her fingers touched the ancient piece of gold she wore on her own neck, the square plate of a Shenu priestess. Inscribed with an ancient spell, the plate had been worn by generations of the Shenu before her, and it looked very similar to the regalia of the people who were gathered here.

Sekhmet made a long piercing sound, nothing like Tiye had ever heard, and glared at everyone as she slowly rotated her body.

"I know what you are feeling. But there is an all-encompassing Maat, and *that* truth is bigger than this feeling." Her voice was melody and power. Tiye recognized the words – it was a slightly accented pronunciation of the ancient language of the star-gods that the Shenu knew.

"Remember what we taught you – there is no end, only its perception. There will never be an end. Life is ever-present. You are ever-present. I am ever-present."

Being the shortest person there, Tiye couldn't see Sekhmet very well, and as she was unwilling to miss anything she looked around for higher ground. She spotted a set of stone steps by the temple wall – they extended upwards well above the heads of the people, disappearing into the darkness of the ceiling. Quickly she climbed the first five steps, which made her only slightly taller than most of the priests, but now she could clearly see Sekhmet in the distance and the effect of her words – the faces in the group gained resolution. Everyone assembled there knew what was coming and what needed to be done – they could not fall into despair, could not give into the unbearable pain of loss.

"When the Flood waters recede, there will be a very different Earth. All the filaments, the crystalline energy structures and the fires of the Spirit that we treasure, will not be here. You will have to persevere in staying alive and awake!"

Tiye inhaled sharply, feeling the tightness in her chest. "Survivors would have to do much more than just stay alive..." whispered Tiye.

Sekhmet continued: "Remember all that we have taught you; remain with a live Mer-Ka-Ba, spinning Light Body! This geometry of Spirit within you will keep your memory intact. The others will only save their bodies, but you will save your awakening!"

The priest and priestesses began to exit the temple. Sekhmet was no longer standing in the middle of the fiery floor. Unsure of what to do, Tiye climbed down the steps and exited the temple with the others.

This was 10,845 BC, the very end of the Age of Virgo, and the Sirian time on Earth was coming to an end. Soon the Age of Leo would begin, ushering in the downward flow of consciousness in the precessional half-cycle, just as the ancient texts had taught her. Tiye stood outside the temple, staring at the lush valley where in her time there was only desert. The huge transparent, pyramid-shaped "bird," which had been sitting over the pyramid for millennia, was beginning to shimmer. Soon it would shift into other dimensions and disappear as though it had never existed. Tiye noticed that there had been other "birds," now departed, the only evidence being partial platforms.

Then Tiye heard a sound – an all-penetrating sound that made the reality of form unsure of itself. The space itself began to vibrate, yet it was not an earthquake. There were people all around her, watching in silence – she could hear their collective sigh as the "bird" disappeared into other realms, and with its disappearance the sound ended. She looked at the faces around her and they reflected patient anticipation of something terrible about to happen, something they could not stop, like the Nile flooding its banks and taking with it the structures built along its shores. No one here had ever seen the pyramid without the "bird" atop it, even though they knew that it could appear and disappear, and the sight of the naked pyramid increased the resolution that the end was coming. Of course it was not the end of the world, but it was the end of the world as they knew it.

"It is the end of Zep Tepi, when Akhu walked the Earth…" said Tiye, exhaling.

*　　　*　　　*

Darkness fell on the ancient town, and Nut-the-night-sky protectively stretched her body over it, shining the light of thousands of stars over the people. Tiye heard the word "come," and when she turned around, saw a girl of no more that twelve urging her to follow. Silently winding through the garden paths, Tiye followed the girl into one of the chambers at the side of the large temple. To Tiye's surprise, Sekhmet awaited her there, seated in an armchair.

They spoke, and Sekhmet revealed many secrets to Tiye. Most of what she was told was already known to Tiye from her studies of the vaults, but there were some secrets she had not known. Then, when Sekhmet looked as though she had said all she wanted, Tiye mastered her courage and asked: "Why did you bring me here, beloved Sekhmet?"

Tiye did not understand when the goddess answered, "I do not know."

How was it possible? How could Sekhmet not know something? But it was not for Tiye to judge the goddess; she was awake enough to let go of her desire for security through this star-god's omnipotence!

Seeing Tiye's confusion, Sekhmet smiled underneath her gold mask.

"I brought you here, Tiye, because you are an important person. But the 'I' who brought you here is not the one who you stand in front of now, for the one who you see does not know why the 'I' from the other time brought you here. I must need your help."

Tiye would do anything for her beloved star-god. She had truthfully answered many questions about her current life, her pharaoh, her position at court, and also about the priests, the land of Egypt and the whole world.

Sekhmet listened intently, then she stood and asked Tiye to walk with her back to the "time-beacon." Tiye could only assume she meant the glowing little pyramid she had seen inside the well – that was apparently the time-gate. She glanced at Sekhmet; she felt that Sekhmet's demeanor was different from when they first met near the well. The goddess's expression was hidden under the mask, of course, but Tiye could swear her face showed deep concern.

Leaving Tiye at the mouth of the well, Sekhmet walked away. Tiye began to climb down the well. As she carefully gripped the rungs of the beautifully painted ladder, she tried to process the events. "The "bird" left, I saw it shimmer away..." Tiye was so engrossed by her thoughts that she scarcely noticed the ladder, missed a step and almost fell to her death. Forcing herself to pay attention to the rungs under her hands and feet, she climbed. Soon she was at the bottom. Walking into the room with the small, glowing pyramid, she struggled to think about what she would tell her Shenu when she returned.

*   *   *

A bright flash of light went through Tiye with a vibrating wave, and when the whiteness dissipated and Tiye could see again she looked for her fellow Shenu, but there was only Sekhmet – right there at the bottom of the well!

"Something must have gone wrong!" thought Tiye. Out loud she said: "Beloved Sekhmet, the goddess in Maat... Why am I here?"

"Because I have brought you here, Tiye, High Priestess of the Shenu."

Tiye had to sit down – here was the same Sekhmet, but her face, illuminated by torches, revealed a slightly different mask. It was lighter looking, thinner. And Sekhmet's body looked different too – there was no gold shimmer in her blue-white skin, and she seemed much denser, heavier, as if every motion caused her pain.

"What happened to you, blessed Sekhmet... if I may ask?" whispered Tiye, watching Sekhmet carefully sit down. Had she climbed all the way down here for me?

Sekhmet told Tiye a long story, a very personal one – of her attempt to support the people; how she stayed behind, unable to convince the other star-gods to remain on Earth; about the suffering of the people; and about her own pain. Tiye's tears ran freely, and she took Sekhmet's hand – the goddess's fingers were long and there were a few dark scratches on her knuckles crusted over with what looked like blood. But there was resolve in Sekhmet; she was not falling apart, her suffering had dignity to it.

Sekhmet revealed that Tiye's visit to Zep Tepi, at the time before the Great Flood, had been initiated by her, Sekhmet, today, so that she could tell herself in the past to remain on Earth. She was glad she had listened to herself, she said. But she was also now aware of something else – a message had come to her, from herself.

Tiye did not understand this, but apparently there was a whole other part to Sekhmet, a cat part. That cat was able to see the future, and after looking at what had not yet happened, she had revealed to Sekhmet what needed to be initiated. That was why, despite the excruciating pain, Sekhmet had come into the well – to tell Tiye what was to come, and what had been designed to be the salvation of the human race.

"I am hardly the person you need to talk to, my beloved Sekhmet! Perhaps the High Priestess of the Shenu will be able to follow your will…"

"You are to be the next Higher Priestess of the Shenu; it is my will and the decision of the Solar Council. But you must let others elect you into that position, and not tell them that you know your fate."

"Oh, Sekhmet, if I am chosen, I must believe I am worthy!"

"You are – because you are brave. Many people believe they are fearless, but all they do is hide from their fear, and one day it will catch up with them. You are truly brave, and that is why you have been chosen. I saw that the Shenu from a future time will come to your time, and it is your duty to help the change they will initiate. They are a sign for you."

After that there were more words from Sekhmet, some of which she asked Tiye to repeat again and again until they were etched in her memory. When Sekhmet was satisfied, she told Tiye to step back into the small room – then the bright flash of light brought Tiye back into her own time, where the other Shenu lay on the floor of the well and she was the only one standing and conscious. No one had felt, seen, heard, or experienced what she had. To them, seconds had passed. To her – at least twelve hours.

*   *   *

Tiye's palanquin suddenly changed direction and the sounds became louder. They had turned into the temple's entrance where commoners crammed the narrow path, hoping for a glimpse of the queen's litter before it arrived at the main temple plaza at the end of the Royal Road. The crowd was screaming now, their hands extended in an attempt to touch her gilded palanquin. The guards' commands became more insistent, pushing the people back. They were almost there…

226

Tiye sighed as she thought of Sekhmet's words now. She knew the prophecy by heart – it was one of the most important messages for the Shenu. She recited it again in her mind, as she had done many times in the last year: *The two Shenu from the other side will open the gate at the beginning of the beginning. The two were chosen by the Council, and their arrival will bring the time for people to remember how to breathe. This begins the end, and people will try to forget. But the will of the Council will be done, and the gate will be sealed until people remember again.*

Sekhmet's words were contradictory, yet Tiye was determined to do her duty well. She understood that higher beings cannot always say directly what they mean because the meaning of such magnitude does not often fit into the words available now. She was sure that Sekhmet was as clear as she could be. The prophecy was recorded. Tiye did eventually become the High Priestess of the Shenu. Strangely enough, her election upset Ay. She knew it was because he had wanted to be the one chosen. But he did not know what she knew...

Tiye had a secret of her own, something she was told during her encounter with Sekhmet. She did not understand all the details of the secret message, but she had spent her entire life deciphering it, studying and learning. Sekhmet had entrusted to her a very important role, and Tiye was determined not to disappoint her goddess. She was not sure how to accomplish what was asked of her – to be a vessel, twice, for the change of Earth. She was meant to generate a pathway for what had to come. The task came with a complicated set of instructions, and it involved Sekhmet and other star-gods. Tiye was the only one who was to know the secret, but Ay was to be involved. Tiye was prepared to take the secret to her grave.

She loved her brother Ay dearly and the gods knew how much they had been through together. Their stories could fill lifetimes! They had shared many secrets, many bizarre and powerful experiences – but who were they to argue with Sekhmet? In recent years he had become more interested in political power. He had wished to be the High Priest of Shenu, and had expressed that wish to her. It was strange, because the top position was always reserved for a woman; such was Sekhmet's will. And having Tiye, a woman, be the only one in recent history to actually step through the gate and, in a sense, be in two different times, talk to Sekhmet in person, see the unsee-able and bring back the prophecy – well, that proved the point. Yet Tiye felt that Ay thought she was "too fortunate," that the only reason she had been given all the social and material wealth that she had, was because she had been groomed to be the High Priestess from the beginning. He intentionally overlooked

Tiye's personal accomplishments and filled his mind with the idea that it had all been done *for* her, that nothing was due to her merit. Tiye sighed, thinking about her brother. He was simply jealous of her status.

"How silly," she thought. "The Shenu are one, we serve Sekhmet, all our wealth is collective and so is our power. The only reason I am in the position I am in, is because this serves Sekhmet's will the best."

The procession stopped and Tiye parted the curtain a little to see why. Immediately the crowds exploded in loud screams. Carefully balancing her golden headdress, Tiye made herself smile. But her thoughts were with her brother.

"I wonder if Ay is here with the Newcomer man? Perhaps they are already in the temple?" Ay and Tiye had always been allies and friends. But lately there had been darker internal currents in her brother that she did not understand. It was as though he anticipated the coming of a dark cloud and was frustrated by his inability to make it go away. "Some clouds are meant to be endured," thought Tiye. It was perhaps because of this frustration with her brother that Tiye had made the decision to see the Newcomers alone at first. Ay had behaved almost rudely in the well, and Tiye wanted her space with the Newcomers to be clear and uninterrupted.

*   *   *

Tiye felt her litter being lowered to the ground. As she carefully stepped out of it, holding her headdress with her left hand, her right was immediately clasped by the High Priest of Ptah who was ready to lead her into the temple's shade. Tiye turned, wanting to make sure her absentminded son had gotten out of his palanquin. He was out, and was looking at her for direction. She sighed. No matter how many times Amenhotep IV accompanied her to ceremonies he never seemed to remember what to do, yet she knew his mind was sharp. "He prefers the sky to the earth," thought Tiye as she followed the High Priest, his white robes and blue skull cap unmistakable in any crowd.

They were at the main entrance to the district of Ptah on earth. Like an impenetrable fortress, its huge white walls surrounded three main temples and many minor ones. There were schools, offering places, storage houses and much more. In case of war the district could stay protected for months once it had closed its massive gates. One of the walls was adjacent to a palace, and on the other side of the palace was a Temple of Ptah, where Tiye had participated in the earlier ceremony. It was the temple her husband had built to honor himself, Ptah, and, on Tiye's insistence, Sekhmet. Gods related to cities, and as the power of priests and wealth of the cities rose and fell, so did the god's perceived power. "People are so very lost," mused Tiye, walking slowly. "Ptah came to be associated with Atum because Atum's priests gained political power. But they did not do it by themselves," she smiled, "they associated Atum with Ra and Horus. This, of course, meant that since they considered Hathor to be Atum's mother, she had to become the wife of Ptah." Here Tiye played her own politics. Sekhmet was worshipped in the Hathor temples as well, and as Sekhmet was associated with Hathor, she became "the wife of Ptah." Tiye enjoyed going to this temple in particular, because it was the place where her husband's statues stood next to Ptah and her beloved Sekhmet.

They walked along the avenue of shining sphinxes and past one of the huge white pylons of the outer wall, which featured statues of eight of the most powerful gods, taking the procession to the large Temple of Ptah-Seker. In front of the temple were large, shallow vessels smoking with incense of myrrh and lavender, and as Tiye joined the priestesses, she also took in the scent of amber. The priestesses of Ptah were the wives and daughters of priests, viziers and generals. They were dressed in more gold than there was on the altars, yet their bodies were covered only by a thin cloth. Tiye was by far the oldest woman among them. She heard the voice of the High Priest of Ptah and saw his blue skullcap ahead of her – he had begun the sunset ceremony. The priestesses followed him, singing and shaking their sistrums, their jangling sound echoing in the large temple. In between the two rows of priestesses walked boys with offerings.

Tiye, with Amenhotep IV beside her, moved to the center of the procession. Together they walked through the long inner temple corridor. The path, adorned with flowers and jars of incense, was filled with a multitude of people, most of them royals of the court. Some had accompanied the queen and young Amenhotep on their journey from Waset to the delta, but most were local nobles. This was their chance to see the queen and the boy, and to honor the gods together. On the ground among the nobles lay the servants.

Walking slowly so as not to disturb the heavy gold headdress, Tiye thought about the Newcomers. She had studied the prophecy for the past twenty years of her life and she was sure that this was the right time. The boy next to her was the Chosen One, the one who would initiate remembrance in the people. How this would come to pass Tiye did not know. But she was sure she was right – she had correctly calculated the time to be in the well when the Newcomers arrived. And so the rest of her assumptions must also be correct. This boy, the young prince Amenhotep IV, has to become the next pharaoh.

This was where the queen ran into a snag in her smooth thinking. Her first son, Thutmose V, was the Crown Prince, not the boy Amenhotep IV. According to the law, and the will of her husband, Thutmose V was to be the next pharaoh. He had been groomed to become one since birth. But now Tiye was sure that this would not happen. Somehow her youngest boy, Amenhotep IV, was the one – the Chosen One.

Slowly rotating her head to the side, Tiye looked at the boy. He was oblivious to the procession, the people, the temple. He was always preoccupied with his thoughts. Amenhotep's dismissal of the royal ceremonies to the gods was one of the reasons Tiye knew he was the One. This was dangerous, this was treason and heresy… but it was the truth. Just like her, he intuitively did not believe that his father or most of the gods of Egypt were really gods. Tiye did not explain anything of this to him and did not help to clarify his intuitive notions. But now she was sure that he would eventually do what he was meant to do. It was her job to make that happen, somehow…

They arrived at the inner altar of Ptah-Seker. Raising her eyes upwards, Tiye could see the well-lit statues of Ptah and Seker, the dark granite shining red in the light of the lamps. Ptah, the craftsman of the world, and Seker, the craftsman of openings – together they held the mystery of creation, reincarnation, and transformation, just as Osiris did.

"Seker of Ro-Setau, what opening do you hold for me?" whispered Tiye to herself. She knew the true meaning of Osiris's transformation, she herself had gone through the secret Shenu initiations, and as she looked at the falcon face of Seker, she felt the weight of what was to come. The well that the Newcomers had come out of was in the land of Seker, in the sacred district of Ro-Setau where the giant pyramids stood. This area was indeed sacred – all was a manifestation of the sky on earth, the land the star-gods walked on. Seker's crooked beak remained motionless, betraying no answer to Tiye's question. She knew that the enormous bas-relief of a mound behind his statue represented Ro-Setau, and Ptah, who stood next to Seker, looked relaxed leaning on it.

"They both protect Maat from being dispersed to the ignorant," said Tiye to herself as she shifted her gaze to the priests. The sounds of singing and sistrum fell silent as the High Priest of Ptah raised his hands in prayer. His fingers held gilded *ankh*, *was* and *djed* and Tiye smiled, knowing that the priest did not comprehend the true meaning of these objects.

When the high priest was finished, the other priests brought the offerings to Ptah and Seker. Together they made a long incantation of numerous petitions for the good health and well-being of the pharaoh Amenhotep III and his son, the Crown Prince Thutmose V.

Thutmose V, Tiye's eldest son, was home, with his father. He was not feeling well and this was fortunate in a way, as otherwise he would have wanted to come along, this being the district of Ptah in Men-Nefer after all. But it was the will of the gods that he was left at home, and so he was. Tiye remembered him playing with Ta-miu, his pet cat... This man, a future pharaoh, was more interested in being a priest than a pharaoh. His official title was the Overseer of the Priests of Lower and Upper Egypt, along with the High Priest of Ptah in Waset. Both titles had been given to him by the priests for completing his initiations. For a while Tiye thought that maybe he was going to be the one. But as she watched him growing up, it became clear to her that he was not. He was religious in his nature, he did not have his own authority; he gave it all to the gods. "Well, mostly to the priests," she remarked to herself. Tiye felt that no one fully dependent on the will of the gods could lead the country. Thutmose V was content with being a priest and playing with Ta-miu. That was all he wanted. Tiye was convinced that Ta-miu was somehow Sekhmet, or at least she was connected to Sekhmet. That cat had been given to Thutmose when he was only three years of age and she had taken his will. Tiye did not know how the cat had done it, but it was apparent. Ta-miu was the most trusted advisor Thutmose had ever had. He insisted on having her carried everywhere he went and he was seen many times talking to her. "The cat made him into a priest," thought Tiye. And Ta-miu was very old, older than even most temple cats. Years ago Thutmose prepared a beautiful limestone sarcophagus for Ta-miu, to honor her life. It was to be placed into his own tomb eventually, so that he could reunite with his beloved cat in the afterlife. And now Ta-miu was sixteen years old. Even Sekhmet could not keep her in the flesh much longer. Tiye had an intuitive notion that when Ta-miu passed over to the Land of the Dead, so would her eldest son.

The ceremony was finally complete. Tiye carried the small bowl of incense to be placed on the altar of Ptah and Seker, and once it was done, followed the priestesses out of the temple. The crowds of commoners were held back by the large gates beyond the pylons, but at the temple's entry hundreds of noblewomen greeted her, tossing barley seeds and lotus blossoms at her feet. The queen was expected to bless the people. Her young son was by her side. Tiye was not sure if he had noticed that the ceremony was over – he was still preoccupied with his thoughts and simply went through the familiar motions.

After the blessing, instead of taking the longer route to the palace, Tiye decided to be done with it all. She felt tired of the crowds. Commanding the guards to walk with her straight to the palace, she knew the people would be disappointed when they saw the royal palanquins being carried away empty, but it would have to be. There were more important events to focus on.

As she walked inside the walled district of Ptah Tiye saw the faces of the Newcomers – the older man Sahed, the woman, and the young man. Ibi was standing next to them, along with their body servants. "Good girl," thought Tiye with satisfaction. "She has already gathered them, and is prepared to bring them back to the palace at once." The previously bound Shenu was not with them. "Perhaps my brother did not anticipate my unexpected exit, away from the Royal Road," she smiled to herself, again with satisfaction. She was not sure why it felt so right to exclude the other Newcomer, sooner or later they will have to talk. But Huy, the Steward of Men-Nefer, was looking for that man, and Tiye was sure he was the one who had bound the servant. It was wise to exclude him, and Ay would have to wait.

Inside the palace courtyard with its perfectly trimmed flowering trees, Tiye finally stopped. Her neck ached from the tension of walking perfectly upright with the heavy headdress over her wig, but she refused to show it. Parting with her son, she kissed him on the forehead. She loved seeing his smile. "Blessed Sekhmet, this is the first moment he has noticed life around him today!" thought Tiye, as young Amenhotep's eyes met hers. His eyes were lighter in color than most of his countrymen, and so was the color of his skin – that lighter tone definitely had not come from her or his father!

Amenhotep IV turned to go to his private quarters in the palace and Tiye was about to do the same, when she heard her name being called: "Queen Tiye!"

It was Ay, and next to him stood the Newcomer man. Her face an unreadable mask, Tiye faced them and waited, as they hurried towards her.

"You never walk through the inner Ptah walls," said Ay in an accusing voice. The man next to him stared at her, breathing heavily, beads of sweat covering his forehead.

232

"I do what I chose. What do you need, my brother?"

"I thought Huy might be occupied elsewhere, while we," Ay pointed at the Newcomer with his eyes, "enjoyed your beautiful ceremony." When Tiye did not reply, he added, "I assume we are meeting in the Audience Chamber?" Although the sentence was spoken as a question, Tiye knew that it was a statement. Ay felt that she owed him for hiding the Newcomer from Huy and he made sure she knew it.

"Of course. Make sure you and our foreign guest do not miss it."

At that Tiye turned and walked away, making it clear who had had the final word.

When Tiye arrived at her private chamber, Ibi was already there.

"I am sorry, my lady, your brother saw us."

"It is all as it must be." Tiye sat down at her table and three servant girls took off her headdress, wig and clothes. Ibi's eyes grew wide when she saw Tiye take the knife out of her sheath, but she knew better than to ask anything, quickly hiding the knife under a cloth so the other girls wouldn't see it. Ibi renewed the queen's make up, wiping off the old kohl and sweat. A bowl of cool water was brought in and a massage servant washed her feet, then gently rubbed sand into them, and then rubbed them again with oil perfumed with myrrh and lavender. Her hands and feet were hennaed by Ibi's skillful fingers.

When she stood up a new white sheath was carefully wrapped over her body, and then a new wig – this one had white fiancé beads braided into it. Quickly placing her feet into sandals with matching braided fiancé, Tiye was ready.

The palace halls were empty, for most nobles, guests and servants were still at the Temple of Ptah-Seker. Her sandals slapping on the polished stone floor, Tiye made her way into the empty Audience Chamber. No petitioners were to be seen today, but servants, at her request, brought in trays of food, which now rested on a low table on the dais. Tiye walked up the dais steps and sat in the gilded chair. The chair was reserved for her husband the pharaoh, but he almost never saw any viziers or petitioners in Men-Nefer. They all had to make the journey to him in Waset.

Tiye sent all the servants away except her most trusted Ibi, and awaited the Newcomers' arrival.

Audience Chamber at Men-Nefer Palace

Vizier Ay gave Mahmoud a meaningful stare when they arrived outside the closed doors of the Audience Chamber. Without knocking, Ay pushed the doors open, and forced his body forward. Mahmoud walked in after him. The first person Mahmoud saw was the queen, seated on the dais in a large armchair. He heard a smirk from Ay, whose face folded into a grimace of judgment as he eyed the queen from the door. The dais was illuminated by many large and small oil lamps, their yellow light wavering on the walls. In one of the walls was a wide window covered by lowered straw mats. Between Mahmoud and the dais there stood a large wooden table. It was as long and wide as any table in a modern corporate conference room, and it was fitted with many chairs. But the table remained empty. The guests, Sahed, Bailey and Craig, were at the other end of the room and seated on the lower step of the queen's dais, munching on food they were taking from a low table in front of the queen. It was filled with fruit and cooked fish, and meat in a red sauce.

Ay quickly made his way past the table to the dais. Mahmoud could see he was angry to have been made equal to the guests – Queen Tiye occupied the only chair on the dais. And so he elected to stand. Mahmoud joined him in a display of solidarity, but finally sat down on one of the low chairs. He was sure he saw the queen hide a smile, and he growled as he chewed on a morsel of lamb covered in pomegranate sauce. "She is mocking me!" Thankfully he still had his handkerchief – imagine if he were to drip pomegranate sauce all over himself! He was anxious, and to cover it up he focused on the food. Oh, he was definitely not a happy man. The dark circles under his eyes and the gray coloring of his skin betrayed the strain recent events had had on him.

No one said a word. Then queen Tiye spoke.

"The prophecy was about your arrival," she said, and her eyes swept over the Newcomers. "I deciphered the time that you would come to be *now*. That was how we were able to meet you in the sacred well."

"Do you know what the prophecy is about?" asked Mahmoud cautiously.

"I believe it is about you. All of you."

"I don't understand…" mumbled Mahmoud. "I am the chosen one, you saw it yourself, I opened the gate."

Tiye looked intently at Mahmoud for a long time. Her eyes moved to Ay, then again returned to Mahmoud. She was silent and Mahmoud began to feel terrified, as if he was being stared down by a cobra. "Why doesn't she say something? Does she not know I am the one?"

Eventually Tiye spoke. "Two Shenu were to open the gate, and I can see that you are one of them. This woman, who claims to have been given the key, is the other."

"I was wearing the locket, the key, on my neck, when we... opened the gate," added Bailey quietly, in response to Sahed's translation.

"This begins the beginning," stated Tiye.

"No, this is the beginning of the end!" exclaimed Mahmoud and stood up. He was becoming more and more frustrated. "This is about the end," he repeated, and he again met Tiye's long, intent and silent gaze, trying hard not to shrink under it.

"No end ever came before the beginning," asserted Tiye after a long pause.

After Sahed's rapid translation into English there was a stifled laugh from Craig, and then a "sorry," as the young man realized that Mahmoud had noticed. "The imbecile!" hissed Mahmoud internally.

Tiye continued: "You have fulfilled your duty to Sekhmet; your names will be praised by eternity."

Then, to everyone's surprise, Tiye stood up. Before Mahmoud understood what had happened, Ay said, "Queen Tiye, is this wise?" Her eyes locked with his in a tense moment, then she slightly bowed her head at the Newcomers, making it clear that the audience was over.

$$*\qquad *\qquad *$$

Bailey sat on the bed in her room, puzzling over the meeting with the queen. She had been hoping for something to be resolved in that meeting, but all the questions of the moment still hung in the air. "Now what?" she whispered. That question, at least, was answered immediately. Nab, holding a white cloak, hurried into the room and over to Bailey. Gesturing for Bailey to put the cloak on, she hustled her out of the room and into the darkness of the halls. Sahed and Craig were already there, each following their servant. Bailey opened her mouth with the intention of talking with them but Sahed, in a tone permitting no appeal, told her to follow Nab. Confused, Bailey decided she had better do as he said and she allowed herself to be led into a beautiful, torch-lit garden, as Sahed and Craig were led in different directions. On the other side of the garden she saw Mr. Halib talking with another Egyptian man. Nab noticed them too, and she suddenly pulled her cloak over her head and, looking directly at Bailey with wide eyes, began to point at the flowers in the garden. Bailey turned her back to the men, pulled the cloth over her head, and went along with the pretense of studying the plants. Glancing over at Nab she could see the relief on her face. As soon as Mr. Halib was gone, Nab pulled on Bailey's arm and they began a mad dash through the palace, like a pair of thieves escaping the scene of a crime.

A few courts down from the garden was a large yard crowded with chickens, and next to that another yard filled with goats. At the next court Bailey halted – this one held a bowl of water and a lion on a chain. The large cat looked hot and sleepy. Bailey stared at him and he looked up, his yellow eyes illuminated by the single small torch at the other end of the court. Nab pulled urgently on her arm – thankfully they didn't have to pass in front of the lion, but slipped through a small side door. Beyond it were more courts and yards. "How big is this palace?" wondered Bailey. Torches and oil lamps lit up the rooms and halls, and the air was filled with the smells of scented flowers and incense in spite of the noxious odors of chicken and goat shit. Bailey was intoxicated with it all. Even the lion was handsome.

They arrived at yet another narrow court, and, after looking around to make sure they were alone, Nab pointed at an open window about six feet from the floor. "What is she pointing at? It just looks like a window… " thought Bailey, hesitating. Nab, seeing her confusion, ushered her to the window and, tucking her foot into a small niche, climbed up and lifted the straw mat covering it. She moved aside and looked at Bailey. Bailey's eyebrows shot up, but she gamely climbed up and into a pitch-dark room, Nab following behind her. Nab seemed to know exactly where they were, skillfully and quickly navigating in darkness. Then Bailey heard the sound of a door opening and Nab pushed her forward.

As Bailey's eyes adjusted to the space, she realized she was on the farther end of the dais in the same room she had been in earlier. Before her sat the queen, in the same chair, with the same tray in front of her on the low table, and around the table were seated Sahed and Craig. The only big change in the scene was the absence of Mr. Halib and the other man, and instead of torches and lamps there was now only a single small lamp on the dais. In its light the locket shone gold on Tiye's chest.

"She wanted to talk to us alone, so she got rid of the other two," whispered Craig quickly.

Tiye smiled as she looked at their faces. Bailey again had the uneasy feeling that she was in trouble, as if she was a very small thing and this woman was spectacularly huge.

"You told them of the prophecy?" asked Tiye.

"Yes, High Priestess. We are here because of it. I am the Shenu," explained Sahed. "I told the father of this woman. He was a Shenu. She was investigating what happened to her father, and we met. She needed to know how he died."

"Her father is in the Land of the Dead?" asked Tiye, looking at Bailey, compassion in her eyes, her hand extending towards Bailey.

"Yes. He died, with her mother, in an attempt to fulfill the prophecy."

"Her mother is also in the Land of the Dead?"

"Yes... I believed that I was one of the people who was to open the gate, and that it was the will of beloved Sekhmet to have it opened at that time. I believed that her father," Sahed pointed at Bailey, "was the other person."

"He was not..." finished Tiye.

"He was not. And my ignorance caused his death," added Sahed quietly.

"All is in the hands of Sekhmet. This woman is one of the two to open the gate. Her father had to be taken by Anubis, so she would choose to open it."

"May I ask you something?" began Craig.

After the first meeting in the Audience Chamber he had been thinking about his role in all of this. "No matter how much each person knows, they only hold a piece of the puzzle. So maybe my role is to put it all together..." This thought had even caused Craig to run into a column earlier, and his shoulder was still sore from it. "Whoa... That's why Sekhmet needed a shaman..." Craig was not sure how a shaman could be useful here, or even what a shaman was, but it felt right to be here and he had learned to trust his feelings. And so he directed his next question towards the queen:

"Mr. Halib said that 'it is all about the end' and you mentioned 'the beginning'... Can you please explain that?"

Sahed translated for Tiye.

"I was the one who opened the gate and talked with Sekhmet."

There was silence in the room.

"You saw a transparent apparition that looked like a tall woman?" clarified Bailey.

"I went through the gate, into a time far back, and I saw life in Zep Tepi. I saw Sekhmet in the flesh, I saw the star-gods depart, and I was given the message. The prophecy…" Tiye took a sip from a small cup and, closing her eyes, recited it, Sahed translating as she spoke: "*The two Shenu from the other time will open the gate at the beginning of the beginning. The two were chosen by the Council, and their arrival will bring the time for people to remember how to breathe. This begins the end, and people will try to forget. But the will of the Council will be done, and the gate will be sealed, until people remember again.*"

"That's a different prophecy!" Bailey bolted up, and in her haste almost toppled the table over. Everyone began to speak at once. Sahed spoke to the queen and Craig pulled on Sahed's arm, asking questions, and Tiye was answering Sahed… Bailey felt her mind spin. She knew that her parents had died trying to open the gate. OK, they didn't open it, but now Bailey and the others had. Here they were… But she wasn't a historian or an archeologist. She couldn't even place this period in time. Craig was saying something about Amenhotep being the current pharaoh, but Bailey didn't remember which one, there was always some number after the name… And even if she did remember, it did not mean anything to her anyway. Why was she here? "Because some 'ancient goddess' called Sekhmet prophesized my arrival? Bullshit!" It didn't make sense. She wanted to scream "I'm the *wrong person!*" This whole thing – the prophecy, the past, Sekhmet – it was all very important to someone else, not to her! They came here to follow a prophecy, but apparently there was also this totally different message that made Tiye go into the well to meet them at the right time. Exhausted, Bailey felt her heart fluttering in her chest.

"What 'council'?" Craig was doing the asking, and his voice brought Bailey back to the present.

The High Priestess of the Shenu began her long answer.

"Zep Tepi, the First Time, was when the great Akhu, the star-gods, walked the Earth. It was the time that Pisces entered the sky, a very long time ago. Akhu came here from the blue star Sirius, and seeded the Earth. Sirius, as beautiful as Isis herself, is the bright star in the sky at the foot of Sahu, Orion-the-strider. Sirius is magical, and it is home for all of us," said Tiye, smiling. "There are round balls in space, circling the magical star, just as our Earth circles the sun. Only these balls are not all in the same sky. And there are people who live on one of these balls."

A loud excited whisper came from Craig. "They know that the sun is a star! And that the planet is a ball, and it's circling the sun. Circling! Whoa, Bailey, can you believe it, these people know about stars, planets!"

Tiye continued. "There are two Councils: the Sirian Council, from the stars, and the Solar from our Sun, governing the Earth. The High Sirian Council and the Solar Council agreed to allow a small group of Sirian people to participate in the Earth Experiment. You see, our Earth was naked then. She did not have people on her body as she does today; there were only the blue waters and green trees, and wondrous animals…"

"What is the 'earth experiment'?" asked Craig.

"It began when the star-gods of Sirius, a small group, came to Earth. They arrived in their large crystalline bird. She was shaped like a pyramid," Tiye looked into space, remembering. "The transparent bird brought the star-gods here from their sky. I was told that this crystalline pyramid-bird was not born by nature, but created by the star-gods. She was almost invisible, so thin were her planes and edges. And she was weightless, because the pull of Earth had no bearing on her. She was a true star-bird, guided by thought and intention," stated Tiye proudly.

Bailey's eyebrows went up as she whispered to Craig in alarm, "A star-bird?" Bailey felt that sanity was slipping from her grasp. "What if the queen is insane? We are at her mercy here…"

Craig ignored her whisper and clarified calmly, as though he were talking about vegetables at the market. "She means the *starship*. Something large, a flying technology… she said 'she was *created*' by the star-gods."

Tiye continued: "And because the star-gods valued their family connections the most, the entire family came to Earth together. They all are connected by thought, you know… as if they are one mind."

"The Sirian star-gods are telepathic?" asked Bailey suspiciously, staring at the queen. She couldn't believe she had used those words, she the therapist was now seriously asking the queen of Egypt, in the past, if the *gods* were telepathic… But Sahed translated her question.

"Yes, that is true, they did not have to talk to know what each of them was thinking," replied Tiye, listening to Sahed's translation. "The pyramid-bird brought a family of thirty-two star-gods. Two of these star-people you know very well, even in your time, I am sure. They are our beloved Isis and Amun-Ra." Tiye was sure that no matter what the future looked like, these two star-gods were well known and honored. "All Sirian people were true gods, they were here and at the same time not here, they were multidimensional…"

"Wow, like in quantum physics," whispered Craig, but Sahed was not sure what that meant, so the words went untranslated.

"…Yet they walked in human form," continued Tiye. "Maybe not so human… but human enough. They ate and drank, they sang songs and told tales, they danced and they made love… I believe that when the star-gods came to Earth, while they were still up in the stars next to our ball in the darkness of Nut, they saw the land of Egypt, a good, harmonious place. Oh, not the land itself, of course, but the energy emanating from this region… The place chosen for the Sirian home on Earth had to be energetically suitable for it to be a stabilizing anchor for their faster consciousness. You see, Sirian star-gods are fast…"

"You mean they think fast?" wondered Bailey out loud.

Confused for a moment by Sahed's translation, Tiye responded: "I am sure they can think much faster than any of us, but it is not the speed of their thoughts I was talking about. They feel faster too, they see faster; they somehow are of a much faster reality than we are. They are of faster consciousness. That means that they are aware of life faster…"

Tiye wasn't sure if this answered Bailey's question or not, but she went on.

"The region of the chain of large lakes in northern Africa, which is this land we are on, had the energy the Akhu needed. These lakes formed a cascade flow into the Mediterranean Sea to the west and into the larger salt waters. The water did not come up as high back then and the Mediterranean Sea was much smaller. Over many thousands of years and several polar shifts the water level rose and the lakes became a river, which we now call the beloved Nile. Part of the land flooded permanently, and the rest became known as Egypt. The Sirian gods, the star people, sat their pyramid-bird in the land of Seker, the Creator of Openings, in the sacred district of Ro-Setau. At that time there were no people like us there, and no pyramids."

Tiye took a sip of orange liquid from her cup and continued speaking.

"We are sitting in the land of Seker now – Men-Nefer city is part of it. And you came through the sacred Ro-Setau, in the desert where the pyramids are. The land of Seker back at the time of the star-gods was warm, but not hot like today, and instead of deserts there were lush forests filled with many living things. Water was everywhere! Away from the land of Seker there were some deserts, but less ferocious than today, not as consuming. This is when the Earth Experiment began. The family of the thirty-two star-gods gave birth to us. The mystery of creation itself is not known to me, but that is how we began… Many people were born then. People met the star-gods and they lived in harmony. The star-gods built the pyramid, you know, the Great One, and the platforms which later were made into pyramids, and the rest of the district of Ro-Setau. They rested their crystalline pyramid-bird right on top of the Great One," smiled Tiye.

"You mean they landed their…. 'bird'… on the pyramid, the Great Pyramid?" blurted Craig, staring at Tiye.

"Yes, their bird sat right on top, I saw it," stated Tiye triumphantly and her eyes shone in the lamp's golden light. "When I came through the gate to see Sekhmet, the bird was still there, like a transparent echo of the stone pyramid. It was almost completely invisible. But if the light was just right you could see it…"

There was silence in the room once again. Only the sound of reed mats gently slapping on the windows could be heard as the wind knocked them about. The golden light of the lamp flickered from the air movement and Tiye moved the lamp to the other side of her chair, away from the windows.

"So, you said this is 'the beginning'…" said Craig, breaking the silence. "But *your* prophecy is not the one we know…"

"The star-gods were always more in the sky than on Earth. Sekhmet is not like that, but even her messages are never given in the language of Earth …" smiled Tiye.

"That's because their vibration is thinner, or faster," blurted Craig. "People who can feel this stuff are always a little weird…" Of course Craig was now talking about himself, and also remembering Abby's mental state. When he looked back at Tiye, her eyes bore into his as though he had himself just given her a prophecy. Uncomfortable, he asked: "Why are we here? – I mean, why did Sekhmet want all of us here?" He was trying to find the missing puzzle piece, and right now it was hidden in Tiye's answer.

"You are the sign I was waiting for," stated Tiye simply, still looking into Craig face. "Now I know what I must do." Tiye stood up. "I thank you for honoring the words of Sekhmet. But tonight you must leave. I have to return to Waset sooner…" she spoke as if to herself, but Sahed translated anyway. "You cannot be here any longer. Especially that other Shenu. "

Sahed stood up and bent over almost to his feet to the High Priestess, and Bailey and Craig followed suit. Tiye bowed deeply to all of them and said quietly, "I will see you again. Farewell!" Then she began to walk to the main door of the room.

*   *   *

It was clear that the audience was over. Sahed watched the queen being swallowed by the darkness in the far end of the Audience Chamber, as she opened the massive door and disappeared behind it.

Bailey stared at Sahed with confusion. Leave? Now? They were not sure why they were here in the first place, and now they were being asked to leave?

Trance-like, Craig looked into space where Tiye had been, and whispered, "Whoa... Now she knows what to do... This is so cool! Life is so amazing; it's a path where every person means something... We had to come to give her a sign... We *are* the sign... And we don't even know what we were a sign for..."

"Right, we still don't know," snapped Bailey. "Can we leave?" she asked Sahed. "I mean, how? We're in this Men-Nefer, but where is the well? Do we go back into it? It's the middle of the night! How do we get a boat to return there? And then what? I don't have the locket..." Her frustration mutated into fear again and Bailey suddenly felt very small. "Where is Mr. Halib? We'll need him with us."

"Tiye didn't want him here. She didn't trust him," replied Craig. "Not as much as her brother Ay does..."

"Which one is Ay?" asked Bailey and then immediately answered her own question: "He must be that other Egyptian man who spoke in the well, he looks like Tiye."

*   *   *

Nab held a basket on her arm filled with the small honeyed cakes Bailey liked, and they walked the Royal Road in near-total darkness, their heads covered by cloaks. When the air began to smell like the river they knew they were nearing the wharf. The silhouette of the massive temple of Ptah-Seker was in the distance, and the flapping of the flags became louder and was matched by the sound of waves. When they got to the river a small felucca boat tied to a large copper ring on the embankment awaited them. Nab spoke quickly to the six men already on the boat.

Soon they had all boarded and were gliding speedily over the water, away from the city of Men-Nefer, only one small lantern lighting their way.

Eventually they arrived to the embankment of Giza, what Queen Tiye called Ro-Setau, with a multitude of dark temples towering over the water. The boat was promptly attached to a pole by the large stone steps and in the light of the lantern they saw a mounted man and horses standing there. Bailey was terrified of these creatures and her heart pounded as Nab helped her onto one, but Craig and Sahed looked very comfortable. Nab with tears in her eyes, handed Bailey the basket with the last of the honeyed cakes. The next moment Bailey realized why – the horses had begun to walk quickly into the darkness and away from Nab, the boat, and the other servants.

The clicking of the horses' hoofs on the stones of the road mixed with the wind, and soon they came to the end of the paved area. Beyond it, there was nothing but sand. After some time had passed the man at the head of the caravan yelled out and dismounted his horse. When all the Newcomers were on the ground, he collected their horses, turned a full circle on his hotly breathing beast while pointing into the darkness, and yelled once more. Then he disappeared into the night, taking all the horses with him. Above them was a huge sky filled with stars, but on the ground they were completely alone.

Sahed spoke first. "We must climb down into the well."

"Without Mr. Council of Antiquities, we won't be able to open the gate anyway. And I don't have the locket!"

"The High Priestess must know something if she brought us back here. We must go. It is that way…"

"That way" was nothing but sand and more sand. Their feet sank into it as they made their way in the direction that the horseman pointed. After almost half an hour of waddling, they noticed the outline of a tent. When they came closer it revealed itself to be nothing but a few staffs strung together and loosely covered with a large cloth. Moving the cloth away they saw the mouth of the well.

They began to climb down the well shaft. Bailey's hands hurt badly – she didn't have enough strength in her body to do this type of climb this often! Finally, they reached the bottom, and to their surprise, it wasn't empty! Two Egyptian men-servants stood next to a body on the floor, illuminated by two small lamps. It was Mr. Halib. There was also a little girl standing next to them.

"Jesus! Is he dead?" whispered Bailey.

Sahed was already asking the men. The men-servants spoke to the girl and then began to climb back up, taking one of the lamps with them.

"What, are they going? Is he dead? Without the 'key' how do we go back home?" Bailey was beginning to get hysterical. The almost all-consuming darkness, the body of Mr. Council of Antiquities on the floor, the little girl standing in the shadows of a room so deep underground, the limited oxygen – it was all too much for her.

"He bound the palace servant... so they bound him as we did," explained Sahed. He looked at the girl, who was no more than five years of age. She stood in the darkness, unafraid. On her neck was the queen's locket.

"They told her that they will come back for her, to carry her back out."

Bailey and Craig looked Mahmoud over – he was alive, if unconscious. They looked up at the little girl. She stared back in silence.

"She has my locket..." breathed Bailey.

"I don't think so," replied Sahed. "I think queen Tiye gave this beautiful, brave child the key so that we could go back home..."

As if understanding his English words, the girl walked to the doorway...

In the next moment everything changed. There was a bright light. Craig moaned and began to fall to the floor, holding his head with both hands; Bailey felt Sahed's hand... Then the light subsided and darkness returned. All sounds in the room disappeared completely, as did the furniture and the little girl. They were back to the room they had left a day ago.

CHAPTER TEN

Current time

Giza Plateau, Egypt

"What could be taking them so long?" wondered Simon in the darkness. He didn't want to shout into the well, but five hours was a long time! He wasn't sure how much time it would take three unfit people to climb down such a deep shaft. "It might have taken them an hour or so just to get down. Maybe they had to rest a little. Then an hour back... Still, what could they be doing for three hours? They were supposed to just assess the situation. Maybe this thing they talked about, the gate or whatever, did open..."

He immediately dismissed the possibility. He felt certain that no paranormal "gate" would be opening any time soon. They had agreed that, since shouting was useless, if something was wrong they would pull on the rope. And as to what was at the bottom of the well – Simon was fairly sure that there was water. "Well, they couldn't have drowned; I mean, that would just be dumb, and they aren't idiots," he reasoned.

"So what could have happened? If the well is not flooded... Was it a much bigger space than they thought?" That was the most likely explanation for their delay. Maybe there were tunnels; perhaps there were artifacts and art, and they had gotten carried away examining it and talking. "Considering how long it takes to get down there, I can see how they might want to have a good look around..."

But now he had waited for five hours, and he felt that he had to do something – it was almost morning! Wiggling the rope produced no effect; talking into the well was equally useless. Checking the guards one more time, Simon carefully opened the rusty metal grill and began to climb down the squeaky ladder.

As he got closer to the bottom of the well he shone his flashlight and even yelled into the darkness a few times – there was no answer. This was alarming, and he pushed his well-trained body to climb down as fast as possible. Surely something was wrong. Where were they? Even if there were large tunnels of open spaces down there, they would have heard him yelling by now and answered back! But the only voice he heard was his echo. It took him thirty-eight minutes to reach the lower end of the well shaft. When he was only about twenty rungs away from the bottom, a brilliant light flashed underneath him. For a moment Simon was almost blinded; it was as if a C-4 explosive had gone off twenty feet from him. He gripped the ladder firmly, but the shock wave he expected never came. Then the light began to subside, and he climbed a few more rungs before jumping down the last five feet.

He was not prepared for the sight he encountered. Bailey and Sahed were grasping each other tightly; Craig sat on the floor, holding his head with both hands; and another man, a stranger, lay on the floor, bound, unmoving, his mouth stuffed with cloth.

For a moment Simon just stared at them. He couldn't hear anything; he was shrouded in silence, as if a grenade had gone off too close to his head. In the next few seconds the residual light faded away and the room became completely dark. But he was trained for situations of crisis, so he grabbed his flashlight and shone it in the direction of the bound man. The man looked unconscious or dead. "Bloody hell…?!" His was the only voice.

*   *   *

Two hours later, just as a pink light was beginning to color the air, they emerged at the surface. The last one out of the well was Simon, who had borne the full weight of the unconscious man. All three had insisted on keeping the man unconscious and taking him with them, instead of leaving him in the well. In the absence of further explanations, Simon obliged.

It was fortunate that they arrived at the mouth of the well at the exact moment of the guard change, and they made their escape to the fence as the young solders joked loudly in the distance. In less than an hour they were riding in Axil's taxi. Six people were a tight fit for the little car, but no one complained. Axil looked terrified. "How did they get him… like that?"

"Damned if I know," replied Simon, still a little out of breath from the climb up. "I have no idea who he is."

"It is Mr. Halib, from the Supreme Council of Antiquities of Egypt," replied Axil, nervously looking at the road.

"Damn…" whistled Simon. At this point he was so exhausted that it could have been the Pope and it still would not have mattered.

"Is he dead?"

"No, from the looks of it he's just taking a nap."

"What took so long?" Axil's voice was a whisper, as if he were trying not to wake the man.

"They were in no condition to talk," answered Simon, ending the conversation.

The unconscious man was successfully transferred from the taxi to the hotel without anyone noticing. At Axil's suggestion, his head and body were draped in a long piece of cloth that Axil had in his car, then he was carried vertically, as if he was a tired old man and needed help. "Apparently this guy from the Council of Antiquities is a very recognizable man," thought Simon, carrying the dead-weight body up to the elevators.

In the hotel room, Bailey immediately disappeared behind a closed bathroom door. Simon carefully lowered the unconscious man onto the floor.

"Is anyone going to tell me what the bloody hell happened down there?" Simon's question had to go unanswered for the time being. Sahed and Craig seemed unable to speak, and Bailey had locked herself away.

"Are you alright?" he asked at the closed door.

There was no answer, but water was splashing, so he assumed Bailey must be at least somewhat functional since she was able to take a shower.

Turning around, Simon took in the room. Sahed was seated in the armchair with his eyes closed, he looked sick with exhaustion. Craig held a bottle of water, his hands shaking violently, his eyes wild. Axil was nervously moving his head back and forth between Sahed and Craig, and to the unconscious man on the floor, but he said nothing.

When Bailey came out of the bathroom, she took a bottle of water out of the mini-bar and sat on her bed. She was trembling as she silently stared at the locket in her hand.

"Is there any food?" said Craig finally.

Before anything else could be said, Axil left the room. It would seem that the emotions of the trio had not quite caught up with their thoughts, and any explanations would have to be put on hold until they did. Simon lowered his own tired body into the other armchair, and silently and patiently waited.

In less than fifteen minutes Axil returned with six large pizza boxes. They smelled delicious. Food, especially cheesy, bready, heavy food like pizza, is perfect for calming an adrenaline response. In a few minutes Bailey and Craig were falling asleep, and Sahed was not far behind them. Axil went down to a café to get coffee and more bottles of water. He could also see the elevators from there – a smart precaution.

Simon checked on the unconscious man. Perhaps he had been drugged. He was solidly unconscious. He fingered the man's bindings, testing their strength, and to his surprise found a gun! The man had been bound – efficiently, crudely and overly tight, but had not been disarmed. It didn't make sense, but neither did anything else. He checked the man's pulse; it was steady. He took away the gun, retied the man's feet to allow for more circulation in his legs, and freed his arms completely. Deciding that the binding over the man's mouth was just too much, he removed the wet, messy cloth.

Then he sat down again in the second armchair – there was nothing to do but wait. These people were useless until their adrenaline wore off and they regenerated a bit.

Three hours later Sahed opened his eyes and looked around. Simon was the only one awake. "Do you think they will mind if I use their washroom?"

As Sahed disappeared in the bathroom, Craig sat up on the bed. He looked green, but in the next few moments he began to change color to a pale white, closer to his natural shade. "Is he OK?"

Simon nodded.

"Why is he still out of it?"

"You tell me."

"We didn't do it, it was… maybe some potion… I don't know, probably Tiye's people…"

"And who might this Tiye be?"

"She's the queen…" As if suddenly realizing how crazy what he was saying sounded, Craig jumped up. "Bailey, Bailey, wake up!" He touched her.

She woke up, groggily looked around the room, and slowly swung her feet to the floor. Then, as if afraid she had lost it, she grasped the locket on her neck.

"Water," – was all she said.

She drank a whole bottle and looked up at Simon. "Am I OK?"

"You look at bit under the weather, but overall you seem to be fine, love. Are you up to talking about what happened down there?"

Before Bailey could answer, Axil entered the room, pushing a large case of bottled water with his foot and holding a tray with a large pot of coffee. Nothing more was said before the dark brown liquid was poured and consumed.

Cleopatra Hotel, Cairo, Egypt

Mahmoud opened his eyes, feeling as if he was hung over. He rarely drank that much, but the few times in his life that he had, he had experienced this same unpleasant feeling of dizziness and nausea.

He heard voices and tried to locate the source of the sound with his eyes. Soon reality came into focus: he was lying on the floor while the other people were sitting up. The memory of recent events came rushing in – he knew who these people were and he remembered that he was bound. Checking his feet, he also noticed that his hands were free and his mouth was empty… as was his stomach. There was an unmistakable smell of pizza in the room. Attempting to locate the pizza, Mahmoud's gaze found his gun – it was on the low coffee table next to a man. He didn't recognize the man. Looking a little farther to the left he noticed one more person. If the first man was definitely European, not American or a local, the second man was surely Egyptian.

"They drugged me…?" he felt too sick to be outraged. "Who in the name of Allah are these people? How many are involved?" Mahmoud couldn't put his thoughts in order, try as he might. His head hurt. To help himself refocus, he cleared his throat… and five pairs of eyes turned to look at him.

"Untie me," said Mahmoud, his voice strained. He sat up on the floor as best as he could with his bound legs.

"I don't think so. Not until I know more about you, fella," said the man next to the gun in an unmistakably British accent.

The "new" Egyptian man stood up and, grabbing Mahmoud underneath his arms, pulled him towards the wall. Mahmoud began to protest the indignity, but shut up when he realized he was being propped up against the wall. Sitting up made his head feel a little better. Next to him was a low table filled with pizza boxes, and he automatically reached

249

for a slice. The Egyptian man returned to his seat and the conversation resumed.

Mahmoud Mukhtar Halib chewed on the left over cold pepperoni pizza and listened. The others were talking about the events in the well, and what occurred after. The infuriating Americans had apparently bragged about the Shenu to this British person and the other, younger looking Egyptian. There was also someone talking through that laptop… that must be the encoded one.

"How dare they! How many know?" Mahmoud was outraged… but not enough to stop chewing.

As the woman explained to the British man something about a "star-bird," Mahmoud suddenly realized two things: first, that what she was saying related to the treasures hidden in the Shenu vaults, and she could not possibly have had access to those; and second, that the old Egyptian man spoke the ancient language fluently, not as an Egyptologist would! Mahmoud had missed that obvious fact – he had been so absorbed with the Americans and so busy trying to deny the man's claim to the Shenu, that it only now fully registered that he could correctly *speak* the language. How could he know it?

"Who are these people?" A chill went through Mahmoud's spine. He felt defeated.

*　　*　　*

"…her name was Azvari, that's what they called the girl," said Sahed, finishing his tale.

"Why would she give such an important thing to a kid to do?"

When no one answered, Simon offered an explanation. "Considering what you told me, Tiye must have either trusted no one and the kid was harmless, or, simply put, the kid was disposable."

"You mean that the gate *killed* her?" Bailey was appalled.

"I don't claim to know how that thing works, but it stands to reason that it could easily have killed the child," ventured Simon.

"No, she wasn't supposed to die," breathed out Craig. "The men said they would 'come back for her,' right? Azvari must have some part in all this, some meaning, like maybe she is also the chosen one or something…"

On the floor, Mr. Halib moaned. Bailey looked at him – his facial expression was that of someone who had just swallowed a big fat maggot. "Is the pizza OK?" she asked gently.

"You imbeciles! Another chosen one? How naïve are you?" spat Mahmoud.

After a long pause, Sahed quietly said, "It is not... complete..."

"Yes, I keep feeling something is missing," chimed in Craig. "We helped the queen and all, but what was this stuff about 'breathing'? Weren't we supposed to 'open the gate to have people remember how to breathe'? Well, we opened it, but we don't remember! Maybe we should ask Sekhmet if she wanted us to do something else, you know, if we missed it? To complete the gate opening or something?"

Bailey was not sure she had heard him correctly. Hell, at this point she was not sure of anything. "He wants to ask Sekhmet if 'there is anything else we can do?! After all we just went through he thinks 'we *missed it*?'" One after another her thoughts began to spin into an emotional black hole.

"That might work, right, Bailey?" she heard Craig say. His voice snapped her back.

"What worked?"

"Check your messages, maybe she already called."

"Who?"

"Abby... Weren't you listening?"

With a heavy feeling in her chest, Bailey understood. If her sister had not been delusional all these years but had actually received messages from the Solar or whatever council, then maybe they had told her something. And maybe she tried to tell Bailey by leaving more messages on her machine.

"I don't think I erased them..." began Bailey. "I mean, my machine is full, she couldn't have left any more messages."

"Then call her!"

Calling the medical facility that housed Abby proved to be useless. Bailey was told she should come and visit, Abby's doctor was unavailable right now, but Abby had skipped her meds again and was now heavily medicated to prevent further damage. Discouraged, Bailey hung up the virtual connection.

"Sorry, dear, I was listening in... and I have an idea." It was Marty. "It might take a day, but it should work. Why don't you take care of your lovely self over there while I take care of this little problem on

my end? Call you back tomorrow, about five in the evening your time."
And Marty's face went off the screen.

Upstate NY, United States

"Well, that should be easy," mumbled Marty, as he pulled up
files on his screen one after the other. The next hour passed agonizingly
slowly. In his manic excitement he didn't feel hungry, even though it had
been days since he had eaten. He had no more food, at least the kind he
knew what to do with. Racing in a high-speed mental tunnel, all his
thoughts were of his final destination: a release form for Abigail Rixson,
signed and approved by two doctors, a psychotherapist and a physician.
Abby was about to be transferred to another kind of facility.

The phone icon flickered on and off and Marty excitedly clicked
on it. To his surprise it was not the facility, letting him know about
Abby's transfer, but Larisa, his maid. The Ukrainian woman was
checking up on him – more than a week had passed since Marty had told
her he needed "a week off." She cared about him, and worried that he
was not alright. Unsure of what to do, Martin tried to hang up, but Larisa
was tough and insistent. She made him feel uncomfortably exposed.
Martin finally told her she could have another week off, and hastily hung
up.

In another fifteen minutes he got the phone call he was waiting
for – the doctors in an experimental brain wave lab that he had some
work done for a while back, had received Abby in their stronghold.
Relieved, Marty took a breath. The request of Abby's transfer into the lab
was a highly illegal one and the lead researcher could lose his license if he
was discovered, but he owed Marty big-time. And he was a medical
doctor, after all, so managing Abby would not be that complicated.

There was a sound. At first Marty could not place where it came
from, so enthralled he was with his own accomplishment. The sound was
repeated – it was an external alarm. Someone was coming to the house!
Changing the screen, Marty looked at the view picked up by the four
external cameras. There was Larisa's concerned face. In a few seconds
she would be right at his door!

No matter what Marty told her, whatever bribes and threats he
made, Larisa could not be convinced to leave. She could hear Marty's
voice through the speakers, and she could tell he had been off his meds
for a while. It crossed Marty's mind that he might be dangerous but he

dismissed the thought – he would never hurt Larisa. Why, he didn't know, but he just knew he wouldn't. The next thought was – food. Larisa could make him dinner. That sounded like a very good idea. And being a Ukrainian immigrant, she knew how to keep a secret – she disliked authorities of any kind, almost as much as he did.

Soon he was well fed and talking with the doctor via computer. Abby was taken off the heavy medication, given some much lighter replacements, and told that Bailey wanted to know more about the Solar Council, whatever that meant. The doctor didn't understand either, but he agreed to record everything she said, to give her paper to write on, and to monitor her to make sure she did not go off the deep end. The last thing Marty wanted was to harm Abby – then Bailey would not like him, for sure!

Cleopatra Hotel, Cairo, Egypt

By the time Marty finally called, Bailey had consumed way too much coffee, haunted by the memories of recent events. Distraught and exhausted, she had not been able to sleep. "Now I know how, and even why, my father died. That's it. I should go home!" she scolded herself. "Do I really want to involve my poor tortured sister in all of this? How desperate am I? It must be so hard for her to remember that horrible time in Egypt…"

"Hello, my dear, how did the day go?" Marty's satisfied voice came up from the laptop. "Would you like to talk to Abby? I have arranged that for you, she is waiting on the other line…"

Before Bailey could react to that question, there was a click and she heard Abby's voice. "Bailey? Are you there? Bailey?"

"Yes, I'm here. How are you feeling?" said Bailey, scrambling to the laptop.

"I like it here, you should come to see me, come visit, I like it here! There's a big bed and it is not white, I have a very red blanket, it's all red and it has a triangle on it…"

Bailey had to think for a moment – Abby's facility was very stark, they didn't have red blankets with triangles on them. "Abby, where are you?"

"I like it here, Bailey, you should come visit, I have a red blanket!"

253

Unsure, she pressed on, thinking to herself that she must have lost the rest of her psychoanalytic mind. "Abby, did you talk to the Solar Council recently?"

There was a pause, a moment of loud breathing, then a whisper: "Who told you?"

Bailey played along. "Oh, you told me, remember, you left me messages on my machine and I just wanted to know more. Abby, can you please tell me more?"

More breathing, but this time there was lots of excitement in it. *"The Solar Council is waiting, the beginning of the beginning will become the end...* Wait?" Abby sounded like she was confused by her own words. She repeated them without the appropriate accents, as if to herself.

"That's good Abby, very good. Did the Solar Council say anything else?"

"No... But Sek-Met... she said *You are not the one,* she said, *you are not the one,* Sek-Met told me, she told me, *you are not the one* she told me, *the enemy is here, beware,* she told me *beware...*"

"I remember that, Abby, you already told me that. I know what it means."

"You do? Oh, you do! I knew you would know! Sek-Met was here, she is really tall! Sek-Met was here, she told me... I tried to tell you, but... the phone was broken." Abby broke off abruptly.

"You talked to Sekhmet? *When?*" Bailey held her breath. She was not sure what she was hoping would come next, maybe that Abby had recently talked to Sekhmet and they would have new information, or that she had not and then this whole insane chain of events could end.

"I talked to Sek-Met... I called you..."

It was clear that Abby couldn't explain the timing any better than that.

"What did she say? Abby, what did Sekhmet tell you?"

"She said *to meet Azhe-Vaari...*"

"Oh my god..." whispered Bailey. "What did you just say?"

Abby happily repeated the words.

"You need to see her so *this beginning won't end prematurely. Azhe-Vaari knows the queen who must be like a king, must not let go yet, they need more time, more time to breathe...* Yes, that's right, she said *you will understand, you need to meet Azhe-Vaari and the beginning will not end prematurely then...*"

"Thank you, Abby, thank you so much for telling me this," said Bailey, trying to stall. She quickly typed the words, afraid she would somehow mess this up. "Did Sekhmet say anything about when we should meet Azvari? Or how?"

"No… she said, Sek-Met said, *to meet Azhe-Vaari,* and you need to see her so this beginning won't end too early… she said *when you understand you should meet Azhe-Vaari…*"

No more information was forthcoming; Abby was beginning to repeat herself – a bad sign. Bailey switched the subject and after a while told Abby that she would come visit her soon. She wanted to talk to the doctor. But to Bailey's surprise, instead of the doctor, Marty got on the line.

"Did you get what you wanted, dear? I think your sister was very helpful…"

"Marty, I need to talk to her doctor. She might be having visual hallucinations – she was talking about a red blanket."

"Err… I had Abby transferred to another place," said Marty, and anticipating the avalanche that was about to come down on him, quickly continued, "Don't worry, she has three doctors looking after her, and she is totally safe. In the old place they just medicated her, you wouldn't want that, would you? You were not there to change what they were doing and it might have been complicated anyway… so I just helped the process along a little. She's in a very good place, all paid for, with good doctors watching over her, but she is much less medicated and more attention is paid to her needs, so she is much better off, she really is much better off right now, Bailey…"

Exasperated, Bailey gave up. "You did transfer her entire medical history there, I assume?"

"Yes, of course, the doctors there know everything about her."

"When did you last take your own meds?"

"Err… I will right now, now that everything is taken care of and you don't need me… I mean, if you need me to do something I can just wait a little, you know, until I am done…"

"Jesus, Martin, how long have you been off your meds?"

"Not too long, not too long… I am fine, really, I am, I was very helpful, you know, my dear, and it would not hurt you to acknowledge that at least a little bit!"

"Yes, Martin, you were very helpful. Thank you. Now please take your medication right away. I want to see you do it" – and she waited until he reappeared in front of the screen with a pink pill and took it.

"Good. Now, where is my sister?" Bailey was trying to sound calm, because she knew if she got upset, Marty would become impossible to talk to and she would get no answers out of him. She had to sound calm.

*　　*　　*

"Whoa! Abby knew about Azvari!" Craig was dumbfounded as he read and reread the message Bailey had typed up. "But I don't get the rest... Didn't the prophecy talk about the end of something, and here she said that the end must not come yet, that it's too early..."

"There must be something wrong," added Sahed quietly. "They should know what to do, but if Sekhmet told Abigail this... They must be in trouble, they do not know..." And then Sahed stood up as if to urge his point: *"We must return!"*

"Yes, it makes sense," responded Craig, who for some reason also stood up. "We should deliver the message and maybe help somehow..."

"What makes you think you would even know who needs that help?" flared Bailey. At that moment she resembled a hissing cobra.

"Bailey, the blokes have a point," said Simon calmly. "This whole thing gives me the willies, but the outline of an objective is here if you look for it. If this Sekhmet, god or not, could tell them back there in that time, she probably would have already done so. If she's telling us, through your sister, then she must not be able to tell them, or somehow they didn't get the message. And she mentioned the queen, what's her name? Tiye? So, it sounds like the queen is in trouble. And if you're asked to help the queen...?" He smiled his wide Cheshire cat smile.

"Cool! We should go tonight then," said Craig, his eyes wide with excitement.

"Why?" Bailey was exasperated with this communal agreement. She was still angry with Marty for transferring her sister without her permission – god knows how many signatures he had had to forge to make that happen! And now this – "go *back* there? Again? Are they nuts?"

"Sekhmet said we have to see Azvari, the little girl, to help the queen."

"Craig, what makes you think we should go now, tonight, versus some other night next year? For all we know, we might have even missed the whole thing by now! Or we already did it – we already saw Azvari, didn't we?"

"Abby didn't get this message until now. She said 'when you understand' and you only now understood, and you didn't understand before now. Not until the moment she told you about Azvari."

"I don't understand anything!" yelled Bailey. She was about to scream, to lash out and fight, but instead something snapped inside, the cobra deflated, and all that came out were tears. Somehow they flew as if some pressure valve had been released on the inside, and they came in rivers. She sobbed and sobbed, hiding her face in her hands.

"We should bring him," said Craig finally, pointing his chin in the direction of the man propped up by the wall. "Without him, we might not be able to open the gate."

"I am not going anywhere! You are insane people, truly insane!" barked Mr. Halib in response.

"Should I tape his mouth?" asked Simon in a very friendly, reasonable voice.

"Do you know who I am? The whole Cairo police force will be out looking for me when I do not come to work in the morning! I had this day off, but not tomorrow, and they will look for me and you will be caught!"

"We know who you are, Mr. Halib. You are a Shenu," said Craig. "And I don't think you will cause any trouble because you don't want others to know what you did last night."

"You are an idiot!" snarled Mahmoud. "No one will believe your crazy stories. You are New Age followers, air-heads, you are not true students of archeology!"

"And you are?" questioned Simon politely. "With all this Shenu business, and the gate, never mind being the 'chosen one'… all of that is pure archeology, of course."

Mahmoud was quiet. With his gun confiscated, he seemed to have lost his edge.

*   *   *

The guards were avoided with surgical precision and with quick and practiced movements they opened the metal gate and began their descent. Climbing down the well was hard. Not so much because of the heat, or even the anticipation of events to come. Mostly for a very prosaic reason: muscle pain. Even for Simon, who exercised regularly, the forty-minute climb down after just recently having done it, and with a dead weight of a man on his shoulders, was a hard thing to do at sixty-four years of age. For the rest of them, it was practically impossible. It took them almost ninety minutes to go down this time. Mahmoud had been partially untied so that he could climb down on his own, with Simon keeping a firm hold of him. Simon was determined to go with the party this time – he didn't trust Mr. Halib for a minute. Plus there was a queen to be helped, and he couldn't pass on that.

CHAPTER ELEVEN

1,338BC

Azvari, the High Priestess of the Shenu, Egypt

The heat of the day subsided and the smell of oils filled the air. Azvari was glad to see the sun set. The sun was the blessing, it brought life, but tonight, as they approached Ro-Setau, the cover of darkness was more appropriate. She was involved in an illegal matter.

A single lantern illuminated the water, the waves gently lapping at the sides of the boat, and Azvari gazed silently into the darkness. Even though she did not appear to be doing anything improper, in such uncertain times caution was advisable. Queen Tiye was a wise woman, and if she had asked Azvari to do this, there was good reason for it. Azvari missed the queen. She had been like a mother to her, and a mentor. Without her Azvari had to be strong all on her own.

"There are the first temples," said the older man. He was seated next to Azvari, wrapped in a linen cloak to protect himself from the night chill. They had left Waset two weeks ago and every night it seemed to get colder. When they had passed the towering Temple of Ptah in Men-Nefer, it actually rained – a fortunate sign of blessing.

"We will be there soon," he spoke again and looked at Azvari, as if to make sure that she had heard him. His name was Ay, and he was the brother of Queen Tiye. He was an important personage at court, he had risen to the official position of Keeper of Records. He was also the current Overseer of the Horses and the Chief Advisor Vizier of the pharaoh. Azvari felt honored to have watched Ay gain more influence – he controlled large amounts of wealth and had a say in the foreign policies of Egypt. She trusted him.

259

The oars slapped the water as the only other person on the boat, a muscular young man, navigated their small vessel into the harbor. The man's name was Nakhtmin, and he was the son of Ay's friend, who was a general. At nineteen years of age, Nakhtmin had achieved much – he was already a high-ranking military officer in the pharaoh's army and well on the way to becoming a general himself. Nakhtmin had inherited political wisdom and the ability to strategize from his father, but also the sensitivity of his mother, who had died giving life to him. But Azvari carried a secret – she knew that Nakhtmin was an initiate… No one besides herself and Queen Tiye knew, not even Ay, who was a Shenu himself. This was the will of the queen – she felt that secrecy would serve Sekhmet best, and Azvari wouldn't dream of disobeying Tiye, or the goddess, by telling anyone. When the queen had been ready to tell Vizier Ay about Nakhtmin, Ay had not been ready to listen. This weighed heavily on Azvari's heart, and she knew that at some point she would have to face it. If the prophecy was correct and the Newcomers did arrive, then perhaps she would have to face it very soon.

Nakhtmin tied the boat to the embankment while Ay helped Azvari to climb out. Covered by hooded cloaks, they approached a man seated alone by a small fire. Without speaking he stood up and began to pack his belongings. Ay walked past him to the horses the man had brought, mounted one and waited for Azvari to do the same. Nakhtmin was left to take care of the boat, while Azvari and Ay rode into the desert, four loaded horses roped together following behind them. The sound of the dunes moaning drowned out the clicking of the horses' hoofs on the stones of the road. The only light came from the stars.

In half an hour the road ended and there was only the sand. As they proceeded into the night, Ay looked at Azvari. There was an unmistakable desire in his eyes. Azvari had known him since she was a little girl, and she knew his intentions were honorable. They had never once wavered since she had gained the appearance of a woman. But she did not share his desire. Ay was fifty-nine years old, and married. He was not the one for Azvari; she knew it, and Queen Tiye knew it. Azvari was not meant to be a minor wife, even if it was of an important vizier. And so Ay kept his distance.

Azvari was twenty-seven years of age and still unmarried. At fifteen she could have chosen a husband and become the mistress of her own house and a mother to her children. Being a priestess did not prevent her from marriage, neither did being one of the Shenu. She would have married whomever Queen Tiye, the High Priestess of the

Shenu, had presented to her. But the queen had left that decision up to her.

A long time ago, when Azvari was only a little girl of five, she met Sekhmet. Queen Tiye had asked Azvari to help her, to go down this very shaft she was again about to descend. She remembered it well... How deep it was... She was carried down in a basket on a man's back. Soon the strangers had arrived. One man was like the people she saw all around her; the other man was similar but dressed in very strange clothes. The other two people were like nothing Azvari had ever seen. They looked different; their skin was devoid of any color, as if they had spent their entire lives underground. The man was as tall as a giant, and his long straight black hair was in a braid. The woman had orange hair, which was very rare in Egypt, and very white skin. When afterwards little Azvari was given an audience with the queen and could ask about these strange people, Tiye answered, "they are guests from another kingdom where all people look like that." And Azvari was told to forget them.

Her name was being called. Apparently she had been weighed down by her thoughts, not looking ahead. Ay was pointing at a tall half buried stone directly in front of them, with a Shenu symbol carved into it, next to a small mound. He helped Azvari dismount her beast, and the animal immediately walked toward a bag filled with food that Ay placed on the ground. Pushing a pole deep into the sand, he tied the horses to it. Then he pulled a wooden palette from his saddle to clear away the sand, and under his efforts the little mound quickly disappeared to reveal a stone enclosure. Ay was an old man, but he was strong and youthful; being a Shenu he knew of many ways to keep himself healthy. They found a cloth over the well's mouth, and under it a copper door. When Ay opened the heavy metal cover, the sound brought Azvari back to the past.

They paused a moment and peered down the shaft. The well Azvari remembered looked very different. When she was a girl, the shaft appeared to be much larger, but now it seemed narrower. She took off her cloak and the chill of the night air wrapped itself around her. Ay gave her an oil lamp with a metal hook at the top – if her hand tired, she could hook it onto the ladder and rest. As she began climbing down, she saw a cloth going over the top of the well, blocking out the starlight – he was erecting a tent. Ay would look like a desert man, resting in a small tent close to his horses.

The last time Azvari had been at the bottom of the well, the people she met there disappeared. They came, stared at her in shock, and then there was such a beautiful sight – the goddess Sekhmet herself came from that light. She was transparent and luminous. Sekhmet spoke to Azvari, telling her that she had chosen her to become the High Priestess of Shenu. She told her about the beginning of the end, and about her future husband. It was an odd combination of information, but who was she to question Sekhmet? Being so little, Azvari had not understood most of what Sekhmet was saying, but she did remember everything.

Azvari smiled to herself as she grasped the ladder. At fifteen, instead of getting married she became a priestess at the Temple of Mut at Waset, following what she thought Sekhmet had meant for her. There was only one large temple to Sekhmet in Egypt and it was not in Waset, but in Men-Nefer. When fifteen-year-old Azvari told Queen Tiye she desired to become a Sekhmet priestess, the queen suggested that she join the Temple of Mut where Sekhmet was being worshipped – it was in Waset, after all, close to the court of the queen.

Many years later Azvari was initiated into the Shenu, chosen by Queen Tiye herself. There was another Shenu, a man, who was close to death, and he asked Tiye if she was raising her inheritor in Azvari. It was true that she was, but Tiye was well and she decided that the sooner Azvari became one of the Shenu, the better. And so that man picked Azvari as his inheritor. The queen approved, and Azvari became a Shenu. Tiye was still the High Priestess, and secretly Azvari hoped that Sekhmet was wrong, that somehow Tiye would stay on this earth longer than Azvari and remain the High Priestess forever. But Azvari knew that Sekhmet was never wrong. Since that time in the well she had talked to her many times. Not in the well of course – this was the first time since her childhood that she had been allowed back in there.

Azvari had a rare connection with Sekhmet. The goddess revealed herself in visions, where she stood in front of Azvari and talked with her. Sekhmet was so tall that Azvari always felt tiny next to the goddess, as if she herself was still only a five-year-old child.

When the visions began, Azvari elected to not mention them to the priestesses of Mut at her temple, but instead to tell the queen. To her surprise, Tiye was very interested. Sometimes she even requested that Azvari ask Sekhmet very particular questions. It was not always an easy thing to do; more often than not there were no answers. But Azvari took her ability very seriously, and she prayed in the Sekhmet chapel every day. She could not call on Sekhmet, but once in a while her prayers were answered and Sekhmet would grant her a vision. These visions did not make sense to Azvari, and surely did not seem to be answering the queen's questions. But Tiye always listened intently and seemed to understand the vision's meaning. There were many things Azvari did not know back then, including why Tiye made her promise to never reveal her ability to others.

Azvari was an orphan. Her parents died from a sickness when she was only an infant. The queen herself took her in. Azvari was not raised as a princess, however; she was almost never seen at public appearances. She was allowed into the private rooms of Queen Tiye, and she played games with the queen's youngest son, who was only three years her senior, and she often won. She also spent time with a girl who was two years older than her, a daughter of Ay. She had known Ay for such a long time...

Azvari was always kept somewhat hidden. Educated better than any princess, her studies kept her more in the temples than at court, though she had been given a place to live in the servant quarters of the palace. When her features filled out, around the age of seventeen, her face resembled Isis herself. And as her willowy body went through the temple halls or the courtyards of the palace, it attracted a lot of attention. But commoners didn't think themselves equal to her social and educational level, and they avoided her. The nobles of the palace were very interested when they saw that she had access to the queen's private quarters, and some even approached her with proposals of marriage. The connection would have been the highest honor – for her, an orphaned commoner, to be married to a noble or even a distant member of the royal family. Azvari cared little for such honors, however; she would have married a donkey if it was the queen's will. But Queen Tiye reminded Azvari over and over, "You know what to do, you were told." She was referring to the time in the well, when Azvari was only five years old. Sekhmet had told her that she would be the chief wife of a foreigner from a distant land, and she would know him by the scar on his face. Many foreign dignitaries came to the land of Egypt to see the splendors of the glorious Amenhotep III, and then those of his son. Because she was at court whenever she was not in a temple, Azvari saw all the guests. Some had scars, but all the ones that did already had a full harem. Azvari was to be the principal wife, and so, at twenty-seven years of age, she was still unmarried. At this point marriage was practically impossible; most women her age had already had at least five children! Who would want to marry her? Perhaps Ay... But he was not a foreign dignitary, and that was that.

"My life is for Sekhmet, and Queen Tiye, who took care of me out of the greatness of her heart. Pharaohs, queens, princes and princesses don't matter. Husbands don't matter!" Azvari told herself.

Climbing the ladder slowly, though, her thoughts kept returning to the possible husband. In a few days dignitaries from Assyria were arriving, and one of them was an unmarried minor prince. "Maybe it will be him... not that he has to be a prince," mused Azvari. "What am I occupying my thoughts with? I am serving Sekhmet. I am fulfilling a promise to Queen Tiye in this very private matter.'

Last year Queen Tiye had asked Azvari to descend into the well at a particular time in the months to come, and to meet the Newcomers. Azvari knew what Tiye meant instantly. "They are returning?" she asked.

"Yes, they must come and see the city. Sekhmet had a reason for telling you that they will come, and her words must be fulfilled." Tiye was referring to a message that Azvari had gotten a few weeks before that, through one of her visions. Sekhmet was adamant that the Newcomers would come back to Egypt, and she had even specified how the stars would be aligned when they returned. Azvari hoped their return would help somehow. She didn't know how, but the gods knew they needed help! "What would you, the greatest queen, want me to do?" she had asked Tiye then.

"You will bring them here. You will know who you can trust and who must not know. Make them unseen. The Newcomer's return is about the beginning of the end. Promise me you will bring them here!"

"You will not be disappointed, my queen, I promise."

How much could happen in a year... She would have not guessed the sorrows... She had thought that surely the pain would break her heart and Anubis would take her! But here she was, slowly climbing down the ladder.

She reached the bottom of the well, and allowed herself a slow, measured breath. Being here, at this sacred place, was an honor. It was hot and moist, and dark, aside from the few feet of light cast by her small lantern. Her heart was beating with the anticipation of something incredible, and she was filled with hope, not fear. Her body ached from the climb, but her Ba-the-soul was dancing. She was early – no one had arrived yet. She unstrapped a small basket from her back – it was filled with ceremonial incense, a waterskin, and dates. Azvari was prepared for a long wait. It might be that the gate would open tonight, but it could also be in a week, or more. Fasting was not new to her. She lit the incense, then took a large sip of water from the goatskin sack. Closing her eyes, Azvari sat still. She knew how to slow down her breathing – a useful technique to know when there was not enough oxygen.

*　　*　　*

There was a bright flash, and Azvari felt faint for a moment. She saw nothing but the white light and she struggled to hear, but could not. A childhood memory came back, and her Ba filled with the anticipation of seeing Sekhmet. But as the light got dimmer, she could see only the Newcomers. No Sekhmet.

After the initial disappointment she focused on who was in front of her. The brightness eventually diminished and Azvari could distinguish not only the contours of the people, but their features. There were five of them this time, not four. To her shock four of the visitors looked exactly as she had remembered them. Twenty-two years had passed, and when she had thought about the old man she was not sure he was even alive, but not only was he alive, he looked unchanged. The other Egyptian man, the colorless orange-haired woman, and the tall younger man also had not aged a year. "Sekhmet truly is powerful," said Azvari, exhaling. "If as a child I thought they were old, now they must be ancient, yet they are well and unchanged."

"We come on the errand of Sekhmet, the Bringer of Truth, the Detester of Untruth," said the old man. Azvari felt her face wet with tears – his voice sounded the same as it did back then, twenty-two years ago.

Taking a deep breath, Azvari spoke: "I am here on the command of Sekhmet and at the request of Tiye, the High Priestess of Shenu. She wishes me to bring you to the great Akhet-Aten city. Sekhmet spoke her wisdom to us, and in that wisdom she brought you here."

After a pause, the old man spoke again. "I am Sahed, and I am honored to meet you. We are here because we also heard Sekhmet's command."

"I am Azvari, a priestess of Shenu. I am to bring you to the palace, unseen."

"Did she say *Azvari?*" said the fifth man, the one who she had not remembered seeing. Not knowing his language, she could only discern her name.

Sahed translated. "Are you the same Azvari, the child who saw us leave the last time we were here?"

"I am. Many years have passed since your last coming. Twenty-two years…"

She heard a whisper that sounded like "Whoa," and other words she did not understand. The white-skinned woman stared at her in shock, and the younger tall man next to her, the one who had the same skin, looked at Azvari with a wide smile as he spoke in their language. "It's good that he smiles," thought Azvari, unsure of why it was good. The two Egyptian men were replying to the smiling young man, but he was not looking at them. The fifth man was older than the young man but seemed younger than the other two, she could not place his age well. He looked at her warmly. After they stopped talking, Azvari asked if they were ready to come up, picked up her basket, and began to climb up.

*   *   *

It was early morning when they emerged from the well. On the surface there was precious little – no big tents, no servants to attend to them. Instead they were greeted by only one man. He was about fifty-five, maybe a little older, and he was dressed as a desert Bedouin. The man looked out of place; he was not someone used to living rough, Simon could see that right away. The man's nails were meticulously filed and his hands looked soft. The skin on his face was pampered, and he had a commanding stance and a fearless, penetrating stare. He was clearly accustomed to wealth and power. Simon speculated that it was a great deal of wealth and power. Could he be royalty? The clothes were a cover, but from whom? Did Azvari know, or did she think he was only a Bedouin? She seemed to be very trusting.

Behind him, Craig emerged from the well and to Simon's surprise went straight up to the man, extending his hand. "Hello, Ay, it's nice to see you again!" And as Bailey clambered out, he added, "Bailey, look, he hasn't aged much, well, maybe some... It's Ay, remember him?"

Azvari spoke to this Ay, and put on a cloak as he began untying the horses. The camp, which consisted of only a tiny tent and some wares, was disassembled in minutes. Ay placed a large copper cover over the well's mouth, then a cloth, and then began to pile sand over it using what looked like a wooden palette. Simon picked up a similar instrument from the ground and began to help him; he handled the palette better than the man did. As Simon shoveled, he noted everything that was happening. From the way Azvari spoke to Ay, it became clear that she was aware of his true position. Soon there was nothing but a pile of sand where the mouth of the well had been. Finished, he noticed a smile on Azvari's face; she quickly turned away to hide it.

Mr. Halib was cooperative. He was no longer completely bound, but as Simon still did not trust him entirely his feet remained tied together. It had been done in a way that allowed him to climb – about two feet of rope hung freely in between his bound ankles. "That is so Mr. Council of Antiquities here can't run, or make any other obvious moves, and we can keep an eye on those hands," thought Simon. No one had a gun this time, and Simon had only brought a knife. He never went on a mission without one. As they were climbing up Simon had thought, "This girl came alone and didn't check for knives or other weapons... Not good," but because she had been alone he had expected a whole legion to be waiting for them on the surface. When he saw that there was only the one man waiting for them, Simon was puzzled. "Why would the queen send this young girl down? Why not this man? Or twenty of them – that would've been a safer scenario." No answer came to him. "Is Egypt in a bad situation? Is there a war on, or something?" He suddenly wished he knew more history.

Simon looked at Bailey – she was very nervous, as if she knew she was about to see something scary and was trying to prepare herself. "Hey, sweetheart, relax, from what you were saying the hardest part is over," he told her.

The man came towards Simon and handed him a white cloth and a brownish shawl. "Well, I guess we're all going undercover here," and he put the clothes around himself, wrapping his head with the brown shawl, mimicking the man's attire. The man, even though his head was wrapped in the same type of shawl, wore a nicely made hooded cloak underneath. "Not much of a cover, pal, if even I, a foreigner, can see it."

Craig was doing the same and he looked excited, swiveling his head all around. He was the first one up onto a horse, and he looked like a real desert man. Bailey was next. Looking around Simon could see Mr. Halib was being helped onto a brown horse, his leg bindings allowing him only a side-saddle position, which he had to be content with. He looked pissed, but Simon was glad that the man had not decided to accommodate him by untying him. Sahed looked like he had seen a horse before now, and he, quickly for his years, mounted. Now the only one still standing on the sand besides Simon was Azvari. Her back was to him, and when he touched her arm to offer to help her onto the black beast, she was startled and almost jumped a step back. He raised his hands in an "I didn't mean anything by it" position and got onto Sahed's horse behind him. "Maybe you can't touch a woman here... I mean, they aren't Muslim, but maybe in ancient Egypt they would cut a fella into pieces for that just the same..."

Soon all of them looked like desert people, quietly swaying back and forth as the horses rode in the direction of the sunrise. In less than an hour they could hear the signs of human activity as they approached the harbor, and Craig blurted out excitedly: "That's the Nile, look! Look to your right!"

Simon turned his head and saw the water, then turned to the left – right next to them was a large, brightly painted stone structure, a temple of some sort, and next to it another, then another, like a street of massive shops illuminated by the rising sun. In front of them was a sizable plaza, and behind the temple roof Simon could clearly see the head of the Sphinx. Emitting his usual whistling sound and staring at the paint on the statue's face, he thought "It is certainly colorful..." Their horses moved along as it looked straight into the glorious sunrise in the east.

The harbor was filled with sailboats and people, the merchants were setting up their wares, and smells of cooked food wafted in the air. Taking pains to avoid notice, their little caravan traveled past all this activity and moved toward a shabby boat with only one man on board. They dismounted and the horses were tied to a pole, as the young man climbed up the stone steps to meet them. He said a few words to Azvari and quickly left for the closest temple. The air was beginning to warm up and fill with the smell of incense from the temples. And sounds, so many sounds came from every direction, voices yelling and animals – horses, donkeys, goats, even geese and chickens! Ay stepped into the boat and sat down on one of the benches, and Azvari motioned for them all to do the same. "Who will row?" wondered Simon to himself. There were four sets of oars and no rowers. The answer was soon apparent – the young man reappeared with four others. One of the men took away the horses, while the other three climbed into the boat. In minutes they were launched out of the harbor, their sail raised. Simon studied the men. Three of them were obviously rowers-for-hire, their eyes held no interest in their passengers at all, and they did their work silently. The young man who had been there when they arrived looked different. Despite the morning chill, his muscular body was covered only by a simple kilt and a white cloth wrapped over his shoulders, but he was no sailor. His intense focused eyes were more that of a body guard than a simple seaman. He moved and rowed with the ease of a trained solder. "Now that's smarter," thought Simon. "At least one of them is prepared." He still thought it was strange that Azvari and Ay had left the only trained man with the boat and had met them alone instead.

Simon listened to the sound of Azvari's voice as she quietly talked with Ay. Azvari was beautiful. Not the type of beauty favored by tabloids, but a breathtaking, everlasting, deep, and ancient beauty. There was something eternal in her face as her gaze swept the harbor.

The morning rolled on and, although they were on the water, it soon became hot. Once they had moved away from the harbor Azvari and Ay took off their cloaks and shawls, and the men undressed down to their kilts. Ay's body was covered by a longer kilt with a white cloth over his shoulders like that worn by the younger man, while Azvari wore a tight white sheath trimmed with gold thread and tied with a wide strip of red linen. When they saw that it was allowed, the Newcomers followed suit. Simon unraveled his head scarf and rolled it neatly. As he turned to Azvari, she gasped. He smiled, unsure of what he could possibly have done to startle her again.

"Ask her, Sahed, ask her," said Bailey impatiently as soon as they took their camouflage off. "What's happening now? Tiye is still the queen, so then her husband is still the pharaoh, Amenhotep III, right? Why are we in this time?"

Azvari seemed frustrated with the questions, but she answered, "You are here because Sekhmet brought you here. This is the time of the beginning of the end. The dark powers are gathering their forces. That is why you were not given a proper welcome, and were met only by me and two other trusted ones. I am a trusted one, and I will try to be of help to you to the best of my ability. The older man is Vizier Ay, Queen Tiye's brother and an important man at court. The younger man is Nakhtmin, a high military officer. They are here to hide you, and must not be distracted from their task."

"What 'dark powers'? Who are they? Are some people after us?" Craig blurted out, surprised by what Azvari had said. "I thought that no one knew we were here except the Shenu."

"It is a very long story and I do not believe that the queen, may she find peace, had the time to tell you all of it the last time," replied Azvari. "When the sun sets, I will tell you more."

It was clear that she intended to sail in silence and that no amount of questioning would change her mind.

They sailed past stretches of grassless land, alternating with green rolling hills dotted with vineyards. Loud bird calls came from the marshes, a heron calling his beloved.

They passed Men-Nefer city by day, and as the sun began to set they arrived at the small harbor of a darkened temple. Sounds of animals and people from a nearby market spilled over the water. Somewhere, a baby was crying. The oarsmen got off the boat to gather wood on the shore, while Azvari disappeared into the darkness in the direction of the market and Nakhtmin secured the sail. Ay stood a little way off and kept watch. When the men returned they started two small fires, settling themselves around one and leaving the other for the Newcomers and their hosts. Azvari came back with a basket of food: duck, honeyed cakes, bread and figs were washed down with a hot liquid resembling tea. The honeyed cakes that Bailey liked so much the last time reminded her of her servant Nab, and she wondered if she would meet Nab again.

"Now can she tell us why we are here?" whispered Bailey loudly, feeling braver after eating.

Azvari met Bailey's insistent gaze as she poured dark-gold colored liquid from a large clay pot into a beautiful little cup. There were many cups in the basket and she filled one for each person and they were passed around. Even Ay and Nakhtmin each took a cup, but returned to their positions to watch the passing people. They took this mission very seriously.

Azvari began her tale. It was a lengthy recount of what Queen Tiye had told them the last time – about the star-gods from Sirius, the pyramid-birds, about people being happy and living together with the star-gods…

"And then Akhu, the Awakened ones, were no more. All peoples of Earth felt Ammit, the devourer of Duat, on their doorstep, falling into such deep sleep that star-gods worried they would never awaken again…"

"Who is Ammit?" whispered Simon.

Sahed quietly replied: "A she-demon of the Underworld who sits by the scales of Maat and watches Anubis work – she devours impure hearts after death. Ammit has a body of á lion, hind legs of a hippopotamus, and a head of a crocodile."

Simon whistled.

"Why is this 'sleep' so bad?" asked Bailey. "Was it like people were falling asleep on the street, while they were walking? Were they ill?"

"No, everything went on as usual," replied Azvari, sipping her herbal tea. "People rose in the mornings and went about their chores, fed their animals and played with their children, and went to bed at night. But perceptive abilities diminished. As I was told, there were teachings by the star-gods about life, about many skies of Duat – the Universe and its Law. The body could become Light, as see-through as a pyramid-bird, and explore other worlds. But all the teachings required the study of the body of light, of the living Mer-Ka-Ba. It is an unseen structure, similar to the pyramid-bird, but composed of two pyramids – one points up, and the other points down. These energy pyramids spin so fast that no one

270

can see them with their eyes. But the internal central eye knows and sees... The awakening and the memory of who we are is dependent on the spinning of the Mer-Ka-Ba. The great sleep that was taking over the Earth was preventing the Mer-Ka-Ba from spinning at that invisible fast speed... And people were forgetting what the true meaning of their life was... They knew not Maat! Instead of Maat – the Truth and Fairness – they only felt the needs of their body, forsaking the spirit! They were becoming lost in their lives..."

"So why didn't the Sirians just prevent it? You know, stop this 'falling asleep' so that people could remember everything?"

"It is a Universal Law that no one can rescue anyone," said Azvari, smiling at Bailey as if she were talking to a child. "The people of Egypt had to figure out a way back to consciousness by themselves, the star-gods could not help them. But the faster consciousness of the star people had created so many energy filaments and sacred grids in Egypt that even though people everywhere else on Earth were falling into sleep, it took over a thousand years for Ammit to claim the land of Egypt. But she did eventually, in Maat of Duat as she was... Egypt fell into sleep, and the people chose to follow... The inner sacred workings of their bodies were shattered, destroying the body's ability to regenerate. People were getting sick, dying... They were terrified and did not remember who they were..."

"You mean that one day everyone woke up and suddenly couldn't remember their names? And who the people around them were?" blurted Bailey.

"Oh, Bai-Ley, your Mer wants to know, but the mind of your Ka won't let you!" said Azvari, smiling again. "People were aware of their names and their surroundings and they went on with their lives as usual, going to the temple, home, market, work... But they no longer connected to Mer-spirit or Ba-soul; they were scared, lost and unsure. They used to do the temple ceremonies for the sake of keeping awake, and out of love and gratitude to the star-gods. After they fell asleep, they repeated the ceremonies as step by step rituals, as something they had to do, but they did not remember why they were doing them. They were alive in their bodies, but they began to think they *were* the body! They almost forgot their Ka!"

"So you are saying that everyone around the Shenu began to act strangely, like they were under the influence of this 'sleep,' but the Shenu themselves were able to keep their Mer-Ka-Ba spinning and stay awake?" Bailey tried with all her will to give this a chance, to make sense of it. She then whispered to Sahed, "I thought that Mer-Ka-Ba was Hebrew?"

271

"The Mer-Ka-Ba knowledge came to us from the star-gods. Many Shenu, including Habiru, were taught its secrets."

The conversation went on well into the night, until finally they slept next to the fire where they were, curled up in blankets. At dusk, Azvari led them back onto the boat and they set sail before the sun was up. Mr. Halib glared angrily at the water.

"This is not so bad," suggested Craig, seeing his frustration.

"We still know nothing!" replied the man.

"Relax, it has only been a day!"

"Ptah created a whole world in a day!" hissed Mahmoud. And to himself he added, "And I must find a way to undo it."

Days passed. They sailed upstream, keeping to themselves. Their meals, like everything else, were basic. They slept on the boat or by a campfire on the riverbank. Large decorated boats resembling pregnant herons were parked in front of the temples they passed. The ceremonies could be heard from the water, as they admired bright, colorful flowers which adorned everything around the temple harbors. And there were chariots! Four brightly colored ones rode quickly past them on the embankments of bright white limestone. To Simon's surprise everything and everybody was fast-moving. He had not thought that in ancient times people lived at such a speed. He commented on it to Sahed, who responded, "Egypt follows the speed of her pharaoh."

They stayed away from the commotion though, docking only at smaller and much poorer harbors. "She meant what she said," thought Simon, remembering Azvari's promise to bring them to Akhet-Aten city unseen.

Darkness came. In another hour they reached a small shabby harbor. The men moored the boat, and Ay went ashore. When he returned an hour later, he said to Azvari, "I talked to the messenger – we must return to Waset. I have to be at the Malkata palace to greet the viziers. I know it is unexpected, but I must be there… Akhet-Aten will have to wait."

Sahed translated as Ay talked.

"Where is Waset?" whispered Bailey.

"Waset is Luxor, and Akhet-Aten is the Horizon of the Light," replied Mahmoud with frustration. The woman's ignorance had no bounds! And she dared to call herself a Shenu! "We just passed it, you saw the chariots there. That was Akhet-Aten. If you know it at all, you probably heard of it as Amarna."

"Wasn't Amarna destroyed?" asked Simon. He remembered reading about Amarna, the lost and then found Egyptian city of light, which had been completely erased by the desert.

The small harbor didn't seem to lead to anywhere but the desert – no houses or lights interrupted the darkness. The oarsmen began to unravel their blankets, making it clear that tonight would be spent on the boat.

Azvari, Nakhtmin and the Newcomers sat by a small clay kiln on the boat, warming their hands by the fire, and talked well into the night. Ay was adamant about not joining the conversation. He felt somewhat undignified by his role – he, the Overseer of his Majesty's Horses and Records, was stuck on a boat wearing poor men's garb, pretending to be a desert man! "But he will bear it, for it is the will of Sekhmet, no matter how much he dislikes it!" thought Azvari, watching Ay sit alone, wrapped up in his cloak.

"How do you listen to all of this stuff Azvari says so calmly?" Bailey quietly asked Simon when he passed her a piece of cooked fish. "It's so crazy!"

"I tend to believe my eyes. And what I see tells me that this is real as far as history goes, and considering the events, the whole shebang of the star-gods and the pyramid-birds might be as real as you and me."

"You're scaring me, Simon."

"Sorry… didn't mean to… But you might want to look at why you fight this so much – it's right in front of you and it certainly feels real…"

*   *   *

Azvari continued her tale.

"The priests and priestesses were able to keep their awareness open for a while longer than the rest of the people of Egypt, but eventually Ammit consumed their awareness too. When their Mer-Ka-Ba stopped spinning, they fell into unconsciousness like all the others. People forgot how to breathe light through their Vertical Column and the eye in the center of their heads. Their life energy began to follow the same path as air, through the nose and mouth, then into lungs and blood.

You see, the perception of Reality is encoded in the Mer-Ka-Ba and in the inner central eye. Once the spin of the Mer-Ka-Ba slowed down and the central inner eye was not supplied with the needed light, we forgot the true Duat. Our Reality not in Maat anymore, but an illusion, a dream. People had known the illusion of duality before, but they simultaneously knew the Maat of Oneness. The sleep changed their perception, and they began to see themselves as separate from what was outside of themselves. People understood themselves as being on the 'inside looking out' from their bodies. In Maat everything is connected, everything is light and there is an *alive* unseen light inside solid things and in between them – everywhere. People lost that perception, trapping themselves inside their physical form.

But Sekhmet did not forsake us. She stayed. Although… it is not my place to say, but I believe she was frustrated with people. She loves us all so much! She wanted us to be braver, to face this darkness and stay awake… She wanted us to try harder. We failed, mostly… You see, when someone is awake, he knows the Maat of Reality, the Truth about things, about Duat-the-Universe. He knows life. He sees what others cannot see… The priests and priestesses could feel the other groups of people, some here in the blessed land of Egypt, others far away, who were still able to stay awake. But there were fewer and fewer of them. And with time even the Shenu were not able to be as awake as Sekhmet desired us to be. Even I… I know Maat, but I can only practice so much of it, I do not see Reality in the way others did before me, practicing what Sekhmet told them. The light on Earth is so dense now, we have less ability."

"Oh, now I get it… she doesn't delegate well!" laughed Craig, remembering the words of his spirit guide about Sekhmet. No one else was laughing, so he chewed on his lip and said, "You mentioned you can still talk to Sekhmet? Even with the light being dense?"

"Yes. My abilities are lesser than those who came before me, but they are still significantly advanced compared to most people. Sekhmet chose me to see her."

"You see visions of her?" asked Bailey cautiously – another person who "sees Sekhmet" made her nervous.

"Yes, she appears to me when she needs to say something to the Shenu."

"Like in a dream? Or right in front of you like we are here?" pressed Bailey, unsure of why this was an important point, but knowing that it was.

"Neither. Sekhmet shows herself to me. She is a tall and beautiful being…"

"And she wears the gold mask of a cat over her face…" Bailey finished Azvari's sentence. Now she was sure that her vision was very important. It held some answer for her, not about her father or Abby, but about herself. Her head had begun to hurt. She was about to blame the headache and dizzy feeling on low blood sugar, when the tears came. She hated crying, especially in front of people, she felt so small and weak. But there was nothing she could do, the tears had their own rules. To her surprise, Azvari placed her hand on Bailey's head and spoke.

"She is telling you that you are back to the Reality of Maat now," translated Sahed.

1,338BC

Waset, Egypt

A few days back, when they had gotten onto the boat, they had finally untied his feet. The undignified position these people had put him in! But Mahmoud consoled himself – he had the knowledge of the ancient language and he had his mind, and that would have to do. He ate with them, listened to Azvari's lengthy talk, and he studied the people and his surroundings.

"This is the time when the Shenu was betrayed," he thought, "and if I can prevent it… it must be my destiny; that is why I was placed in this position, why I had to endure this indignity! Sekhmet was testing me!"

They continued traveling south, until finally they arrived at Waset, the City of Amun. It was early morning, before the heat of the day took hold. Wrapped in their Bedouin camouflage, they came onto shore. Nakhtmin quickly sought out four men who appeared to be waiting for him. Mahmoud recognized the white kilts, the wide leather belts and arm-protectors – these were soldiers in the pharaoh's army. Mahmoud suspected Nakhtmin was too, and it became clear from how he talked to the men that he outranked them.

Ay had abandoned his desert shawl but was still covered by his cloak. He made eye contact with Azvari, turned around and speedily walked away from the boat. The Americans were, of course, gawking at everything, wide-eyed. Mahmoud contemplated bolting away into the morning crowd, but one look at the man who called himself Simon was enough to know that would not be a good idea. He snarled and waited.

Hidden by their clothing, they were led through the city, following two soldiers who kept up a fast pace in front of them. The other two men picked up the rear, their eyes scanning the crowds. Waset was magnificent, a truly powerful sight, and the archeologist and historian in Mahmoud grasped at the details – there were obelisks with their golden tips pointing to the sky, fires and incense, people running with baskets and large pots on their heads, everything alive with activity and very clean. There were chariots too. They passed two stationary ones, but they were walking too quickly for Mahmoud to read the hieroglyphs etched into the copper inlays.

Strangely though, the colorful temples looked deserted.

"Oh, I might be too late!" thought Mahmoud desperately.

The soldiers stopped at a small gate, said farewell to Nakhtmin, and left. Nakhtmin opened the wooden door at the opposite side of the street, and let everyone in. He quickly walked ahead. They stepped into a yard filled with goats and chickens. Following Nakhtmin through the droppings and scattered grain they entered what appeared to be a kitchen. Pots hung over fires, and six headless chickens were laid out on a large wooden table. The American woman gasped loudly and backed up, almost running into Mahmoud. Azvari urged them to hurry and they followed her through the other doorway, then through another courtyard, several corridors and more courtyards. The rooms were becoming cleaner and better decorated. "We are moving to the front of the house," guessed Mahmoud silently. Finally they arrived at a lavishly decorated courtyard, and stopped.

"This is where you will rest. You will be sent for later," said Azvari. And she quickly departed. They were left almost alone in the courtyard, the servants rushing by giving them only a passing look. "Yes, we look like Bedouins, we might have come here to deliver a message from a distant oasis, and so we are to be treated well, but without any special consideration," thought Mahmoud. He was puzzled. "I wonder why, and from whom, we are being hidden?"

Soon house servants ushered them out, repeating "Master must rest, Lady must rest." But rest, of course, was the last thing on Mahmoud's agenda! Yet this time he decided not to deviate from the plan presented by the locals – he had been drugged the last time, after he bound that servant. He lay on the uncomfortable pillow-less bed and stared at the beautifully painted ceiling. A scarab stared back at him. Mahmoud wanted to walk around, to explore the building, but he knew better. He had to be content with studying the ceiling.

After almost two hours two young man-servants entered the room and Mahmoud sat up on the bed, growling with impatience. One of the men held a copper bowl of water, the other came in with tray of fruit and a tall vase. Mahmoud was washed, feet to head. Then he ate the fruit and rinsed his mouth with water from the vase. He was dressed in his own clothes now – he didn't want to wear that Bedouin scarf a moment longer. Luckily he was not made to. One of the servants led him out of the room.

Meeting the others in the hallway, Mahmoud again saw Nakhtmin. He gave each of them a long, light, and almost transparent white cloth. Encouraging them to wrap themselves up in it, Nakhtmin couldn't hide a smile at their clumsy efforts. They soon looked like odd walking mummies, but it hid their identities, and that was the point after all. Nakhtmin then led them out of the palace.

"Whose palace was this?" asked Mahmoud, coming close to Nakhtmin.

"This is Vizier Ay's palace," was the reply.

"Did Ay have a palace the last time?" thought Mahmoud, struggling for a moment with the idea that twenty-two years had passed here, while for him it had only been a few days. "No. Time is the same everywhere," he thought, correcting himself. "We just came out of the well twenty-two years later."

History was not an exact science; it could still be the time of Amenhotep III, with Tiye being his Chief Queen. "A longer time than officially thought, but what do we know?" he mused. This time period was sketchy in the Shenu records…

They had rested through the heat of the day, and now the sun was setting and torches and lamps were being lit everywhere. The city was alive again. People were rushing about, pushing and pulling, riding donkeys, calling out… A man shouted for people to move – the street was being cleaned! They crossed the freshly cleaned plaza to the Temple of Amun. There was little activity there. Smoke rose from large shallow bowls, filling the air with incense. But torches were few and lit only in the main gallery of Amun, and the offering tables were empty.

To the others, Nakhtmin said in a quiet voice, "We are in Ipet-Sut, in the precinct of Amun-Ra, his temple."

Sahed nodded, but seeing the blank stares on the faces of his other companions, the Egyptologist in Mahmoud took over: "Ipet-Sut means, 'the Most Select of Places,' it means Karnak, which is part of

Amun's district in Luxor. This was the largest temple at Karnak, and it was dedicated to Amun-Ra."

They walked through the dark temple to the east, towards a tall doorway. There, behind a white-washed mud-brick wall, they saw, in the remaining light of the setting sun, another temple. "Oh, the gods of Egypt!" moaned Mahmoud.

Unable to contain himself he ran around the others and through the east doorway, past the white wall and into that temple, hardly able to believe his eyes. He was standing inside the Gempa-Aten, the temple built by Amenhotep IV. "Before he went mad," he commented to himself. In the current time the temple was completely ruined, with nothing left but a few hundred talatats and the broken outline of the foundation. Mahmoud was speechless. Forgetting all his suspicions for a moment he raced farther into the temple, looking in all directions and craning his head. There was no ceiling; the sun had set and he could see the stars. The tall columns reached high into the sky, and were beautifully decorated.

Four priests dressed in white robes busied themselves lighting the many large bowls of oil in the temple. Within a few minutes the dark outlines were brightly illuminated, and Mahmoud was so overcome. He hurried from one area of the temple to the next, looking. "It's gigantic!" The temple ruins had suggested a much smaller size. "There must be almost five hundred feet this way, and it's probably seven or eight hundred ahead to the west..." The walls were yellow and white, with many scenes painted on them. When the middle of the temple became illuminated, Mahmoud almost stopped breathing. Directly ahead of him was a huge, red granite sphinx with a beautiful face. In front of it stood a large offering table, also of red granite, with fruits and flowers piled on top. For a moment Mahmoud couldn't get his legs to move and he just stood there, staring at the sphinx. He felt the others catching up to him. They passed him and continued walking into the middle courtyard, a rectangular space surrounded by square pillars. He followed them on autopilot, his eyes jumping from column to column. Then he moaned again. In front of each column was an enormous statue, a red granite likeness of Akhenaten and Nefertiti.

*　　*　　*

"Whoa!" exclaimed Craig as he entered the central courtyard. He stared at the reddish face of the sphinx illuminated by the fires, and it stared right back at him. "Simon would love this!" He hoped that in whatever form his spirit guide could exist in the material world, he could witness this sight. "This is soooo cooool!" he whispered. His gaze fell on the large statues. They were red granite forms, wide at the hips, with elongated bodies, long necks and large-chinned faces. Each wore a different headdress, and every other one had its hands crossed over its chest, holding crook and flail. "These look like Akhenaten, like the ones in the Cairo Museum," thought Craig. Suddenly he realized what he was looking at – he was so amazed that he could only utter another "Whoa!"

In less than half an hour, Azvari arrived, Ay next to her. They joined Sahed and Bailey in the main gallery, far back from where Craig was standing. From there they couldn't see the statues and they could only glimpse the sphinx. The only person in the large open space under the stars was Mr. Halib, and he seemed to be as awestruck as Craig. He and Craig looked at each other, and Mr. Halib smiled for a few seconds – a lost, mad sort of smile – at Craig.

The priests brought food. "Too bad it's offerings to this sphinx guy, I could use some food." To his surprise the food was not deposited on the large stone table, but placed on the floor. There were two large copper trays, filled with fruit, eggs, bread, and something that resembled hummus. Azvari invited them to eat. Delighted, Craig came over to the trays and sat on the blanket. Eventually all seven of them gathered around: Azvari, Ay, and the Newcomers, as the ancient Egyptians called them. Nakhtmin must have left earlier, he was not around. As Craig ate he continued to survey his surroundings. They were in a small side enclosure of the temple, between the columns of the side entrance. He couldn't see beyond the rectangular opening; there was nothing but blackness. But he felt a breeze, which indicated there was some open space beyond. The sphinx was behind them to the left, its lit-up face visible between the pillars.

"The ceremony will not be performed until sunrise, when the rays of the sun enter the temple and enlighten the face of the sphinx. We have time to talk," said Azvari.

"What did she call this place?" Craig asked Sahed as he chewed on nuts.

"It is Gempa-Aten, which means something like 'The Sun Disc is Found in the Estate of God Aten.' It was eventually destroyed," answered Sahed.

"Who is it for?"

"It is in honor of Aten, the god of the sunlight. Akhenaten built it," replied Sahed.

"Akhenaten? What happened to Amenhotep?"

But at that moment Azvari began to talk, and Bailey's question had to go unanswered.

*   *   *

Azvari had stayed away from mentioning current events on their journey to Waset. But now it was time to explain what was going on, and so she did.

"The great pharaoh, Amenhotep III was taken by Anubis fourteen years ago. His eldest son, Thutmose, who also is with Osiris, went even before his father. His younger son, Amenhotep IV, is our pharaoh; this is the glorious thirteenth year of his reign."

There was a loud intake of breath – it was Mahmoud. "I am too late… Oh, Sekhmet, why did you send me here now? Why not just a little earlier?"

He caught Azvari's intense stare and tried to think straight. "I am the chosen one, the significant one in Sekhmet's plan," and he took a piece of flat bread into his mouth and slowly began to chew it, trying to look dignified and indifferent at the same time. There was an avalanche of questions from the Americans, and Mahmoud tried to return to his train of thought. "Maybe I failed Sekhmet… Maybe she sent me here the last time to prevent what was about to happen but I was too dumb to do it… And now it is done. What can I do now? How can I help matters?" The bread was soon gone, and he took another piece. Chewing helped him to think. "Perhaps she wants me to make sure… to find the one who betrayed her… Maybe the Shenu here do not know about it. Maybe the only reason the Shenu survived is because of my actions!" Suddenly Mahmoud felt very significant again. He could barely contain his desire to ask the questions tumbling around in his brain, but he stopped himself – whom could he trust? This was not the time to ask questions.

The boy, who never seemed to shut up, again inserted himself into the conversation. He aggravated Mahmoud to no end, but for some reason Azvari tolerated him easily. She answered his questions with patience.

"Our beloved Queen Tiye, may she live in eternity, passed into the Land of the Dead a year ago," said Azvari as she looked intently into their eyes. "She was equal to her pharaoh in many ways. She was truly an amazing person…" Azvari looked wistful for a moment, as though she missed her. Her wet eyes looked into the past.

Mahmoud could hardly believe his ears – Azvari spoke of the queen as being "equal to her pharaoh." That had to be a blasphemy by the standards of her time, yet she said it openly in front of Ay, an obviously powerful man.

"My sister was more than a Chief Queen; she was the High Priestess of the Shenu. Her role was to guide Egypt in the direction laid out by the most powerful Sekhmet. Tiye convinced Amenhotep to give proper honor to the goddess, and he erected over *seven hundred and thirty statues* dedicated to Sekhmet during his reign. Tiye's power was mystical, intelligent and political. The Shenu needed to have influence over the neighboring kingdoms. Foreign kings dealt with my sister on many official occasions – they wrote letters to her as an equal to Amenhotep III. Her gender and humble birth did not fool them. It did not matter to them, so powerful was she in the court. They knew that the scribes and viziers could be bribed, changing the translation of their letters into whatever was politically useful to the priests of Amun. But by the time Tiye was in full power, she spoke and could read and write in eight languages: Hittite, Assyrian, Babylonian, Aegan, Mitanni, Hurrain and the Nubian dialect, besides her native Egyptian. She met the foreign dignitaries in the Audience Chamber as an equal to her pharaoh – two thrones were set on the dais." Ay smiled with sadness. "The queen could speak to the foreign messengers directly, whereas Amenhotep III had to have a translator…"

Azvari smiled. Thoughts of Tiye were obviously pleasant to her. "Yes, the women of the kingdom were raised in power by the example of our beloved Queen Tiye. It became fashionable for noble girls to be educated in languages," she added with pride. "Women are treated with far more respect in Egypt than in most other countries, and many women of foreign lands who come to live in Egyptian harems find this almost unbelievable until they arrive."

"Statues of Queen Tiye are part of home shrines, and large ones are placed throughout Egypt to remind people of her glorious queenship. These are larger than most statues of queens, you know? She is alongside the pharaoh, her Amenhotep, and carved as large as he is – that is a sign of immense honor. It was an accomplishment for all Shenu to have our High Priestess elevated this high in the kingdom."

Mahmoud listened for signs of the information he craved. "Plagues of Egypt! She is speaking as if the Shenu is an organization for female rights!"

"What about…" said Mahmoud, trying to change the subject "…Akhenaten? He dismantled Waset – I saw the empty temples to Amun today!"

"Our glorious pharaoh Akhenaten and his most beautiful wife Nefertiti praise Aten, the god of Light," replied Azvari. "Akhenaten was exposed to the knowledge of the Shenu and shown the key to the well. He went into the sacred well with the Shenu who chose to reveal themselves to him. He returned the key to Sekhmet. He believes she gave him a mission and he is following it. And so he dismantled the power of Amun."

There was silence as four pairs of eyes stared at her.

Azvari continued: "This happened a long time ago, before the new city was built. The young prince was crowned in Waset, there," she pointed to the west, the large and dark Temple of Amun-Ra, "crowned… as Amenhotep IV."

Then, to everyone's shock, Ay added with pride: "My daughter, Nefertiti, became his Chief Royal Wife. She has already given him six beautiful daughters."

"Yes, beautiful ones!" exclaimed Azvari with a smile, ignoring the confused looks. "The family lived here, in Waset, and worshiped at the Temple of Amun-Ra, while the Temple of Aten, the Light, was built."

Ay continued: "Once this temple was opened, people could see the power of Amenhotep IV. Secretly the pharaoh had a desire to let go of the other gods of Egypt, keeping only Aten in power. This temple became the main and only active place of worship in Waset. The priests of Amun-Ra did not like this…" Ay smiled as if to himself. "They controlled most of the visible wealth in Egypt, more than the royal family itself."

As if trying to move away from an uncomfortable subject, Azvari went on: "In the fourth year of his glorious reign, Amenhotep IV taxed the temple of Amun here in Ipet-Sut of Waset, and all the other temples. In the fifth year he disbanded the priesthood, diverting all the income from the other temples to his powerful god Aten. This is also when he became known as the servant of Aten and changed his name to Akhenaten, right in this temple in front of the red sphinx. He publicly spoke of the 'center of Egypt,' the place that is the middle of the whole kingdom, that was to be the new city of Light, Akhet-Aten."

"Akhet-Aten is what you know as Amarna," reminded Sahed in English.

"The City of Light, Akhet-Aten, is the brightest and the most beautiful, you will see! All the powers of gods of Egypt, including Amun-Ra, are merged into one, Aten!"

"So this Aten is the sun, right? Like Ra was before?" asked Bailey.

"The most powerful Aten is not the sun, it is the Light. Our pharaoh teaches us that images of the gods only distract us from the true god inside us, and so he banned all the images of the gods, except Aten. Glorious Aten is shown as rays of light, coming from the sun. Aten is the breath of eternity..."

"...and people will remember how to breathe..." mumbled the tall youth quietly. Shocked, Mahmoud stared at the boy – how could he possibly know Sekhmet's words?

"You can see the Light," Azvari stood up and pointed at the wall carving just above her. "This is Akhenaten and that is his beautiful wife Nefertiti. See the little ankh being held by the hand on the end of the sun ray? It is being held to both their faces – that is the symbol for the eternal breathing of Light."

Mahmoud hadn't known that, even though he had studied many pictures similar to this one from the abandoned talatats of Amarna. He stood up to look at the ankh. It was true – there was a sun disc with many rays, a few of the rays had hands on the end, and the ones by the faces of the pharaoh, his wife and their daughters had little ankhs in them. The archeologist in him was again fascinated.

"The kingdoms of Mitanni and Babylon, Assyria and Hatti – all of them study this transformation of god. They sent their dignitaries and princes to Akhet-Aten city just a year ago, when our pharaoh celebrated his festival. He taught them about Aten and received tribute from all the foreign lands." Azvari sounded really proud to be a "progressive Egyptian."

Ay added, his voice slightly annoyed, "Egypt is at peace with most of these kingdoms, and many dignitaries arrive every day to view the City of Light." His face clearly showed that he had to deal with these dignitaries, and that it was not an easy job. "The pharaoh just completed a campaign in Nubia in the south, it is his biggest military achievement..." There was sarcasm in Ay's voice and a smirk on his face, and it was not hard to see that he did not think much of Akhenaten as a military commander.

"So Amenhotep IV changed everything and became Akhenaten because of the Shenu?" asked the boy. Yes – this was the direction

283

Mahmoud wanted the conversation to go, but he didn't want to be the one directing it that way. He had to preserve his own secrets.

"It is as you understand," said Azvari, once Sahed had translated Craig's words. "A few of the Shenu revealed Sekhmet's locket to the young pharaoh. He then chose to descend into the sacred well himself. When he returned, he changed his name from Amenhotep IV to Akhenaten and moved his capital city from here at Waset to a new city, built in the desert, the City of Light – Akhet-Aten." Azvari smiled, remembering. "He refuses to worship the gods other people worship. The Shenu were furious when they realized what had happened. The pharaoh had gone into the well and he gave the locket back to Sekhmet, for it was lost to the Shenu. He does not have the locket, the Shenu have searched everywhere. He effectively locked the time-gate forever, and he made the Shenu's political goals obsolete! They had to deal with him now!"

Mahmoud could not tell if Azvari was frustrated by this fact or not. She was passionate as she explained the events, but was it from fury or excitement? "Were they found? The betrayers?" asked Mahmoud finally. This was what was essential, the information he had to know for his mission, this was how he could serve Sekhmet. But Ay and Azvari only looked at each other and said nothing. For some reason all the others were looking at him.

"No," finally replied Azvari.

*   *   *

"Guess we know now not to talk about the True Shenu in front of him!" whispered Craig into Simon's ear. "Mr. Halib still has no idea who we are."

Mahmoud was walking far in front of them with Ay, impatient to get into the boat. Because the temple was on the Nile embankment the masts of felucca boats soon came into view. Craig tilted his head up. Somehow the night's blackness seemed blacker and the stars seemed brighter here.

"Do you think Azvari knows about the True Shenu? She didn't sound too excited about the whole heretic-pharaoh thing," asked Simon quietly as he came next to Sahed.

"I am not sure, but I do not feel her to be of the false Shenu. I am less certain about Ay, he might be one of the false ones, or he hides it well – for what reason I do not know…"

Nakhtmin awaited them at the shore with a small sail boat, and they boarded. Mr. Halib was already seated, anxiously looking around, trying to see more of the embankment. In the distance were many more temples, but none were illuminated as brilliantly as Gempa-Aten.

Sailing the Nile downstream at night was peaceful, the river supporting them as if their boat was a feather. They sailed through the night, and as the sky began to light up with the approach of morning a pot of tea was prepared and dates and fruit were spread out on a tray. With the sun came the heat. The white cloth they were wrapped in was helpful protection from the sun, but they were hot under it. Towards evening it began to cool on the water, and as the sun set they arrived at a small harbor.

The embankment was filled with people who seemed to be dismantling their stalls. The people on the shore yelled something at them, and no knowledge of the language was needed to know they were trying to sell them their goods. Ay and Nakhtmin purchased some bread, hummus, ducks, and water. The ducks were luckily already cooked, their bodies black and warm from the fire. The flies attacked the basket with the ducks, and Nakhtmin waved them away again and again.

Bailey was afraid to try the duck, but Craig took a slice that Ay had cut. Simon was skillfully dissecting the other duck with his own knife. Ay nodded in approval.

"This is not bad, Bailey, you should try it!" said Craig, chewing enthusiastically. The meat was tough, and a little stringy. "Maybe this isn't duck…" Craig had not seen many dead birds in his life, other than pigeons, so a featherless and headless bird could be anything. But he was hungry. This was the first time they had eaten since the night before, in the temple, not counting a few dates on the boat.

After they ate, Nakhtmin maneuvered the boat into its position for the night.

*   *   *

Everyone was asleep except Craig and Ay. Craig felt frustrated because not knowing the language prevented him from talking to Ay. Truthfully, Ay didn't look like he wanted to talk – he was resting his back on a vertical mast at the front of the boat, facing the harbor.

"He is the night watch," Craig realized.

Too many things had happened for Craig to be able to sleep. This was the first time he had had a chance to process recent events.

"So, what do we have? Queen Tiye is dead, and so is Amenhotep. Akhenaten is the pharaoh, and he threw out all the other gods except this Aten the Light, and even that is a metaphor. He is married to Nefertiti and they live in Amarna... Why am *I* here?" Craig was lying flat on his back, and with the sail down he could see the whole sky. The only sound was the lapping water on the sides of the boat.

"I have to talk to Simon, the Cat will know," Craig decided. "Well, he'll know, but he might not tell me," he thought, remembering Simon's way of teasing him. But in the end he felt it was better to try. "What was it that he told me? That I can do this without the candle and even the medicine bundle? It is the *inner light...*" repeated Craig, recalling the words.

And so he closed his eyes and tried to focus on a candle inside himself, moving that light vertically through his body. At first nothing happened. As he kept focusing, his neck began to hurt, yet Simon-the-cat was still nowhere near. He was about to give up and open his eyes, when he realized he was no longer lying down. He looked around his mind – there were the familiar trees and moss, and sounds of birds in the distance. This was their usual meeting place, except for the last few times when Simon for some reason insisted on the room at the bottom of the well. "I can't believe this worked without the candle and everything..."

Craig felt himself relax. He loved this forest, it reminded him of something very safe, even though he could never remember if he had ever been to a forest like this in person. Soon Simon came out from under a large pine tree, meowing as he walked towards Craig.

"I need your help."

"Hello to you, too," replied Simon.

"Sorry, hi, how are you? Would you like me to pet you?"

"Yes please," the Cat said, and flopped over by Craig's feet, ready to be petted. After that activity had been exhausted, Simon sat up and stared at Craig – this was a clue to start talking.

"Ok, so, I need your help. I am, we all are, in Egypt, back-in-time in Egypt I mean..." he stumbled. "Sekhmet gave Abby a message, Abby can hear these things. The message said that we have to meet Azvari again and help her, otherwise something will end before it supposed to."

"Was there anything else in that message?"

"Yeah, something about the queen... But see, that's the problem, the queen is dead. How can I help that? Who am I supposed to help? You told me that Sekhmet needed a shaman, so..."

"You only know one queen?" purred Simon.

"There is another one here, Nefertiti, she is Akhenaten's wife."

"Maybe she needs help?" offered Simon.

"I thought it was Azvari, but she never asked for any help, and she doesn't seem to need me... But she keeps insisting on going to this City of Light – we are going there in the morning."

"Do you know why she wants you to go there?"

"No... should I?" – now Craig felt scared. This shaman business never fully made sense to him since he didn't know anything more then he normally knew, so how was he supposed to be a shaman?

"Use your mind, you odd child! What did the message say about the queen?"

"Something that she... *must be like a king... must not let go yet, they need more time to breathe...*" recited Craig. "Wow, it's not about Queen Tiye! It's about Nefertiti!"

"Now you are back on the path," purred Simon with satisfaction.

"So, she is the right queen here, she is supposed to not let go of something, otherwise something will end... and to do that she should be like a king," continued Craig, ignoring Simon. "Nefertiti must be a pharaoh! Wait, she can't... Can she?"

"In this time it seems like most rules have already been broken, why not this one?"

"Do you mean I'm supposed to convince her to become a pharaoh? But Akhenaten is alive, he is her husband and there can't be two pharaohs... Maybe she can be like Tiye, she was very influential but still a queen?"

"Did the message say 'influential' or 'the king'? Don't invent the wheel here."

"I don't understand..." Craig felt defeated.

"It is because you do not have all the information," explained Simon. "See, there is a secret they are not telling you, Azvari and that man, Ay... There is a sickness in the City of Light. People are dying and the populace believes it is the wrath of the gods, the gods who were rejected by Akhenaten. The priests of Amun, who lost their power, are stirring things up. People are scared and they will believe anything if they think it will help this sickness go away, so if it means throwing away Aten and going back to their favorite statues, so be it... There is a danger of revolt – that has never happened in Egypt, since pharaoh is a god, right?"

Craig could swear Simon was smiling. "Are you telling me we are going into the city when there's an epidemic? Where everyone is dying?!"

"Well, maybe not yet... I'm not sure exactly where you are, remember, my time is not like yours... Maybe the sickness is just beginning... If it was ending, there wouldn't be a City to speak of – no one would be left; anyone who could, would have deserted it. Most of it was also burned eventually, in attempts to contain the sickness."

"Shit! ... Sorry... So Amarna will be burned and it's because the gods are mad at Akhenaten?"

"I just told you that people believe that, must you join the crowd?" Simon scratched his nails on the tree trunk and stretched. "It is the second sickness, you know?" Craig obviously did not know, and so Simon continued: "The first sickness was what you call the influenza virus – once people started to get sick from that, more ships with supplies were ordered to come into the harbor – the priests thought that maybe the food was contaminated and if people had new food, fresh, they would get better. But on the ships came the black rats, all the way from Punt and India, with spices which were supposed to kill the flu, you know...The little vermin eventually arrived to your City of Light..." Simon scratched his side. He obviously enjoyed the conversation about rats: "But really, it is all about the fleas... Egyptian rats have fleas that carry the plague, but they were used to these fleas and immune to that disease – a balance of nature. The visitor black rats were not used to the sickness carried by Egyptian fleas – those rats got sick. The flea and the black rat together concocted a very deadly plague... And cats and dogs ate those rats, before they were dead of course. And animals like goats and cows were bitten by these 'modified' fleas, and so were people..."

"What is it? I mean, are we safe?"

"Have you ever heard of anyone getting sick by going back in the past?" smiled Simon.

"No... but I never heard of anyone going back to the past either."

"The pharaoh is sick. He isn't dying, he is just under the weather. But one of his daughters is very sick, and the little one might not make it..."

"Oh... But if they stay alive, then why this 'premature end'?"

"It won't be, if you do your job."

"What is my job? Simon, please tell me!"

"You'd like it all laid out for you, step by step, with explanations and footnotes, wouldn't you? Too bad," and he rolled onto his right side. "You will get the pieces, from many people, mind you. Being a shaman means you have an ability to put them together. Use it."

Before Craig could ask anything else, Simon was gone, and so was the whole forest. A loud bird cry made him open his eyes – the sky was still black. It was close to morning, he could feel it.

"I can put this puzzle together... That is why Sekhmet needed me, to help others make the right steps, but they don't know what to do, and I somehow am supposed to know... Whoa..." In his amazement about his own importance Craig almost forgot that he was no closer to understanding the puzzle than before.

Akhet-Aten, Central Palace, Egypt

Light had begun to spill over the blackness but it was still dark, and they needed a torch to get out of the harbor. By the time they arrived at Amarna the sun was almost over the horizon. The embankment of bright white rocks glittered in the sun, and Craig walked up the high steps as if into a dream.

Facing them was an open expanse of flat white stone – it was the biggest plaza they had ever seen, and it was packed. It was also loud – music was being played, and there were thousands of voices, and birds and horns. To the right, perpendicular to the shore, towered a huge double pylon with a wall extending on either side. Enormous gold-plated statues of Akhenaten and Nefertiti were placed in front of it.

Seeing Craig's amazed face, Nakhtmin explained: "This is the Royal Arena. Pharaoh and his queen ride chariots in there. The horses of the most select breeds are kept in these stables."

"Nefertiti rides chariots?" was all Craig could mumble back.

Farther ahead was an even bigger double pylon with an even larger wall. There were ten flag posts in front of it, long strips of linen sluggishly waving in the morning air.

"That is the House of Aten – the Great Temple of Light," said Ay, pointing.

Making their way through the crowd, they eventually arrived at the Great Temple's walls. The entrance was even more imposing than it looked from far away. The music, which at first had seemed to come from the temple, was actually coming from somewhere to the right. Ay walked purposefully in that direction and they followed him. The street was as crowded as the plaza, like a highway during rush hour. Everyone was trying to get a glimpse of the procession.

It was still early in the morning, and torches blazed on either side of the massive street. The tall trees made it appear dark, and in the fires of the torches the faces of sphinxes on either side of the road were illuminated.

"There must be thousands of sphinxes!" exclaimed Bailey.

"This is the Royal Road, our pharaoh rides his chariots from here to the North Palace," explained Nakhtmin as, following the procession, they turned onto the road. On the left were the temple's tall walls, and on the right, the arena. Craig turned around – his height put him a head above everyone else, and he could see as far as vision allowed. The Royal Road just went on and on in a straight line. Then someone pulled on his arm – it was Sahed, telling him they must go. Craig wanted to protest but he noticed that the others were already very far ahead. He and Sahed hurried after them.

The seemingly interminable line of sphinxes eventually ended at an intersection with a large gateway on the right and an open road to the left. In front of the gateway stood four tall Nubians, long spears in their hands, and four Egyptian soldiers with large knives on their belts. Ahead of them, in the distance, was a beautiful, two-storied wall with many openings. Sahed translated Ay's explanations:

"That is the Royal South bridge, it connects the Central Palace on the right," and he pointed to the guards in front of the gateway, "with the Offices of the Pharaoh on the left. Above the street is the Window of Appearances, one of four in the city. This one is used for giving important news firsthand to the commoners."

The sound of music from the procession came from somewhere beyond the bridge now. Ay turned into the palace gateway until protests from Craig successfully stopped him.

"We have to see what's going on! Please! We have to! Please!"

Nakhtmin spoke to Ay and then waved them all to follow. From the expression on Ay's face it was clear he did not care for the change in plan.

They walked underneath the bridge and came to a road lined with tall, connected buildings. The crowds had been left behind, but the music was louder here. To the left stood a large temple with many tall pylons one behind the other. To the right, towards the Nile, was an open plaza the size of a football field, with many shapely trees and a short row of sphinxes leading up to the temple.

They followed the music into the plaza and saw a group of beautiful women arranging themselves in a line. Craig counted thirty-nine of them. The women were naked save for a few bracelets and bright diadems, and each held a musical instrument which they shook to make a pleasing sound. Behind them men in short kilts blew small trumpets; that sound was not as pleasing this early in the morning.

Nakhtmin moved quickly, going up a small flight of stone steps and continuing through the temple. Eventually they stopped next to the furthest pylon. They had walked the entire length of the temple and now stood on a high balcony overlooking the altar area.

Ay explained in a loud whisper: "This is the Royal House of Aten, a smaller temple for the royal family built in honor of Akhenaten."

"I would hardy call it 'smaller'," whispered Bailey to Simon. "This thing is as big as the House of Aten back there."

Mahmoud, his eyes wild, whispered to himself, "…the mortuary temple, the Mansion of Aten…" and grasped the stone railing as if willing himself to awaken from this dream.

The temple had no roof, only beams positioned atop painted columns. The columns rose up in the sky like shoots of live lotuses welcoming the sun's rays, though as the sun was not yet high enough to penetrate the space most of the temple remained in deep shadow. They watched the procession as it climbed up the incline until it was only a few feet beneath them. A girl of about fifteen led it, clutching three long-stemmed lilies. She was wearing a thin, white, transparent cloth that barely covered her body and a large necklace that extended over her shoulders. Her arms and wrists were adorned with gold bracelets, and on her head was an odd wig with a large gold cobra affixed to it. The hair was short at the front and progressively longer at the back. Her face was very beautiful, the eyes almost magical, with long eyelashes that made her look a little sleepy. But she stared ahead intently. Four priests wrapped in white cloths followed behind her, and they hit tambourines with every step she took.

The procession arrived at the easternmost altar at the same moment the sun was high enough above the horizon to suddenly spill light onto the columns, the central altar, and the girl. The timing could not have been better. The girl lifted her hands up and sang, then the priests sang too, and after a while the rest of the women began to sing the same words. The girl faced the main path where light entered the temple and prostrated herself until she was almost flat on her face. The priests also knelt, and the naked beauties lay on the floor. After a long while the girl stood up. The priests handed her one tray after the other, presumably to bless, which they afterward placed on the altar.

Ay immediately motioned them all to leave and they quickly retraced their steps.

"Who was that girl at the front?" asked Craig. Sahed, a little out of breath, translated.

"It is Meritaten, the princess, she is also Priestess of Aten," replied Ay without slowing down.

He wanted to ask more, but there was a loud cry behind them and Nakhtmin was suddenly pushing him and the others towards the palace wall. Craig turned just in time to see a gold-colored chariot speeding past them, red cloth waving. Behind the charioteer stood the girl.

"And that was princess Meritaten being taken back to the Northern Palace of Light," said Ay, answering Craig's unasked question.

Akhet-Aten, Central Palace, Egypt

Ay led the way to the palace gateway, and the soldiers parted to allow them in. They walked through a long, high-ceilinged hall lined on each side with brightly painted columns, and emerged into a walled courtyard so vast it resembled a plaza. A chariot passed quickly in front of them, and then another. Bailey stopped and Craig almost ran into her. Servants with baskets on their heads hurried by, and two men carried a large cedar chest.

Four tall posts held long white and red flags flapping loudly in the morning breeze. To the left of the courtyard was a tall, colorfully painted columned wall more than five hundred feet long, with a huge columned portico in the middle. The wall was lined with colossal red granite statues of Akhenaten and Nefertiti. Craig counted ten on each side of the portico. There were more statues along the other walls, but those were seated.

Ay strode confidently ahead, yelling for them to follow.

"What is this place?" shouted Craig over the noise of the chariots, which rode up and down the ramps, in and out of the wall openings, crisscrossing the courtyard.

"This is the courtyard of the Central Palace," answered Nakhtmin instead of Ay, who was determined to press forward. "These are messengers," he continued, pointing at the passing chariot. "In there, behind this wall, are ceremonial courtyards, waiting areas for foreign dignitaries, the Great Hall for the feasts and the Audience Chamber for petitioners."

The smell of water wafted to them on the breeze as they crossed the courtyard. At the opposite end of the courtyard was another gateway

– the twin of the one through which they had entered. Everything was symmetrical. Both gateways had flags flapping over them, and both were painted bright red and covered with beautiful gold drawings of a sun disc. They passed through the gateway and into an identical columned hall, which led to a wide, limestone-paved path leading outside, to the water. A huge, colorful vessel, inlaid with gold and silver, was moored at the harbor, its enormous rectangular sail in the process of being rolled up. Thirteen gilded ebony oars protruded from the boat's sides. Craig and Simon stared, fascinated.

"What do you think?" said Simon. "Probably two men per oar, two sides – that's fifty-two men just to move this thing out of the harbor."

Instead of going outside, however, Ay turned right, and Simon and Craig had to tear themselves away from the boat.

Inside was dark and cool, and they followed the red-and-blue floored hallway into the depth of the building. Eventually a man in white robes met them, bowing deeply to Ay and Nakhtmin, and guided them to a smaller courtyard which had as its centerpiece a flower-covered fountain. The roof of the courtyard was a mesh of small beams, creating a lattice work of broken light.

So far no one seemed to be sick; that was good. Craig had noticed a few people coughing and sneezing, no more than was normal for a city, and they didn't seem to have anything more serious than a cold.

Servants brought out trays of food. The men were covered only by a cloth over their hips, and the tight sheath the women wore ended just underneath their breasts. Craig tried not to stare and luckily he was given a male servant to attend him. They ate together, sitting on pillows laid out on the stone dais. Simon proceeded to question Ay about the chariots, but Craig was quiet. He could think only of what his spirit guide had said.

After the empty trays were cleared away, they were invited to rest.

"Wait a minute, is one of Akhenaten's daughters sick?" Craig blurted out.

As Sahed translated, Ay and Azvari looked at each other, then she answered, "Yes, Meketaten is sick. Her elder sister, Meritaten, was just praying for her in the temple. Blessed Meketaten is only thirteen years old, there were thirty-nine dancers for each year of Meketaten, to triple her years. How did you know?"

"Simon told me…"

"No I didn't," said Simon before Sahed could translate.

"Never mind… Is anyone else sick? Is there a plague?" pressed Craig.

"It is not called *that*. We are praying for the sickness to depart soon, but many people are afflicted," replied Azvari with concern.

"It will pass like everything else," added Ay.

*　　*　　*

"No, it won't," Craig thought as he walked away. He was beginning to understand what it really meant to be a shaman. For so many years he had felt lost on that score – it was just a mysterious title that really didn't do anything for him. He accepted it as fact and recognized that it came with a lot of responsibility, and he was willing to take it on, but he had no idea what he could be responsible for. He had strange dreams for a long time before he was told he was a shaman, and he sure had visions, but he had never attached any particular meaning beyond "having access to other worlds" to the term shaman. Being a shaman never clouded his view of himself; his ego remained uninvolved. A shaman had abilities and Craig assumed that that was all it meant, but now that he saw the proof of what a chat with his spirit guide could bring, he was amazed, excited, and scared all at the same time. He desperately wanted to help, to do the "right thing," but he got the feeling that there was nothing he could do to save princess Meketaten. A while back his spirit guide had told him that being a shaman didn't mean he could change the future. That could happen only under very specific circumstances and exceptions were rare. Of course, Craig asked what "extreme circumstances" made changing the future possible. Apparently, he could only affect the future if it was allowed. He didn't understand that – allowed by whom? – but Simon had not been forthcoming with answers. That Cat seemed to always insist on Craig learning everything himself, giving him only the slightest suggestion, an outline, never telling him what to do. Over the years Craig learned to respect that, and to actually enjoy it – when he eventually did answer his own question, it was that much more satisfying.

The servant took him to a small, clean room with a bed. Craig looked at the white linens piled on the bed appreciatively, and started opening them up to use as blankets or pillows when a servant girl, wearing only a shawl around her hips, walked into the room. She stared at him, and for a second he stared back at her. With a deep breath he made himself look away, only to hear the girl giggle. "Oh, what the hell!" he told himself, and looked. She was very pretty. Her breasts were round and firm, with dark areolas. Her nose was a little too long... but who cared about noses? He was a young man, not yet twenty, and she was beautiful and practically naked! She seemed to understand his desire, and moved closer. Craig wasn't sure how it happened but the next moment he was sitting on the bed and the girl was on his lap, her arms around him, and they were kissing. His hands were touching her in every place he knew he shouldn't. "What am I doing?" he thought as she pulled him down to lie on the bed. Immediately, he released her. He could almost hear Simon-the-cat saying, "Are you ready for the consequences of having a child centuries in the past? You do know they don't have condoms here, right?" Right. And so, taking a deep breath, he made the girl stand up. She did, without comment, and seeing his embarrassment, left the room.

"OK, good call, man," Craig told himself, exhaling.

Before his heart could return to its normal beat another girl was hurried in. She wasn't as interesting to him as the previous one was, but she was naked – no loin cloth this time. Craig's head spun, while his body responded to the girl's nakedness in not-so-subtle terms.

"Shit!" His psyche wasn't ready for all this, but the girl seemed perfectly at ease. She came closer and began to stroke his penis through his pants. He jumped away and the girl fell to the floor, as if in apology.

Confused, freaked out, and very embarrassed, all he could say was, "Ah... sorry... please leave me...?"

She seemed to understand him, and left immediately.

Relieved, Craig took a breath. His heart was going a million miles per hour. He had never had a girlfriend before; no one had ever touched him in a sexual way. But before he could make sense of these events, a youth, aged about fifteen, was pushed into the room. His face had stunning symmetry, his skin was a deep brown color, and he was completely naked aside from the many bracelets he wore on his wrists and ankles. He walked towards Craig, sat down and calmly closed his eyes. Staring at him for a moment Craig didn't know what to do... then he realized what was expected, and flipped out. It was about time to flip out, right? In a loud whisper he told the boy, "Go, leave now!" and pointed to the door. The boy's eyes flew open and his beautiful face looked surprised, but he left.

The servant came in again and started talking quickly, all the while looking at the floor. Craig had had enough. No more girls! Or boys! He told his servant to go away, and after he left threw himself onto the bed, squeezed the linens together to make a pillow, and tried to think of something other than the first girl's breasts.

"OK, think, Craig, think! You are the shaman, it's all up to you!" That last thought was absolutely terrifying to Craig, but at least the terror took care of the erection. "Maybe I can't save the little girl, but can I save the city?" he thought, shifting on the low bed. "Is it too presumptuous of me, to think I can save anything? Or is it exactly what's expected of me?"

Saving the city was probably not allowed – surely that was something that Sekhmet would have told them. "If she wanted this thing, this city, to not end prematurely, all she needed to do was to stop the plague, right? But she said something about the queen being like the king..." He thought very hard but there were no clear answers, and eventually he drifted into sleep. His male servant quietly entered to cover a square window with a reed mat, making the room almost completely dark – the only light filtering through the reed curtain.

*   *   *

Mahmoud refused to be led into a room, like a donkey, to sleep. There was too much work to do! He had to find out how much was known and he had to act, do something, to fulfill what Sekhmet required of him.

He lingered and looked around. Above them was a balcony-gallery with red columns circling the perimeter of the garden court, and there were doors to more rooms. "There must be at least twenty rooms in here," he thought, amazed. "And this garden – what a luxury..." Except for the meshed ceiling of the garden court, most of the palace was covered by a flat roof. The sound of trickling water added to the cool tranquility of the space.

Mahmoud, however, did not feel tranquil. Waving away his servant, who was becoming insistent, he looked around and locked eyes with Ay. Ay was a Shenu with correct ideas, and he might just be the ally he required. And he could really use an ally!

"I have some business to attend to," stated Ay. "You may come along if you wish."

Oh, yes, Mahmoud wished it. Ay led him through multiple inner halls to an enormous court with flags, statues, chariots, servants, hurrying officials and women covered in gold jewelry. Everyone seemed to have somewhere to go, and moved quickly despite the heat. Mahmoud's pulse was racing, and he swore to himself – worrying and running around in the heat was not conducive to good health. At least inside the building the air was cooler, the shade was a blessing. He could use some fan-bearing girls about now! "But it's not like I'm not used to the heat," Mahmoud told himself as they walked from under the shade of the building into the blinding sunlight. It was very hot indeed.

Ay too walked at a fast clip, determination in his stride, and Mahmoud pressed forward. He was physically here, in Akhenaten's Central Palace – in the middle of history – this was the era of the heretic pharaoh, before it disappeared. He tried to take it all in.

The walls had openings large enough for a chariot to ride through – which they did with incredible accuracy and speed. On the other side of the yard, more than five hundred feet away, stood a sixty-foot double pylon with flag posts and an enormous image of a golden sun disc on each side. The discs shone like powerful projectors, reflecting the sun, and for a moment Mahmoud was blinded. As his eyes adjusted, he saw two monstrous ramps, larger than any he had seen so far, leading up to the opening between the pylons. The sight of it took Mahmoud's breath away and froze him to the spot. But he could not allow himself too long an interlude, for he had a mission to accomplish.

Ay didn't seem to want to accommodate Mahmoud's interest, and he continued without slowing. They exited the palace onto the Royal Road. In the full sunlight Mahmoud could see all the details he had missed in the morning. The road was more than thirty feet wide. Ay crossed it and continued ahead. Mahmoud couldn't contain his questions any longer.

Apparently Akhet-Aten had three palaces. Two were for the pharaoh and his chief queen Nefertiti – the palace they had left was the central, official, palace and the one in the north, called the North Light of Aten, was where the royal family actually resided. The North Light was about four miles from the Central Palace. The third, smaller, palace was for the other queen, Kiya, and it was also in the north, close to the North Light palace. Besides these there were two "sunshade palaces," which, Ay said, were large garden enclosures with lakes, fountains, terraces and columned halls. Maru-Aten Sunshade was also for Queen Kiya; the other one was originally built for Tiye, the widow and dowager queen, and she rested in it when she came to visit.

"Did Queen Tiye come here often?" asked Mahmoud.

"My sister enjoyed living in both cities, in Waset's Malkata palace, and here, in Akhet-Aten. She usually stayed in the Central Palace, but to get away from all the gossip, she would go to her Sunshade. It is ten minutes by chariot to the south of here," replied Ay. "Living in two cities was the best political solution," he added. "After her passing, the Sunshade was re-dedicated to my daughter."

The city of Akhet-Aten was divided into districts and inhabited by over a hundred thousand people. The north of the city was thickly populated – all the highest officials and royalty bought villas there, to be close to the pharaoh's palace. Nestled in the desert hills, the villas had been built according to Akhenaten's specifications. They were connected by roads and gardens, with the largest villas set closest to the Royal Road.

Here in the central area were the temples: the Great Temple of Aten and the smaller Royal Temple where they had seen the ceremony that morning. The Central Palace was where members of extended royal family and the minor wives of the pharaoh resided. The main banquet hall, where the court met a few times per week, was also in that palace. The Central Palace was connected by the bridge to the Offices of the Pharaoh, government bureaus and archives, police, stables, storehouses and the barracks behind them. There were also houses belonging to the most important officials in the area. According to Ay, the closer a house was to the temples, the better. The main sculptor and artist, greatly favored by Akhenaten, also lived here, and Mahmoud held his breath, realizing it was Djutmose, the one who made the famous bust of Nefertiti! Panahesy also lived here – Mahmoud knew of him.

"Is Panahesy a priest?" asked Mahmoud.

"He is the High Priest of Aten, responsible for the cattle and the offerings. Of course, you'd think he was responsible for the sun itself!" said Ay, swearing. "The other High Priest is Meryra, he oversees the grain."

To the south along the Nile were villas belonging to lesser officials, and these were, according to Ay, "built wherever people pleased" – an indication that it was a less affluent area. Still, most were also well adorned and connected by an extension of the Royal Road to the Central Palace area and the temples.

Ay hurried on, and Mahmoud was told to sit on the shady bench. He waited for over an hour. When Ay emerged he held a papyrus scroll and a seal in his hands, and behind him a teenaged boy carried a large bundle of scrolls. Ay told the boy what to do with the scrolls and he replied, bowing deeply, "Yes, High Vizier Ay." Two older men came up to him, also bowing deeply, and Ay talked with them, ignoring Mahmoud, who had gotten up from the bench and was nervously hovering. "I thought he was the general of the charioteering division, not a high vizier," thought Mahmoud, his irritation at the long wait fading away.

When the other men finally left, Mahmoud asked, "What does your position entail?"

"I run the country," hissed Ay, walking to the entrance of the columned hall. Mahmoud hurried after him, thinking that if Ay had finished his sentence he might have said something like, "while pharaoh serves his Aten." A high vizier in ancient Egypt was equal to a prime minister in modern times.

They crossed the tree-lined court and emerged onto the street once more, but instead of returning to the Central Palace as Mahmoud had expected, Ay turned right.

"I must see Nakhtpaaten," explained Ay as he walked in the heat.

"Who is he?"

"The other high vizier. He oversees the city, all the construction, and the trade."

Passing the Offices' tall wall, they turned into a narrower street. Most of the walls here were sides of courtyards, and through openings in them Mahmoud saw stables, workshops, kitchens, and storehouses. Richer houses seemed to have thicker walls and larger gardens. "It must be to control the heat, it's the same way we build now."

"Wait here," said Ay, quickly passing through large wooden doors and leaving Mahmoud in a small square courtyard. He returned just as quickly.

"Was that Nakhtpaapten's house?" asked Mahmoud, as they walked back, in the direction of the Central Palace.

"No, he lives in the southern part of the city, in a very large building," smiled Ay. "We were in the Bureau of Correspondences of the Pharaoh, next to the House of Life."

"What is the House of Life used for?" Mahmoud felt like an idiot asking, but the archeologist in him was hungry for information.

"All the letters addressed to the pharaoh go to the Bureau of Correspondences. There they are sorted by importance and language. The ones needing translation are moved to the House of Life where the scribes copy them into our language. Letters of the highest importance are then carried to the Offices of the Pharaoh where the viziers can review them, or to the palaces. Any important document of a political, architectural, magical or medicinal nature is copied in the House of Life.

All the papyri scrolls of importance are stored at Per Medjat – the library in the Central Palace."

Soon they were back on the Royal Road. Three chariots appeared, a loud voice making their presence known. People hurried to get out of the way as the chariots sped past them.

"That was the Central Palace Overseer and the Women's Quarters Overseer, returning from the port. A large shipment of cloths and spices came to harbor this morning," explained Ay.

"Who is that?" asked Mahmoud, looking at a strong middle aged man riding a chariot without a charioteer. All the other charioteers were half his age. As he maneuvered his chariot out of the palace entry onto the Royal Road, Ay stopped and exchanged a few words with him.

Mahmoud walked a few steps ahead so as not to be in the way, and stood in the shade of a building across from the palace wall.

Now in modern times, no buildings were left standing in Amarna. The entire city was built with unbaked mud-bricks, and only the foundations of important buildings had a stone base – as if they knew that Akhet-Aten would not be forever – they built quickly. All that remained in modern times were stone pillars and the fourteen boundary stelae that Akhenaten erected, and of course the stone talatat. When the city was abandoned, the talatat were dragged back to Luxor and reused by Horemheb and Ramesses II as filler material for pylons and foundations. Mahmoud had been asked to supervise the project to rescue these talatat. "As if they were captive!" he had fumed at the time. Nevertheless, tens of thousands of decorated stone talatat had been recovered and photographed, and the scenes on them reconstructed. "What a waste!" thought Mahmoud. He didn't like the idea of dismantling a standing temple to find out what was inside its pylons and floors! But the truth was deeper still – Mahmoud as a historian did want to preserve all the history that could be salvaged, but he was afraid of the information hidden on the talatat. All it would take was for one of those pictures to show something that was supposed to be hidden, and they would have a huge mess on their hands. Many small details that should have remained hidden had already been discovered, and Mahmoud, in his position at the Council of Antiquities, had worked swiftly to make the discoveries go way. "But one can never hide it completely," he sighed to himself. "There are always the ones who post everything online and claim that we're hiding the truth… If they only knew the truth!"

"That was Ranofer, Senior Charioteer. He is delivering news about Princess Meketaten to the North Light Palace. The royal family resides there, but they brought the princess closer to the temples. She is in the Central Palace, where we left your friends."

"They are not my friends!" hissed Mahmoud.

"All Shenu are one," stated Ay quietly.

What was he supposed to say to that? That those Americans are not the Shenu at all? But they knew so much! And if they were not the Shenu, well, that only made him look like an idiot for not knowing anything about them. How could he have allowed the information to get into their hands? Jonathan Rixson was dead. This was not supposed to happen!

The people parted, letting by a small group of important personages, bowing deeply. The shorter ancient looking man at the center of the group seemed to be a priest; he was very dark skinned and was wrapped in white robes with a sun disc embroidered on it in gold thread. He was limping a little on one side and with every step was forced to put weight onto a staff with a gold disc on the top. Next to him were a few other men, dressed similarly, and they all walked quickly and talked to him, probably trying to get his blessing. On his right side walked a taller man, about forty years of age, his hips covered with a short white, also gold embroidered, kilt, and his face and chest were scarred in a few places. Mahmoud was about to look away, but to his surprise both men stopped in front of them.

"The ceremony was most beautiful this morning, Meryre. All thanks to Aten and your priestly duties," started Ay.

"I didn't know you attended," replied the old man, squinting his eyes at Ay. "May eternal Aten bless Meketaten with its light!" He was standing very close to Mahmoud, but didn't seem to notice him. All his attention was focused on Ay. "May our glorious pharaoh Akhenaten and his beloved queen Nefertiti, your lovely daughter, and all their children be blessed by Aten," said the priest, raising his hands to the sky. His old neck was adorned with only one thing – a gold disc about five inches in diameter suspended on a shiny metal ring. The light hitting it almost blinded Mahmoud. He tried not to flinch.

"Blessing to you, Ay, High Vizier and Overseer of the Charioteers." The voice of the taller man was low. "I trust you will make it known to me if any foreign guests of Akhenaten were to come to Akhet-Aten – so we can give them a proper welcome, of course." The man's bare chest displayed a rectangular plaque and Mahmoud strained to read a hieroglyph on it as he finished his sentence. Mahmoud looked up, only to meet the man's eyes.

"Dear friend, I will introduce you to the Mitanni officials in two days, as soon as they arrive to Akhet-Aten," said Ay. "We can never be too careful," he added in a low voice. The bare-chested man did not look fooled, but he did not question Ay.

As they walked away, Mahmoud's gaze followed them. "Who are they?"

"Meryre, the High Priest of Aten, and Mahu, the Chief of Police of this city."

"I don't think that Mahu believed you – he knew immediately that I was not from here."

"You are an Egyptian and that is enough," said Ay, smiling. "You are not a foreigner who he has to watch out for." There was something in the way Ay said that that left Mahmoud unsettled. He was being told that he could blend in, but at the same time he had a feeling that Ay was babysitting him, watching him, even studying him. "The last time we traveled back in time... he walked me around the palace in Waset... and now he is walking me around Akhet-Aten..."

"So this is the capital in every way then?" asked Mahmoud to change the subject.

"The capital is where pharaoh lives, and Akhenaten lives here. Most of the administrative offices, with the agricultural and tax-collecting viziers, are still at Men-Nefer. Akhet-Aten is a city of palaces and villas. Mahu scrutinizes all who enter the city. No one is allowed in who does not have an audience at the palace or the temple, or who wasn't invited by one of the families living here."

"What about the poor people, the commoners?"

"They do not have their own village, only the workers do. All the servants and slaves are integrated into the households of their masters. All inhabitants of the City of Light, the royal family and its extended relatives, the nobles of the court and the priests of Aten, have a set function, a duty. Everyone else is connected to trade, but through one of the families – there are craftsmen, artisans, musicians, gardeners, fishermen and builders. Only the builders live outside the city boundary."

Mahmoud had not known that and he listened with interest. It had always been assumed that the city was wealthy but nothing was known about its inner workings.

"The west side of the city is the Nile, and no one can dock their boat at our port without the appropriate sign. The rest of the city is surrounded by markings that no one can cross."

"Where do people buy food?"

"There is one market on the embankment in front of the Great Temple of Aten and the Arena, we saw it in the morning. And the officials of the city are paid in grain."

"Are those for grain?" asked Mahmoud, pointing. Large whitewashed silos stood behind the walls of private houses, and behind the massive temple wall were over ten of them, sticking upwards like beehives.

"Yes. The grain is then further used to pay their free servants and artisans, and also can be exchanged for the goods they want at the harbor market. It is used to feed their families, the slaves, and to give offerings to Aten. Of course, those offerings can be eaten at the end of the day," smiled Ay, "not like before with other gods. They might have been angry at hungry people if they took food from their altar, but Aten enjoys people eating from his altar."

That was a very odd thing to say and Mahmoud had not known about this practice. Was Ay mocking Aten? Was this the sign Mahmoud was waiting for? Was Ay an ally and could they together find the betrayers of the Shenu?

Unaware of Mahmoud's thoughts, Ay continued: "Additionally, nobles and workers are paid in beer. Bread and beer are the pride of Egypt."

They walked along the wall of the Arena and Mahmoud could hear the loud voices from behind it. Seeing the question on his face, Ay answered: "The soldiers are riding in the Arena, it is entertaining for the court ladies."

"In this heat?"

"It is the way of things."

Suddenly Ay pulled on Mahmoud's arm – they had to step aside, as did all the jewel-laden nobles, to let a large herd of swine pass by them.

"Pigs are acceptable to eat?" asked Mahmoud. He thought they would be considered unclean in ancient Egypt just as they were by Muslims.

"The workmen's village is in the east, inland, outside the city wall in the desert. The herd is going there. They have many more herds to support themselves in addition to the provisions they receive from the state."

"Why do they get provisions?"

"They are brought here from Waset and paid very well, some even in gold – they are the artisans and the construction specialists who built this city and the tombs farther to the east. Their village is surrounded by a wall, they have houses provided for them, and food is brought in for them along with any supplies they need."

Mahmoud remembered that the British had excavated that site and found dense housing and extensive traces of pig husbandry. The pigs were economical; they served as food and removed waste. "These people are like those in the village of Dier El-Medina at Luxor, the specialists who worked on the royal and private tombs on the West Bank..." thought Mahmoud. He had always been proud of these simple people who had the talent, skill, and will to dig deeply into the rock and paint beautiful burial decorations for tombs.

"No Egyptian god or goddess, no prior king, could lay claim to this place. It is virgin land and our pharaoh says it is the exact middle of Egypt," smiled Ay.

"You know as well as I that it is *the exact* middle of Egypt!" snapped Mahmoud. "Only the Shenu possess such calculatory techniques, Akhenaten isn't supposed to know them!"

Ay smiled again. "It is a well chosen balance point, unspoiled and untouched land, a pure environment for the rays of Aten."

Mahmoud was not sure if Ay really believed all this Aten stuff, it was heresy after all! "Or perhaps he is just being a skillful politician," he thought. "It is probably illegal to not praise this Aten nonsense..."

"The city is only on the east side of the Nile. Our pharaoh does not see the west bank of the river as the Land of the Dead, you know? He says there is no such location; instead we are to connect to ourselves where we die, wherever we are. And so the west bank can be filled with wheat fields to sustain us."

The new city was built from the ground up, with an original plan. There were too many components in this city that were not supposed to exist, that people should not have known, and Mahmoud knew they had to have come from the Shenu. "Did the betrayers let Akhenaten see the inside of the vaults?" Mahmoud shook his head vigorously in anger. "That would be preposterous!"

They finally passed the Arena and came to a large embankment plaza paved with white stone. Onto it spilled a bustling market with stalls and tents filled with imported merchandise and haggling customers. There were goods for women, from kohl paste to glass bottles of rare perfume; hundreds of wigs for men and women in every possible variation of style and length; linens in all the colors of the rainbow; and sandals, from plain reed to extravagantly beaded leather. Two semi-permanent buildings housed a pavilion of glass and pottery, respectively.

The glass shop glistened with vases, bottles and beads, and the pottery shop was stuffed with bowls of every shape and size.

Farther inland were food stalls. "Come to buy some lamb, High Vizier? I give you the greatest cut!" shouted a meat seller, his large table covered with salted raw meat, the flies fanned away by two young boys. Ay waved him away. Conflicting scents of spices were carried on the breeze from the next stall. Men holding small cups of grain, and women carrying baskets with flowers headed in the direction of the temple with their offerings. One of the women recognized Ay and bowed down in obeisance. He let her kiss one of his gold rings and she gifted him two lilies, uttering a blessing. Beyond the market there was a forest of masts at the wharf, where many officials checked ship captains' "papers." Mahu's golden square plate shone like the sun itself on his chest, even though he was very far away. A man with a pot belly hurried out of the Great Temple and towards the wharf, shoving aside a servant who had the misfortune of not noticing him.

"That is Panahesy, the High Priest of Aten," snarled Ay, watching him.

"I thought you told me Meryre was the High Priest?"

"He is. Meryre is responsible for the granaries, and the offering of bread and beer. He lives in the north city next to the North Palace. Panahesy is responsible for cattle, and the meat offerings. He lives in the central city, not far from the Central Palace. All the bakeries and breweries of Akhet-Aten are under Meryre, all the slaughter yards are under Panahesy. They compete in everything. I'm sure Panahesy can't wait for old Meryre to be taken by Anubis. Meryre is wealthier, but Panahesy received a special dispensation from the pharaoh to build inside the Great Temple walls," smiled Ay sarcastically.

"He lives in the temple??"

"He wishes! Panahesy had a cattle court and the butcher's tables built in the temple yard, exactly on the path from the northern entrance to Akhenaten's favorite stela of himself. It was an easy way to catch the pharoah's eye. Meryre nearly joined Osiris when he had heard that Panahesy had gotten this building approved! That was years ago, but they are still rivals. Panahesy built a house for himself next to the temple wall; probably so he can be at the temple on short notice, while Meryre would have to come all the way from the north."

"Do they both perform ceremonies?"

"Akhenaten and my daughter perform the ceremonies, the priests only assist. And yes, both of them do it."

"Are people here happy with Aten?" asked Mahmoud cautiously. He was almost sure that Ay would not be outraged by this question.

"Everyone is here *because* of Aten," answered Ay.

Unsure of how to proceed, Mahmoud walked silently ahead.

"The nobles are not happy, neither are the..." Ay suddenly looked around as if to make sure they could not be overheard, "...the priests of Amun. When the priests of Amun fell, so did many wealthy families. Now there are new nobles who won't give up their new power at any cost," he whispered. "And people are in confusion. They are not sure how to believe what our pharaoh is asking them to believe. They aren't awake enough to understand... Salvation in the afterlife is now believed to depend on the well-being of the pharaoh and his communication with Aten. This makes people very nervous."

The afterlife was the most important subject for all Egyptians. Tombs were made in advance, decorated with the correct texts from the Book of the Dead and of course multiple representations of the gods. This was the accepted way to make nice with the gods so that they would allow a happy afterlife. But during this period, Aten was the only god allowed to be represented, and even he could not really be painted, for he was the light – no wonder people were scared! Mahmoud's knowledge of this period was sketchy because most of the artifacts didn't survive. "The Shenu had a lot to do with that," he thought with satisfaction. As much as he was a historian and a man of science, he felt that this period of Egyptian history was best erased – the information of the Shenu had been exposed at this time and if the Amarna records survived, people might find out that ancient Egyptians were not as dumb as was commonly assumed. And that was dangerous.

Mahmoud's thoughts were racing, but before he could say anything Ay asked him a question: "In your time do you not worship Aten?"

Mahmoud had almost forgotten that Ay had no idea that Akhenaten would disappear from history in the next four years! In another ten his name would be obliterated from all the monuments in Luxor and Memphis, and this city would be reclaimed by the desert...

*   *   *

Craig woke up startled. He could swear he had just been talking with Simon. The Cat had been sitting right next to his head on the bed, he could still smell his fur. But now, sitting up, Craig could see that Simon was not there. As the confusion of the moment began to wear off, the memory of the dream came into focus. Simon was asking him why he thought that Sekhmet meant for Amarna to be saved. He couldn't remember the answer, but the question itself was intriguing – why did he think that she meant Amarna? "What else could she have meant? To prevent the premature end... it had to mean this city..."

As he spoke out loud, a realization began to surface: it was something the queen had said the first time they came, and then again what Azvari was saying... "Tiye said that Sekhmet gave her a message, and it was a little different from the one Sahed knew... Something about two people opening the gate and the beginning of the end..." Craig struggled to remember – without the laptop he was like a man without arms! "She said... those chosen by the Council would come and people would remember how to breathe... I thought it was us. But we aren't teaching anyone how to breathe, we don't even know ourselves! And people are not suddenly starting to breathe here; in fact, they might be all dying..." thought Craig. "So maybe it's not us. Maybe someone else is the chosen one and that person is supposed to help bring back this memory of breathing ..."

Completely confused, Craig sat up. His small room was hot now, even the stone floor was warm. Walking to the silver pitcher, he poured himself some water, drank it all and poured more. The servant wasn't around, he was probably waiting outside. Not wanting to bother him, Craig sat cross-legged on the floor in the shade by the opening in the wall. The movement of air made it a little cooler. He tried to return to his thoughts. Who else could be the chosen one? Tiye? If she was then it was over, because she had already died. Azvari? Maybe, but Craig had no idea how to help her or even what help she needed. Besides, she didn't ask for any. He went through all the Shenu he had recently met, trying to figure it out. No chosen ones sprang to mind. "Mr. Halib thinks he is, but he's just creepy..."

Then Craig jumped up with lightning speed, spilling his cup of water.

"It's not one of the Shenu! The chosen one is not one of the Shenu! It is Akhenaten! It has to be. It all makes sense now..." Craig paced back and forth, having to reverse the direction every three or four steps. "He was chosen by the Solar Council to do some job, to begin something – and look what he did! He got rid of all the gods and tried to tell people there was only one god, and not even the sun, but light itself! And this premature end is not the end of the city but the end of the pharaoh! Is he really that sick?"

As he drank the rest of the water straight from the silver pitcher, he froze in the middle of the room. "I've got it! He's not sick enough to die, but because of the plague people think that he was wrong to get rid of the gods. He has to fix that, he has to change that idea. And if the city can't be saved, then he has to fix it some other way. And the only way he can do it, is to abdicate – which he cannot do – pharaohs don't retire. But they do have co-regents! But anyone who Akhenaten could make a co-regent would be a rival to him, and probably change everything right back to the other gods... So it has to be someone he trusts, who can change things up politically, but still be loyal to the one god – and that person has to be Nefertiti. He has to make Nefertiti a king, a co-regent! Not a man, but a woman!"

It was an absolutely insane thought. "But it makes sense... that is what the message said – the queen needs to be like a king. Not to *be* a king, but to be *like a king* somehow... I need to talk to Nefertiti!"

*   *   *

Mahmoud was not sure how to answer Ay's question. "Do people in my time worship Aten?" Ay wouldn't believe the answer. "Not only is Aten forgotten, all the gods of Egypt are forgotten. We are now servants of Allah," he thought bitterly. He had nothing against Allah, but he also knew the truth about the gods of Egypt being from the stars and so did this man in front of him. "How do I explain to him that in my time the Egypt he knows is no more?"

"Can I see the temple?" It was better not to answer.

They walked towards the Great Temple of Aten. Its front wall ran for over a hundred feet and it was enclosed by almost a thousand feet of outer wall. The façade was adorned with ten flagpoles. "More than at Karnak," observed Mahmoud. He had recently done a documentary about the Karnak temple, and he had mentioned that the eight flagpoles in front of its main pylons were the largest number in Egypt – but apparently not. The brightly colored flags flapped strongly in the wind from the Nile, and the front double pylon was decorated with much bright paint. Akhenaten, together with the royal family, was depicted on the walls, but there were at least as many images of Nefertiti alone. Overall the images seemed to be of the triad that Akhenaten and Nefertiti formed with Aten. The historian in Mahmoud was remembering the famous triad of Waset, Amun-Mut-Khonsu, and the triad of Memphis, Ptah-Sekhmet-Nefertem. These traditional Egyptian triads made little sense because quite often the gods were unconnected, chosen to be together because of the politics of the priests rather than for suitability of the gods. But here it kind of made sense – the royal couple and their god were as one. Everything was so colorful! High walls on all sides sheltered the enormous temple, but it was open above to the sunlight. Passing the main pylon, they were inside the outer court, which felt more like a garden than a temple. In front of them was a ramp leading to a flat platform about five feet high, which overflowed with offerings. Beneath the pillared walls priests in short white kilts fanned away the incense smoke, while placing more flowers onto the side altars. Well maintained citrus and pomegranate trees trimmed the large courtyard, and flowers grew between the columns in small square openings in the stone floor. Beyond the main temple walls, but still inside the large enclosure of the temple grounds, Mahmoud could see hundreds more offering platforms with flowers and food, and beyond them a sea of sunflowers, their black and yellow heads cheerfully greeting the sun.

"This is the House of Rejoicing," commented Ay, placing the lilies he had been given onto one of the altars. The sun spilled freely into the yard through clerestory windows in the ceiling above the columns. Even the doorways, and they walked through many, had broken lintels, while the processional way through the middle of the columned hall had no roof at all. Wherever they went they were in contact with the god, sunlight. There was no holy of holies, no sanctuary for an earthy cult image of the god fashioned out of costly materials such as gold or precious stones. Instead the space was filled with hundreds of low, square offering platforms, culminating in the middle of each yard with a pedestal on which stood a gold and ivory chair with bent carved feet. Mahmoud noticed four things on each of the chairs: two large gold cups and two shallow gold bowls.

"There is wine representing fire and barley for air in the cups, and meat representing earth and water for water in the bowls," explained Ay. "The most basic, yet essential, gifts. By means of his rays Aten fills the space with himself." As soon as the sun rose in the morning, it filled the temple, and instead of representations of familiar gods there were statues of the royal couple and paintings of the royal family, and paintings of the sun disc with many rays. Aten's effect on the temple and the people was through light; his life-giving hands were present everywhere in the sanctuary. Where there would have been statues in the niches there were offerings of fruit, wine and beer, geese, and bowls with meat, interlaced with flowers. The smells of incense, flowers, and raw meat were an odd combination for the senses.

Watching Mahmoud's face, Ay commented: "Aten enjoys flowers the most, we are told. Their beauty is similar to light itself. Although Panahesy would have us believe otherwise. As his butcher's yard is behind the temple, Aten will never go without fresh meat."

Mahmoud couldn't tell if Ay just had an odd sense of humor, or if he was openly mocking his god!

Exiting the temple, Mahmoud felt Ay's strong hand pushing him to the side and was about to protest, but then he realized why – Mahu, the Chief of Police, and the middle-aged man who earlier had been standing next to the high priest Meryre, were approaching them. Stepping into the deep shade behind a beautifully decorated column, Mahmoud felt uneasy – he was used to being in the public eye, he wasn't used to hiding!

Ay left Mahmoud behind the column and walked straight towards the men. They appeared to have been waiting for Ay; Mahu had been told that Ay was in the temple.

"I trust you are in control of the situation?"

"I am always in control," said Mahu. "This is our world after all," he added in a whisper.

Mahmoud began to sweat – the man said he was in control of Egypt! He had to be a Shenu, like Ay. And the second man with them – he would not have been allowed to hear that if he was not himself privy to the information, and he was smiling with satisfaction.

"That man who was with you earlier, who is he?" asked the middle-aged man. "I haven't seen him at the palace before."

Mahmoud felt panicked, and then the meaning of the situation emerged in his brain – Ay and these two men were meeting. They were Shenu. But somehow Ay had decided they were not ready to meet Mahmoud. Why? He is a Shenu! And the chosen one! And he is from the future, he might be able to help them in ways they could not foresee.

Ay was blatantly lying now about who Mahmoud was, his voice dismissive. "He is hiding me!" Alarmed thoughts ran through Mahmoud's mind.

Unless he misunderstood their words, Mahu and the other man saw this pharaoh as a disaster, and they were actively mocking Aten. It was done in a subtle way and very quietly, but Mahmoud was sure about what he heard. He had found his Shenu. If he could only step out from his dark shelter and tell them, explain to them what happened in the future. Help them!

They parted ways. Ay began walking in the opposite direction from them, and then circled through the temple to arrive behind the columns where Mahmoud was left waiting.

"Why didn't you tell them who I am? I am the chosen one!"

"And you could easily be killed if they had found your story too preposterous to be the truth."

"But the prophecy? The chosen one coming here..." began Mahmoud.

"That already happened twenty-two years ago. You already came, the Shenu has already seen you. The will of Sekhmet was already fulfilled."

"But I am here now!"

"Yes, and you can easily be killed. On whose errand are you here?"

"I came because of the prophecy..." said Mahmoud, struggling with the words. He was beginning to see what Ay was pointing out and the thought was frightening him – there was a prophecy and it had already been fulfilled, so how come they were here now? Again? Mahmoud had been brought here, bound and against his will, pretty much as the means of entry for the Americans and their guide. There was no prophecy about their arrival, none! Yet somehow Azvari had known to meet them in the well... Somehow the Americans had known to return at that time... His head was spinning. What is going on?

"You see now that your role might not be the one that you envisioned?" continued Ay.

What did he envision? He thought of his whole life, his training as a Shenu, the secret vaults and the artifacts... It was all real, he was sure. But then this American woman's sister knew to tell them to come now... Mahmoud winced, remembering the old pizza.

The situation was becoming clearer and clearer. He, Mahmoud, was chosen by Sekhmet to find out who the betrayers were. He was going to do what he could to fulfill that task, to offer his modern expertise. But he already knew! By the sons of the pharaohs, he already knew who the betrayers were! Oh, it was all so simple, so perfect, it was all placed in front of him so he could not miss it. And he had almost missed it! This Shenu woman, Azvari, and the Americans, and their old guide... They were the traitors! Azvari had to be the one! She had been only a little child, but she grew up in the royal court, she said so herself. She must have been initiated into the Shenu, but then betrayed them by stealing the locket from Tiye and giving it to Akhenaten, who was then still Amenhotep IV. Oh, yes, Mahmoud could see clearly now! All he

311

needed to do now was to find out if Ay knew about what Azvari had done.

"Is Azvari the High Priestess of the Shenu now?"

"Yes, she is. She will be the last," replied Ay. The Shenu had already made the decision to not allow women into it, for it was seen that they could not handle the secrets. The existing female members would be the last ones, their inheritors were to be men.

"Do you know then who betrayed the Shenu? Who exposed its secrets to Akhenaten?"

"Nothing can be known for sure. But I suspect my sister."

"Tiye?" Oh, now it was even clearer! Azvari didn't have to steal the locket, Tiye and she had together betrayed the Shenu! "Tiye told him… it makes sense."

"There is no proof."

"I can tell you something, something you don't know," Mahmoud whispered, excitement in his eyes. He grabbed Ay by the elbow to pull him closer. "The traitor did not die with Tiye. There are others. She must have told someone besides Akhenaten, or he told someone else who told others. There are people in my time, in the future, who know about the Shenu!"

"Of course there are, you are one of them," replied Ay calmly.

"I am a Shenu. They are not! They claim to be of the Shenu, but they are not. I personally know every one of the thirteen and they are not in that group."

"What are their names!" snapped Ay angrily. Finally, he was beginning to understand the weight of the situation.

"The names will have no meaning to you because it is far in the future. But you know some of them – all of the ones who came with me. The Newcomers, and there are more of them, at least three more that I know of, back where we came from…"

"And you allowed this to happen?!"

Mahmoud had not foreseen this turn of events – was this man going to hold him accountable for the spread of the information, him personally? How could have he known? It was not his fault! He had done what he could to protect the Shenu.

Frustrated, and now scared, Mahmoud went into attack mode. "This began in your time! Not mine! It is *you* who allowed this to happen! It is you who were blind about your queen being the traitor! Your own sister! And now it is you who is being blinded by your feelings towards Azvari. I saw how you look at her! She is attractive, isn't she?"

Ay looked angry and terrified. Good, Mahmoud thought, I'm almost there. "She is the traitor! I know it. Azvari is the one who Tiye converted. Isn't it true that she was raised by Tiye? She was at court all the time. She is now the High Priestess of the Shenu because she was placed here by Tiye. She is the two-faced spy! She will tell others who will tell the Americans..." Mahmoud realized that this wouldn't really make sense to Ay. "I mean the people who came with me — they are all inheritors of Azvari and Tiye!"

"You are lying!" hissed Ay, and abruptly turning around, began to walk away.

Mahmoud could not allow him to leave, he had to get his attention, he had to convince him that Azvari was the traitor — he could probably even prove it if they put her under surveillance! Mahmoud hurried after Ay and grabbed his arm to stop him. His fingers slipped over the large gold bracelet Ay wore over his bicep and it moved, revealing a tattoo hidden under it. The image was that of a beautiful girl, kneeling in prayer. The word "beloved" was inscribed at her feet, and Maat feathers were positioned above her head.

Mahmoud froze, staring at it with widened eyes. He found that suddenly he could not breathe.

"Never do that again!" warned Ay in a stern voice, pushing Mahmoud's hand away.

"When did you do this?" whispered Mahmoud, struggling to inhale.

"Eleven years ago," replied Ay, working the bracelet back into its original place.

Mahmoud finally inhaled. His thoughts were racing. Oh, fate, why are you so cruel? Looking at Ay's embarrassed face as he struggled with the bracelet, Mahmoud knew immediately that the tattoo represented Azvari. It may as well have said her name! Eleven years ago she would have been sixteen, the age Ay might have asked her to marry him. *Follow the beloved... do not stray from Maat... you are the beginning of the end...* Oh, Sekhmet, am I to follow him and that traitor, Azvari?

*   *   *

The servant entered through a small side door, and swept a low bow. He had heard movements in the room and was presenting himself to his charge. When he raised his head he froze, seeing Craig standing in the middle of the room. There was no fear in the man's eyes, only curiosity. Craig rushed to him.

"I have to see Nefertiti! I have to see her, I have to see Nefertiti, do you understand?"

To his surprise, the man bowed his head and gestured for Craig to follow him. He was shown into the side room which the servant had just left. There was a curtain covering the entrance. "She couldn't possibly be in there," thought Craig, moving the curtain aside.

The room was a ten by ten square, with a partition wall about three feet from the back wall. The beautiful bright blue and green fiancé tiles with paintings of fish lined the walls about four feet up. Many silver and red fish swam to the right, between the tall grasses, drawn on the painted wall above them. On his left was a sink – a beautifully carved light green stone bowl, filled with water, held there by an ornate stone stopper. The sink stood on three metal legs, and underneath it was a metal bucket. On a shelf next to the sink were placed flowers, some beautifully carved jars, and a thin copper knife. Above it on a hook hung a large cloth – a towel. In the right wall was a stone square, three feet high, with a low drainage hole and an opening a little higher than the floor. Craig realized this wasn't really a bathtub; it was more like a shower. Water was poured over the bather – there were three large metal vessels on the floor next to the tub. But what really got his attention was the contraption behind the partition wall. It looked like a seat with a hole in it, and the circle of the hole had a stone frame – the same light green stone as the sink and with the same carved design on it.

"Wow! It's a toilet!" Somehow Craig had not expected to find a toilet in 1,338BC! Yet there it was. "I thought we didn't get those until after the Middle Ages?" Craig poked around, unsure of what to do and almost ran into his servant – the man had stepped in quietly behind him and was waiting for instructions.

Seeing the confused look on Craig's face, he began to pick up objects to show Craig how to use them – the knife was for shaving, the water for hand and face washing, the cloth was to dry it. The servant even jumped into the tub for a moment, picking up the tall vessel, as if ready to pour water over himself. Craig found this funny and his own gestures began to repeat the servant's, which only encouraged the man to do more. The man hovered over the toilet to show how this is to be used. Craig could not stop laughing – he had urinated twice in a room he had found behind the garden since it had pigs and chickens in it and already smelled, when this bathroom with a toilet had been right next to him! "If I'm going to see the queen, I better wash up," he thought. There had been no such opportunity since they had arrived in this ancient time.

Being half Native American was a good thing in the way of shaving – he didn't have much to shave, even at nineteen. So that was easy. The copper knife was as sharp as a razor and it did the job very quickly. He brushed his teeth with a mixture of myrrh and mint – it did a surprisingly good job. With the help of the servant, who poured the water over the tub partition, Craig washed not only his face and body, but also his hair – the dust had made his black hair grayish. To Craig's surprise, most of the washing was not to be done with water, but with oils. The water was for shaving, washing the face and hands and pouring over the body to purify it. But the rest of the "washing" was done by massaging the skin with a paste, then with oil, and then toweling it off. The paste reminded Craig of Bailey's exfoliating cream, which he had once used mistakenly when his own shower was broken and she allowed him to shower in her bathroom. The oils smelled like lemon, musk and lavender. His servant showed Craig that lavender was for the face, musk for the body, and lemon for the feet. Skillfully manipulating Craig's hair, the servant poured oil over it for shine, then made one braid, wrapping the end with a copper wire. There were four little charms on the end of the wire and the servant winked at Craig as he pointed them out. Finally, Craig finished up by using the toilet and was ready to go. He was given white linen to cover himself with, and the servant, after watching Craig's bungled manipulations, took the linen and wrapped it over Craig's naked hips himself. The rest of his body was left bare. Perfumed with oils and massaged, Craig felt oddly aware of how transparent the cloth on his hips was. The servant wore more clothes on him than Craig, but there must have been a reason for it. To finish things up, the servant asked Craig to lift his arms, massaged some incense into his armpits, then picked up a blue flower and stuck it into the top part of Craig's braid. He stepped back, viewing his work with approval, which for some reason made Craig feel embarrassed and he smiled sheepishly.

His dirty clothes were stuffed into a cloth bag, which Craig carried with him as he followed the servant through the house, into the garden court where they had been before and through a columned hall with a painted floor. To the left was a huge open courtyard with chariots, and to the right was the Nile, with bobbing sails and a royal boat, bulbous and brightly painted, gleaming gold in the sunshine. The servant turned neither left nor right, but continued walking ahead, farther into the building.

They arrived at a larger rectangular garden courtyard with four stone fountains positioned one after the other. A loggia balcony ran across the perimeter of the courtyard on the second floor, the roof over it supported with wooden columns painted a deep red. There was no ceiling in the center, and the fragrant flowers of the garden were bathed in sunlight. In awe, Craig followed his servant through a stone doorway, which led to a dark, cool corridor and into yet another open courtyard, its walls completely covered with paintings. The courtyard was about forty feet square, with ramps on all four sides and chariots rolling through it. Craig couldn't begin to guess its purpose. Then they stepped through a doorway with a gold sun disc over it and suddenly it was cool and dark. Adjusting his eyes Craig could make out square columns supporting the roof forty feet over his head. The large hall was also square, and the middle had a sunken floor and no roof. A massive column of white light shone through the ceiling opening high above, illuminating a red granite statue of a sphinx – it had a female face. "This is a Nefertiti sphinx," thought Craig. He heard the servant calling and followed him into another even bigger but similar looking space – to the right further away the steps led to a platform with two large thrones on it.

His servant pointed to a set of stone benches in a dark alcove. Craig sat down on a cool bench and was handed some fruit juice. It was a flavor he didn't recognize, and musing over the juice, he barely noticed when Bailey, Sahed, and Simon entered the space and were escorted to similar benches. They exchanged a few words about their experiences, and settled. When Azvari arrived Craig fully expected her to bring Mr. Halib, but he was not with her.

"Ah… I have to talk to Nefertiti, can I meet her?" asked Craig, unsure of the polite way to make such request, hoping that Sahed could put it into the right words.

*   *   *

"I have to tell you – there is a lot you do not know!" Urgency was clear in Azvari's quiet voice. She sat on one of the benches, Sahed next to her, then Bailey. Simon decided to sit on the floor in front of them. This was a strategically sound position; it allowed a clear view of each flank of the hall beyond the columns. Craig plopped himself on the floor next to Simon and crossed his legs as if he was preparing for a vision quest, intently staring at Azvari.

"You are the Shenu and so you must know…" she began. "Tiye was the one who exposed the Shenu to Akhenaten, her son. Only two more people, also the Shenu, know this. Your arrival was her sign. The beginning of the beginning – her son was to step forwards as the One.

316

But there was another truth given by Sekhmet to Tiye. The *chosen one is two* was Sekhmet's message, delivered to her through me much later. Tiye alone knew it to be about her offspring."

No one spoke, so Azvari continued.

"Tiye followed Sekhmet's will. She knew the prophecy about the beginning, but when you left, I was met by Sekhmet. I was a little girl then..." she smiled. "Sekhmet told me many things, but she also gave that message – *the chosen one is two* – and it came with a complicated set of instructions." Azvari smiled to herself, remembering. "I repeated everything to the queen, and she knew what to do. She and her brother, Ay, performed a sacred ritual, exactly as Sekhmet instructed, so 'the two' would come..."

"You mean Akhenaten and some other child?" asked Craig. "I thought she had four daughters... Oh, and one son first, right? But he died..."

"She didn't know at the time which children would be the 'chosen two,' and she had three sons and five daughters. But this is about the pharaoh and his queen," said Azvari.

"You mean Akhenaten and Nefertiti? But he is the only one who is her child."

"They both are her children in a matter of Maat if not fully of her body. They are the descendants of the star-gods, brought into this world through Queen Tiye and Vizier Ay. They are from Mer and of one Ba, brother and sister."

"Wait, Akhenaten and Nefertiti are siblings?"

"Yes. But not like we would be, not of the body. They are of the star-god light."

"But Akhenaten's father is Amenhotep III..." Bailey was trying to comprehend.

"Tiye alone knew he was not fully so..."

"How can somebody be 'not fully a father'?"

"We are not made of flesh alone, our Ka and Ba are from somewhere else. The flesh of our pharaoh came from Tiye and Amenhotep III, but his Ka was brought here through the sacred ritual by Tiye and Ay – they opened a divine tunnel for his Ka to enter. This was the will of Sekhmet and the Solar Council, and it is Tiye's secret as well."

"But Ay referred to Nefertiti as his daughter... I doubt he could openly have a kid with the queen!" said Craig.

"When Tiye and Ay brought the pharaoh's Ka here, it did not come alone," smiled Azvari. "The 'one who is two' – one Ba but two Ka! The second Ka had no flesh to anchor in and so it hovered. Both Tiye and Ay had insistent dreams of a child, a girl. The queen had thought she might be carrying twins, so heavy was her body! But when Akhenaten was born, there was no twin, and the dreams did not stop. Then Ay's wife became pregnant. At the same time Tiye found out about an affair that her brother Ay had with her elder daughter Sitamun... Ay was Sitamun's tutor and the sixteen year old girl fell in love with him. This was not Ay's proudest hour! His wife was pregnant with his child, and young Sitamun could not possibly become his minor wife! To protect the princess, and Ay, Tiye hid Sitamun away from the palace gossip. The child in her was as heavy as the one Tiye had carried earlier, and Sitamun was unwell. As Hathor would have it, both babies came only a few days apart, both too early... Ay's wife's baby was taken by Anubis and she was inconsolable. Sitamun gave birth to a daughter, herself barely escaping Anubis while giving life to her. And thus Sekhmet's plan became clear – Sitamun's daughter was 'the other'. It would have been impossible for Sitamun to raise her, she was so weak and had to be nursed back to the land of the living for a long time. But Ay's wife had so much milk to give and no baby – thus she became a nursing mother to Sitamun's daughter. Ay raised the girl as his precious daughter, Nefertiti the beautiful. Even his wife does not know that Nefertiti is Ay's child and queen Tiye's grandchild..."

A triumphant smile adorned Craig's face – he knew the answer! But no one was particularly interested, and he decided to wait.

1,338BC
Akhet-Aten, Egypt

Her eyes hurt. How much crying could she do? Princess Meketaten lay in her room, a private sanctuary filled with her favorite things brought especially for her from the Northern Light palace. A warm breeze circled through the room, picking up the myrrh incense and carrying it to the princess's nostrils. Yet with each breath Nefertiti's heart became heavier. Her daughter was not well, and she recognized the symptoms. The sickness that had traveled through Egypt had reached Akhet-Aten. The suffering in the City of Light was only beginning, but more and more people were succumbing to the sickness. Nefertiti cared deeply about the city and its well-being, and so she had made a point of regularly receiving all news of it. Lately, the main news was the sickness.

Meketaten stirred and Nefertiti came up to her.

"How is my beautiful flower feeling?" Nefertiti asked the girl. Her answer was a prolonged and wet cough. There was no blood on the cloth the girl used to cover her mouth and so Nefertiti held the hope that her daughter could recover. Yet the young princess, who should have been enjoying herself playing in the garden, was lying in her bedchamber, her back supported by cushions, her face swollen and her eyes red.

"Anubis already has taken my youngest daughters, I won't let him take another one!" Despite her resolve, Nefertiti felt fear creeping into her Ba as if the crocodile god Sobek was near. Setepenre would have been almost five years old now, but two years ago she had passed to the Land of the Dead after contracting this same sickness. Only a year after her death, Nefertiti's fifth daughter, Neferneferure, became sick with similar symptoms. "What is this?" Nefertiti had asked their royal physician then, but he had not been able to answer. More offerings to Aten, more grief and more pain... And more potions!

Nefertiti was only twenty-eight years old, but her body showed the effects of six childbirths. "All this grief is not making me any younger..." she whispered to herself. A girl, seated next to her, touched Nefertiti's hand. Her name was Mutnodjmet, and she was Nefertiti's step-sister.

Meketaten stirred on the bed. Again Nefertiti was pulled away from her thoughts to tend to her daughter. "Only thirteen years on this earth, and she might not see another year!" As if trying to push away that thought, she adjusted an amulet in her daughter's head. Meketaten coughed some more and looked at her mother with pleading eyes – she was getting weaker and weaker by the day. Nefertiti wished she had the power to make her daughter better, but all the gods of Egypt, including Aten himself, could not seem to help.

"Maybe we should tell the officials, the viziers?" suggested Mutnodjmet, as she poured the potion into the cup and gave it to her older sister. What she was referring to was a secret they kept – the young princess was not only sick, she was also pregnant. Meketaten and the youngest son of one of Amenhotep III's wives were in love, and their relationship had already resulted in pregnancy. Luckily Meritaten had noticed her sister's condition right away, when only a little more than a month had passed. But what could Nefertiti do? She could not bring herself to force her daughter to drink herbs which would rid her of the child. What if it didn't work and instead a baby was born sick? It was decided that if the child was a boy, the young princess Meketaten would be immediately married to the sixteen-year-old lesser prince.

But there was another problem. Meketaten was the second daughter and so Meritaten, the eldest and most royal one, had to be married first. But Smenkhkare, the only prince royal enough to be worthy of Meritaten, had already married. And Nefertiti's first daughter would not be anything less than a Chief Wife! Four months ago though, Smenkhkare's wife died in a horrible accident, run over by a horse. Immediately preparations had been made for a Royal Wedding – Meritaten would be made Smenkhkare's Chief Wife. Akhenaten desired to have a very large ceremony the next year, to make the marriage officially known to the whole of Egypt. He reasoned that by then Meketaten would have given birth and would feel much better, and she could be easily married off at that time. And by then she could actually enjoy the ceremony, the gifts, and the visits of the officials and priests wishing her and the baby a long and happy life.

"Of course he is right," thought Nefertiti back then. "We just have to survive this, the baby will be born and she will be well. The first pregnancy is always the most dangerous. But my daughter is strong." And then the sickness came! The father of Meketaten's baby became very ill and passed to the Land of the Dead just a month ago. Meketaten did not carry the pregnancy well, as she was grieved by the death of her lover. In addition to her grief she began to cough, sneeze and have trouble swallowing because her throat swelled. Now she was becoming weaker and weaker every day, no matter how many potions and prayers she received.

"So much death!" thought Nefertiti. In the beginning of this year Queen Tiye passed to the Land of the Dead, joining Nefertiti's two youngest daughters. Tiye was powerful and wise, and without her guidance the weight of protecting the throne fell on Nefertiti. It was a heavy responsibility but Nefertiti was up for the job, even if it meant suppressing her own heartache.

Nefertiti was the matriarch of the royal family now, equal in power to her husband. He was so strange, so hard for people to understand, so sensitive and loving to her – she felt she had to protect him. People loved her; her likeness was depicted on the temple walls as often, if not more often, than Akhenaten. They followed her, and she stood by her husband. Indeed, she was his protector.

"My beloved husband's head is in the sky!" she thought in frustration. "Who, if not I, will protect him now that Tiye is gone? I must do something!" She had already done much, and was known among the court nobility, priesthood and even the foreign dignitaries, as a fierce advocate of her husband's interests. She was the proud inheritor of Tiye's power at court. Akhenaten honored her loyalty and had immense trust in her. Indeed, in the Great Temple of Aten she was shown in the traditional pose of a pharaoh: standing before Aten, smiting a foreign enemy with a mace. Such depictions were usually reserved for the pharaoh alone, and yet Nefertiti had earned this representation. Even though the image related to foreigners, many people at court knew it to be a symbol for her readiness to destroy anyone who attempted to destabilize her husband.

She thought about Akhenaten. He was in such grief over the death of his mother Tiye, still recovering from the pain that her passing brought to his heart. "How could we bear one more death?" The tears began to run down her cheeks. Putting a hand on Nefertiti's shoulder, Mutnodjmet tried to comfort her sister.

"Maybe we should tell the officials?" she said again.

"You think it would be better for the power of Aten to see Meketaten die from an unfortunate pregnancy than from this sickness?"

"I don't know. You avoid talking about the sickness, everyone does, yet more and more people are afflicted."

She was right, and Nefertiti knew it. The sickness was dangerous, but even more dangerous was people's fear. She had to think about the kingdom! If it was announced that another royal daughter had died from the sickness, people would panic. "My dear husband might not want to see it, but I know – people are scared, and the priests all over Egypt are angry." Nine years ago Akhenaten disbanded the priesthood of Amun and the other gods. Every god of Egypt had hundreds, even thousands, of priests serving its needs. Without the gods, Egypt didn't need the priests. Royal and noble families had traditionally supplied the priesthood with their own children for generations. There were lineages of priests, honored and powerful. And now they were all out of a job. Only a few had converted to serve Aten and retained their position, and most of those, Nefertiti knew, had made a political move, not a pure-hearted one. Over and over she had told her husband, "You must not trust the priests, even if they serve Aten." Akhenaten almost always followed his wife's advice. He trusted her completely, not only with his heart but with his life, in eternity. Why else would he put bas-reliefs of Nefertiti on the four corners of his coffin? These were positions reserved for the four goddesses, Isis, Nephthys, Selket and Neith, but now it was to be Nefertiti's role alone to protect his mummy.

"He is so gentle and sensitive..." thought Nefertiti. They were married when she was almost fifteen, as young as her step-sister Mutnodjmet was today. Akhenaten was only a year older than she was, and having grown up playing with him, she knew him well. He would stay caught in his thoughts for hours while the rest of the children played or studied. Akhenaten was not like anyone she knew. She felt so very close to him; she could *feel* him, she knew all the nuances of his moods. It was as if they were one entity in two bodies. She always had his respect and his heart.

In the first year of his reign, Akhenaten changed. He summoned the strength that Nefertiti had always suspected was in him. He became confident and assertive. Nefertiti was sure that her aunt Tiye was the reason. Akhenaten began building the great Gempa-Aten temple in Waset, next to the Temple of Amun-Ra. "Our faith is a mixture of politics," Akhenaten had once said to her. "Great Ra-Horakhty is a merging of Ra and Horus, and when Amun's priests became so powerful, Amun was joined with Ra, becoming this Amun-Ra. He is not a true god, not as they see it." Now, this was an outrageous statement. Nefertiti had felt the weight of the moment – her young husband had just stated, with certainty, that Amun-Ra was not a true god. He could be killed by the priests for such speeches!

Nefertiti was a beautiful wife, and she was also an intelligent one. She saw that the statement was not a random one made out of annoyance with the priests from their meeting in the Audience Chamber that day. There was something else behind it, a certainty. Nefertiti spoke to Queen Tiye about it in confidence, and Tiye also showed no shock or fear in her expression. Nefertiti was convinced that Tiye had known about her son's odd comment before Nefertiti told her about it. This meant one of three things: either she had someone spy on them, or Akhenaten had talked to her about his views, or she had told him something that led him to those beliefs. It was unlikely that the queen needed to spy on her own son, and it was also unlikely that he would have told her about it because he did not feel ashamed of his statement and only his guilt would have made Akhenaten mention it to Tiye. This left the third possibility – Queen Tiye herself had somehow convinced her son that Amun-Ra was not a true god! As preposterous as it sounded, Nefertiti knew the power that Tiye possessed and it was possible that she knew much more than anyone at court, the priests and her late husband included.

Nefertiti spent a long night on the Malkata palace balcony at Waset that night, struggling with her decision. She was the person most trusted by her husband but he now knew something she did not. She could allow it to pass and remain only the Chief Royal Wife. But if she wanted to retain her position of confidante, she had to support her husband, no matter how strange and even heretic his beliefs might be. She had to know the source of his views. And so Nefertiti made one of the most dangerous decisions of her life. She would confront her husband and ask him what the basis was for his statements. If he intended to keep this information away from her, especially if it was somehow Tiye's secret, she could lose everything. But if he trusted her as much as she believed he did, she would become irreplaceable. She did love him, and if he stepped onto the path of insane heresy, he would be dead within a year without someone like her to protect him. Queen Tiye was old, who knew how long the gods would allow her to walk this earth, and when she died, who would stand as ally to the pharaoh?

Nefertiti spoke to Akhenaten the next morning. He requested time to think – Nefertiti knew immediately that he wanted to ask permission of his mother Tiye. At night he came to her bed chamber and commanded the servants to leave. Doors closed, they spent an entire night quietly talking. What he told her was beyond the impossible, it was insane. But the confidence in his voice, the stern, calm face of Tiye the day before, and her own heart told Nefertiti that this was Maat. The truth was ever-present in Akhenaten's words. He was chosen by the beings from the stars to change the course of history. He was shown that the *neteru* of Egypt are real beings, star-people, the archetypes of consciousness, and not just deities. He was told that their power was immense and their position had been usurped by false gods; that these false gods wanted people to be weak and herd-like, so that the false gods could be shepherds. Only two of the usurpers had people's interests in mind, Ptah and Hathor, all the rest were false. And he was told that there were real star-gods, Amun-Ra and Isis, who had dwelt in Egypt a very long time ago, but they were not the ones to whom they had built their temples. Nefertiti listened quietly, and with every new piece of information she was amazed at the confidence in her husband's words. There was more. He told Nefertiti that Sekhmet was a person, one of the true star-gods, and that he had met her! Akhenaten would not tell her how or where this had occurred, but she could see it was true. He cried as he attempted to express the magnitude of that event. When he became quiet Nefertiti offered a suggestion: "Why don't we build a temple to Sekhmet? The biggest one ever built..." But as her eyes met the wet gaze of her husband, she knew that this was not the correct course of action. He explained how people had been misled. "We are the gods ourselves," he said, "and even though we are now at a much lower level, we can eventually become more and more god-like. The true star-gods wanted us to know this. But the usurpers wanted power over people, wanted to be gods and the people to be the slaves."

"Aren't we all servants of the gods?" ventured Nefertiti.

"We are not meant to be servants. We are meant to be students."

"How will they teach us if they are not here?"

"I know the truth and I was chosen by Sekhmet to lead people in remembering."

"My dear husband, you will be seen as insane, or worse, killed by the priests the next morning, if you tell them that the gods of Egypt are not to be worshipped!"

"The priests have become political; they hold the gold of Egypt and the fate of its people. This has to change."

"The people of Egypt might not support you – they love their gods, false or not..."

"They love statues! Idols in stone! There are no gods in the statues! They pray to false gods!"

"Even if this is true, it cannot be changed. People follow traditions."

"They will follow their pharaoh." Akhenaten suddenly did not sound as confident, and Nefertiti realized that here was her new role – she would have to shield her husband from his own insecurity. He knew the truth and he had a vision. But for his vision to succeed he had to believe he could do it, that he could change Egypt. He could not waver. Nefertiti would have to support his belief by protecting him from negative news, from the confusion and fear of other people. He was to know nothing of it unless Nefertiti deemed it to be appropriate. Over the years she had inserted herself more and more into the official business of running the country – she attended the Audience Chamber more often than the pharaoh. She entered into the ceremonies of the priesthood as regularly as she did into the dealings with foreigners. She was determined to shelter her husband from any uncertainty on his path – because if he wobbled, even for an instant, he would not live to see the next day. Adversaries and conspirators were constantly circling, always ready to pounce on any weakness. And so publicly Akhenaten was to have no weaknesses, he was to be the picture of confident purpose.

Together they devised a complex strategy of events that would need to happen in order to change the flow of history. Nefertiti was not really sure it would work, but she knew that her role was to support her husband and she believed in his words. She had never found out if her aunt Tiye had anything to do with it all. As she sat by Tiye's deathbed, Nefertiti felt her aunt's hand on hers – she was patting her! Tiye wasn't distant, but she had never been this affectionate. Then Tiye said, "You have earned this queenship, wife of my son. I am proud of you, dear daughter." She died a few minutes later, her hand still on Nefertiti's hand. Nefertiti cried and cried after that – Tiye had never before called her *daughter*. It was the most powerful sign that Tiye approved of her that Nefertiti could ever hope for. If Tiye approved of Nefertiti, that meant she also believed in Akhenaten's path – and thus she would watch over them from the Afterlife.

*   *   *

As she watched her sick daughter sleep, Nefertiti thought of Kiya. Kiya was Akhenaten's other wife – the Greatly Beloved... Kiya's sister, princess Gilukipha, was sent from the Mittani kingdom to marry his father, Amenhotep III – she came to Egypt with three hundred and seventeen ladies-in-waiting! Two years before his death, the aging pharaoh had received princess Kiya as an assurance of the alliance between Egypt and the Mittani kingdoms. She was thirteen and had an odd name, Tadukhipa, and Amenhotep III began to call her Kiya instead. Two years later he died. All of the aging royal wives lived in the Women's Quarters in Malkata palace in Waset. But beautiful Kiya was quickly whisked away, by Tiye, Nefertiti suspected, and married to Akhenaten in the year he changed his name to honor Aten. Kiya was a Mittani princess and she became a royal wife once more. She was seventeen when she bore him a daughter. Nefertiti had endured that affair. Kiya had a spell over her husband, taking not only his interest, but his heart. Nefertiti knew she herself was irreplaceable and that Akhenaten would always respect her and care about her, but he was *in love* with Kiya! In only two years Kiya gained substantial influence at court and over Akhenaten – he built her a sunshade, Maru-Aten in the south of Akhet-Aten city, where all the walls were decorated with likenesses of Kiya and her daughter. Nefertiti thought of this as one of the darkest times of her life. When Akhenaten spent time in Nefertiti's bed chamber, his heart was not there. When she was carrying his fifth daughter, Nefertiti decided to not name her in honor of Aten, for he had allowed Kiya to take her husband's heart. The right to name a child was always the mother's and so, holding her baby in the birthing pavilion that day, Nefertiti announced her as Neferneferure – the Most Beautiful One of Ra. Akhenaten nearly stopped breathing, but it was done. Kiya lived in her own palace, a little south of their North Light palace, but that day she came, strolling thought the gardens with her daughter as if mocking Nefertiti. Akhenaten was oblivious of this, so happy he was, holding his new baby. He loved every one of his daughters. Kiya gave him one more, and so did Nefertiti, again not naming her to honor Aten. "What does it matter now, Setepenre and Neferneferure were taken by Anubis!"

The style of art in their time called for true likenesses, and Nefertiti's statues now reflected her slightly aging body. Just like Queen Tiye as a matriarch was always depicted with the signs of age, now Nefertiti had inherited this role. The position of the Most Beautiful One was transferred to Meritaten, the eldest daughter. Normally she would have supported the transition, she always rejoiced in the artistic honesty of the current art. But Kiya had been a thorn in her side for years now, and it did not help to see Kiya's statues reflecting the youthfulness her body retained after only two children. A mere two years older than Kiya, Nefertiti had already had six.

"Am I in competition with her?" Nefertiti asked herself in frustration. "She knows nothing of the pharaoh's destiny, she is only a passing interest of my husband!" It was painfully slow in passing, but it would eventually pass.

Mutnodjmet called her. Nefertiti had been staring into space for hours now. The sun would be setting soon, the servants had already lighted the oil lamps, and she had not noticed.

Mutnodjmet repeated her words. "Dear sister, there are people in the Audience Chamber to see you, and Azvari says they are from very far away."

"I do not have any space in my heart for foreign dignitaries right now, Mutnodjmet. Can this wait until at least tomorrow morning? Hopefully I will have slept by then and my appearance will not scare them..." She smiled a sad smile.

"Sister, you will always be the Most Beautiful One in the kingdom! There is no shame in your tears."

Nefertiti sighed: "Who are these people?" Azvari was one of the trusted few who knew about Meketaten's pregnancy and her being afflicted by this sickness. She would never have brought them here now, reasoned Nefertiti, unless... "Did you see them?"

"No, sister, I only saw Azvari. They are waiting for you in the Audience Chamber. I will watch Meketaten and call you if there is any change at all, I promise."

"Did Azvari say anything about these people?" pressed Nefertiti.

326

"Azvari only said that these Newcomers do not worship false gods, sister."

Nefertiti stopped breathing, staring at her sister. "What did you say?"

Mutnodjmet repeated Azvari's words. Of course, they seemed completely normal to her, since in her mind they probably referred to the dignitaries' awkward attempt to express their love for Aten, Egypt's only god. But Nefertiti's intuition, which she always trusted, was screaming that Azvari, her long and trusted friend, a priestess of Sekhmet and now Aten, who knew the anguish Nefertiti felt about her sick daughter, would never, under any circumstances, bring people to see her at this time. It was simply inconceivable. What was Azvari, a simple priestess, a commoner, doing with foreign dignitaries? And what they said about the false gods… Those were the same words that her husband Akhenaten had used twelve years ago, words that were based on a secure knowledge he would not reveal. Those words had changed the course of history…

Nefertiti stood up. After a quick freshening up in the bathroom, she took off her blue cap and replaced it with a thick black wig, and looked at herself in a silver mirror. She did not look good. But she did look determined. Maybe Sekhmet, the star-god her husband had met years ago, had sent her help. Maybe there was a way to save Meketaten… She would do anything! Although Nefertiti held no illusions – her little daughter was probably not very important in the larger scheme of changing a world. She placed a gold band over the wig to secure it, the cobra on the front looking particularly resolved. Taking a deep breath she forced herself out of the room.

*　　　*　　　*

A tall woman entered the hall. Not tall compared to Craig, of course, but she was definitely taller than most people they had so far encountered in Egypt. She was wearing a thin white cloth over her shoulders, tied with a red sash so that it hung like a robe, only the cloth was so thin that everyone could easily see her entire body underneath. "Wow, Azvari must be the only woman in Egypt who still wears clothes," thought Craig.

The tall woman's face was beautiful if a little stern, and definitely tired. Her features were very similar to the girl he had seen earlier in the ceremony and Craig realized he was looking at the queen.

Queen Nefertiti wore only a few thin gold bracelets on her wrists and a necklace of fiancé and gold beads. There was no other jewelry. Her head was adorned with a wig similar to the one the princess at the temple had worn. It was rounded at the front, went past the shoulders, and had a long bob-like extension at the back. A gold band with a large cobra wrapped around it at her forehead on the front. She walked about ten feet into the room and stopped. She appeared to be oblivious to the presence of other people.

Azvari quickly bowed in obeisance. By the time Craig had copied the gesture, Azvari was already hurrying towards the queen. The absence of servants was strange.

The queen stepped onto the dais and sat down in one of the thrones with a plush pillow. Azvari helped her get comfortable. Soon she waved for the others to come up. The hall was cavernous, and the queen was seated almost at the opposite end of it. Sahed fell to the ground, saying something to Nefertiti, Simon bent on one knee and Bailey just stood and stared at her.

"She is much older than I thought she would be," whispered Craig. He could see the effects of gravity on the queen's body – nothing major, but she did have a pot belly, her breasts were not as perky as they might have been when she was young and her face was showing some age. "Well, I guess six children would do it! I wonder how old she is? Looks like forty, but she might be younger..."

"I am Nefertiti, the queen of Akhenaten, the Servant of Aten. Have you brought any good news to our City of Light?" Her voice sounded tired, as if she was only going through the motions of an official greeting.

Looking closely, Craig could see now that she had been crying. "Oh, her daughter! What is her name... Meketaten?.." He asked out loud, "How is your daughter Meketaten feeling?"

Nefertiti's eyes welled up with tears, but she refused to allow them to flow. She breathed and answered, "Aten is watching over my daughter, she is unwell..."

"Our prayers are with you, dear queen," offered Simon.

"I honor Newcomers who pray for my daughter," she bowed her head slightly. "Why have you come?" Her eyes were suddenly focused and staring at them as if she could see all the way through – a lioness stalking its prey – the truth.

No one spoke and Craig decided that this was his time – Sekhmet had chosen him, the shaman, to help in this situation and he had to be brave, leave his insecurities behind and do his job. He repeated in his mind the words of his spirit guide "I know what to do, I know what to do..."

"Queen Nefertiti, your city has a sickness in it, right?" he began.

"Yes..." she answered, tossing a quizzical look to Azvari, who shook her head.

"I know that's supposed to be a secret, and we are not going to tell anyone. Your daughter is sick with this same sickness that people in the city are?"

"Yes..."

"And she is also pregnant?"

There was a long pause as Nefertiti stared at Craig. There was such exhaustion in her eyes that he felt guilty for asking. Azvari said something to the queen and Sahed translated to them that Azvari had told the queen that she had not disclosed this secret. "Secret? It was a secret?" thought Craig, about to back-pedal. "No! I know what to do, I know what to do..."

Out loud he said, "I am very sorry for asking this stuff, I know this about your daughter only because my spirit guide told me. I speak to a spirit being, you understand?"

"You have visions of a god?" asked Nefertiti after another long pause.

"Nah, he's no god..." laughed Craig, then realizing that this might be inappropriate on many levels, finished by saying, "He has great knowledge and he guides me in my visions."

"Can he bring health to my daughter?"

"Ah...." Craig felt horrible, knowing very well that her daughter probably would not get well.

"Why are you here?" demanded Nefertiti, reading the answer in his eyes.

OK, this was his moment; it was now or never.

"I know that you must become a king, to change Egypt, you have to be the one to rule. You can't let all that Akhenaten has done disintegrate this early, there is more to be done. It is very important." Craig was not sure if he had said it all in the right way.

The next moment he realized that all four of his companions were looking at him in surprise, and they were joined by Azvari and the queen as Sahed translated.

"I am the queen. Akhenaten is my king. Why and *how* will I be a king??"

"OK, it's a long story... and I can't tell you all of it because I don't have all the pieces either. But the main point is this: there is supposed to be a 'chosen one,' but it is not one, it is two; it is you and your husband. He is chosen, but you also were chosen…"

"Chosen by whom?" Nefertiti asked in a way that meant she was humoring him, but in her eyes Craig could see that she already knew the answer.

"I think you know, the Solar Council." When no reaction was forthcoming, he added, "The people from the stars, the real gods… you know?"

Again there was silence. Azvari looked uncomfortable, but she had brought them here and she herself did not know why – maybe it was for this?

"Go on," commanded the queen.

"OK, so the Solar Council, these star-gods, especially Sekhmet, they chose your husband Akhenaten, and you, to help people come out of their asleepness, because people forgot who they are… I am probably not explaining this very well…"

"You're doing just fine, mate." To Craig's surprise, Simon was encouraging him. Simon was watching the interaction between Craig and the queen closely, as if readying himself to act quickly if it was required.

"Ehh… OK, so this asleepness that has afflicted people has been here for many thousands of years, right, and in order for people to wake up they have to have something… I think you are this something! You and Akhenaten, you make this point in time that will not last, but will do something so people can wake up later on… that is where we come from." He finished, unsure if what he said made any sense at all.

Again there was a long pause. Nefertiti's eyes bore into Craig. Finally the queen spoke. "You are from the time that has not yet come to pass?"

"We are from there, yes," answered Sahed.

"Has Aten brought you here?"

"Sekhmet brought us here," answered Craig. "She brought us for a purpose, to tell you that now is *not* the time to end this yet. She sent us."

"Sekhmet, the Bringer of Truth, the Detester of Untruth…" mumbled Nefertiti to herself, but Craig recognized the ancient words, he had heard them many times now from Sahed, Tiye, Azvari, even Mr. Halib.

"You said that this will not last… Is my land in trouble? Will this plague take all the people of Egypt to the Land of the Dead?" asked Nefertiti finally, ready to bolt out of her chair forward.

"Ah... no, Egypt will still be here... But Akhet-Aten... I am not a prophet, queen, I don't know..." But then, as if realizing this was not the way a shaman should speak, he added, "I don't think that everyone will die, but ... eh..."

"My daughter will not live," stated Nefertiti.

"I didn't say that, I don't know!" protested Craig.

"I talk to spirits of my own..."

"Oh... sorry... I meant the city, and everything you and Akhenaten have built here – it is all good and it is what Sekhmet and the Solar Council wanted you to do, you did it well." Craig tried to sound encouraging, but seeing the tears in Nefertiti eyes he knew it wasn't working. She took a visible breath and said something to Azvari, who immediately poured her some liquid from the vessel on the low table near her chair.

When the queen composed herself, she spoke.

"You bring the blessing of Sekhmet? She approves of what we have built?"

"Yes, and the Solar Council too," replied Craig with confidence he did not know he had.

"What is this about the *end* that must not come?"

"Oh, that... that is the whole reason we're here, you know," explained Craig as Sahed translated. "We were told, Sekhmet told us... that this whole thing, this... event in time... will end, and it is OK. It's supposed to end, you see. It's supposed to be a short thing that allows something to begin here... Something from the stars, from the Solar Council, so that people in the future can wake up. And they can't wake up, apparently, without what you are doing here."

"The false gods of Egypt will be worshipped again," stated Nefertiti. After a moment of silence, she added, almost as an afterthought, "In the time you come from, this City of Light, our beloved Akhet-Aten, is no more? It is forgotten?"

What could Craig say? That people in his time had not even known Amarna existed until a hundred years ago? That there were no monuments from this city left standing? He had difficulty believing it himself, as he looked around the large hall.

To Craig's surprise, Simon spoke again, this time to the queen. "You see, dear queen, nice things like this have a way of reappearing, even after they have been forgotten, so nothing is really lost... And people are very interested in this city."

331

She smiled at Simon. Then, changing her facial expression to stern, she faced Craig: "You said it should not end, yet you are telling me it will be forgotten?"

"Ah... It is supposed to end, as I said. But it has to exist for some time before it ends... I think... This is what Sekhmet and the Solar Council are saying – that everything you built has to exist longer, not end right now." He was making sense to himself, and gaining confidence as he spoke. "The sickness in the city – many people will die from it and not only here, in the rest of Egypt also. And that tragedy could easily cause the end of Akhenaten's new way of living. But this must not happen. They are saying it is too early. What you have built will end, but now is not the time. And they say that only you can stop it."

"I can prevent the sickness? Is this what Sekhmet said? How?!" Pressing forward, Nefertiti almost stood up.

"Ehhh... no... I don't think so..." Craig felt cruel cutting down Nefertiti's hope. "But you can prevent the fall of Akhenaten and his way of life, this stuff he is teaching about Aten, and that the other gods are not real. You can have people believe this a little longer, just enough so whatever is supposed to happen will happen."

"I do not understand... I am to prevent the end of my husband only for a short time so something can happen much later?"

"Yes, and not only in Egypt but in the whole world!" explained Craig with excitement. "The whole world needs to remember how to breathe life, the Mer-Ka-Ba in people has to work again... And it hasn't been working for a long time. It will never work unless the teachings of this time stay alive long enough. And Sekhmet was worried that it was not going to last long enough. People will get scared about the sickness and they might blame the pharaoh... and then this whole teaching will end. But it can't end yet!"

"You said I can prevent this premature end of the rule of Aten. How?"

"You have to become a king. I don't know how to do this, but this is what Sekhmet said: the queen must be like a king."

"Then she did not say I have to become a king," stated Nefertiti. Craig was about to protest, to defend his shamanic discovery, when she added: "She said I have to be of a king's likeness, not *become* a king."

"Oh... what's the difference?"

"In your time do you know of Hatshepsut, the great queen of the land of Egypt?"

"Yes, she was a female pharaoh." Craig was glad he knew!

"She was a queen who made herself into a pharaoh. It is a dangerous position and I do not have the political support of the viziers, or the priests, to do it... But maybe I can..." her voice trailed off and Sahed stopped his simultaneous translation.

Craig was about to ask what she meant, when she stood up – it was clear that she had made a decision. "Is there anything else you have to tell me?"

"Eh... no... That was it."

"I have to return to my daughter's side. I honor you, Newcomers, for your truth. Maat is here today, in Sekhmet's words. Come to the North Palace of Light tomorrow, we will return there."

And Queen Nefertiti walked out of the room.

No one said a word for a long while, they only looked in the direction she had left. Somehow her presence was very potent, and when she exited the columned hall it was as if she had left a hole in the room and everyone had fallen in.

"She is tall..." That was all Bailey could say.

"Maybe because she has star-blood in her, as Azvari told us," suggested Craig.

"She didn't look like an alien to me," smiled Simon.

"I didn't say she was an alien," defended Craig. "But she is definitely taller than anyone here, she is even taller than Bailey." Bailey was five feet five inches tall, so being taller than her was not a huge accomplishment, but in ancient Egypt they had seldom met a person, man or woman, much taller than five feet. Sahed fit right in, but Simon and especially Craig, who was over six feet, looked like giants. "I wonder how tall Akhenaten is?"

"You did well, mate," said Simon, patting Craig on the back. "I knew you had it in you. Glad you found it, *shaman!*" Craig felt a moment of happiness – he had been able to be a shaman, whatever that meant!

Simon stopped, looking at Azvari. "Sahed, would you tell Azvari that we can explain to the queen anything she needs us to?" Simon could see that Azvari was worried, nervously looking in the direction of the doorway Nefertiti had walked through. "We don't mean to get her in any trouble."

Before Sahed could finish translating it, a beautiful girl walked in through the same doorway. She spoke to Azvari, calling her by name, and although she looked at them with curiosity she didn't approach them, but retreated into the darkness.

"Who was that?" asked Craig.

"This was Mutnodjmet, Nefertiti's sister. She told us to come and watch the ceremony at the Temple of Aten tomorrow, and then ride with them to the palace."

Craig could see the resemblance – Mutnodjmet looked about sixteen and was very beautiful, with similar features to Nefertiti, but she didn't have a commanding presence, and she was much darker and slightly shorter. "She doesn't look like Tiye either," thought Craig. "Maybe she is a half-sister?"

*   *   *

The entrance to the Great Temple of Aten was decorated with flowers, and there was music – tambourines, chimes and singing. A tall couple led the procession, their only apparel was transparent cloth loosely set around their bodies, large gold pectoral-necklaces, tall cobra-fronted blue crowns, and bracelets on their arms and wrists. The pharaoh's face was exactly the same as the image carved into the red granite sphinx they had eaten under at Gempa-Aten in Waset – almond-shaped eyes under perfect kohl-painted eyebrows, a straight nose with balanced nostrils, full lips, high cheekbones and a prominent chin. Akhenaten's torso was thin, his thighs were heavily muscled and his shoulders were wide. The royal couple was followed by three girls, their daughters. Their youngest had the same light brown skin color of her mother, while the pharaoh and Meritaten had darker, redder complexions, and Ankhesenpaaten was somewhere in between. Nefertiti's head was shaved to allow a tight fitting blue crown to stay on, and the girls wore wigs.

Akhenaten, Nefertiti beside him, walked through the House of Rejoicing at the front of the temple and up the ramp onto the stone pedestal, and raised their hands up in obeisance to the sun. Everyone following behind them did the same. Then Akhenaten began to sing, Sahed translating what he could:

"Beautiful, you appear, great and shining... high over all the land... that you have created... the people are awakened and stand on their feet, for you have roused them... their arms are raised in prayer and they are blessed. Women turn liquid into people... You keep a child alive in the mother's womb and quiet his tears until they dry up... You let the child be born and provide for her every need... You have created the land of Egypt and also all the other lands and you are One God, the universal principle for Love and Light. There is no war in your presence... Tongues differ in speech, so too their characters and skin colors, for you distinguish people... but all are equal in your Light... You remain in my heart, and there is no one else who knows you, except for your son Akhenaten, and who loves you, Nefertiti, whom you have taught your nature and your might..."

"Much like Moses of the Hebrews, and what Jesus said in the Bible, no?" whispered Bailey.

"Sounds like it... I mean, he's talking about 'one god' and this business of 'god is the same for all' ..." offered Simon.

Sahed continued his translation: "We are one with you, Aten, for you are the light of who we are... there is no other light, no idol, we all are one being... with different bodies... we are one body with different faces... we are one Light with a multitude of sparks of your love... We belong to ourselves, through you, the Light Aten. Your children, the people of Egypt and of other lands, forgot the Light, forgot your likeness, because of the fear in their hearts... They fear standing alone, standing in their godhood as you have shown us – you are the godhood in people, you are eternal! You alone are the Light inside and outside our bodies! Your children were lost and fear overtook their hearts; they looked for a shepherd and found an usurper, they became lost... but they are found in your Light, dear Aten! We are led by you, through the stars and their guidance to the wisdom of breathing your Light, to add to the air we take into our chests...There is no one else but you, the all-penetrating, all-permeating Light of Maat..."

"Oh, Jesus, is he telling them about the false star-gods? The 'usurpers'?" whispered Bailey.

Akhenaten's voice, supported by the voices of the priests now, grew stronger as they chanted the blessing of Aten. Meritaten, Ankhesenpaaten and Neferneferuaten-Tasherit – Nefertiti eldest, third and fourth daughters – watched her mother for the clue to join. Once the prayer to the sun was over, Akhenaten added a poem that he had written just that morning, about Aten's love caressing his sick daughter Meketaten. Nefertiti put flowers onto the altar, then the girls did the same.

Sahed continued his translation as soon as Akhenaten resumed singing: "Those who pass on do not abandon us, they receive life of another kind, they are as alive as we are, but in your light, Aten... My wife whom I love, is Neferneferuaten Nefertiti, who lives and is rejuvenated, and my daughters, Meritaten, Meketaten, Ankhesenpaaten and Neferneferuaten-Tasherit, who walk this Earth with us, give them your wisdom and the light of your love... Meketaten, be in her body as one with her soul... And to my daughters who are souls, and have other bodies, Neferneferure and Setepenre, hold in love and peace for they are with you, Aten… May all the children of the land be in your Light, awakened into knowing of their inheritance… We are one with you, Aten, we open our eyes and we are not afraid to see Maat…"

Akhenaten's voice went surprisingly very high and then, abruptly, he stopped singing. The energy of the moment was intense, the presence of true spirit was palpable. Bailey looked as Sahed.

"Maat means *truth* and *fairness*, remember…" he said.

Descending the pedestal, the royal family walked the length of the temple, followed by the entire court. They stopped at each niche while flowers were placed on the already overflowing altars. Then with a final burst of singing, and while the music was playing, they turned around and began to walk back in the direction of the Nile, out of the temple.

Azvari waved at the Newcomers to follow her out of the temple, but there were hundreds of people surging around them and they were carried away from her by the swell. Women waved palm branches and held their little children high over their heads, shouting praises as if Aten himself had descended upon the city. Bailey felt Craig's hand grasp hers – he was the only one tall enough to see where everyone was – and he pulled her first towards him and then towards Sahed, and the three fought their way to Azvari.

First to pass them, in individual chariots of gold, were Akhenaten and Nefertiti, quickly followed by their daughters. Akhenaten tossed gold deben to the people and they reached out to touch his horses and catch the deben. Boys ran after the chariots, picking up what they could. But strangely, the women, crowded on the Royal Road, were chanting Nefertiti's name and tossing lilies before her chariot. Cries to bless them in the name of Aten followed her until Nefertiti's tall blue crown disappeared in the cloud of dust after Akhenaten.

Azvari, observing their confused looks, whispered, "She is the goddess of the people, they love her – Akhenaten and Aten are too distant for them; they can not touch Aten, but they can touch her. She praises Akhenaten and Aten, and they praise them because of her."

Nobles, viziers with their wives and daughters, ladies-in-waiting and other dignitaries, were being helped into the rest of the chariots parked by the temple.

Craig was on the verge of asking Sahed if it was alright to get a quick close-up look at one of the chariots, when an official looking man spoke with Azvari and then ushered them all ahead. To their surprise, they were each being asked to board one.

"Oh, no, no way!" protested Bailey. "How far are we going? I'll walk! No way am I getting into one of these!"

But Sahed and Azvari had readily complied and were already in a chariot, and Craig quickly pulled Bailey into the second one. Only three people, maybe four, could fit into it. In each chariot stood a Nubian charioteer holding onto the reigns to control the horses. Craig excitedly examined his chariot. It was pretty much an open box with nothing on the back, a taller front and shorter sides. And nothing to hold on to.

The chariots began to move amidst a tumult of people yelling and singing and horses' hoofs hitting the stone embankment – such a frenzy of activity! Because so many chariots had left the temple at the same time, they were somewhere in the middle of a long chain of them. Bailey trembled as she clutched the side, and wished she was brave enough to hang onto the charioteer – he was the only part of the chariot that looked solid!

As their chariot moved faster and faster, Bailey began to think that the inhabitants of the City of Aten must experience their pharaoh mostly through a cloud of dust! In about three seconds she couldn't see anything through the dust raised by the train of chariots. She closed her eyes, and, in spite of herself, screamed.

They rode the length of the embankment, but no one inside the dust was able to see that. Finally the chariot came to a halt, and Bailey opened her eyes and stopped screaming. She could see absolutely nothing.

"Come on!" She felt the pull of Craig's hand on her elbow.

"How can he see anything in this mess!" wondered Bailey, but as she stepped down and looked around, she realized that she too could see. Crowds of servants were gathered there, cloths and pitchers in their hands. They quickly wet their cloths and washed off the riders. Bailey welcomed that service, and soon she was clean and out of the cloud of dust.

"The North Palace of Light is inside the universal Love of Aten," stated Azvari.

"What do you mean?" Bailey was finally becoming fascinated. She looked around. They were on the Royal Road, the north end of it. To their left was a towering wall with an even bigger, squarish entrance. Following the direction of her gaze, Azvari added: "That's the entrance to the palace, above it is the other Window of Appearances."

The nobles of the court and whoever else was in attendance at the temple were now welcomed through the palace gates. The Newcomers joined a line to the gate, following behind a group of young noblewomen. Full of curves and sparkling beads, they chatted loudly, and the malachite paste over their eyes, accented by the heavy black lines of kohl, shimmered in the sun. The women were more interested in their conversation than in keeping up with the flow, and as the Newcomers passed them they were enveloped in the women's perfume. Instead of walking though the large gateway in front of them, though, Azvari followed the dignitaries of the court as they strolled to the left, seemingly around the large palace. There they found gardens and avenues lined with acacia and sycamore trees as far as the eye could see, all the way to the Nile. Shaded stone benches appeared inviting and calming. A glass-tiled path, bordered by irises and fragrant jasmine, led to tiled bathhouses and fountains. A pond was surrounded by the images of fish swimming on the colorful tiles. Beyond the bathhouse and the pond were the Women's Quarters. Craig picked up a pebble and tossed it into the pond, awaking the birds in the tall grasses in the waters.

"There! Look!" exclaimed Craig. Looking in the direction his arm was pointing they could see a tiger! A real tiger was lying in the shade of one of the enclosures, and there appeared to be no kind of chain on his neck. Bailey's eyebrows shot up.

"The pharaoh says that they will not attack a pure soul," said Azvari in response to her questioning look.

There were many creatures living in this idealistic environment. There were monkeys and lions, tigers and antelopes, large birds, and even three hippos! Behind the hippopotamus Bailey spotted a fluffy black and white goat and behind that, a towering giraffe. This was a formidable zoo, but she saw no cages or fences. "Why don't they just eat each other?" she wondered, as they walked on a limestone path amidst the gardens.

"The exotic animals are tributes to our pharaoh from foreign lands," explained Azvari.

After a while, Azvari finally felt it was safe to leave the courtiers and return to the palace. She led them into a side entrance, past the servant quarters and through a long columned hall. Servants ran back and forth, folded linens in their hands.

"What's happening?" asked Bailey.

"A weekly feast in the Great Hall. I don't think we can gain an audience before that, unfortunately," said Azvari. "You will rest before the meal," she continued firmly.

They were met by four men who served them water along with some fruit. Later a dark-skinned Egyptian girl entered, her heavily made-up eyes looking at Sahed. She walked straight to him, smiled, took him by the arm and they walked away, as all the rest of Newcomers, including Bailey, stared at her swaying hips perfectly visible under the transparent cloth. Unsure of what was happening, Craig, as if hypnotized, followed them to the doorway and almost ran into a stunning, tall Nubian girl. Hundreds of little blue fiancé beads were woven into her short wig, the same beads making up a necklace and a wide, low-slung belt – otherwise she was completely naked. She smiled at Craig, took him by the wrist, and led him out of the room before he could protest. When another woman walked in, she looked at Simon.

"Oh, no, I don't think so," he said out loud, looking at Azvari, who hid a smile. She didn't understand his words but the meaning behind the raised palms in front of his chest was clear – she spoke to the girl, and the girl was gone.

"Thanks."

When the sun began to set they were summoned to the torchlit gardens, where they met up with Sahed and a very much disheveled Craig. Through the wide-open pillared façade they could see the courtiers slowly making their way into the Great Hall, attended by servants in gold kilts. The limestone floor glistened under the sandals of the guests bowing before important viziers, and women in bright makeup whispered to each other.

As the courtiers waited, the royal family was seated on a dais in the far end of the Great Hall. Old men stopped playing senet to watch them. Close to the dais musicians performed, and many people were already feasting. The daughters of wealthy men imitated Nefertiti and her daughters in dress and makeup, and flirted with the viziers and officials.

Azvari led them away from the Great Hall and up a flight of limestone stairs to the roof terrace, where they were alone. The setting sun bathed the city below in cardamom-colored light and the gold rooftops of the Great Temple of Aten and the Central Palace shone brightly far in the distance. Along the water, large houses glittered with hundreds of winking lights, and in the east hills white villas, like pearls, reflected the sun's orange glow.

The servants came up with trays and two large vases. Placing these on a low table, they retreated the way they had come.

They sat on pillows around the trays, and Azvari explained what was happening: "We can not bring you into the Great Hall to feast with the court, too many questions will be asked. I had the servants bring us some of the food from the Great Hall here so you can eat."

There was roasted gazelle and honeyed lamb, slices of fish, barley bread and almonds. Figs and some bright yellow fruit were laid out on the other tray, and one of the vases held spiced pomegranate wine. A warm breeze pleasantly caressed their bodies while they ate.

Eventually a servant girl came, bowed and whispered something to Azvari.

"It is time," said Azvari, standing.

They followed her down the stairs and past the Great Hall, filled with loud chatter, music and the clattering of dishes, and through dark columned halls and open courtyards. As they approached a set of huge copper-inlaid doors, a servant pulled them open, and Azvari led them in. The doors closed heavily behind them.

They were in a large rectangular chamber with a polished mosaic floor, and on the west wall windows swept from floor to ceiling. Through these curtained windows a large columned balcony could be seen, and beyond it the Nile. The sun's orange light slanted through the curtains, illuminating odd shapes on the floor. A fire crackled in a large brazier, the flame dancing in the night's breeze and illuminating the figures of Akhenaten and Nefertiti. They sat on a dais in large pillow-stuffed chairs and their eyes glowed, reflecting the fire.

"Newcomers. This is the pharaoh of glorious Aten, Akhenaten," said Nefertiti in a very ceremonial way. Her voice sounded tired.

Following Azvari's direction, they all bowed deeply.

"You may rise," said Sahed, translating for Akhenaten as they straightened. The pharaoh's voice was deep. It was hard to believe that he was the same man who had hit that very high note at the temple ceremony earlier.

"Are you the one who said that I am chosen to awaken people to breathing Light?" he asked, looking at Craig. "What is your name?"

"Yes, I told Nefertiti that... I'm Craig. I told her because Sekhmet said that," answered Craig clumsily after a pause.

"Is Sekhmet above Aten then?" replied Akhenaten with a smile, as if testing Craig.

Was this a trick question? Craig had to come up with an answer and soon – no one else was speaking. "Shit, if I say yes, maybe he will kill us!" But Craig remembered that Sekhmet had picked him because he was a shaman, and so he spoke up with conviction: "Sekhmet is a true star-god. She is the one who initiated the Shenu."

There was a very long pause, so long that Craig was not sure if Akhenaten had understood what he had said. Craig had not mentioned the Shenu to Nefertiti, but he remembered that Azvari said Tiye had told Akhenaten – so he should know of them.

"Hopefully your code name did the trick," came a tight whisper from Simon, who was thinking the same thing.

"You are on the errand of Sekhmet, the Lover of Truth, Detester of Untruth?" said Akhenaten finally.

"Yes, we are. She told us about what is happening here and she brought us here through the gate, the gate you... used... also." Craig was not sure how much Nefertiti knew and he did not want to say more than he should. The shaman in him was walking a very thin line.

"She has given you a message for us?"

"She said that this will *all* end prematurely," Craig attempted to show with his arms the "all" he was referring to, "unless... Nefertiti becomes 'like a king.' I'm not sure what that means," added Craig, looking at Nefertiti for help.

"Will I be called to Aten soon? Before the next Sed festival?" Akhenaten inquired.

"Ah... I don't know... I know that people are sick, though, and that they might blame you for it, because you made them stop worshipping their statues..."

"They are only statues!" Akhenaten stood up. He was taller than Nefertiti and seemed as tall as Craig. Craig felt his Cat spirit guide pushing at his leg – were it not for that, he would surely have stepped back. But he held his ground, staring at Akhenaten, the only man who matched his own height in all of Egypt. In a confident voice Akhenaten continued, "They are empty idols of false-gods! They are put there to worship only to encourage people to forfeit their inheritance, to *not* breathe the Light of Aten!"

Craig swallowed and thought, "Wow, he is really agitated... I better watch how I phrase things." Out loud he said, "If Queen Nefertiti can be like a king, it will please Sekhmet. It will prolong the reign of Aten and allow what you have started here to do the job it needs to for the people of Earth, now and in the future. It is what the Solar Council and Sekhmet want..."

There was a pause, and Akhenaten spoke softly to Nefertiti. She replied, but when everybody looked at Sahed for a translation, he just shrugged his shoulders – he could not discern what they had said to each other.

Finally, Nefertiti spoke. "I will take the role you speak of," she said. Then she stood up and almost launched at them: "Now, leave!" Azvari quickly got up, and ushered everyone out.

*   *   *

"Jesus, that was scary!" exploded Bailey as soon as they left the large chamber. She couldn't believe what just happened. She had seen and heard Akhenaten, the famous pharaoh, the man who had held her locket all the way in the past. "What am I saying, so did Queen Tiye, and Azvari, and every other priestess before and after them…" The reality of the present and what it might mean was catching up with her and she stopped, staring breathlessly into space, her thoughts racing. "Where do I belong in this? *Who* am I…?" she thought, and it was an odd question for Bailey, as she had always felt secure in who she was – the daughter of a selfish man who had caused the death of her mother and the mental condition of her sister; a therapist who knew ways to help people. She had grown independent and responsible because she had to take care of Abby, and she had done a very good job of it.

Yet now Bailey felt weak and faint, and had to sit down. They were back in the garden courtyard, noisy from the music and laughter in the Great Hall nearby and with its only light spilling in from the same source. She lowered herself onto one of the benches and stared at a large pink flower, trying to focus. Simon and Craig were watching her, their faces full of concern. She heard Craig speak, his voice sounding far away. Repeatedly he said, "belong to truth, belong to truth…," but she felt dizzy and nauseous and couldn't seem to grasp their meaning. "I think I'm cold now… Or am I overheated, from earlier in the day?" Then she began to laugh as she remembered when in Luxor she had dragged a semi-conscious Craig upstairs into their hotel room, and how everybody had been telling her he was overheated. Her laugher sounded nervous and a little insane, even she could tell, but at that moment everything seemed out of place, so why not her laughter?

"Belong to truth? What is he talking about?" she thought, struggling to stay on top of it. "What truth?" She felt she might vomit and she must have looked it because Simon pushed a bowl under her chin just in time. Then there was water, a warm wet cloth washing her face, people's hands holding her, her face being fanned by an almond-eyed servant girl… None of it mattered. She was a rag doll, without a spine or any other bone. The tears began to flow. "I'm so weak! I'm not responsible at all! I don't know anything!" She was given a pitcher of water but seemed to have forgotten how to drink and only stared at it. "The truth is that I am alone! I don't have any family, they all left me!" She felt herself crying but the pain she felt was so much bigger than the tears that they barely seemed related. "I was wrong about everything, my father was not a selfish monster, Abby isn't crazy... I don't know anything anymore!" She wasn't sure if the words had come out of her or if the screaming voice that she vaguely recognized as her own was inside her head. Luckily, the noises from the Great Hall drowned her out and no one came to investigate.

Finally she remembered the water – cold, could it be cold? Yes, the silver pitcher was blissfully cold, and she couldn't understand how it could be or who was holding it, but she drank it hungrily. Someone put a piece of ginger in her mouth and she chewed on it. It felt good; she felt like she was stabilizing, the spinning was beginning to slow down. Her body felt better after purging the contents of her stomach. "Maybe... I ... was... poisoned..?" she thought lazily, unsure of anything at that moment. Nothing seemed to matter anymore, and she was suddenly so very tired.

"Focus, Bailey! Focus! You have to look at it, you are almost there!" This was Craig, his face inches from Bailey's and his eyes staring at her resolutely from the darkness.

"Wow, his eyes are so black..." thought Bailey vaguely.

"Focus, damn it, Bailey, pay attention!"

"Did I say that out loud? What is he talking about... almost where?" Bailey's mind felt like jelly, wobbly and unstable, and she could not trust it. As if to answer her unasked question, Craig's voice came again: "Trust your feeling, just go with it, focus!"

Bailey attempted to focus on his words. Truth? The pharaoh Akhenaten and Craig just had a totally legitimate conversation about Sekhmet, the star-god. Her truth, the very truth on which she had based her life, her career, her power, her very identity, was shattered. Bailey had not been abandoned by a selfish parent, she was actually part of something amazing. There was meaning in events, they had not happened randomly. She had not pulled an unlucky straw in life, having to be raised without parents, having her twin be out of her mind. She was actually a part of something... She was important, but not in the way she had ever considered herself to be. Her father loved her and cared for her, and he was not selfish but actually a very brave man – he had dared to believe! Her grandfather was part of this secret, the Shenu... And if anyone had listened to Abby, this whole insane thing could have been prevented – Abby's messages meant that it was Bailey and that man, the one from the Antiquities Council of Egypt, and not her father and Sahed... *She* was the chosen one! Again Bailey felt herself laughing, but she wasn't sure if it was laughter or an anguished cry, nothing was concrete. "Maybe this is good? My whole life I've wanted things to make sense, and just when I thought I had gotten to that point, when everything was fully predictable and solid, it all collapsed in this bizarre sort of way! I'm the freaking *chosen one??!...*" Bailey felt the anger now, anger at herself for having been such a closed-minded and rigid idiot for so long! She could have looked into this before now; years ago she could have examined the locket in the safety deposit box, years ago she could have figured out that Abby was not insane! "What kind of psychologist am I? I can't even tell if my own sister is delusional or delivering a message from Sekhmet! Or the Solar Council!" Bailey felt insane. The insane part was not how delusional she felt, but how normal current events seemed – *she was walking and talking to people thousands of years back in time*, and she was totally OK with the concept that she was chosen by someone called Sekhmet! So yes, she was ready to believe the idea that Sekhmet was real, and that she was from another planet. "Jesus, aliens? Sekhmet is an alien? I've definitely lost it!"

"You haven't lost it, love, you're just overwhelmed. This is a hell of a situation!" That was Simon's voice. She tried to locate him but either her eyes were not functioning, or her head was in the wrong plane... she couldn't tell if she was vertical or not. She felt drunk. The floor was cold. "Cold? Am I lying down?" Yes, she was lying on the cold stone floor. It was helping a little, although it kept tipping to the right. So she gripped the tiles with her nails to stop herself from sliding off.

"You have to face it! You have to! Focus!" That was Craig again, whispering earnestly. "Face what?" Bailey couldn't understand what he meant. All she knew was that she was not who she had been before she came to Egypt. She couldn't be a little girl mad at her daddy anymore, she had to let that part of herself go. She had to deal with the reality of the situation. And reality was *unreal!* Her father was a good man, and her sister was talking to real people, well, alien people maybe, but she was actually *talking* with somebody... "Oh, this is the truth Craig talked about!" She got it; the truth was that she was somebody else, not the person who she had constructed. She had to belong to herself! That was the point of this whole mess. She was free now, finally free. Bailey smiled as she lay on the ground. She had wished, for as long as she could remember, that she could be free of the hatred towards her father, the pain about the events that had involved her whole family. And she finally had that chance. She had it now, right now! If she could only believe that

344

this was real... What was it that Simon said? Something about believing what is right in front of his eyes... Well, this was no delusion, or vision, of whatever the hell they call it – it was real, at least as real as Bailey thought a thing could be. Over the past few days she had felt alive and awake. "I wasted so much time being angry... No more! I will believe, I have to! This is what we do, right? Humans are an intelligent species. We investigate, and when something feels real to us, we believe that it is real, until proven otherwise.... How can someone prove to me that this is not real?" She scratched the stone tiles with her fingernails, which hurt from the pressure. "This is not a dream. This has got to be legitimate, if my body hurts... I just met Akhenaten, I saw Nefertiti, they are real, and we are in Amarna, a place that doesn't exist!"

Bailey sat up. She could finally locate Craig – he was sitting on the floor facing her, looking into her eyes expectantly. "I know who I am. I'm just not sure what to do with it..."

Craig immediately hugged her, Azvari too, then Simon. Even the servant girl was smiling with relief. Bailey felt so very different. Hugs had never felt comfortable to her before... When they released her, she looked at her hands, as if she was seeing them for the first time. Simon helped her to stand up and they began to walk out of the palace into the gardens. Surprisingly, there were many people wandering on the winding paths. A young woman giggled by the lotus pond, entertained by the affections of a young man next to her, some people were quietly laughing on the benches by the fountain, a few men were walking aimlessly, their eyes searching for company.

Azvari walked confidently on the tiled paths, eventually arriving at the wharf. Roped to a tall post, a small boat bobbed up and down on the water. The ramp to it was very narrow, Azvari and Simon went on board first, then Craig used his hands to guide Bailey onto it. On the last step Simon lifted her into the boat. She was still a bit out of it, but strangely not embarrassed by the whole incident.

"Are we going home now? Where is Mr. Halib?" she mumbled weakly.

"Azvari sent a message to Ay, he will take care of that," answered Simon.

Bailey had not realized she had said the words out loud. Well, at least the business of delivering Sekhmet's message was over!

345

*   *   *

Their boat was inconspicuous and even smaller than the one they had used to come into Amarna. It seemed that now they had to be even more careful not to be seen. But, from the garden, they had been followed. Simon noticed them immediately and told Azvari – he believed she should be informed. To his relief she had noticed them too. Simon knew that they went in circles before finally arriving to the boat undetected. Climbing onto it quickly, Simon followed Sahed's directions and released it from the dock. Without other people on board, it was up to Simon and Craig to keep the boat moving, while Azvari watched for pursuers. Light came from the only lamp and in the darkness of the night Simon hoped that the river ahead was clear since he could see nothing. The lights of the North Palace fell behind them as the boat found the current – they were moving downstream, north. Away from the shore the wind was strong, Sahed and Simon raised the sail and the boat picked up speed. There were lights along the eastern bank and they stayed parallel to it.

Simon could sense that something was wrong and it could soon develop into a very bad situation. He didn't like the look of the two men who had followed them through the gardens. There was something very different about those men, Simon could feel it in his bones. Not that they looked inconsistent with the other Egyptian men, but they had a particular look in their eyes – a look of hatred. Simon was very familiar with that look. He had seen it in Somalia, and in many other unstable places in the world. He knew that the men who had followed them were not simply doing a job. That would have been simpler; people following orders, without any particular personal involvement. Twice he had locked his eyes with those men and he knew in the core of his being that those men were intelligent and they had a very personal reason for the hatred in their eyes. It was a vendetta, and they didn't bother to hide it, which meant they were even more dangerous. No help was forthcoming. This time there was no Queen Tiye who could offer protection. "Well, this time they have me, and I'm a force to be reckoned with."

Days went by; their Bedouin wrappings came on and off. Simon had paid attention, learning the basic words for "food," "water," "danger," "look" and the like. He could now converse with Azvari on a rudimentary level, using his hands and facial expressions when words were absent. This was as much his mission as it was hers. He was determined to apply his expertise. Twice he had seen men watching them in ports where they stopped – men that Azvari missed. He taught her as much as he could, pointed to her what she missed and why. He even had to incapacitate a man in one of the harbors – the man was way too curious, and Simon suggested to Azvari that she challenge him, and signal Simon if he gave a bad response. It was bad – his hand flew to a knife on his belt and Simon, who had discreetly followed him wrapped in Bedouin rags, had to make his move quickly. In seconds the man was unconscious, but alive, appropriately tied and gagged, and laid out in the niche of a large temple. Their journey down the Nile to the Delta was, indeed, a long one...

Finally they arrived to the "Land of Seker," as Azvari pointed out. The Temple of the Sphinx was impossible to miss. They could see its head from a distance, the painted face a bit grotesque, in Simon's opinion, and he turned away.

"Aren't we going to that harbor?" he pointed.

Sahed pointed to another dock, "Azvari said that friends are waiting for us at that port."

They moored at a little harbor to the south of the Sphinx's large plaza. Small temples and many traders populated the site. It was a market of sorts, but not a typical one – this was a place where worshippers could purchase their offering to a god, if you happened to have not brought one with you. Everything, from flowers and carved statuettes to young cattle, was available, as long as you had the deben. As they picked their way through the loud mess of the market, Simon noticed a man trailing them. He was about to go investigate, when he felt the tight grasp of small fingers on his wrist. It was Azvari; she said only one word, and he knew that it meant "friend." The man following them was making sure that they were not being followed before making contact. That was a tactic Simon understood. After three more blocks through a cacophony of animals, birds and people, they arrived at a tiny temple. The inside was almost completely dark, or so it seemed before their eyes adjusted from the blinding sunlight. It was also, thankfully, much cooler. An older man stepped out of the darkness and hugged Azvari. It was Ay! Next to him was Mr. Halib, who looked slightly tired but unharmed. Mr. Halib stared at Azvari with such intense interest that Simon had to take a second look. There was nothing new about Azvari to warrant Mr. Halib's curiosity, yet he glared at her with a mixture of fascination and hatred. "Ok, better watch him, and Ay is a part of this whole game too," thought Simon, as he watched Ay and Azvari talk. Ay's eyes betrayed his desire for Azvari, even when they were talking business. That Azvari did not share that desire was clear.

Simon thought of Azvari often. He had been intrigued from their first meeting and somehow he had ended up spending more time next to her than anyone else on the trip. Bailey was being attended to by Craig, and Craig liked to chat with Sahed. Mr. Halib had not even been around most of the time. Azvari's inner light, confidence and power fascinated Simon, and he felt drawn to her as steel to a giant magnet.

There are some who wish for their entire lives that they could be like Mother Theresa, or the Dalai Lama, or that they could simply be a good person, standing up for the ideals they subscribe to. But most people stop right at the wishing. It was so easy to say "well, I'm not Mother Theresa!" and have that statement become a convenient excuse for making a life for themselves in a cage, to lug comfortable furniture and pillows into that cage and live happily ever after, knowing that they could not be their ideal, so why bother trying. Then there are people who do what they can, and as often as they can, to match the ideal, to follow the light, to do good deeds. They know they are not perfect and they might never match the ideal, but at least they take every opportunity to attempt it. Simon was one of these; he knew he was not perfect by any means, but after Elona's, his wife's, death he had fallen into the "why bother" group, and he hated himself for it. If it had not been for Bailey, he might have stayed there. But he had recovered from that low point, and now he was the type who did what he could. Azvari... she actually was an ideal, a person to follow. She was bright eyed and awake, and she was not afraid, she was a leader. She was living the life he was striving to live: a life of "paying attention" and being on course.

They spent the whole day in the small temple, until the sun began to set and its orange rays permeated everything in sight. Simon acknowledged the sound decision of moving out at night. They, with the addition of Ay, Mr. Halib, and the young soldier Nakhtmin, who they had met earlier, made their way to the Temple of the Sphinx. There, horses awaited them. Soon they again took on the likeness of desert Bedouins, riding their beasts straight into the sunset. The desert beyond the pyramids was extensive. Not one structure in sight, only miles and miles of undulating dunes. As the sun set, they began to turn, eventually arriving at the well. It was just as they had left it – a mound of sand. Simon would have had a hard time recognizing it, but somehow the men knew. It was uncovered and opened in minutes. Bailey turned to Azvari and Azvari nodded her head – yes, she would go down into the well with them, since she had the locket of Sekhmet on her neck and they would need the key to initiate the opening of the doorway.

CHAPTER ELEVEN

Current time
Upstate NY, United States

One day was already over and the next one was beginning. Martin opened his eyes and stared at the clock – the bright red numbers showed 2:08AM. It was late morning in Cairo and he could not wait to call. No one had answered for a while, a whole day actually, and Martin was very worried. Luckily, Larisa had reminded him to take his pills – normally he would have ignored her, but he had been off his meds for too long and nothing was required of him for the moment. So for almost two days now Martin had been medicated. It made him feel paranoid, because he couldn't tell if everything was alright or if he was just not aware that something wasn't right. He had been calling Cairo once every hour, but no one picked up on Bailey's computer. She was either not there or someone else was in charge of the laptop. This was too depressing a thought, and Martin waved it away with a loud swear. That left only one other prospect – they had not yet returned. How could that be? Last time it took about four hours in his time, while they had a whole day on the other side of the well. But already a day had passed here. Did that mean they had been in ancient times for a month now? Martin was nervous, and probably would have gone mad with worry, were it not for his medication. Larisa was coming every day now, making sure he ate and slept. She seemed to have adopted him as a pet of sorts, making taking care of him a reason for her being. He paid her well and she had told him a while back that she couldn't take that much money for nothing, it was not how she was raised. And so she did what she considered would match the money he paid her – she essentially moved in, and washed, cleaned and cooked. Now she was also reminding him to take his medications. She could see that Martin was spiraling into something deep and probably unpleasant. He had worked intensely on projects before and those times had led him to some unstable behavior, but there had never been anything like this. Martin was absolutely sure of her loyalty. That was a new feeling...

There was still no answer on Bailey's laptop. Larisa walked in with a large cup of soup. It was his favorite, Martin absolutely loved that soup – he didn't know what was in that Ukrainian concoction, but it was phenomenal. Spoon after spoon, the warm liquid disappeared, and so did the vegetables and pieces of chicken. There was a loud beep – so sudden that Martin almost spilled the soup. The screen was alive with the square frame of a webcam, and Craig was looking at him. "Martin, are you there?" He could hear Bailey's voice in the background, "I told you, it's too early, we have to call later..."

It took a few seconds for Martin to recover from his surprise and answer.

What he was hearing was absolutely incredible! The Shenu, Akhenaten and Nefertiti, Amarna, and Azvari, a woman now... Oh, there were so many questions!

But soon Marty felt faint. "You did what? You let him go?" His voice exploded over the speakers. "No! No...." he wailed, "that was a mistake! Oh, dear god... no, he'll definitely come after you. Jesus, he'll imprison you – get out of there now!"

They had let Mahmoud Halib go! How could they? Why? What would stop that man from calling the police and saying that they had stolen property? Or worse, fabricate evidence against them!

1,338BC

Giza Plateau, Egypt

The Newcomers had departed. While Nakhtmin tied up the horses at the wharf Azvari approached Ay, touching his arm. To her surprise, his eyes showed anger.

"You have not been truthful with me, High Priestess!" he snapped.

"I am trying to be. You do not make it easy!" she snapped back.

"What do you mean? I always take your counsel..."

"There is a lot you should know, but you refuse to see Maat!"

"My sister betrayed the Shenu!" whispered Ay.

"She never betrayed Sekhmet!" Azvari whispered back forcefully.

"The Shenu is of Sekhmet!"

"Are you certain?"

"What? You knew! Tiye told Akhenaten and you knew! You probably even helped her..." Suddenly Ay sounded defeated as he looked into Azvari's almond eyes.

"Dear Ay... Tiye, may she have peace in eternity, wished to tell you. She believed you were not ready... She made me promise her that I would tell you when I saw that you were ready for Maat... And I believe you are ready now..."

Taking Azvari by the elbow, Ay pushed her in between the boats arranged on the wharf for repair. Checking to make sure that they were alone, he looked at her face expectantly.

"Sekhmet had you and Tiye bring the double *Ka* of the star-gods into human bodies. Akhenaten and Nefertiti are the 'One who is Two.' They are here to bring Maat forward. The only way for them to do so in the very short time allowed to them was to change what people believe. For that to happen, our pharaoh Akhenaten had to be introduced to the idea of one god, had to trust his vision in Aten, and our queen Nefertiti had to follow it…"

"You know for sure those two are… the 'One who is Two'?"

"Akhenaten's body is of Amenhotep and Tiye, and Nefertiti's is of yours and Sitamun's, your niece's blood, but you can see how unique they are – Nefertiti resembles Akhenaten, not you, and Akhenaten resembles Nefertiti. He does not have Tiye's short stature or Amenhotep's square jaw."

Ay sat down on one of the turned over boats, as if his knees had been bent by the weight of the truth. He knew that Tiye and he had twice been involved in a ritual. Both times it was because Sekhmet had wanted it, or that was what Tiye had said. Both times, Ay had drunk an herbal mixture. He didn't remember either of the occasions, only the fact that it had happened. He had raised Nefertiti, thus she felt like a daughter to him. But she carried nothing of him in her appearance, and neither did Akhenaten of his parents.

"I assumed you knew…" whispered Azvari, placing her warm hand on Ay's shoulder. "You were there after all…"

"You said 'One who is Two'?"

"Yes. One star-god chose to come into two bodies, each with unique qualities to support one another. They are the 'beginning of the beginning' as has been prophesized."

Nakhtmin had found them and Azvari waved to him to come closer. He slid between the boats.

"He knows too?!"

"He has known all along, Ay. He helped Tiye and myself."

"I trusted you…" Ay looked at Nakhtmin. He had thought of adopting the young soldier, son of a dear friend now passed to the Land of the Dead, the boy who had never known his mother.

"And you still can. Azvari is telling you the truth."

"The Newcomers brought another message from Sekhmet – *this cannot end prematurely*, she told them. And it will end – they revealed to us that the city of Akhet-Aten will fall…"

"What? They cannot know this! You cannot know this! This is preposterous!"

Nakhtmin suddenly reached forward and slid aside the cuff bracelet on Ay's arm. A beautiful girl in a Maat outfit, with 'beloved' inscribed under her feet, was revealed for the second time in a few hours.

"This is Azvari – I know it! It is from the time you asked for her heart and she told you she could not give it to you. Yet you still had this permanent image painted on your body – it is because she knows Maat! So follow your beloved now!"

Taking a deep breath, Ay lifted his face to Azvari – there were tears in his eyes.

"What does Sekhmet desire of me?" he whispered, looking into Azvari's eyes.

"You are an important man at the court and what you say to viziers will matter. You must support your daughter, your queen – Nefertiti is to become the co-regent of Akhenaten, and Meritaten is to take her place as the Great Royal Wife. It is already decided – I was there to witness it."

A wife as a co-regent to a *living* pharaoh? This was beyond heresy; it was impossible. The Shenu would never support it. Somehow Ay was to make them believe he was against the change, all the while helping his daughter? Could this even be done?

"Dear Ay, I know what you are thinking. We are both of the Shenu and we both have to pretend so as not to be discovered. I have no fear of letting go of this body in the name of Sekhmet, but I pray I will have enough time on this Earth to fulfill her will. And you must too! We have to protect Akhet-Aten."

"You just told me it will be destroyed – by the sickness I presume…"

"Yes, I guess so, although the Newcomers did not say. We have to protect the legacy, it has to remain."

"The Shenu will erase all traces of it as soon as it is possible," stated Ay with certainty.

"Yes, that is why we have to appoint another desert vault in a separate location, to hide what we can – for the future. But right now what matters is that Aten the Light does not fall prematurely."

Ay took a few deep breaths.

"I will do what Sekhmet asks of me."

CHAPTER TWELVE

Current time
Cleopatra Hotel, Cairo, Egypt

The events of the last few days had been intense and almost overwhelming. It was an incredible adventure, and Craig wasn't sure if he wanted it to keep unfolding, or to be over.

They decided to let Mr. Halib go. After all, why keep him? They would soon have to leave the country, and he would have to stay. Simon thought of keeping him prisoner as a tactical advantage – they could probably use him as insurance, to make sure nothing happened to prevent their going. But somehow that didn't seem right, and Craig felt that they should let him go. He had Bailey's support – perhaps being American tourists had something to do with it, but neither of them could envision keeping the undersecretary to the Supreme Council of Antiquities of Egypt tied and gagged for any length of time. Sahed was opposed to releasing him, but not intensely; he was sure he could disappear and stay safely hidden from Mr. Halib. Axil, to Craig's surprise, supported letting Mr. Halib go – he reasoned that Mr. Halib wouldn't be able to talk about most of what had happened, he wouldn't be able to find him or Sahed, and he already knew who Bailey and Craig were, so the decision, he thought, should be Bailey's and Craig's, and their choice depended on whether or not they felt safe letting him go.

And so, upon their arrival into current time, Mahmoud Halib was allowed to leave the taxi. Axil even went so far as to drop him in downtown Cairo where he would have easy access to other taxis so that he could get home. Back in their room, Craig sat on the bed and stared through the window. He was shaken by Marty's reaction. Craig had anticipated that he might not agree with them, but he hadn't expected such a passionate response. Bailey was curled up on the bed, asleep, her head covered with the blanket, and Craig knew that in her clenched hand she was holding the locket, afraid that it would disappear again. Simon was seated in the armchair, as before. Even asleep he looked as if he could be fully awake in a moment and ready for anything. Mr. Halib's gun had been confiscated by Axil and Sahed – just in case Mr. Halib decided to charge Craig and Bailey with possession of an illegal weapon.

Craig couldn't sleep. Cairo was alive, the sounds and smells of the city wafting in through the open window. They had decided to not turn on the AC because Bailey had been complaining that she was cold and shaking since they got out of the well.

He looked over at his bag – a part of his medicine bundle was sticking out of it. Somehow that little piece of cloth transfixed him, until finally he plucked it out. He thought that it felt heavier than before. He wanted to use it; the balcony seemed like a good place for a vision quest. As he quietly made his way through the room, he saw Simon open his eyes. He continued to the balcony door, and seeing his determination, Simon closed his eyes again.

It was almost chilly outside. The night should have been warm, and Craig was sure that it was. But his skin felt the wind, and the chill went straight through his spine. Resolute, he sat on the floor of the small balcony, his feet against the railing, and unwrapped his medicine bundle. He took a breath. The air was filled with spices and the scent of insect-repelling candles. He closed his eyes, not sure what he was looking for. Perhaps it was simply comfort he sought – there were so many feelings churning inside his being. Feeling the Cat's fur had always made Craig feel safe.

When Craig opened his eyes, he was in the woods next to a fir tree, with sounds of bird calls high above. He was back in his favorite forest. The Cat spirit guide came up from behind him, purring. Oh, Craig was so happy! Falling onto his side and rolling, with the Cat jumping over him, Craig found himself laughing. This was hope, this was peace, this was finally safety again!

He lay on his back and looked into the bright blue sky. A few perfect puffy white clouds floated in it, and through them a large bird plummeted into the forest. Craig turned his head in time to see that it was a hawk going after an unfortunate rodent. His eyes locked with Simon's – the Cat flopped to his side, displaying a white-orange belly.

"Do you think you are done?" Simon inquired.

"Yeah… I guess… I think I convinced Nefertiti to be a king. Oh, you should have seen it! I was so confident! I sounded like I knew what I was talking about!" Craig was so excited he sat up. He almost never felt confident, so it was definitely an event to mention!

"So, do you think you are done then?" repeated Simon.

"Ahh…" Suddenly Craig felt unstable. "You don't think so?" Caution was always a good strategy when talking with his spirit guide. Most of the time Craig had no idea what he was doing but it would be too embarrassing to let the Cat know that, and so he always made sure he fished around before he answered.

"Sekhmet wants to see you."

"Is she here?" asked Craig, quickly looking around.

"No, you odd child, she is not here! But she, for reasons beyond my comprehension, wants to see *you*. She says you are supposed to weave something… you know, that Soul Contract thing I mentioned earlier…"

Craig remembered that, alright. It had come up in a conversation he and Simon had had years ago, on Craig's third ever quest. He was told that he was a shaman, and he wanted to know what that meant. The Cat had answered, cryptically as usual, that he was meant to weave realities, that this was his Soul Contract. Craig had no idea what that meant, but he thought it might be embarrassing to ask, and so he had not.

"Sekhmet wants to meet me because I'm supposed to do something for her?"

"Not for her, for yourself. I told you before: everything you do is always for you first. If it's not, then it's not worth doing. All actions affect others, some more visibly than others. You people tend to only acknowledge the actions that you can see had an effect. If it was a positive one, you assume you did well, or you judge yourself for a negative outcome. But really, everything has some effect…" Simon stopped talking, busy biting at his side.

Craig bent over and scratched the Cat, who blissfully let go of his side and lay down again, stretching.

"Sekhmet wants you to do what you need to do for yourself, because it's what you decided that you needed to do before you got into that tall body of yours. She just wants you to do it sooner rather than later."

Noticing Craig staring at him with his mouth open, Simon added, "It's no biggy, it's not like it will save the world or anything… But it might help."

"How will I know what to do?" Craig was beginning to get nervous again. "How do I meet Sekhmet?"

"Well, this vision quest stuff is not really her thing… You need to go through the well."

"Go back?! We can't! We let Mr. Halib go, and without him we can't do it…" Oh, Craig was so disappointed with himself. The one time he needed to do something important, he screws it up by insisting on releasing the man who was half of the entry ticket!

"When the end comes, the key should be returned. After all, you people need to finally think and breathe for yourselves."

Craig was going to ask what that meant, but Simon was suddenly nowhere to be found. Getting up, Craig looked around, but that only ended the vision – and once again he was sitting on the balcony in Cairo.

When he walked back into the room, the laptop was beeping – Martin was trying to get in touch. Simon-the-man was already in front of the laptop answering the call.

CHAPTER THIRTEEN

Sixth-Dimension, Sirian Space
Sekhmet

T he light flows like a river, smooth and sparkling. Bright points shine brilliantly, punctuating the light – these are intersections of lines of consciousness, and they are filled with direction and desire. One of the points glows red-orange. It is Sekhmet. She has returned to her dimensional home, her Sirian anchor. Her golden cat-body is meditating; it sits like a statue in perfect stillness, staring into space. But the cat isn't looking at what is in front of her. She has opened a multidimensional window, and she is looking through it at Earth. All Sirian felines can create windows like this, but Sekhmet is half-feline. It had taken her eons of pain, sorrow, and misery to learn how to do it. The cat purrs quietly – she is free, she is home. Reality makes sense again, she feels no entrapment. Yet she cannot stop being curious or caring. She stares at the sister world of Earth, at the confused, asleep children who create war and suffering for themselves over and over again. They believed the imposters, and they forgot the star-beings... Sekhmet had let go of the children, but she couldn't let go of the vision: Maat is encoded in the very matrix of these children, therefore it can be awakened. It must be awakened! This is what prompted her to visit the Solar Council meeting, to put forward the idea of a repair for the Experiment. She was sure that a solution could be found, and she was not wrong! She purred louder, knowing her vision was true, rejoicing for the children of Earth.

Because she was outside of time, Sekhmet could open a dimensional window into any timeline. The key was to follow the one timeline that was anchored in matter and ignore all others that were not.

357

They all had equal value, were all equally real, yet only one was anchored in the form that lived the actual experience.

Sekhmet looked at Egypt, her beloved second home. The period of awakening had been such a tiny spark in time, a moment of clarity inside a black sea of unconsciousness. But it had happened; it had worked.

Sekhmet's female form shifted, aligning its vertical matrix with the portal the cat part of her had just opened. She found the girl with the red hair, and now she had to follow that timeline until the right moment. "Linear time can be so infuriating!" flared Sekhmet.

Finally the moment is right – the red-headed woman is in a white room, all alone. She is sitting at a table, drawing.

Sekhmet smiled. She had so much love in her heart for this woman – she would always think of her as a girl, the child she had tried to tell that her father was not the right match for the gate – Sekhmet had not wanted anyone harmed, but it had happened. The girl couldn't anchor the full energy of Sekhmet's message, and so she had never grown up. Now here she sat, drawing a large tree on a white piece of paper, her legs folded under her, her tongue sticking out, as she carefully made lines with a green crayon. "She looks older but she is the same child she was back then..." mused Sekhmet.

The female Sekhmet weaves gold with her fingers and soon there is a familiar lion mask in her hands. "It is so much easier this way," she smiles, remembering that in Earth's dimension someone would have had to make the mask for her. At first she had found it fascinating, not being able to create through intention, having to have matter shaped by someone else. But she had grown tired of it over time. Putting on the golden lioness mask, Sekhmet looked through the dimensional portal at Abigail.

Current Time, NY, United States
Abigail

This new room was very nice, and the soft blanket of deep red color was even better. And they let her draw all she wanted without asking her what her drawings meant! Abby was positively delighted. She had almost completed the picture of her favorite tree – the large one she had always seen outside her window in the other place, the tree around which she had seen the floating white figures the last time.

Engulfed in her drawing, Abby almost didn't notice that she was not really at the table in the white room anymore. She lifted her head and saw only the tall woman in the golden lioness mask. The woman just stood there, looking directly at Abby. Her amber eyes were warm and pretty, and Abby smiled. She felt no fear. She was about to show this pretty tall woman her drawing when she stopped herself, suspicious. "This is not really happening. This is a vision, but it's not happening…" Real visions only happened when she was off the medication. And she had faithfully been taking her little white pills since she had moved to this new house. But the tall woman was persistent, saying the same words over and over. When she placed her hand on Abby's shoulder, Abby knew she should pay attention. The hand felt hot, and Abby was not sure if she was in trouble now. She tried to concentrate on the tall woman's voice. "She must have come from very far away, I can barely hear her," thought Abby, as the tall woman dissolved and the room returned to normal around her. But she did hear. The words were less clear than when the tall white people who called themselves the Solar Council spoke, but they were clear enough. Abby understood alright!

She ran to the man in the white coat and told him she had to talk to her sister. Now!

*   *   *

"Bailey, are you there? Bailey?"

There was no camera where Abby was, so Simon and Craig were looking at Martin's frustrated face. Bailey had been woken up and was now sitting in front of the laptop.

"Yes, Abby, are you OK?"

"She came, Bailey, Sek-Met came! She told me, Bailey, she told me!"

"Is everything going to be OK?" Bailey surprised herself with the question – she must really believe that Abby is actually in communication with Sekhmet! Loud breathing came from the other side of the line as Abby collected herself in her excitement. Bailey took a breath herself, thinking. They had to get out of Egypt. They were too exhausted after the climb up from the well to catch a late flight back to the States and they wanted to spend the night in their beds, but they were fully expecting to be in the air in the morning. Did Abby know something? Would Mr. Halib try to stop them after all?

"I don't know," said Abby finally, sounding lost. "Are you OK? Bailey, are you?"

"Yes, yes, I'm just fine. Are you OK?"

"Yes, the room is so nice and I can think now! I remember so much and it's not scary at all!"

"Good, good... What did Sekhmet say to you?"

"She said that *as the guide joins the beloved, the key must be returned or people will always rely on it.* That's what she said."

"Whoa! We *have* to go back!" This was Craig's loud whisper behind her shoulder. Bailey turned and glared at him.

"What do you mean, go back? No way!"

"That's what Sekhmet means – return the key, meaning return the locket, and she can only do it if we go back into the well."

"Bailey, are you there? Who are those people talking? Do they also know Sek-Met?" Abby's voice sounded nervous.

"Yes, I'm right here. Tell me again... Sekhmet said we have to return the key?"

"She said *it has to be returned*," recited Abby diligently, "*so people stop relying on it.*"

The rest of the conversation went nowhere. There was nothing else to find out from Abby, and Bailey couldn't tell her where she was – she was afraid to worry her sister. Cutting the connection, Martin spoke up. "I'm afraid to say 'I told you so,' but you do have to go back, apparently. And somebody just let go of the means of getting there!"

"Forget that, how do we know when to go?" said Craig. "*As the guide joins the beloved...* what does that mean?"

"How should I know? You are the shaman, I'm told!" snapped Martin.

True, thought Craig, he was the shaman and he should be able to come up with an answer. Who could be the "guide"? The only guide they knew here was Sahed, but he was not joining anyone. The other options for a guide were Azvari, of course, and even Ay or Nakhtmin. But there was no way of knowing if any of them had joined their "beloved." Should they just go and see what happens?

There was a knock on the door. In a split second Simon was on high alert, standing sideways by the door. Craig asked, "Who is it?" From the other side of the door came the familiar voice of Axil Narmy. Letting him in, Simon checked the hallway. Axil did not look well...

"What happened?" asked Bailey, staring at Axil's ashen face.

"Sahed Ashi has joined his beloved wife in the afterlife..." breathed Axil, and lowered his body onto the chair.

"Oh my god!" whispered Bailey staring at him. "What did you just say?"

360

"Sahed passed on two hours ago. I just came from the house where his body rests."

"No, not that, you said he had *joined his beloved...?*"

"Yes, Sahed always talked about the day of his death as the time when he could finally join his beloved wife in the afterlife."

"We have to go back now!" interjected Craig.

"I am not crawling down that thing one more time! I just can't do it!" hissed Bailey, desperately staring at everybody. Yet even as she said the words she knew she would go back. She had to finish it.

CHAPTER FOURTEEN

1,321BC

Ay in Waset, Egypt

I t had happened. Ay had hoped that time would be good to them, but Anubis, the jackal-headed god of death, must have had other plans…

Ay was over seventy years of age now, yet well in health and vigor thanks to the Shenu secrets of regeneration. No one dared to oppose him at court – for someone to live this long, the gods must favor him! "What could Sekhmet want? This would not have occurred if she disagreed…" He smiled sadly.

He sat on a low gilded chair, lifting his gaze to face the messenger's terrified eyes. The other viziers looked on, trying to conceal their eagerness.

"Tell me how our pharaoh fares," commanded Ay.

"The pharaoh Tut-ankh-Amun, may he live in the love of Amun, is propped up on his bed. His fever fire has burned for three days now, and each day it burns hotter…"

"What do the royal doctors say?" inquired Ay. These were the doctors who three days ago he had himself sent to the desert camp where Tut-ankh-Amun lay feverish, coughing and spitting blood, his broken leg turning from red to purple to black. He was not yet nineteen years old.

"The maggots live in the pharaoh's leg, but they are not strong enough to eat up the sickness. The fire burns hotter, so the royal doctors have been applying salt to the pharaoh's skin…"

The messenger did not speak again, confirming by his silence the negative result of the new treatment. A buzz of whispering erupted amongst the viziers. Ay stood up, grasping his ornate cane, and stormed out of the room, glaring as he made his way past the viziers. Their faces registered confusion – Grand Vizier Ay had always been their ally, so why was he angry now?

"I'd better keep my temper to myself and Sekhmet!" whispered Ay under his breath. "I must keep their support!

Despite the cane Ay moved swiftly through the Malkata Palace to the empty Festival Hall. The doors were silently opened for him, and then closed behind him. He stepped out onto the Hall's balcony, taking a deep breath of fresh Nile air and grasping the stone railing tightly until his fingers hurt. Slowly, slowly, he forced himself to loosen his grip. This was a disaster! He had done all he could to follow the path Sekhmet had laid out for him, risking his life many times over to do it – and he thought he had done well. Oh, he had been so successful: he had returned Egypt to its gods – the false gods! Ay slammed his fist hard into the railing – so hard that the stone made a gash in his ring. The pain was helpful; now he could focus. He rubbed his hand, thinking.

"I am too old for this, Sekhmet, too old! Find someone else!" He thought the words but he knew he didn't mean them. He would do all he could to secure what had to be.

Malkata Palace was vast, and the balcony overlooking the artificial Nile-water lake spanned its entire east side. Staring into the waters, Ay took another deep breath. He was not sure how to deal with this problem. He was a master problem-solver, but this problem might just prove too much for him. If the pharaoh died there would be an empty space in the court, a space that Horemheb would surely fill. And this could not be allowed!

The sun shone brightly as usual. In the distance he could see farmers in small boats overflowing with emmer wheat and other goods on their way to the Temple of Amun in central Waset just a few harbors away, not knowing the fate of their young pharaoh but praying to the gods for his health.

Ay massaged his hand... Oh, he was not even sure if Nefertiti, his beloved daughter, had known the whole truth while she was walking the earth. He suspected that even though she was not part of the Shenu, Akhenaten had told her enough. "And if he didn't tell her, she was intelligent enough to figure it out..." Ay smiled again, this time with satisfaction.

Ay hated that the gods had taken his magnificent Nefertiti into the afterlife before him – no father should outlive his daughter! After the Newcomers left, Nefertiti became bolder. She was unafraid politically and in spirit, as if she felt the power of Sekhmet behind her propelling her actions forward with passion and conviction. That same year, the fourteenth of his reign, Akhenaten made her his co-regent – a very bold move indeed. She took the name Ankhetkheperu-Ra Neferneferu-Aten, adding Ra to her new name to pacify the populace who were in an uproar because they believed that Aten had failed to protect them from the plague. Her own name, Nefertiti, was never mentioned again. Promoting Meritaten into the position of the Royal Chief Wife to take her place, she was free to rule, equal to the pharaoh in all matters, when Akhenaten became ill. "Meritaten's beauty distracted the priests, while Nefertiti ran Egypt! The priests were more lustful than they were willing to admit," smiled Ay. "Meritaten served as the legal official consort to the ailing Akhenaten and she did her job well – who would dare to challenge a 'divine marriage?'" smiled Ay. "They knew it wouldn't be wise to stand in Nefertiti's way." Ay liked his granddaughter Meritaten, but she had a mind of her own and he secretly distrusted her – she had a stronger allegiance to her mother than to Egypt! In some ways that was good, and in other ways bad...

Nefertiti went further still. When Akhenaten died and the next pharaoh had to be named, she knew she didn't have enough support to become one herself, and Tut-ankh-Aten, whom she had trained, was too young. So Nefertiti made an even bolder move, one that the priests didn't expect – oh, his daughter was so wise! – she supported Smenkhkare's rise into the position of pharaoh! As the heir to Amenhotep III, he had a legitimate claim, and he despised Aten. The priests of Waset, those from the temples of Amun and other gods, loved him – this stubborn, narrow-minded boy-man. He knew nothing of the real world, only what had been presented to him by the priests, and his mind had been manipulated. He took the male version of Nefertiti's regent-name, calling himself Ankhkheperu-Ra Smenkhkare. Meritaten had been maneuvered into the position of Smenkhkare's Great Royal Wife after his first wife died, and Ankhesenpaaten was married to Akhenaten instead. As Smenkhkare's wife Meritaten had access to his most private thoughts and decisions, and she faithfully reported everything to Nefertiti. "That boy lasted only seven months as a pharaoh, even with the help of all the priests of Egypt!" spat Ay. He had never liked Smenkhkare – he was immature and sheltered, and he didn't have the core power required to rule Egypt.

Singing rose up to Ay from the felucca boats, and turned his thoughts to Mutnodjmet, Singer of Hathor and priestess of Amun, a mature woman of thirty-two years who knew Maat. He felt proud of Mutnodjmet too. She was his younger daughter, Nefertiti's half-sister. She was pure in spirit, and Ay loved her dearly. She was married to Nakhtmin, Ay's adopted son and trusted advisor – a man she loved and who loved her more than the land of Egypt! But another man circled Mutnodjmet like a vulture – Horemheb. Horemheb, the high general of the pharaoh's army, coveted Mutnodjmet. She wasn't interested in him, and Nakhtmin, a general under Horemheb, appeared to ignore the situation. Horemheb, a commoner by birth, had become the Adviser to Pharaoh, almost equal to Ay himself. Ay smiled silently. He knew that Horemheb was not really his equal, not by any real measure. Ay was an excellent politician and a great vizier. He had been in the court for his entire long life, starting from Amenhotep III and going through the reigns of Akhenaten, Smenkhkare, Nefertiti, and now Tut-ankh-Amun. No, Horemheb was no match. He was an ambitious and brilliant man – Ay himself had helped his rise by praising him over and over to Tut-ankh-Amun. Horemheb's negotiations in Nubia had made him a legend, had made him prominent enough, he seemed to hope, for Mutnodjmet to notice. Ay was sure that the entire campaign had been orchestrated to show off in front of his daughter – Horemheb kept forgetting she was married! She was faithful to her husband. Horemheb had no chance.

But Ay had not known then what he knew now. Back then he was not even sure if following Aten was the correct way for Egypt – dismissing all the other gods seemed odd to him, if not heretical. But once Azvari revealed that this was the will of Sekhmet, he had understood the mission – to perpetuate Aten. That was why he had not understood it when Nefertiti took Smenkhkare as a co-regent and allowed him to publicly dismiss Aten! She herself accommodated the Amun priests in small things, but Smenkhkare, directed by these priests, was never seen in the Aten temple after Akhenaten's death. Ay had no special love for Aten, but if Sekhmet wanted Aten, how could his daughter ignore Sekhmet's wishes? But the end was meant to come. His role, it seemed, was to make that end graceful and peaceful. Ay was not sure he could do it, but if Sekhmet was on his side, who could stop him?

The day Smenkhkare died, Nefertiti proclaimed she would not take a husband or have another co-regent, instead placing Meritaten once again by her side. Oh, his daughter was nothing if not daring! "Meritaten does not have a living child by Smenkhkare, but we must prevent the end from coming prematurely!" she had told her father in the back recesses of the temple, while the priests were confirming that the body of Smenkhkare was cold. Nefertiti remained Ankhetkheperu-Ra Neferneferu-Aten. There was no opposition – the priests were still in shock from all the events of the last year and thrown into confusion by Nefertiti's action. Nefertiti, who had supported Smenkhkare, her opposer in faith, had now claimed the throne, and in the name of Aten? Ay did all he could politically to secure his daughter's power. Oh, he had lived such a long life, so much had happened! "Sekhmet, I am too old! Let me go!" he whispered passionately. There was no answer, only the calls of birds carried on the Nile breeze...

Ay thought back to the time when Tut-ankh-Aten turned nine. Many were not sure he would be allowed by the gods to walk on this earth for much longer, but year after year the boy lived. His weak constitution and recurrent sickness prevented him from military training, with the exception of archery, and he made little progress in his studies. Nefertiti had already ruled as a single power for two years by then, with Meritaten as her official consort, but the boy had finally come of age. She probably could have made him a co-regent to her, but Ay knew his daughter was spent. After all she fulfilled her duty to Sekhmet, and she had groomed the boy correctly. He was the son of Smenkhkare and his first wife, Akhenaten's sister, and so, being the grandchild of Amenhotep III, he was a legitimate heir. The Amun priests supported Tut-ankh-Aten to the throne, loving the fact that he was not related directly to Akhenaten and Nefertiti, who had only had daughters. Aten of the Light was too much for the uneducated population, and nothing could erase the memory of the plague that ravaged Akhet-Aten. The end was coming, and the old gods of Egypt, true or not, had to return. The nine-year-old boy-pharaoh needed guidance, of course... and so Nefertiti, in her eternal wisdom, provided that guidance yet again.

"That little child had no idea what he should do!" thought Ay with frustration. "All he wanted to do then was play, just as he does now... and it has brought him near death!" It was too late for second thoughts; what was done was done.

Ay smiled sadly, looking at the large boat passing under him. It belonged to one of the viziers and was carrying cattle to the Temple of Amun, to sacrifice for the sake of the pharaoh's health. The whole of Egypt was concerned – their "god" might soon be taken by Anubis.

The path Ay walked was narrow. He had to be very careful! When, many years ago, Azvari had told him the Newcomer's message, he almost didn't believe it. But all the signs were there, and over time Ay

366

saw Maat. If Sekhmet herself did not want this to end prematurely, who were they to oppose her? This meant that Ay was forced to betray the Shenu! Many long nights were spent in front of the Sekhmet statue, as he attempted to talk to the true goddess, asking her for guidance. The goddess gave no further directions. Tiye, Azvari and Nakhtmin – his sister, his beloved and his adopted son – had betrayed the Shenu. The Shenu didn't know that the pharaoh and his wife were designed by Sekhmet herself to circumvent the Shenu's power of gold deben and dusty leather-bound scrolls. Tiye said the prophecy was fulfilled when the Newcomers came, signifying to her that it was not Thutmose, but her second son, who must become the pharaoh of Egypt. And so it was – Akhenaten and Nefertiti, divine children who barely resembled their parents, ran Egypt. Those two managed to alienate the entire pantheon of Egyptian gods. "No pharaoh can rule on his own!" Ay had raged back then. "Without the Amun priest's gold, you mean?" Tiye retorted to him. Ay was speechless at first, so infuriated he was with his sister. "If the priests of Amun fall, so will many wealthy men who control Egypt! He cannot do this!" "My son thinks he can," was her answer, said in a quiet, calm tone. The next day Akhenaten announced his plans to move the seat of power out of Waset to his new city Akhet-Aten. Without Waset there was no priesthood! The power of the priests had been effectively erased by moving the capital to Akhet-Aten. Ay had had many doubts back then...

Current Time

Cairo, Egypt

Mahmoud was sweating as he exited the lecture hall. There was really no reason for it, the venue was a five-star hotel and the AC was functioning just fine. Yet the sweat poured off him. He suspected the cause – terror. When the Americans had allowed him to leave, he immediately took a taxi home. The first thing he did when he got there was shower. The second thing was finish what was left in a bottle of scotch. He was exhausted on many levels but even with the help of whisky sleep was not forthcoming – how many nights now had he gone without rest? His social calendar was overflowing; his secretary had called his house twice, which was unheard of – she must have been really worried. Mahmoud called his office, explaining that he had "phone difficulties." Apparently he was booked for a lecture, to be video-recorded, the next day. He agreed to keep the commitment – diving back into his normal life might make him feel normal again.

He was wrong; the diversion did not bring a feeling of normality. He had pushed himself to focus on his presentation and it had not been a complete disaster – at least he could ask to have the errors cut out of the recording later. If only other things could be so easily erased!

Finding his car in the parking lot, he got in and locked the doors in an attempt to feel safe. But instead his cell phone beeped, and when he saw the number his worst fear was confirmed. It was a coded text from the Shenu – they were asking him what progress he had made on the situation.

"Progress? Not only did I allow the Americans to get into the well, I was transported into the past, twice! I saw the people of the Shenu and the royals of the time. And I was told by Sekhmet to follow that woman Azvari, who I know betrayed the Shenu, and Ay, who probably did too!" he whispered. "What am I going to do?!"

He had nothing to report – so far he was actively avoiding dealing with everything that had happened. Like a man in a trance he went through the motions of his life, afraid to face all that had happened. Was he being asked to betray the Shenu? "Who am I kidding? I already did by not keeping them informed!" He had been proud to be part of the Shenu, one of the few who knew and protected the truth. But what was the truth? Unable to make himself go home he drove to his office, where at least there were stacks of work to occupy him. The building was still open, visiting hours would be over in only half an hour. Lying that he had forgotten something, he raced into his waiting room. He was not prepared for what he saw there. Three people were sitting in the chairs, awaiting his arrival – the older British man and the Americans!

"No…" moaned Mahmoud.

"Mr. Halib, we need to talk to you," said Craig, jumping up from the chair and coming towards him.

"You are preposterous monsters! You do not know what you are doing!" exploded Mahmoud, but noticing the stares of his coworkers lowered his voice. "Darkness will come, and it will consume us all!" He walked into his office, and they followed him. Mahmoud closed the door. Now what?

"There's no point in complaining about the dark, if one refuses to do anything to turn on the Light, is there?" said the older man.

"What do you want of me?" asked Mr. Halib, defeated.

"We have to go back, Mr. Halib," said the young man, looking intently into his eyes. There was no question in his stare and Mahmoud knew this was not a request as soon as he switched his gaze to the older man. His eyes betrayed no worry, he was calm and in control. What was Mahmoud to do? Of course he could have these three arrested, but that would hardly play in his favor. Before he could think the answer shot out of his mouth: "OK, we will go."

"Great!" said the younger man, pumping the air with a celebratory fist. The red-headed Bailey woman and the older man didn't seem as convinced that there was reason to rejoice, and they were silent. Soon the younger man quieted himself, and silence filled the room.

Mahmoud sat down behind his desk – the familiar position made him feel somewhat in control. But his thoughts were still playing hide and seek. He had successfully avoided dealing with the events of the past few days, but now both evils were knocking at his door – the Shenu required an answer and these people were asking him to go back! *Follow the beloved… do not stray from Maat…* Oh, he knew he had to go, there was no question. Did this mean that he himself was the traitor? Mahmoud could not believe that. Yet he was the only member of the Shenu he knew of who had experienced anything like this. What did it mean? "Would they even believe me if I told them I went *through* the time-gate? Back in time?!" Mahmoud intuitively knew the answer – they would not. It was one thing to have all this happen before the age of the Internet and psychiatrists, when people like his father were more likely to trust that time travel was real. But now? The men of the Shenu would certainly not believe him. He had no proof – no other Shenu member had witnessed his travels, and he had brought no artifacts. It would be his word against established reality – and he would surely lose! "Oh, Sekhmet, why did you bring this into my life?"

"Because you are the chosen one," said the older man, as if mocking him. Being so tired, Mahmoud had not realized he had spoken the last words out loud, much less in English. The man was right – he was the chosen one, and it was time to face his destiny.

"When do we go?" he asked with resolve, looking at the woman's freckled face.

"Now," replied the younger man. "We got another message from Sekhmet…" he added in a whisper.

1,321 BC
Waset, Egypt

When he felt the hand on his shoulder, Ay flinched. He immediately relaxed once he realized who it was – Ankhesen-Amun, the current Great Royal Wife. She was still beautiful at twenty-six years of age, despite the pain of having two daughters born without breath. Ay smiled as he took her hand. Her eyes were red from crying. Since news of her husband arrived three days ago she had been worrying about the man whose health only seemed to get worse and worse. "She has aged a year in a few days," thought Ay. "Perhaps she does love him…" It was hard for Ay to believe that. Nefertiti had groomed her daughter, Ankhesenpaaten, to marry the future king, and when the girl was seventeen she was given in royal marriage to the new pharaoh Tut-ankh-Aten, right at his coronation ceremony – why waste the flowers? Her mother had raised her well. The princess understood the need to secure the throne, and marrying the pharaoh was a sure way to do it – even if the pharaoh was a nine-year-old child. Age didn't matter – in the eyes of the public he was a god, and the eyes of the public always had to be shielded from Maat, because they would be blinded if they saw it. To Ankhesenpaaten, the boy was simply useful. She cared for him, playing with him and sharpening her skill in archery for hours every day. But she also cared for her studies while he did not. Ankhesenpaaten wanted to be awake; she was the true daughter of Aten the Light, while her young husband cared only for games and entertainments. "All this name-changing…" thought Ay, looking at Ankhesen-Amun's face and holding her hand. "In the second year of Tut-ankh-Aten's reign, Nefertiti knew she was soon to leave this Earthly world. To secure her daughter's future, she had to secure the position of the pharaoh. And so she reinstated the gods of Egypt and reopened the closed temples. She supported the priesthood's overwhelming plea to change the pharaoh's name from Tut-ankh-Aten to Tut-ankh-Amun, and then of course Ankhesenpaaten became Ankhesen-Amun. It was a good move, and Ay congratulated his daughter in her wisdom. They were finally able to move back to Waset, leaving Akhet-Aten to lay barren in the desert…"

"What will happen to Egypt if Anubis claims my husband?" she whispered.

Ay thought for a moment. Was this the time to end the reign of Aten, the perceived heresy? Or did Sekhmet demand more of him? How could he know? He could only try to continue favoring at least some of Aten's priests. If that was not what Sekhmet desired, it wouldn't work anyway... "And what is my life in the balance of human history?" Out loud he said, "Dear child, my beloved granddaughter, what do you want?"

"I want my king to rise and be well," she answered immediately, but Ay could see that this was only the appropriate answer. He squeezed her hand, looking into her eyes.

"I want to continue the path laid out to me by my mother. I believe Aten should not be forgotten..." she whispered, conviction in her eyes. Ay knew right then what he needed to do. This child understood the direction of history.

Servants ran through the gallery, shouting. Ankhesen-Amun jumped up, ready to run back to the Audience Chamber – a new messenger had come with news of her husband.

She looked back at Ay for permission, and he waved her to go ahead. She needed to run, and so she did, while Ay slowly began to walk in the same direction. There was nothing to rush for – he knew what he would find at the Audience Chamber. The messenger would tell them that the pharaoh had passed to the Land of the Dead. It was his leg, Ay knew. That leg was not favored by the gods from the beginning, his limping became a fashion statement at the court – everyone had carried now a beautiful staff and wore sandals with backstraps. The boy had had too much recklessness in him, without cool reason to balance it. "His head was as hot as his heart, there was no thinking!" Ay muttered to himself as he limped through the gallery. Three days ago Tut-ankh-Amun's chariot tipped over at full speed during another race, or hunt, or whatever the youths did these days... Tut-ankh-Amun was taken back to the oasis camp immediately, but he was badly bruised, his head swollen, his leg broken, and they were a full three days' walk away from the palace at Waset. He could not be moved. He was laid at the camp, general Horemheb at his side. Horemheb had been on the same hunt, proud of the respect the young pharaoh had shown him by including him. So while Horemheb was stuck with the dying pharaoh, sending messengers to Waset, Ay had sent the royal doctors to the camp. The bruises began to heal, but the leg did not.

Ay had spent the last nine years, all the years of Tut-ankh-Amun's reign, protecting his person and his soul. "Yet it was not an enemy from inside Egypt, or from foreign lands, but this boy's own stupidity that killed him!" spat Ay as he limped towards the royal chamber.

Current time
Giza Plateau, Egypt

Unsure of what to think of the ease of the present circumstances, Bailey sat silently in Mahmoud's black Mercedes. Axil had gone to attend to Sahed' funeral, while she, Craig, and Simon had returned to Mr. Halib's office at the Council of Antiquities. She was sure now that going back was the correct course of action – an internal current was sweeping her in that direction. Bailey had no logical explanation for what she felt. The truth was, she had changed. The lights of Cairo sped past her window, or was it Giza? Her clients, her practice in the States, seemed so far away and so irrelevant considering the events of the last few days. How could she ever return to that life? Would she die in this last attempt to travel back in time? This was an odd thought and no matter what state she was in, she had to analyze it. "Die? Why would I die?" She soon attributed this thought to the change – the part of her who had fueled the therapist had died, and that was why she was not sure if she could ever return to her practice. Her ability to analyze people had always been based on the stability of her comprehension of herself – her abandonment by her parents by their deaths, her resentment towards their "irresponsible" behavior, her own sense of inner justice and responsibility towards her mentally ill sister... It was all a lie. "Nice" mommy was bitchy and mistrustful of her husband, the "selfish" daddy had been following the path laid out by an ancient star-being, or alien, and her "paranoid" sister was actually in contact with that very star-being. Oh, Bailey knew she could not go back. If she did, her practice would have to look different. Could she do it? This was not the life she had signed up for! Or was it? She had this nagging feeling that somehow this had all been her own design. If nothing else she was a smart person, and this mess smelled like something she would come up with – so multifaceted and complicated! Bailey always complicated things, overthought and overanalyzed them – it had always been her way of coping. And now? Try to analyze going back in time and meeting an Egyptian pharaoh! She smiled to herself – she was amazed at her own calmness. This inner peace was highly inappropriate from her mind's perspective, yet she knew she was OK. Somehow the peace was true and the mental alarm was false. "I must be developing this thing Craig calls a soul..." she mused. It made sense: the soul was the cause of this peace and illogical knowing, while her mind was more of a past-referencing mechanism – unable to make sense of events, it sounded an alarm.

372

The lights of the city were moving farther away. "We must be coming close to the site now," she thought. No one had said a word during the drive. She tore her gaze away from the window and looked at the others. Mr. Halib was grasping the wheel tightly and silently; Simon rode in front, carefully watching Mr. Halib drive. Craig sat next to her on the back seat, staring out the opposite window. The only sound was Mr. Halib's heavy breathing.

1,321BC

Waset, Egypt

Tut-ankh-Amun had passed to the Land of the Dead. The whole of Egypt would soon be in mourning for its young pharaoh, but Ay had other concerns. Pharaohs were seen to be directly descended from the gods, and people assumed that the gods gave him special powers that enabled him to maintain the cosmic order of Earth. Ay had always thought this to be preposterous. As a Shenu he knew about other empires, those from the past and of incredible power; he knew of other kings and queens, and even "circles of elders" who ruled their lands. Ay knew Egypt's role in the history of Earth, and it was no more and no less than it was. Believing the pharaoh to be the "cosmic ruler" seemed almost equal to a mockery. Yet this was what people believed, and they could not be disappointed. The politician in Ay knew that their views could be changed, but they could not be re-directed too abruptly or they cease following the shepherd… Upon the death of the reigning pharaoh his successor had to be named immediately, so that the world's cosmic order and the protection of the gods would continue unbroken.

Horemheb had been named heir to the throne because Tut-ankh-Amun could not have foreseen that Ay would outlive him. After Nefertiti's death Ay became the pharoah's most trusted advisor, but he was also over seventy years of age. Horemheb was the High General; he commanded the army, he had the support of the soldiers and the priests, and he had the official seal of *idnawu*, the Deputy of the Lord of Egypt under its pharaoh – Tut-ankh-Amun himself had given him the seal, making Horemheb his successor. Horemheb had even planned to make Mutnodjmet, Ay's daughter, his Chief Wife. The fact that she was still married to Nakhtmin did not seem important in his scheme. He had positioned himself well. "What have I done?" whispered Ay, once he realized the situation that he had helped create. The last thing he had assumed was that this ignorant child-king would get himself killed so soon! But what was done, was done. Horemheb could not be king, not yet anyway, no matter what his level of legitimacy. Like Ay, Horemheb was a commoner, he was not of royal blood. Ay had himself promoted the man again and again, believing him to be worthy of political power. Yet Horemheb was not Shenu and he did not see Maat – that could not be ignored!

Ay stopped to take a deep breath and think. Once he stepped into the Audience Chamber where all the viziers and priests waited, there would be no turning back – he had to know what to do *now!* He knew two things: Horemheb could not be allowed to claim the throne; and Horemheb was three days walk away with the deceased pharaoh in the desert hunting camp – he was not here in Waset!

When Ay entered the Audience Chamber, everyone's eyes turned to him.

"Speak" he commanded the messenger, although he could read the news from his face.

"Tut-ankh-Amun, may his heart be light and may Anubis guide him, has passed to the Land of the Dead. His Ka is free, awaiting the judgment of his heart, weighing it on the scales of Maat against the feather..."

Ay had to act before the messenger said anything else. He spoke. "We will not abandon Egypt to turmoil, it will be protected by the new pharaoh. I am the chosen one by the young pharaoh and the viziers, the priests of Waset temples support me. I claim the throne of Egypt."

There was a moment of silence but Ay stood, waiting. He knew that they had to think and that was why there was no action. The worst that could happen was that he would be killed on the spot. But he doubted he would be slain. He knew that everyone was aware that the royal seal of *idnawu* had been given to Horemheb, and that was why they were shocked at Ay's announcement. But the viziers trusted Ay; he was a known commodity, while Horemheb was younger and uncertain. The Amun priests liked Horemheb because he had wanted to give all the power back to them, to dismantle Aten's temples. "If it was up to him, Akhenaten would *not* be remembered!" Ay often thought. But the priests were also afraid of change and they had known Ay for over twenty-five years. He was also old, and they could assume he would not be able to change too many things in the time left to him. This was probably Ay's riskiest move yet, but he glared at their faces as if he had the power of Sekhmet behind him. In truth he was not sure if he had, but his reasoning stood – if it was her will, it would be done; if not, then it did not matter.

The High Priest of Amun came towards Ay and fell to the floor, saying the words proclaiming Ay the next pharaoh of Egypt. Then all the priests and viziers did the same, and all the noblewomen in the room followed.

After speaking the appropriate words, Ay walked out of the room – he needed to leave, to return his thoughts to order. As he walked to his private chamber through the Malkata Palace, a wave of whispers followed him – the servants were relaying the news: the young pharaoh had been taken by Anubis, Ay is the next pharaoh, he will be crowned in the spring, seventy days from now…

Storming into his private chamber, Ay collapsed onto the large armchair and summoned Ankhesen-Amun – in the Audience Chamber he had watched her face when the messenger was relaying the news of her husband's death. She was hurt and she needed to grieve, but Ay knew she was strong and would be able to focus – he needed her to.

Ankhesen-Amun rushed into the room "You wanted to see me, grandfather Ay?"

"Yes, my dear, we have much to discuss…"

Ay dismissed all the servants and gestured to her to sit next to him. He had nothing to lose, he would have to trust Ankhesen-Amun. She was Nefertiti's daughter after all, groomed to have the proper vision. If she betrayed him, he might have to have her killed, but he hoped it would not come to that. He had to risk it; he had no other choice. He told her about the true star-gods, the true meaning of the god Aten and what her parents really did, politically and spiritually. Ay revealed the secrets – not all of them of course, and he did not mention the Shenu.

"I see no other course of action, my grandfather Ay," said Ankhesen-Amun with resolve. "You must marry me."

Ay looked at her and exhaled – he had not realized he was holding his breath. The girl was the inheritor of her parents and, if she continued this way, she would become the inheritor of the Shenu's secrets as well.

"Please say something, grandfather Ay! Please see the meaning in my words! You must marry me – I am a widow now, but being my husband will secure your position as heir to the throne in the eyes of the people!"

"Yes, my dear granddaughter, we must set up the royal wedding so that it happens as soon as the burial rites are completed in the spring, at the time of my coronation. Horemheb should not be given the chance to oppose me."

"He will in time…"

"I do not have a lot of time left to me, Anubis sleeps at my doorstep… But if Sekhmet will allow me only a few more years, I can serve her well, I can secure the future!"

Current Time

Upstate NY, United States

Sitting on the bed, Martin closed his eyes. Larisa's hands felt wonderful on his shoulders. She stood behind him on the bed, her knees bent, massaging his aching neck. Martin could obviously afford any masseuse he wanted, but he had never trusted anyone to touch him, professionals included. Even his doctor came to visit him at his house, for a generous donation to his medical practice, of course.

Larisa was not a professional but she was trustworthy. And there was something else… Martin found himself actually enjoying having her hands on his neck. That was surprising, because Martin didn't enjoy anything besides math. Larisa was that one complicated equation Martin couldn't figure out. She cared. He had tried to trick her many times into revealing her "true nature," convincing himself that she cared because she was paid to care. But Larisa did not seem susceptible to tricks. Also, she didn't pity him. Martin could not stand pity; he despised it when people were nice to him simply because he was a cripple. That was one of the reasons he had stopped going out in public – he felt people were secretly laughing at him, while politely assisting him out of pity. His psychiatrist, of course, diagnosed these thoughts as paranoid fantasies stemming from his initial insecurities, and exacerbated by his car accident. Martin's answer to this was the creation of the fortress he called home. Larisa came into his life much later, and she did not pity Martin. She admired him in a way, respected him, and cared for him, almost like a mother would. Strange that although she was close in age to his fifty-six years, Martin often felt she was so much more mature when it came to practical matters! He could always play the genius card, of course, and money helped him to be seen as eccentric instead of nuts. But the truth was that Martin Shwabster was disabled, terrified, and very alone. Somehow Larisa's presence always helped him. Their banter over food or

376

security measures could go on for hours and Martin secretly treasured those moments. Those were the only times he felt somewhat normal.

He moaned, immediately stopping himself.

"Good?" asked Larisa.

"Yes, thanks," mumbled Martin and prepared to transfer himself to the chair. He was embarrassed that he had let go his control. Larisa simply moved the wheelchair closer towards him. Then he asked, looking at the floor: "Why are you here?"

"You need help," she answered simply. Martin loved her simple answers – it could be because English was not her first language, or just a sign of her character. He could talk enough for both of them; it was nice to have this simplicity.

"But I did not ask you to come, remember, you are on vacation, Larisa," pushed Martin. She had been coming every day since she realized that he was not taking care of himself. But she also stayed much longer, hours at a time, late into the evening and sometimes through the morning, quietly sitting on the sofa, reading a magazine, while he worked on his computer.

"You need help," repeated Larisa. She smiled, looking at him, and patted his shoulder. She had never done that before. Martin felt himself blush – luckily the room was somewhat dark, the only lights were the monitor and a small table lamp.

"Ehh... Mmm... Maybe you would like to stay?" Martin heard himself say. He was so scared that he was not sure if those words had come from him, yet he knew he said them.

"You not feel good? You need something?" for a moment Larisa sounded worried.

"No, I'm fine." He was about to dismiss the whole thing, glad she had not understood him, when she spoke again.

"But I will stay. You don't have to be alone," and she smiled, again gently touching his shoulder.

"Ok, that's good, glad we figured that out, whew!" Martin could not stop talking, any change always created so much anxiety in him. "I have that other bedroom, it's just a room, I'll get a bed and some other things for you – no, you get them, I'll give you my card, just go and pick what you want and have them deliver..." Martin stopped, realizing that this meant people would be coming into his house in large numbers.

"There is a bed in that room, it is fine," replied Larisa. "But if it's OK, I will change the curtains..."

"Of course, anything!" Martin actually felt happy. This whole time he had been worrying about being excluded from the events in

Egypt. Bailey was going into that damn well again, she was going back into the past! Oh, Martin would have given anything to be able to go himself, but the thought of sitting on the plane next to strangers, or the dust in the well itself, never mind being carried, immediately discouraged him. Thanks to the talkative Craig, Marty was privy to all the little details of their travels: the people, the events, the environment. "That is enough," Marty told himself. It had to be. He knew there was no way he could get over himself and go – he would have a nervous breakdown and end up in a hospital, which would surely kill him! And so he watched from the sidelines, terrified to be dismissed, trying to make himself irreplaceable. Almost a week ago Martin had been so riled up that he told Larisa the whole story – he was surprised she believed him, instead of thinking it was one of his paranoid delusions. She was a good listener and a way better helper than his psychiatrist ever was! She had even pointed out that he only gave Bailey the money so she would need him. He knew Larisa was right. But it didn't matter, it was better than not having access to Bailey at all! The last few days had been insane, and Martin was so nervous and exhausted that having Larisa with him was a blessing. And he had just asked her to stay...

"A hug?" He heard Larisa's voice, and then what she said, and before Martin could reply, she hugged him. He found his own arms wrapped around her as she held him. When she finally let go, there were tears in Martin's eyes. He knew she saw it, but she didn't comment, just politely proceeded to help him off the bed and into the wheelchair. "She is perfect..." thought Martin, trying not to sob.

1,321BC
Coronation at Waset, Egypt

Only seventy days had passed since the death of the young pharaoh, but the whole of Egypt was in a different mood. The royal barge had brought Tut-ankh-Amun, his body bathed in resin and perfumed oils, to join his Ka on the west bank of the Nile. Once the judgment was done, his body would rejoin his soul so he could step into the Afterlife with all his wealth and wisdom. "Not much of the second, I am afraid..." thought Ay as the royal crown was fitted to his head. He stood rigidly upright, his hand on an ornate cane. At this crucial moment he couldn't show any weakness, so he would have to walk out onto the balcony of Malkata Palace without the cane. He could hear the crowd roaring outside, the loud voices of singers and announcers rising above it. Bright sunlight spilled into the room – the sun was getting high, they better get on with it! A mild obstacle in the course of the coronation proceedings was the damned cane – instead of him walking the whole way back from the temple where he was crowned as the new pharaoh of Egypt, Ay had to be carried in an ornate litter. He would have preferred walking, but such was the consensus of the viziers – he was to walk only when it counted, but without the cane, and sit when it did not matter if he walked.

"Damn bureaucrats, may Anubis take you away!" swore Ay.

This was the second half of the ceremony and the gold paste was being reapplied to his aging skin to give him a glowing appearance. Some of the paste had come off with sweat and where he rubbed against the sides of his palanquin while he was being carried. "We can't have that, can we?" spat Ay, knowing full well that the priests were right – he had to look perfect, no matter what his age.

The whole of Egypt was celebrating. People had stopped mourning for their young pharaoh when the new one was elevated to the throne. And there was one more cause for celebration – a royal wedding, no less! Ay would walk out to board his boat and sail after the boat of his bride on the royal lake to the Temple of Amun. Ay smiled as he thought of her – she was twenty-seven, but her beauty was still very apparent. The wedding was to be witnessed by more than a thousand noblemen and women, foreign dignitaries, priests and viziers, and the hundreds of spectators watching from the east shore and the royal barges, boats and small feluccas parked in the Nile between the temple and the palace. The common people would see Ay and Ankhesen-Amun sailing to the temple and after the wedding, when the priests had performed the ceremony. The marriage would be considered official when Ay carried Ankhesen-Amun over the threshold of his chamber in Malkata Palace.

Releasing the cane, Ay took the gold regalia of kingship into his hands and slowly walked towards the roaring crowds. For a moment the sunlight almost blinded him. Staring straight ahead, he felt the magnitude of his actions. Most Egyptians knew him, and Ankhesen-Amun was beloved in all Egypt – together, no one dared oppose them. Ay had made an enemy in Horemheb, but he had to do what must be done.

Ankhesen-Amun came out onto the balcony, bending her beautiful body low to the ground. When she stood up, Ay could see her determined face – she was well aware of what she was doing. Ay was old and he could not hold the throne for long. And when Horemheb finally got his turn to be a pharaoh, he would dispose of Ankhesen-Amun, seeing her as betrayer because she chose to side with Ay. By this wedding she was effectively signing her death warrant. But that didn't matter to the daughter of Nefertiti. She would stand by Aten the Light as long as she could take a breath.

Ankhesen-Amun's boat held only one person, Nakhtmin. He would row the boat through the royal lake, into the Nile to the Temple of Amun. Traditionally Ankhesen-Amun's parents would sit next to her, but she was an orphan now and so she went alone. Ay descended into his boat, also rowed by one man, Nakhtmin's friend. Ay's parents were long gone and there was no one to accompany him either. His boat traveled after Ankhesen-Amun's and the crowds cheered, throwing lotus blossoms onto the lake.

In the Temple of Amun, Ay watched as the smaller crown of Egypt was placed on Ankhesen-Amun's head. When she married the child Tut-ankh-Aten, her mother Nefertiti had changed the traditional bridal crown by adding the golden wings of Isis over young Ankhesenpaaten's wig, and the two feathers of Maat behind the crown.

The ceremony was complete. They walked out of the temple, Ankhesen-Amun conspicuously helping Ay walk. "No one dared to question Nefertiti then, as no one would question Ankhesen-Amun's actions now," thought Ay with satisfaction, noticing the feathers of Maat sticking up over the golden wings of Isis on his bride's wig. The crown of Egypt looked almost less significant than the golden feathers shining in the sunlight. "As well it should be," thought Ay, taking Ankhesen-Amun's hand. "Maat should be above all, including political power."

They both stepped forward onto the royal barge – the wedding ceremony was complete. The crowds watched them sail back to the Malkata Palace, rejoicing with loud singing, wishing the new pharaoh a long healthy life and his beautiful wife healthy offspring.

"Dear grandfather, Mutnodjmet is not well," whispered Ankhesen-Amun, while bowing slightly to the crowd. Her face wore a fake smile, she had been trained in state duties by her years with Tut-ankh-Amun, but her eyes showed her true concern for her aunt.

"Is my daughter in labor?" inquired Ay in a quiet whisper, also smiling and waving to the crowds.

"We don't know…"

Mutnodjmet was pregnant again, and it was not going well. The political situation was the least of her concerns right now, and Ay was glad she had not attempted to attend the coronation. She was carrying Nakhtmin's child, but Horemheb had made so many advances towards her, openly disrespecting Nakhtmin, that there were whispers in the dark temple recesses and in the long palace corridors, whispers saying that her unborn child belonged to Horemheb and not Nakhtmin. "If Horemheb had ever taken her body by force, she would have told me!" thought Ay furiously. He would have had Horemheb killed if it was so! Her absence at the ceremony on Ay's coronation day was construed to be because she was ashamed to face her father knowing she was carrying Horemheb's child! "How dare they say such things!" fumed Ay, when he had spoken with Nakhtmin just before the wedding. Nakhtmin's reaction was a wise one: "Let it go, you cannot control rumors or the feelings of others. I know my wife is carrying my child. And she would have confided in me if Horemheb had dared to take her body by force."

Nakhtmin now stood at Ay's side, helping Ankhesen-Amun aid Ay to walk out of the barge into the palace. There still was a wedding feast to endure...

That night Ay, in his first ruling as pharaoh, designated Nakhtmin as heir to his throne – a wise precaution, for Egypt could not be left without its cosmic protector for even one moment, and Ay was at an advanced age.

1,317BC

Giza Plateau, Egypt

Strangely enough, no one was waiting for them in the well once they went through it. Bailey was half-expecting Mr. Halib to start complaining that they must have picked the wrong time, but he did not. Coming up to the surface seemed easier this time. Simon went first, of course wanting to make sure they were safe.

Bailey could hear Simon's voice, but not what he was saying. Soon Mr. Halib joined them. Apparently they had almost scared to death a young man who was stationed by the well's mouth. The well was covered by a tent, which the young man was sitting in. Mr. Halib was able to understand what he said – something about "the glorious pharaoh, Ay" and Azvari. That was all they needed to hear – this boy had been sent by Azvari to sit by the well's mouth in case they did show up. Apparently he had been there for almost a month now, slowly eating dates from his bag. Someone was bringing him food and water, but he was not to leave the tent no matter what.

The boy was hurrying now, talking non-stop. Mr. Halib ignored him and looked past him at the horses. There were six of them, their eyelids were half-closed. He spoke to the boy and prepared to mount a brown horse, but the young man stopped him. He looked embarrassed and terrified as he tried to finish tying up the tent and help Mr. Halib with the horse all at the same time. Simon and Bailey saw it, and yelled at Mr. Council of Antiquities to stop. He stopped, resignation on his face, and just stared. Exasperated, Bailey went to help fold the tent – this guy used to scare her, but now he simply annoyed her. "I must have changed!" thought Bailey, helping Simon with the rope.

In a few minutes the entire site looked just like any other sand dune. Mounting their horses they followed the nervous and excited young man. He continued talking, apparently not noticing that no one responded to him, or that only Mr. Halib could understand him.

The first sign of civilization they saw was the head of the Sphinx, brightly painted, flags on tall posts in front of it. In less than half an hour they were on the familiar embankment, the avenue of the temples, thronging with people and animals as usual. The Sphinx glared down at the Newcomers patiently as they boarded a small boat. Its captain, a Nubian man in his late forties, did not speak much – it seemed the arrangement had been made ahead of time for them to use his boat that was just big enough for him, the four of them, and the boy from the well.

They pulled away from the embankment's steps, Simon helping the young man with the sail. Leaving the noise of the busy street behind them, the calmness of the water brought Bailey back to herself. She realized she did not know where they are going! And Mr. Halib was definitely not giving away any information; in fact, he was not talking with the young man at all. Craig and Simon seemed to have picked up a few words from the last time they were there, and were conversing with the boy. Well, if one could call pointing and saying a word a conversation! Bailey was not that good with languages and her stress prevented her from memorizing much of anything except visual stimuli.

Bailey wondered why such a young man had been allowed to meet them alone. He was hardly a Shenu... Nakhtmin, the young man who was here the last time, was twenty or so, and a strong soldier, very leveled and calm, present and tough, and he knew exactly what to do. This boy looked like he was barely sixteen, and he was struggling to keep up with the river, never mind the circumstances. "Things must be very tight!" guessed Bailey. "If this boy is all they could spare... Where is Azvari?"

She repeated her question to Mr. Halib, who after a pause repeated it to the young man. Even in ancient Egyptian Bailey could hear the annoyance in his voice. But Sahed was dead and Mr. Halib was all they had for a translator. Bailey had not had the time to register emotionally that Sahed had died, too many things were happening at once. Normally she would have been very sad about someone's passing, but here she felt no grief. If anything she was kind of happy for him. "I must think he's better off dead!" she thought.

Bailey had not realized Mr. Halib was speaking to her. "...to Waset, that is Luxor; and she will meet us at one of the harbors, he does not know which one yet."

"OK, so we are going to Luxor again," thought Bailey, "and Azvari will meet us there somewhere... How far are we in the future? Wait, what am I saying, the past... Can we go into the past? Damn, we are in the past... Can we end up in the past of the past we already went to? Or is this the future of that past?"

Craig must have read her mind, because he was already asking Mr. Halib what time period were they in. His reply was short: "Ay is the pharaoh."

"Ay? I didn't know he was ever a pharaoh?!" exclaimed Bailey. "What happened to Akhenaten? Is he dead? I thought that Tutankhamun was the pharaoh after him? When are we...?"

"There!" pointed the young man, as if answering her question. It was a brightly decorated harbor not far from the place they had just left, with a beautiful barge parked next to it.

Mr. Halib translated: "This is the barge of dowager queen Meritaten, she and Mutnodjmet performed a ceremony at one of the temples there."

"Meritaten, as in Nefertiti's daughter?" asked Craig.

"I do not know another one," snapped Mr. Halib.

"And Mutnodjmet is the young girl we saw, Nefertiti's half-sister, right?"

Mr. Halib said nothing, but from his face his surprise was clear – he had not had the chance to meet Mutnodjmet the last time he was there. Bailey guessed he had not seen Nefertiti or Akhenaten either, and so far he had not been told that she and the others had.

1,317BC
Five weeks earlier, Egypt

Azvari opened her eyes, her body perfectly still. She had sat on the cushion on the temple floor for the past three hours in front of the statue of Sekhmet. Night had descended over Waset hours ago, and now the only light came from the two braziers by the temple walls. For the past four nights she had been dreaming of Sekhmet. It was as if the goddess was trying to tell her something, but the message did not come. Finally Azvari elected to sit in the temple in the quiet of the night, alone in the huge structure. She had been correct in her assumption that quiet space would help – the vision unfolded in front of her eyes as clear as crystal. And now, opening her eyes, she did not want to disturb the precious feeling of connection with Sekhmet. There was so much to do, so much to face. She had to talk to Ay.

Led by a trusted servant she entered his private chamber, and stopped short. There were no fires burning except for a small bowl of smoking, glowing herbs. Ay was sitting on his low chair and Azvari immediately recognized that he had not gone to bed either. Sleep was a rare commodity these days…

"Greetings to you, wise pharaoh," she said quietly. When he dismissed the servant, she added, "How are you feeling?"

"I am as well as Sekhmet allows me to be. But you did not come here to ask about my health – I believe that could have waited until sunrise."

"Forgive me for disturbing you, Ay." There was neither an apology nor anger in her voice, and Ay smiled. She knew very well that he had not yet gone to bed. Just as he knew she would not have come to see him if it was not important.

"Say what you came here to tell me."

"I had a vision of Sekhmet. I do not choose to share it with the rest of the Shenu."

"What did she tell you?" Ay had worked hard to preserve what was left of Aten, while returning Egypt back to its multiple gods. He believed he had done well. Yet seeing Azvari's face he knew the news would be hard for him to hear. He repeated his question.

"Sekhmet said: *All will end soon, very soon, the Newcomers will be the sign. The Shenu are to know nothing about Maat of the One who is the Two, they are to remain blinded. But the secret must go on – the future of the human race depends on it.*"

"We will take the secret to our tombs," agreed Ay.

"*The secret must go on* – we have to choose our inheritors," said Azvari quietly, carefully studying Ay's face for his reaction.

"Begin another Shenu?" he whispered, adding, "Sons of the pharaohs, the Newcomer told me about them. He said that these other people with him, the white-skinned people, are the descendants of Tiye and you…"

"Our children?" gasped Azvari.

"I don't believe so. The meaning was unclear to me then. I knew my sister Tiye had no children that would inherit this new line of Shenu, and so I assumed the Newcomer was lying to anger me, to stain your name…"

"Then the Newcomers are the Shenu who we initiated in secret," continued Azvari, ignoring his last words – the wound of her rejection of him might never heal.

"Secret initiates?! We have done no such thing!"

"Yet. We are now told to do so by Sekhmet herself."

"The Shenu will dispose of us, even my position as pharaoh will not protect us."

"They don't have to find out. We choose our inheritors for the Shenu as expected, while entrusting the secret to the new Shenu – we both already know who will become our true inheritors, there are only three people we trust who have not yet been told all the truth…"

"My youngest daughter Mutnodjmet, my elder granddaughter Meritaten and my wife and grandchild Ankhesen-Amun…"

"As the High Priestess of Shenu I agree with you, Ay, and as your humble servant I am very glad you agree with me," she smiled.

"The High Priestess of the Shenu is a traitor… twice!"

"Traitor to the Shenu who strayed from Maat, never to Sekhmet!"

"Your proposition is to show a masked face to the Shenu themselves, while revealing the true face only to the ones who will know the secret? Oh, Sekhmet, how many more trials will you ask me to go through?"

"Ay, remember your strength," said Azvari in a quiet voice.

Ashamed of his outburst of weakness, Ay changed the subject. "Does this mean the Newcomers will visit us again then?"

"It would seem so, Sekhmet has foretold it."

"So be it. Do you, in your wisdom, know what Sekhmet meant by the *end?*"

"You will have to give Egypt to Horemheb, such is Sekhmet's will," she stated.

"The land of Egypt itself will be enslaved by the priests of Amun… Horemheb does not know the truth… He will erase the legacy of my family, of Aten! From the time of Amenhotep III the priests controlled more land and wealth than the royal family! If Akhenaten had not changed the rules, they would still have more power than any pharaoh of Egypt! And Horemheb will bow to the priests like every pharaoh that came before Akhenaten!" Ay inhaled sharply, his eyes glowing, looking at Azvari. She had power in her stare. She met his glare, and he knew to pay attention. He had been in love with this woman for as long as he could remember, the tattoo on his arm being the proof of it – and now his love was telling him that they had to 'give up'?

1,317BC
Five weeks ahead, Egypt

Their little boat sailed into the harbor and docked. The young man said a few words to the Nubian captain, jumped off in a hurry and disappeared in the harbor crowd.

"Where did he go?" Mahmoud was stumped by their reception this time – the last two times they had been very carefully taken care of, protected. This time they were allowed to stay dressed in their own clothes and only a boy was sent to greet them. The Nubian man tied his boat to the dock and began to fold the sail.

The tall American, Craig, was already off the boat, and he bolted in the same direction as their guide before Mahmoud could say anything. Mahmoud quickly jumped out and followed him – this time he was not going to miss anything! He soon found Craig standing in front of a woman wrapped in a beautiful shawl. She looked very familiar and coming closer Mahmoud gasped, realizing it was Azvari. She had aged, and now looked at least ten years older. But her beautiful features were still radiant and no passage of time could ever mask the fire in her eyes. She greeted the tall boy with a smile. Then she looked into Mahmoud's eyes and bowed her head. He couldn't stop staring at her – she was the "beloved" whom he was to follow. "Fate can be so cruel!" he thought.

Azvari paid several deben to the Nubian captain and they were led to another boat. This vessel had not one, but three sails, two white and one red. The sides of the boat were painted white, with copper edging on the railings and the wooden, copper-covered face of a lion shining in the sun at the front. Wasting no time, they got in and sailed off. Besides Azvari there were three men: the young one who had brought them to her, and two adults. The men had stern expressions on their faces and confined themselves to tending the boat, showing no interest in anything their guests were doing.

"I am glad to be able to greet you, for Sekhmet allowed me one more glimpse at your faces before I travel to the other side of life," she said as Mahmoud translated.

"You're too young to think of such things, lady," said Simon, grinning.

Azvari smiled at the translation. "Seventeen years have passed since you were here last. A lot has changed... I see that Sahed has been taken by Anubis..." she added, looking at Mahmoud.

"Wow, she looks great for forty-four! I thought she was your age," whispered the tall youth to the redhead.

Azvari opened a box the men had brought on board. It was filled with bread and fruit, and had a large vessel nestled in the middle. The British man, Simon, helped her to pull it out. Soon they all were drinking from it – it was something very similar to beer, a little on the sweet side.

Their small boat was skillfully navigated by the men. Its three sails propelled it over the water, and they passed many other boats.

"Whose boat is this?" asked Bailey.

"This is a Mut-Sekhmet temple boat, I am a priestess there," answered Azvari.

After the meal, she began to talk.

"You were last here at the time of glorious Akhenaten, you saw his beautiful Akhet-Aten, the City of Light. It is no more..." she said with sadness in her voice.

"Is Ay a pharaoh now?" asked Mahmoud.

"Ay is the pharaoh of Egypt, following the path laid out by Sekhmet."

"What happened to Nefertiti, is she alive?" interjected the tall youth.

"Nefertiti, may she have peace, followed the path also. Your visit the last time foretold her actions, and helped her grieve over the passing of young Meketaten... Nefertiti did what Sekhmet asked of her."

"What did *you* tell her?" Shocked, Mahmoud turned to Bailey Rixson.

"We told her of the prophecy..." mumbled the woman.

"What prophecy?!" Mahmoud knew he had been kept out of the loop, but now he realized the extent of it – these people had traveled back in time and had told Nefertiti something that had directed her actions and perhaps changed history! And *he* is the chosen one!

"Well, it was more of a message, not really a prophecy," explained the tall man, tying his long hair into a ponytail. "See, Sekhmet told Abby that *the end cannot come prematurely*. And you already know about the *beginning of the beginning* prophecy, right? That was why we came here the first time, to signify the beginning to Queen Tiye. The second time was because it was going to end too early, from the plague in Amarna and all that, and Sekhmet needed Nefertiti to *be like a king*. So we came to tell her…"

Mahmoud could only stare. These people were in communication with Sekhmet, and they had affected the history of Egypt… Or was it Sekhmet who had…?

As if sensing his question had been answered, Azvari continued. "Nefertiti's name was erased from all official records, and Akhenaten took on a co-regent with whom he shared the throne of Egypt. Taking a new name to signify the change, she became Ankhetkheperu-Ra Neferneferu-Aten, but did not attempt to change her appearance. She was not masquerading as a man, she was a woman and a king at the same time, just as Sekhmet asked of her."

"What an odd name…" said the redhead.

"It means Aten is Radiant as Ra Because the Beautiful and Perfect One Has Come," explained Mr. Halib as if to a child. History was becoming clear to him – so many unanswered questions had been explained in Azvari's last few sentences! Even the Shenu didn't have much knowledge of this period – they had systematically erased any mention of Akhenaten. But if these people were telling the truth and Sekhmet had not wanted this cult of Aten to "end prematurely," to the extent that she had asked Neferiti to become co-regent, then… Mahmoud felt faint. "That means Sekhmet initiated the heresy; she supported Akhenaten and Nefertiti and this whole Aten nonsense…? But why?"

Azvari continued: "Nefertiti became co-regent to her husband, while her role as queen consort was taken over by Meritaten, her elder daughter. After you left, Akhenaten built a temple in the City of Light to himself and to Nefertiti as Ankhetkheperu-Ra Neferneferu-Aten, so that the people could see the two pharaohs guiding Egypt. To make it even clearer to the people and foreigners, he erected four commemorative stelae with carvings of himself and his co-regent, both wearing the royal crowns of pharaohs, only they were labeled king and queen, male and female, and a third cartouche identified them as two kings in one…"

Mahmoud moaned. He was the only one in their group who knew what Azvari was talking about! Only small fragments of these stelae survived, and no part of the temple had made it at all. And the Shenu had had a lot to do with that!

"After you had left, Nefertiti stayed in Akhet-Aten for three more years, while the sickness ravaged the city. It was slow at first and only the workers died from it outside of the city bounds. But in the third year after you visited, the plague entered the City of Light. Precious temple animals were killed and burned. People wept in the streets, and died by the hundreds. Their bodies were covered with sand in the desert, buried without amulets in mass graves instead of being placed in tombs in the proper manner. Akhenaten also died – not from the sickness... We think his heart gave out from the pain of watching his children die, his temples desecrated. The royal family and the court escaped and moved to Waset. Akhet-Aten was set on fire, every house, every temple – all that was not of stone – burned... Boats and barges were not allowed to leave the harbor so as not to spread the sickness. So many people perished... Anubis spared me from the sickness and I was allowed to secretly leave. I took with me who I could, whoever was not sick – two female servants, five little orphaned children and one temple cat – I carried her in a basket..." Azvari had turned away, wiping her face.

Composing herself, she continued: "To appease the priests Nefertiti took Smenkhkare as her co-regent. Meritaten was married to him at that time, but after seven months on the throne he was poisoned – the gods know, not by her! Once he was gone, Nefertiti herself ruled Egypt for two more years as Ankhetkheperu-Ra Neferneferu-Aten, until young Tut-Ankh-Aten came of age. During those years Meritaten acted as a ceremonial Royal Wife – Nefertiti didn't want to remarry and give the power away to a king, neither did Meritaten. Neferiti attempted a reconciliation with the old cults, without the erasure of Aten and the memory of the City of Light – the city was left in the desert, mostly uninhabited... When Tut turned nine, he was crowned as a pharaoh and married to Ankhesenpaaten, Nefertiti's third daughter. The pharaoh-queen had lost her family to the sickness – all her daughters except Meritaten and Ankhesenpaaten, and her husband, were dead. Nefertiti was hated by the viziers and priests alike, and she had withdrawn from official court life. She became the shadow power, the influence behind Tut-Ankh-Aten's early years of rule. She tried to teach him to keep the path of Akhenaten alive, even though a return to the old gods was inevitable. But eventually the priests and viziers won him over, and she was not in good enough health to prevent it – our young pharaoh changed his name to Tut-Ankh-Amun, erasing the power of Aten. Her daughter had to follow the rule of the court and she changed her name to Ankhesen-Amun," finished Azvari. Then, as though it was an afterthought, she added, "At her deathbed *shawabti* Nefertiti commanded that her own name and titles be inscribed as they had been in the time of Akhenaten, that being true to what she knew to be Maat."

Everyone was silent for a moment, digesting this information.

"The young pharaoh Tut-Ankh-Amun lived for nineteen years, when he passed into the Afterlife after a fall from his chariot. His body had many sicknesses throughout his life, and after his leg was broken, he burned with fire and passed away. Horemheb was the named heir, but we…" Azvari stopped, as if unsure how to continue.

"You placed Ay on the throne instead!" finished Mahmoud. He knew the Shenu was powerful, but even he could not have imagined this.

"Ay took the throne, and he married Ankhesen-Amun, the widow. This was four years and one month ago… Horemheb hasn't forgotten the usurpation, but he couldn't fight us at the time. He dove into politics, spreading hatred of Ay's policies among the priests and the generals alike. He was even overheard saying he would erase Akhenaten's *heresy* from history once he got the chance!"

Mahmoud moaned again – he knew the history recorded from this period on…

"Of course Ankhesen-Amun and Ay never consecrated their marriage, it was only a political alliance – there was not going to be an heir. Knowing this Ay designated general Nakhtmin, his adopted son, to succeed him as pharaoh. You met Nakhtmin the last time you came here. He is an important man in the court, the Commander General, and he is now married to Mutnodjmet, Nefertiti's younger sister…"

The day passed in silence, their boat gliding over the water.

"Have you met Sekhmet?" asked Mahmoud suddenly. His mind had finally caught up with the information.

"I have seen her. But I have not traveled through the gate as Queen Tiye had, may she have peace… or you."

"Tiye went *through* the gate? Where did she go?"

"Queen Tiye was taken by Sekhmet to the time of the last polar shift, when the star-gods were leaving Earth," said Azvari simply.

"She *went* there?" Mahmoud couldn't believe it.

"Yes, Sekhmet met with her in the land of Egypt a long time ago, when the pyramid-bird was still here."

Mahmoud knew exactly what she was talking about, but it was one thing to know it from records and a whole other thing to have actually been there and seen it...

"The star-gods had left Egypt before the polar shift which had brought the Great Flood. People survived the flood and began life again at Edfu, and the masters started mystery schools. Sekhmet was the only star-god who stayed behind. Oh, she raged about people falling asleep! She started to fall with people – she cared for us so much! One day Sekhmet found the pleasure of her fire again and was able to return to her realm. But as a gift she left us the Shenu. And as a promise of her care she left the locket, the key..."

"We know about the locket... What did you call that time, before the star-gods left... the 'polar shift'?" asked Bailey Rixson.

"Every now and then Earth changes her energy. Earth does so with awakeness and by choice. Her energy garment has opposites, or poles. The polarity of her energy can be changed," explained Azvari. "Earth shifts these polarities to accommodate her consciousness. Sometimes the poles reverse; sometimes they move only a little. Every time the poles move, people feel the changes..."

"Like weather changes?"

"The weather is also Earth's clothes, so yes, it changes too, sometimes very much. It is a magical time of transformation! A lake can become a desert and a barren plain can turn into a lush forest. But the more apparent change is in people's awareness. After a polar shift it can be very hard to spin the Mer-Ka-Ba, although sometimes it becomes much easier... And without the spin people forget who they are."

"So the last polar shift happened when the Sirian star-gods left?" repeated Bailey.

"Yes. That polar shift marked the end of the Egyptian Golden Age of Awakening. The polar shift also brought lots of water, because Earth had changed. She melted frozen water and everywhere was flooded. The Nile almost erased the whole of Egypt for more than a year! By navigating their large boats many priests and priestesses survived that flood. Common people were also instructed in boat-building, and most listened, but some did not, preferring to perish with the land. The people who survived the flood lost their memories, the continuity they needed to know who they were, since most did not have a spinning Mer-Ka-Ba. They were tired and battered and consciousness was still falling, so their Light Bodies were dark. These people began to rebuild their culture from nothing. Much of the knowledge of mathematics, sacred geometry and its application to architecture, that which had been taught to all of us freely by the star-gods, was lost. Egyptians forgot how to build pyramids. They began to bury people in the ground and cover them with a stone slab."

"That is why what we know of history begins not with what you are talking about, and it doesn't mention star-gods or pyramid-birds... it shows basic beginnings – pottery, graves with stones... and the idea that the pyramids came much later..."

"The Shenu were one of the few who remembered... There were other orders of magi and priestesses who survived the flooding waters and held on to the knowledge. But common people did not retain much. It was during this time that the imposters came in..."

"Imposter-gods, from somewhere else?" asked Bailey.

"Yes. They fought their own wars, using people in them. Can you imagine true gods who fight *each other?* The imposters were like children compared to the star-gods! They taught people to take sides in their wars. They were not evil, simply immature... They were ruled by pride and they taught people how to be prideful."

"So they were probably after you then?" added Craig.

"These imposter-gods raised the civilization of Egypt again, but in a different way. The order of Shenu was noticed, but not interfered with. The new gods knew about the powerful one, Sekhmet, and did not dare harm her people. The Shenu eventually came to know the new imposter-gods, and recorded their history. To the people of Egypt the new gods were the real gods, because nobody remembered anything from before the Great Flood; theirs was the only civilization they knew of. But the Shenu remembered. Their mission was to protect the knowledge of the gods, the real history. By the time the pharaohs began their reigns in Egypt, the true gods were long gone and so were most of the imposter-gods. To a pharaoh the gods were mere idols. But the Shenu always knew the truth. Their knowledge was encoded into the priestly rituals resurrecting Osiris, his son Horus crossing the Winding Waterway, and travels in the Duat to the Land of Seker, to the district of Ro-Setau – just like the sun from the Great Archer in the sky crosses the milky river of stars to arrive at the paws of Ra-Horakhti, the Lion in the sky. The whole of Ro-Setau is built to accommodate this transition, the memory in stone... Most pharaohs were not initiated in this sacred knowledge though."

Azvari glanced at Mahmoud, then continued, "Some pharaohs were very obsessive about the Shenu's secrets, knowing them to contain great power. Khufu spent years of his life attempting to decode Ro-Setau, searching for the Shenu's knowledge, for the "secrets of Thoth,"

392

desiring to gain power equal to Sekhmet and Thoth and to unlock the pyramid. He never found it, the Shenu never revealed themselves to him."

Finally Mahmoud spoke in a hoarse voice. "Akhenaten was chosen by Sekhmet?"

"Yes. Your first arrival revealed this truth to Queen Tiye, may she have peace."

"But his Aten religion...?" mumbled Mahmoud.

"It broke the spell of the imposter-gods over the people. Akhenaten was brought here by the star-gods to remind people of Maat."

"...*do not stray from Maat... follow the beloved...*" mumbled Mahmoud in ancient Egyptian.

"What?" whispered Azvari, to Mahmoud's surprise.

"Nothing, never mind..." he said, waving her off.

"I know those words," she said with certainty, as Mahmoud stared at her in surprise. "I said that to Ay twenty-eight years ago, when he asked me to marry him."

Mahmoud swallowed.

"Ay had them inscribed onto his arm, as a permanent reminder of Maat."

"...and you... Sekhmet told me those same words..."

They looked at each other for a long while, thinking. Finally Azvari went on. "Now you understand why the Shenu did not like Akhenaten? They feared this descendant of the true gods, for he would not tolerate lies!"

"We didn't know he was appointed by Sekhmet," whispered Mahmoud.

"The Shenu were political, they would never have tolerated a lessening of their power, and they still don't. They love nothing more than to have one of their own on the throne – Queen Tiye and now Ay. But they do not know Maat!"

"Tiye and you betrayed the Shenu, exposed the secrets to Akhenaten..." whispered Mahmoud without any venom. The word "betrayed" seemed to have lost its power.

"It was Tiye and I, and Nakhtmin. We have never betrayed Sekhmet. But after Nefertiti's death, the Shenu manipulated Tut-Ankh-Aten into changing his allegiance from Aten the Light to the 'gods'. He was young and feared powerlessness, he desired to be in no way associated with Akhenaten and his heresy. With pride he recorded his lineage from Amenhotep III, as if Akhenaten and Nefertiti had never existed. He transferred the official capital back to Waset and, hungry for the support of the priests, he and the Shenu obliterated any reminders of Akhenaten in the City of Light and in Waset – they destroyed his tombs, his priests, his relics…"

"So little has survived…" whispered Mahmoud.

"This too was foretold – that is why you are here now, is it not?" Confused, Mahmoud looked at Azvari.

"Your visit signifies the end."

"*I am the beginning of the end…* the end of what?" whispered Mahmoud.

"The spark in time burned brightly and it will be gone soon, but its legacy will go on. I am the begining of that legacy, and you, Mahmoud, are the end of the Shenu."

Malkata Palace

Waset, Egypt

Ay lay on the ornate bed, his shoulders supported by linens. The left side of his body was paralyzed, and his speech had become odd. The doctors had seen this illness before and believed it to be the beginning of death. Ay himself was not sure, but he could tell that running Egypt from this position would not be possible for long. His paralysis was a weakness – and a pharaoh of Egypt could not have such an obvious deficiency. He would be replaced soon. "Hopefully Horemheb will wait for my death before claiming the throne," thought Ay, knowing full well it was unlikely. Horemheb was impatient as it was; he felt that the right to rule Egypt had been denied him – he would not find it beneath him to poison the old man in order to gain this ultimate power.

The viziers of Egypt had gathered by his bed, each attempting to act as if their pharaoh was not ill. Ay found them more annoying than useful. There were a few old men amongst them who had served under the previous two pharaohs, and Ay trusted them to some degree. The rest he did not. The younger men were loyal to Horemheb.

Ankhesen-Amun walked into the room and sat by his bed. From her expression Ay understood that the Newcomers were close. He swept the chamber with a glance, trying to take in everyone's face – oh, he knew he couldn't trust most of them!

"You may leave," he pronounced the words with difficulty. The viziers turned to the queen in surprise.

"Leave us! Have you not heard your pharaoh?" she repeated, outraged at that they had questioned Ay. Before the illness not one of them would have dared! Turning to Ay, she said, "Dear grandfather, how may I ease your pain?" There was suffering in her eyes.

"I am not in pain, dear child," lied Ay. "Anubis took half of my body but Sekhmet must have me do one more act for her, so she kept the other half of me here." Seeing tears in Ankhesen-Amun's eyes, he took her hand.

"They are here, grandfather," whispered Ankhesen-Amun. "They are *all* here."

She called her body-servant and in a minute the girl brought in six people. The Newcomers were here, but without the old Egyptian man. With them walked in Azvari and Nakhtmin. Ay was about to greet Azvari when two more women walked into the room from another entrance, their faces hooded by cloaks. Ay exhaled when he saw who they were – Meritaten, his oldest granddaughter, and Mutnodjmet, his youngest daughter. These two would inherit the knowledge of current events, they had the right to be here.

"My trusted children, this was not wise," he whispered, knowing how dangerous their action was. "Someone might have seen you."

"And if they did, what of it? We have come to visit our divine relative in need!" said Meritaten, her voice as confident and strong as it ever was – consort to three pharaohs, Akhenaten, Smenkhkare and Nefertiti, she knew what power was! She felt it was beneath her to hide. And Mutnodjmet, even though she was quiet, looked no less sure.

Ay knew that arguing with these two would not work in his favor. He needed them, and he was too old – he would lose. The girls were over thirty years of age, they would have to make their own mistakes. Ay hoped that none of those mistakes would get them killed by Horemheb's hand.

They had enough troubles without Ay complicating their lives further. Meritaten had suffered greatly from the death of her mother. Nefertiti had always been her anchor. Knowing the truth about her mother's actions, the reason for co-regency and her own role as the Royal Consort, gave Meritaten peace – Ay knew she was better off knowing than not. And his lovely daughter Mutnodjmet, how much suffering had come to her! Anubis had taken four of Nakhtmin's children, girls born prematurely. She had love in her life, for the gods of Egypt knew Nakhtmin loved her. But with each daughter's death she had died a little inside. Knowing the truth gave Mutnodjmet a direction, a path. If the gods did not grant her children, she could be the mother of an entire land by knowing its secrets and protecting them.

"We are here on the errand of Sekhmet," said the Egyptian Newcomer called Mahmoud. He spoke with a strange accent, but everyone could clearly understand him.

"Speak," Ay commanded, remembering the man.

"Our visit, it would seem, is a sign for you to... end," he said awkwardly.

"Does the legacy of Sekhmet go on in your time that has not yet come?"

After thinking a moment, Mahmoud answered, "Yes."

"What is *your* belief?" Ay remembered clearly the mistrust in the man's eyes the last two times he met him.

Again Mahmoud fell silent. What was he to say? That he no longer knew what to believe? He had to answer; the silence was becoming palpable.

"I know now that Sekhmet initiated Akhenaten... and Aten."

"Does Maat affect your heart, or only your mind?" asked Ay in a tired voice. He could see from the faces of his allies that they knew what he was asking.

Mahmoud listened to his heart. It was not beating. How could this be? No, it had to be beating, just not as hard as it had been earlier. "Sekhmet chose the heresy... So that means it is not a heresy?" Afraid, Mahmoud put a hand to his heart.

Ay coughed, and the women tended to him. For a moment, everyone forgot about Mahmoud, who stood silently in the middle of the room in front of the pharaoh's gilded ebony bed.

"The Shenu betrayed Sekhmet!" said Mahmoud out loud, amazed himself at how odd his voice sounded.

"You are the end of the Shenu!" stated Azvari, righting her body from tending to the pharaoh. Everyone stared at Mahmoud. The words had been said in ancient Egyptian, so the Newcomers could not understand them, but from their faces it was clear that they got the meaning.

"Yes... I am..." agreed Mahmoud quietly. Then, as if he had been woken by this realization, he suddenly fell to his knees. "Ay, great ladies of the court, I am your servant..."

"You will serve us by serving Sekhmet," said Meritaten slowly, her voice regal.

"I serve Sekhmet, the Lover of Truth, the Detester of Untruth! I will end the Shenu!" Mahmoud turned to the Westerners and repeated his last words in English. From their suspicious faces he could see they were not convinced and were confused by his kneeling on the floor. "I will serve Sekhmet!" he repeated. "*I will end the Shenu!*"

"And the Shenu will quickly end you. From what I've seen, they don't have any trouble disposing of people, do they?" said the British man. "How do you propose to avoid that?"

"I won't tell them…" Mahmoud looked possessed now, his eyes wide. "I will not expose you to them, I will cover up what has happened, I will allow some information to come out, only small amounts here and there, they won't notice, I will hide my allegience…" Abruptly Mahmoud realized he had always hidden his true allegiance! From the beginning he had believed that the artifacts in the vaults should be exposed, that the information hidden there would change the world. But he had allowed himself to be manipulated by the others, all because of his damned insecurity! He was so afraid that he was not a Somebody, and he thought that protecting the secret gave him strength. He had always felt like an imposter himself, hiding among the great ones, fearing that one day he would be discovered and they would send him back to where he belonged – that village in the middle of nowhere. No more! He would not bow to his shame any more! He was chosen by Sekhmet! This time there was no pride in his acknowledgment, no superiority attached to it, simply the understanding of responsibility. He knew what he had to do. He was ready!

Unexpectedly, a loud stern voice exploded from the far end of the hallway, behind the closed doors: "I have come to see pharaoh! I demand to see him now!" No one moved.

Without even turning her head to the doors Meritaten said, in a tone suggesting no appeal was possible, "The pharaoh is busy."

A servant ran into the room through a side door, panic in his eyes. Soon it became apparent that one of the young viziers, accompanied by a someone in a cloak, was requesting admission to the royal chambers immediately and would not take no for an answer.

Ankhesen-Amun stood up to defend her husband's peace, but Ay stopped her. He knew Anubis had come for him – it might as well be like this, in his own royal chambers. He knew who the cloaked man accompanying the vizier was. Looking into Azvari's eyes, he understood that she also knew Maat. He squeezed her hand – it was all he could do to proclaim his undying love for this magnificent lady who should have been the queen of Egypt!

Before Ay could speak, Azvari was in action. Speedily she moved everyone into the neighboring robing room, which was connected to the washroom, and farther, the garden. Ay knew that Azvari, the Newcomers and the two royal princesses would be whisked away before anything happened in his chambers.

The young vizier entered and announced: "The General of the Army Horemheb is here to see you."

Ay struggled to sit. Ankhesen-Amun rushed to help him. She was so close to him her wig brushed his face, but Ay waved her away with his good hand. He was still the pharaoh and a man.

Horemheb entered the room and took off his cloak. Ankhesen-Amun stood up – an unconscious reaction owing to her fear of him. "This is not good at all," thought Ay. Horemheb had gained more and more control, but Ay's Ka was still connected to his body and he would be damned if he allowed the promise to Sekhmet go unfulfilled!

"Leave us," Horemheb commanded Ankhesen-Amun. She hesitated, looking at Ay, tears in her eyes. Ay was sure she didn't understand the meaning of Horemheb's visit, but she felt it, and her feelings were too apparent. "It will get her killed!" he thought desperately. He whispered to her: "Get out, my queen, Egypt needs you. I will be fine."

He knew very well it was a lie.

"We have to go!" whispered Nakhtmin, pulling Azvari's arm. The Newcomers were already out, led by the servant, and Meritaten and Mutnodgmet had gone with them. The older Newcomer and Nakhtmin waited on Azvari, who was leaning against one of the large cedar chests in the robing room, unmoving. For the first time in her life she knew with absolute certainty what was about to happen. Ay was never going to walk out of that room. All the pain of not being able to return his love welled up in her heart – she knew he was sacrificing himself to keep their secret safe.

A firm hand grasped her arm. "Death there. You live." These were the words whispered into her ear by the Newcomer called Simon. His Egyptian was simple and clear enough – Azvari turned her eyes away from the spot on the curtain leading to Ay's room and looked into his eyes. He looked right back, and she knew that he understood. "You live," he repeated.

He didn't try to pull her away; he was giving her the power to decide, only keeping his eyes fixed on hers. She turned to Nakhtmin – he stood silently by the garden exit, looking away from them.

Only Anubis knows for certain what happened after Azvari left the robing room. But Azvari was among the ones who believed that when judgment day came for Horemheb, his heart would not outweigh the feather of Maat. Whatever the truth is, that day the pharaoh of Egypt Ay died, and a new pharaoh, Horemheb, rose to take his place.

* * *

After a mad dash through many corridors of Malkata Palace they spilled out onto the Nile embankment. A small boat was waiting for them. Simon helped Azvari to board it; her face was ashen and she was shaking. The princesses had gone their own way, back to their own palaces. There was no one to comfort Azvari, and she sat in silence, her eyes unseeing. Nakhtmin and Simon took care of the boat, but once it was sailing, Simon could not help but return to Azvari. She had not moved or spoken. He crouched down so that his face would be in front of hers and looked into her eyes – she pulled the linen hood from her face, and it was wet with tears.

Simon didn't know enough ancient Egyptian words to express his support, and so he simply hugged her. She was reluctant at first to allow it, but the moment she relaxed, the sobs came.

Nakhtmin put Craig in charge of the rope holding the sail and busied himself with his bow, shooting wild geese and diving for them. They moored on the grassy riverbank close to a small town to buy pomegranate wine and bread and gather wood for the fire. Simon sat next to Azvari and when the night grew cool, he wrapped his blanket around her for warmth.

When they arrived at the harbor near the Sphinx a servant met them, horses at the ready. Simon found he didn't want to take his arms from around Azvari, and only reluctantly released her. She gave him a quick glance of gratitude and hastily mounted her black horse. "She is an incredible woman!" thought Simon, his heart hurting. Getting onto his own horse, he followed the others into the desert. Nakhtmin led the caravan.

A huffing of horses sounded in the distance behind them. Simon twisted his body around and squinted to see who was approaching. The riders were dressed in Bedouin robes and they were driving their horses hard in the direction of the little caravan. The hairs stood up on Simon's neck. "Danger!" Nakhtmin reigned in his horse and turned the animal around. Mr. Halib shouted something in English, but Simon didn't hear – he smacked Mahmoud's spotted horse and shouted "keep going!" The heavy horse jumped, almost causing Mahmoud to lose the reigns, then began to run. Bailey and Craig were frozen. Simon was familiar with this type of situation – the dynamics of "protect the unit" were simple. Shouting at Bailey and Craig to keep going, he turned his horse around to stand by Nakhtmin. He understood what Simon was doing; the gratitude showed in his eyes.

Simon's heart sank when he heard Azvari's voice behind them. He couldn't understand what she was saying, but he caught Nakhtmin's reply. He was telling her to go, but from the sound of her voice it was clear she planned to stay.

Desperately assessing the situation, Simon looked around. They were unarmed. Four men were coming toward them. Four against two were not bad odds, it could be worse. Hearing Nakhtmin speak, he turned to him and was handed a small saber, or a large curved knife, depending on the way one chose to look at it. "Ok, this is doable," thought Simon, a little relieved. Turning to Azvari he said only one word: "Go!" Yet she did not waver. She had a thin long black knife in her hand.

"So be it." That was all that Simon had time to think, because the four desert men were already there. He and Nakhtmin faced them, Simon positioning himself as best he could to protect Azvari. The men's sabers were longer, and they were young and quick, but Simon and Nakhtmin had the advantage of experience. One man was immediately killed; Nakhtmin was knocked off his horse, but he dragged the other man down with him. Feeling he was at a disadvantage on the unwieldy beast, Simon jumped off and lunged. In a moment two of the assailants were dead on the sand. Their robes spread out around them, exposing their golden kilts – they were royal guards. "Horemheb's," thought Simon as he struck at the third man. There was movement behind him and he felt rather than saw the knife coming at him, but there was no time to move. He took a blow and fell; now he should be dying but he was only winded – the thrusting knife had been stopped by the flat of Azvari's blade. She shouted at the guard in a voice that was not hers, glaring at him from the height of her black horse like some dark avenging demon. Jumping up, Simon grabbed the distracted man's leg and before long he was down and dead. Looking around he found Nakhtmin. He had killed the third guard, but it was done at a high price – a blade protruded from between Nakhtmin's ribs. One look told Simon he would be dead in under a minute. Jumping off her horse, Azvari ran to Nakhtmin and grabbed his face, speaking quickly. Simon couldn't understand if she was praying or making him a promise. In a few seconds Nakhtmin had taken his last breath, and a string of blood came out of his mouth. Azvari continued holding his face and talking. Breathing heavily, Simon looked around – were these men the only ones, or were there more on the way? So far the horizon was clear; all he could see were dunes.

Feeling uneasy on the open plain, Simon eventually touched Azvari. "We have to go…"

"Leave me, you must go. It will end – this is my fate!" she replied.

Understanding "go" and "my fate," Simon smiled a sad smile. "Not if I can do something about it, lady. It's too soon for you to die." His decision was made.

The horses knew the way, but Azvari wanted to be sure the Newcomers had made it to the well. Reluctantly she lay Nakhtmin's head on the sand and jumped back onto her horse – she will return for his body later. They rode as fast as they could to the well. It was uncovered, and there were no sounds. Azvari took the locket from her neck, while Simon yelled into the well: "Are you there yet?"

"Simon? We are half way down, I think…," came the reply, a distant echoing voice.

"Go without me. I'm dropping the locket in," he yelled, quickly taking the locket from Azvari's hands and wrapping it in one if his scarves. "Get the locket and go. Go!"

"Without you?" said the confused voice. There was a pause. "I got the locket, but… you won't be able to go home… Simon?"

Looking at Azvari, Simon smiled. "I am home," he said, and began to cover up the well. It was best to disguise the site while they assessed the danger. They would return for the locket later. To his surprise Azvari grabbed his face with both hands and kissed his lips. Hard. And long. He willingly gave in, holding her tightly, wishing he would never have to let go. When they finally parted, she softly touched the scar on his forehead.

"…my foreign dignitary…"

CHAPTER FIFTEEN

Multidimensional Space
Outside of Linear Time

The bright flash of light does not end in the usual darkness. Instead the light persists, bright and all-encompossing.

"Did it not work?" asks Bailey, her voice muffled and distorted.

"Where do you think we are?" Craig wonders.

They cannot see each other, or anything else for that matter – there is only the whiteness. Their bodies feel strange, as if they were suspended by many tiny particles. Yet there is no perception of direction; it is as though they are floating in a vacuum, a very bright vacuum...

"If you could feel the electrons move inside your body, this is probably what it would feel like," thinks Craig.

As the light begins to subside, it does not disappear completely. In the lower intensity of the dimmed light their bodies find gravity, suddenly feeling a bottom to this place. But this gravity is not the same as the usual gravity; they are not standing on anything, but only hover with an awareness of up and down.

Craig's eyes adjust and through the white mist he sees Bailey's figure floating to his right. Turning his head he sees Mr. Halib's body floating to his left. As if in slow motion, he extends his hand and tests his fingers – they work, but the sensation in them is not the same. It feels... as if this is not his body! He stares at his extended hand, and right in front of it, suddenly materializing from the mist, is the large head of a lioness. Craig is startled, but he cannot jump back, instead his body jerks strangely.

402

"Whoa!" is the most he can say.

"You might want to be more polite." That is his spirit guide's voice. Unable to move away from the glowing amber eyes of the large lioness, Craig asks inside his mind, "Simon, where are you?"

"Here, you odd child, you better pay attention," replies Simon-the-cat from somewhere behind Craig's head. "This is the One I promised you would meet, so be polite! She hired you, after all!"

"Oh...? Oh! Sekhmet!"

He could swear the lioness smiled, in the next moment turning into a tall woman, a gold mask appearing on her face – only the amber, glowing eyes remain the same.

"Oh, Jesus..." mumbles Bailey.

The next moment the light dimmed again and they were standing in the same room at the bottom of the well. It was definitely not the well in ancient Egypt – there were no torches in the niches, no tables or candles. There was only some leftover rope from the time when they bound Mr. Halib. Gravity was almost back to normal, they were certainly not floating anymore. Turning his head, Craig saw Mr. Halib bent over on the floor, and in front of him stood an eight foot tall glowing woman in a shiny mask.

"Wow! Bailey, she's still here!" he whispered.

"She can see that. Be polite as I told you!" hissed his spirit guide. Craig could see him now, sitting by his feet.

"Hello, Sekhmet. It's very nice to meet you... finally..." began Craig courageously.

Sekhmet looked at him. Craig had never felt anything like it, even when he looked into the eyes of his spirit guide. Pictures, feelings, thoughts, memories – an avalanche smashed through his mind.

"We'll decipher those later..." purred Simon softly, rubbing on his leg.

"You have done your job well, I honor you," Sekhmet's voice sounded in his head. She started a ring of fire around herself.

"Whoa, pyrokinesis!" whispered Craig.

"What?" whispered Bailey.

"It's the ability to excite objects on a molecular level – she can start fires with her mind," answered Mr. Halib. He was still on the floor, but he was sitting up now.

"Is this real fire?" asked Bailey cautiously.

"Perception is the key to transformation," they telepathically heard Sekhmet say. "You can easily pass through solid matter – what you perceive as solid matter – which in truth is mostly empty space."

The fire expanded and suddenly in a flash passed through all of them. Whipping their heads around they saw the flames reach the walls of the semi-circular room, surrounding them. The room glowed a warm reddish hue, yet it was still cold.

"Do you know the feeling of time repetition?" asked Sekhmet.

"She means déjà vu," whispered Craig. "We've been feeling it all the time!"

"It is a protracted pliability of time-space, you don't know about it yet," she communicated to them, and smiled under the mask. "Your linear perception of the progression of events is an illusion. In Maat, each choice leads to a new path, creates a new reality. When you feel this déjà vu, you are allowed a glimpse into the other path, the one your body had chosen not to follow, but which your consciousness sees as an option. It occurred somewhere, in the other Maat."

"I do not understand, oh glorious Sekhmet!" said Mahmoud.

"There is more than one of everything, including reality. Maat is both subjective and moldable. If you can dream a better world, you can make a better world. And travel between them… You have helped to open up the options for the human beings of Earth, so that they eventually can have the chance to join the dimensional community."

"Why did you kill my father? And mother?" asked Bailey, her voice shaking. She couldn't believe she was asking this, but she was here in the same room with a star-god, so why not complete this insanity by asking an insane question?

"I took no one. They were part of the path."

"An accident…" whispered Bailey.

"There are no accidents, only choices. We move slowly but intentionally, changing the space we are in by means of sensing, knowing and feeling, from a very slow dimension to a very fast one, or the other way around," answered Sekhmet. "But changes of a large magnitude require brave actions."

Sekhmet extended her hand, her long fingers pointing to the locket on Bailey's neck. Bailey grasped it, she no longer knew if this was "her" locket, or the one Azvari had thrown into the well and Bailey had worn over her neck to open the gate.

"We have to give it back to her, remember?" said Craig.

Then, without knowing how it happened, the locket was on Sekhmet's chest, shining as brightly as her gold mask.

"Nobody can walk this line for us, nobody but us can say what is here…" she said, pointing to her chest. And the next second there was a bright, shimmering, moving structure around her, vibrating so strongly they felt it inside their bodies. It looked like a collection of pyramids and circles, but the shapes were moving so fast the details were impossible to distinguish. Sekhmet's hand still pointed to her body – the *breathing Light Body*.

As she disappeared from the room they heard her say: "Remember the edge between the Light and the Dark, it is your path…"

EPILOGUE

Current Time
Over the Atlantic Ocean

"This says the pharaohs went like this: Amenhotep III, then Akhenaten, then Smenkhkare for less than a year, then someone called Ankhetkheperure Neferneferuaten for two years..." read Bailey from the page on the screen of her laptop. While they were waiting in the Cairo airport Craig had downloaded many files of official historical data about the period of time they had just witnessed.

"That must be Nefertiti..." said Craig. "Azvari told us she was the co-regent of Akhenaten for four years, then Smenkhkare ruled for seven months, and then she took the throne because Tutankhamun was too young."

"This says," continued Bailey, that "since Ay was already advanced in age upon his sucession, he ruled Egypt for only four years, succeeded by Horemheb. During his short reign he facilitated Egypt's return to the old religious ways, while preserving the Amarna legacy. He constructed a mortuary temple at Medinet Habu for his own use. Prior to his death, Ay designated Nakhtmin, his senior military officer and adopted son, as his successor. The inscription carved onto the funerary statue of Nakhtmin, made during Ay's reign, clearly gave him the titles of *rpat*, the crown prince, and *zanzw*, the king's son."

"Well, he obviously didn't make it..."

Bailey continued reading: "Horemheb was the last pharaoh of the 18th dynasty, although he was not related to the preceding royal family and is believed to be of common birth. Before becoming pharaoh,

406

he was the Commander in Chief of the Army under Tutankhamun and Ay, which is how he was able to seize power. He removed the claim of his rival Nakhtmin, an official heir, and arranged to have Ay's tomb desecrated by smashing the latter's sarcophagus into several pieces and systematically chiselling Ay's name out of the tomb walls, and he is presumed to have destroyed Ay's mummy. Because originally Tutankhamun had chosen Horemheb as his successor, Horemheb spared Tutankhamun's tomb from vandalism. Upon his ascension to the throne Horemheb reformed the state and religion, and began offical action against the preceding Amarna rulers. Horemheb demolished the monuments of Akhenaten and reused the remains in his own building projects, and usurped the monuments of Tutankhamun and Ay. Horemheb also took for himself the mortuary temple at Medinet Habu, built by Ay, erasing Ay's titulary on the back of a seventeen foot colossal statue by carving his own titulary in its place. Horemheb presumably remained childless, his Chief Wife Mutnodjmet or other lesser wives produced no children for him…"

"Wow, he married Mutnodjmet? That is after he somehow got rid of Nakhtmin, her husband, right? She probably married him to stay influential…Yes, remember even Nakhtmin was saying that they had four stillborn babies… I'm sure she had no children with Horemheb."

"Hold on, there was something about that before…" Bailey scrolled up the page. "Here: The name and titles on Nakhtmin wife's funerary statue were intentionally erased, although her beautiful features can still be seen..."

"That was Mutnodjmet. Horemheb did not want anyone to know she was Nefertiti's sister and previously married to his enemy."

Bailey continued reading: "Horemheb appointed his vizier Paramesse as his successor. After Horemheb's death Paramesse assumed the throne of Egypt as Ramesses I, beginning the Ramesses dynasty… So that's how Ramesses came to be…"

They sat in silence. Their seats in first class, which Marty had insisted they take, were comfortable. They would be in JFK airport soon, there were only a few hours left of the flight.

"It's so strange that somehow all those things we saw were almost completely erased from history, as if they never happened. Ay is historically a minor pharaoh, but we saw how important he was. Azvari is never even mentioned anywhere, Tiye is barely spoken of, and Tutankhamun is practically a cult figure, and he was a nobody!"

"It was supposed to be forgotten. Even Sekhmet said she and the Solar Council were not hoping for it to remain. She said it was supposed to be a 'spark in time.' But it changed everything."

"Like what?" argued Bailey. "No one knows anything about it, Mr. Halib will mostly continue hiding what he knows, and the True Shenu practically doesn't exist anymore."

"Not true. Mr. Halib will do what he can to start changing the Shenu, and will probably leak some information whenever he can…"

"He will just get himself killed," replied Bailey, sipping her apple juice.

"He seems to be smart enough to avoid that, Bailey," smiled Craig. "And Axil and the two of us are now the True Shenu in a way…"

"I'm not sure I want that role! I'll have to rearrange my whole life as it is," whispered Bailey hotly, "…now that I know…"

"Sometimes what we have woken up, we can't put back to sleep," answered Craig. He was amazed at how confident he felt. Life made sense – for the first time ever!

THE END

www.ingramcontent.com/pod-product-compliance
Lightning Source LLC
Chambersburg PA
CBHW020927020726
47495CB00002B/386